Disney
STAR DARLINGS

BECOMING STAR DARLINGS
CINESTORY COMIC

Published in the United States and Canada by Joe Books Ltd
489 College Street, Toronto, ON, M6G 1A5

www.joebooks.com

First Joe Books Ltd edition: November 2016

Print ISBN: 978-1-77275-451-3
ebook ISBN: 978-1-77275-472-8

Adaptation, design, lettering, layout, and editing by First Image.

Library and Archives Canada Cataloguing in Publication
information is available upon request.

Printed and bound in Canada
1 3 5 7 9 10 8 6 4 2

BECOMING STAR DARLINGS

CINESTORY COMIC

Based on the characters created by
Shana Muldoon Zappa and Ahmet Zappa

JOE BOOKS LTD

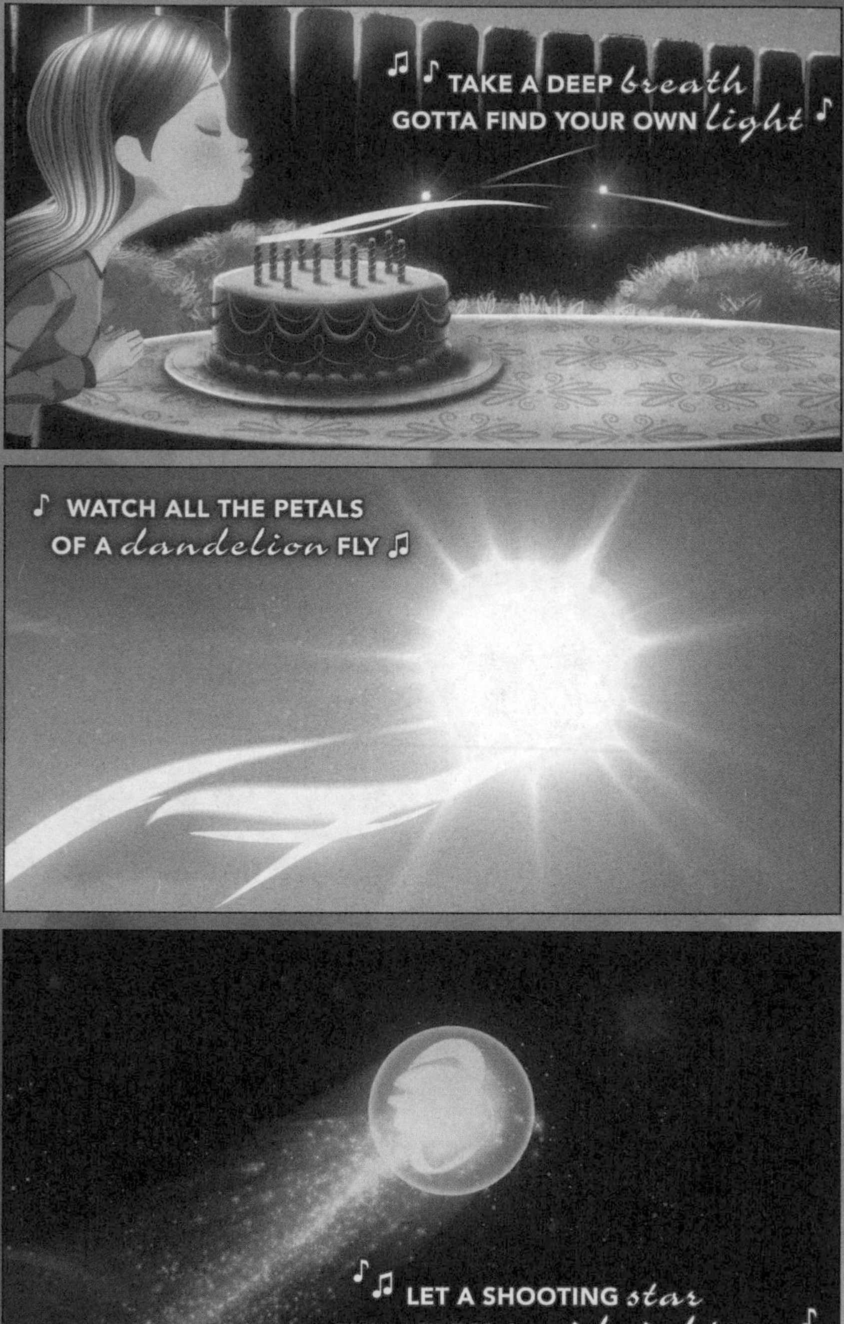
♫ ♪ TAKE A DEEP *breath*
GOTTA FIND YOUR OWN *light* ♪
♪ WATCH ALL THE PETALS
OF A *dandelion* FLY ♫
♪ ♫ LET A SHOOTING *star*
RUN ACROSS A *midnight* SKY ♪

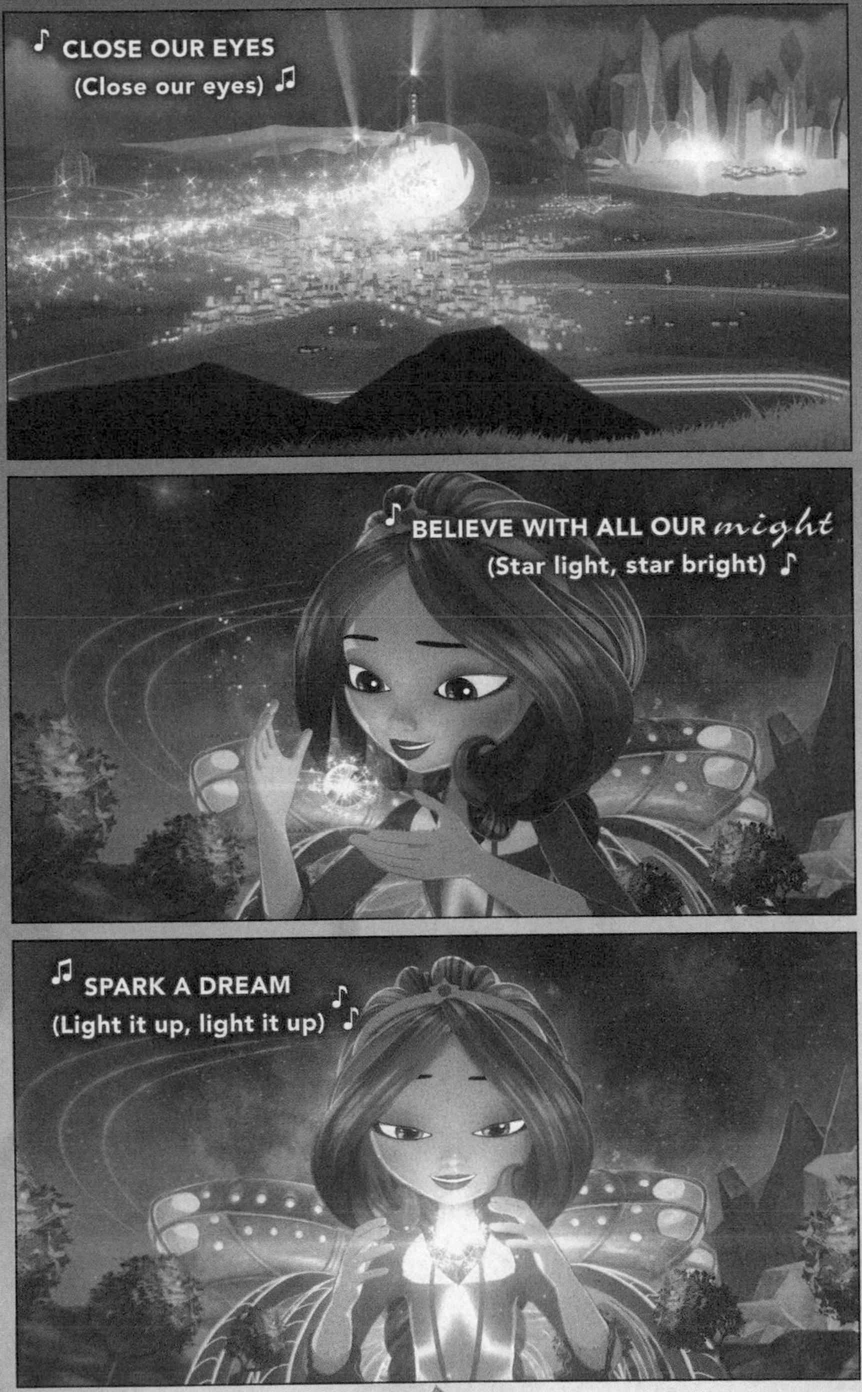
CLOSE OUR EYES
(Close our eyes)
BELIEVE WITH ALL OUR might
(Star light, star bright)
SPARK A DREAM
(Light it up, light it up)

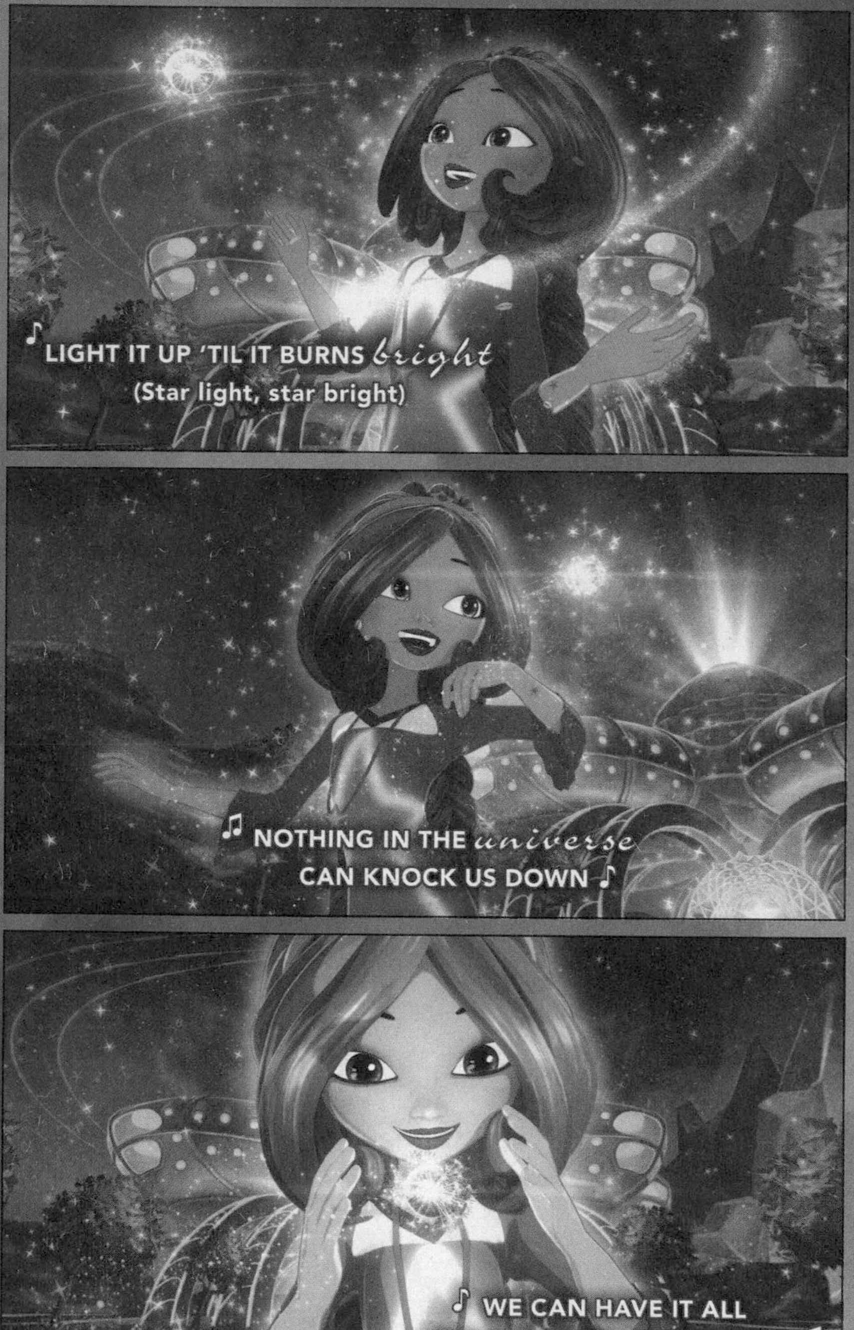
♪ LIGHT IT UP 'TIL IT BURNS bright
(Star light, star bright)
♫ NOTHING IN THE universe
CAN KNOCK US DOWN ♪
♪ WE CAN HAVE IT ALL
WE GOT EACH OTHER now ♫

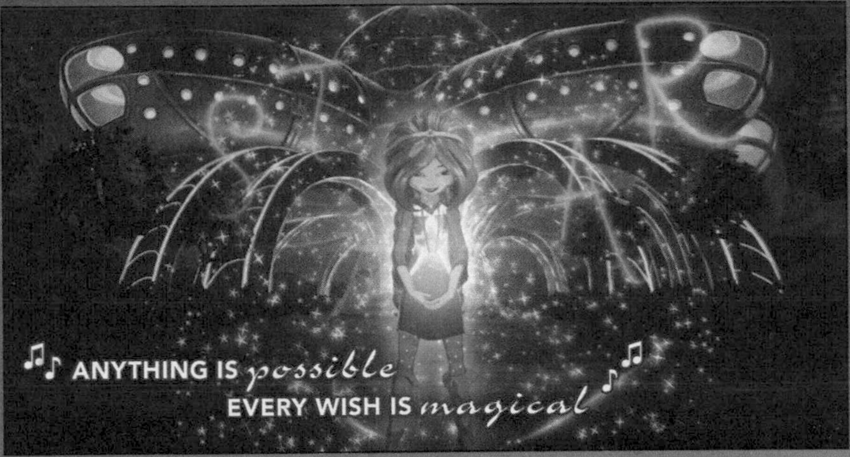
ANYTHING IS possible
EVERY WISH IS magical

Disney
StarDarlings

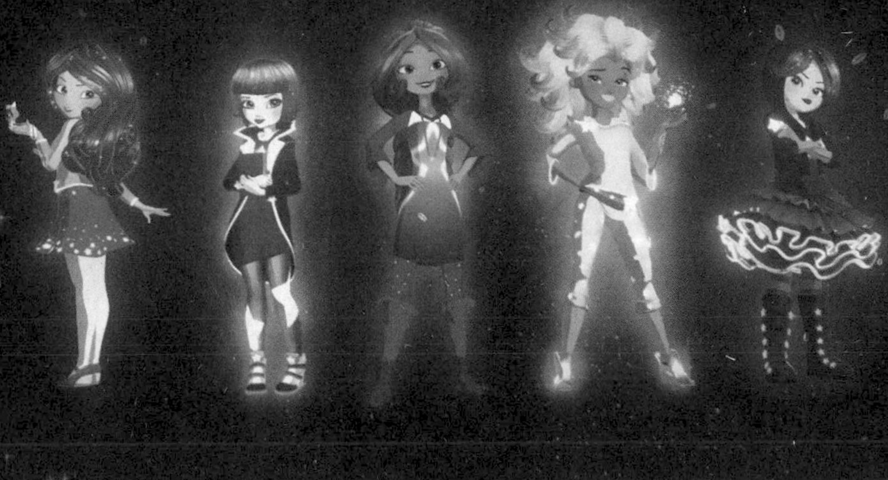

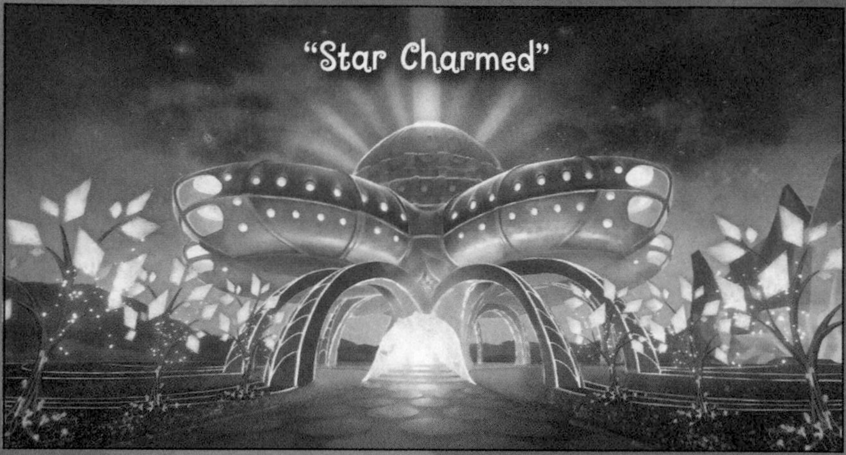
"Star Charmed"

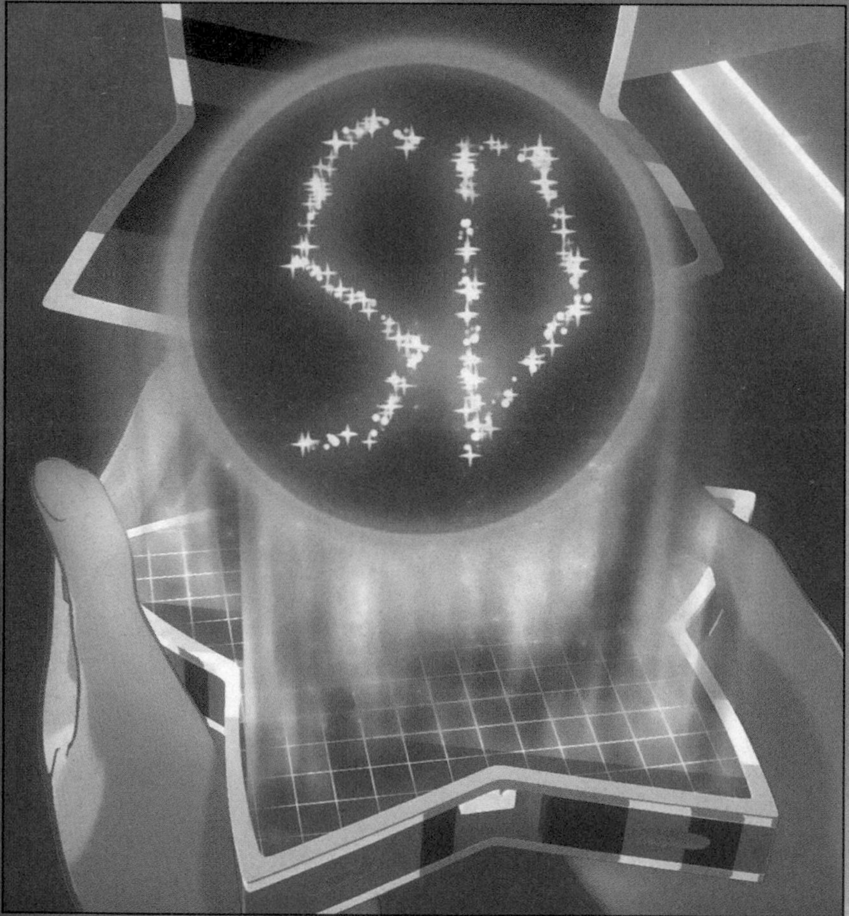

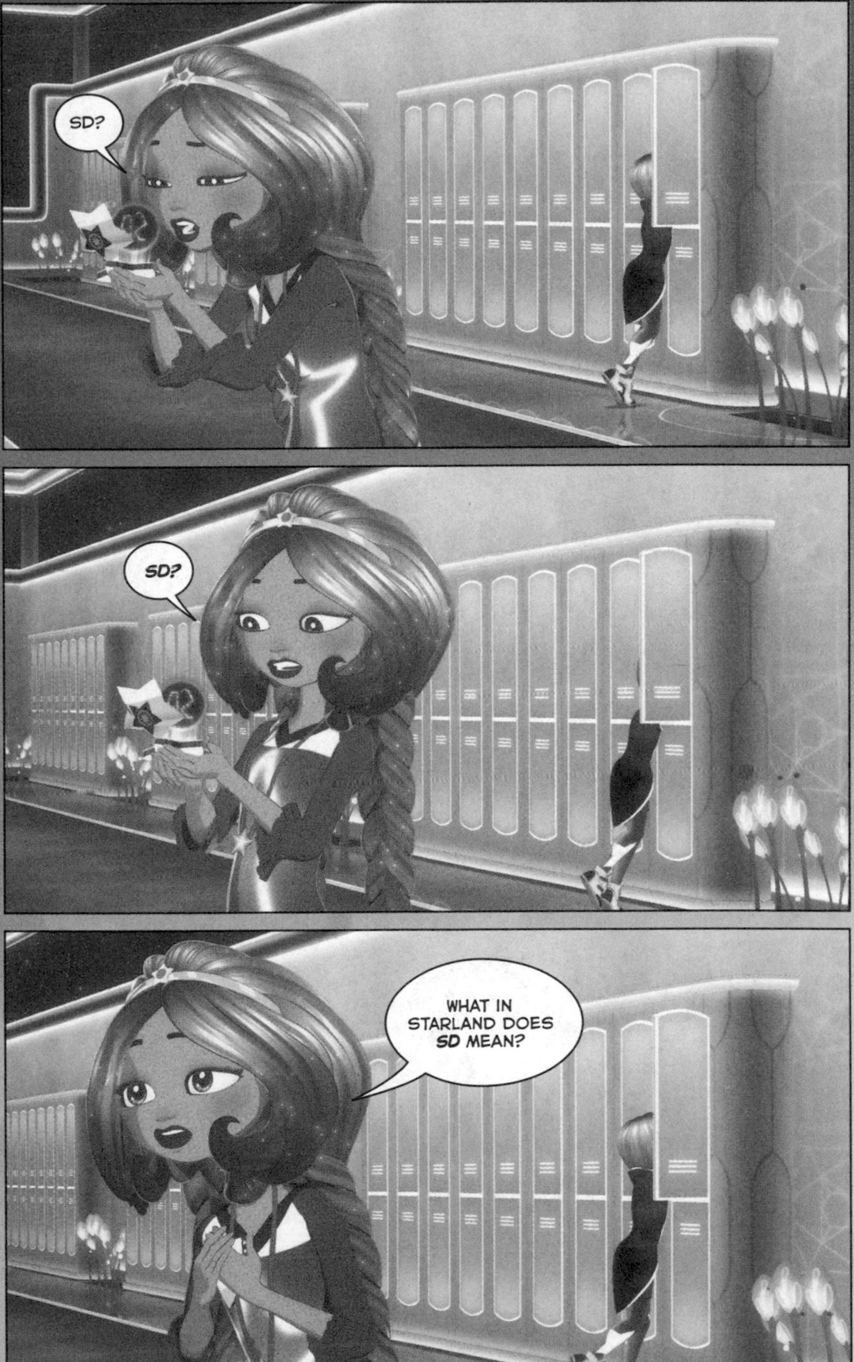
SD?
SD?
WHAT IN STARLAND DOES SD MEAN?

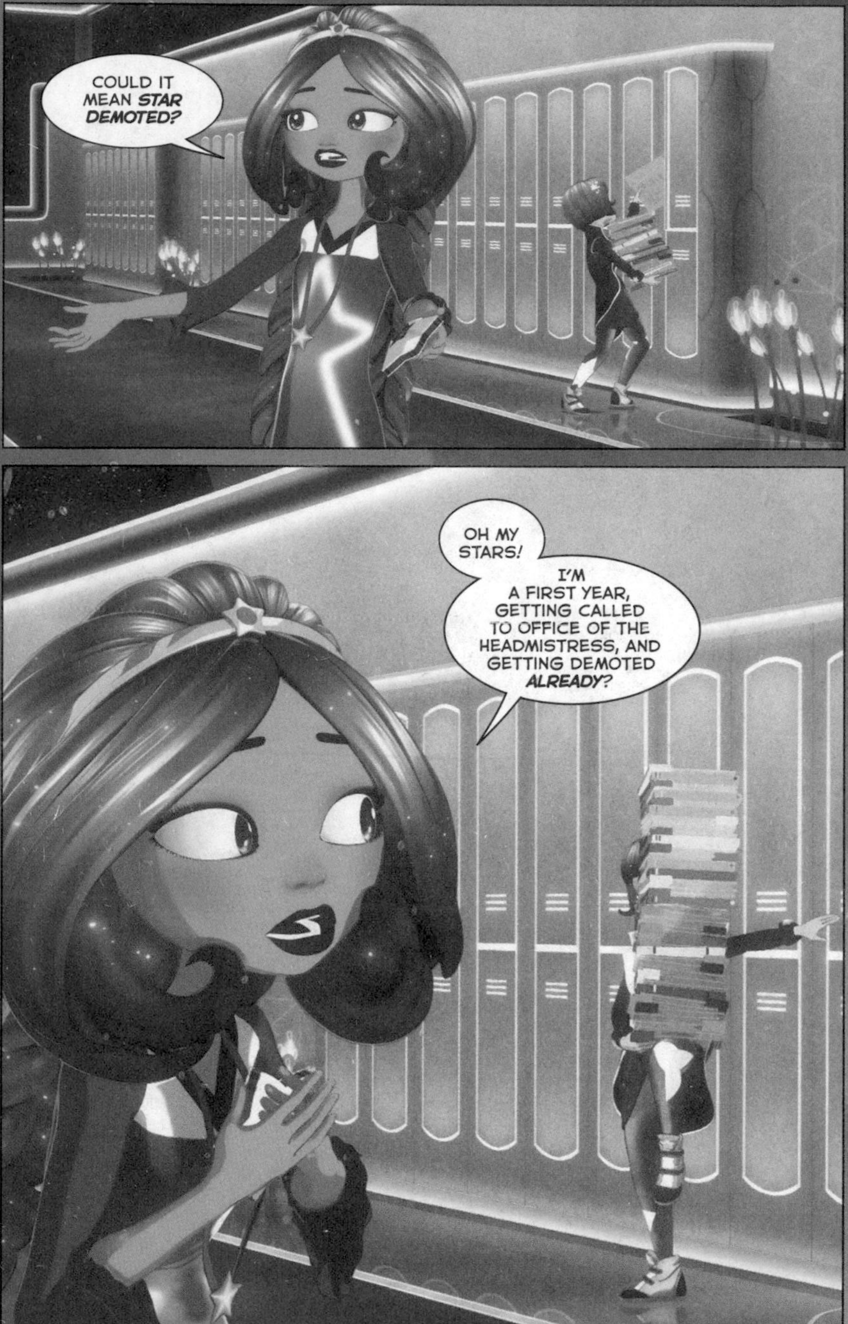
COULD IT MEAN ***STAR DEMOTED?***
OH MY STARS!
I'M A FIRST YEAR, GETTING CALLED TO OFFICE OF THE HEADMISTRESS, AND GETTING DEMOTED ***ALREADY?***

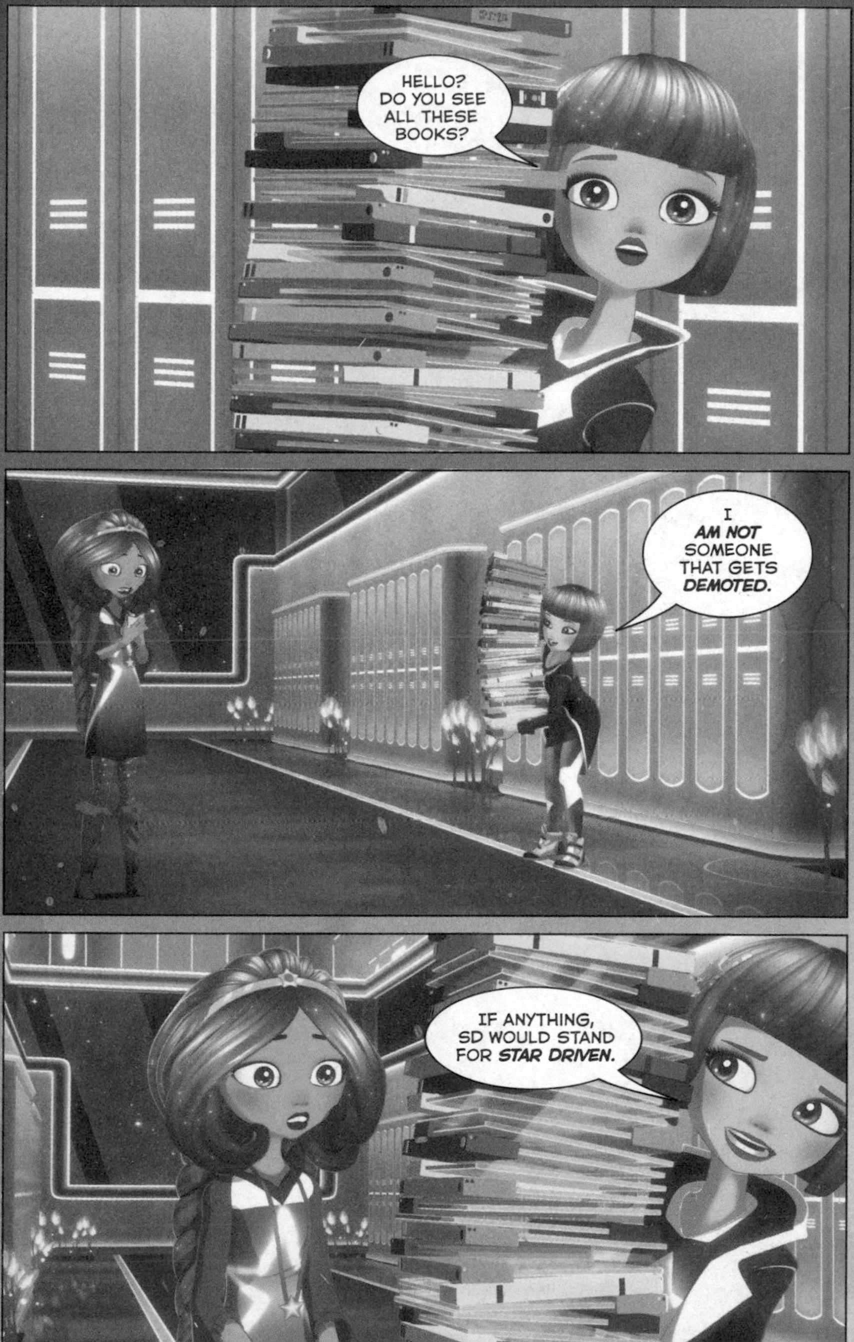
HELLO? DO YOU SEE ALL THESE BOOKS?
I **AM NOT** SOMEONE THAT GETS **DEMOTED.**
IF ANYTHING, SD WOULD STAND FOR **STAR DRIVEN.**

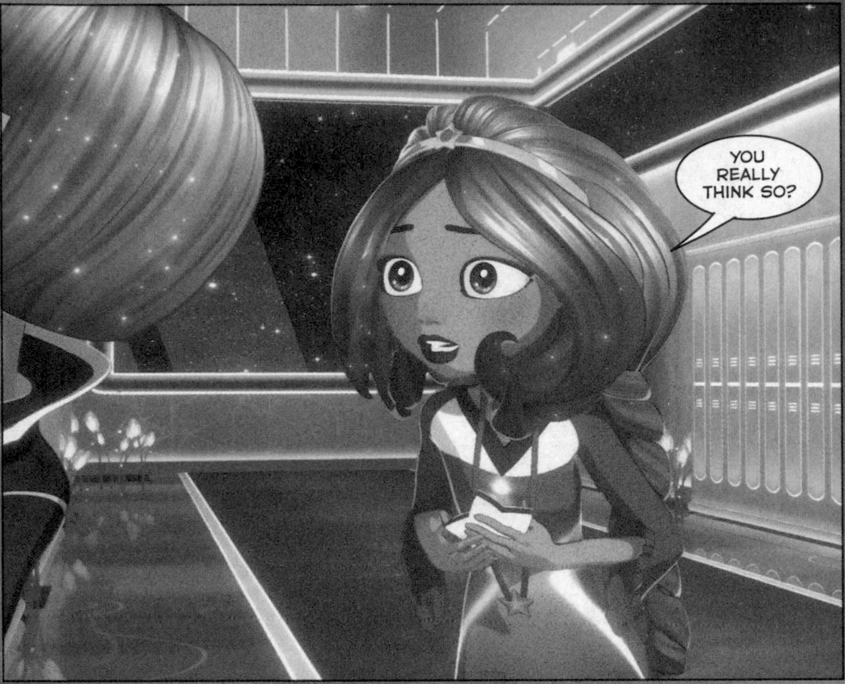
YOU REALLY THINK SO?

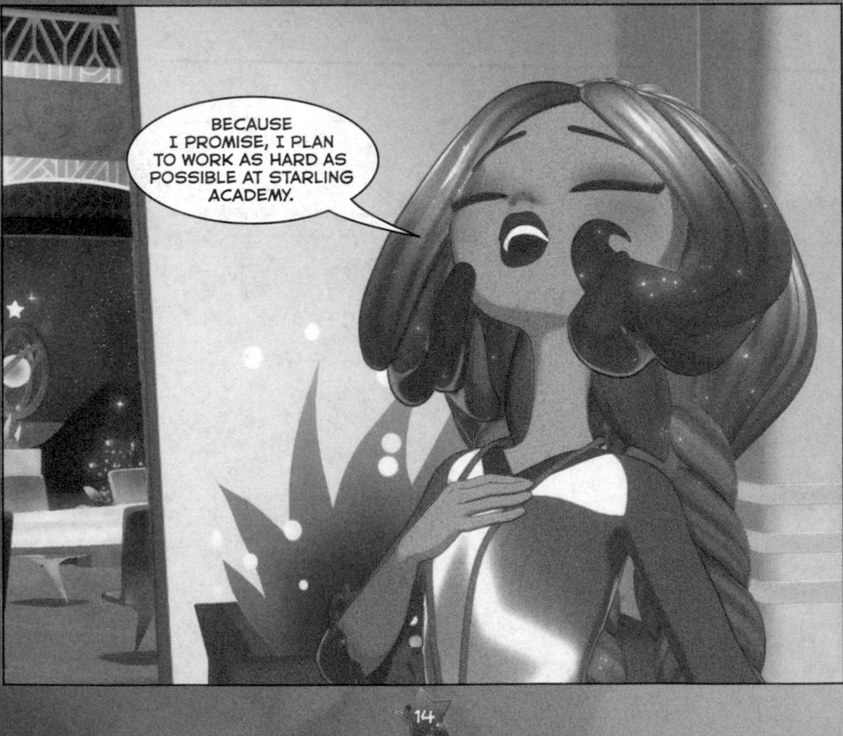
BECAUSE I PROMISE, I PLAN TO WORK AS HARD AS POSSIBLE AT STARLING ACADEMY.

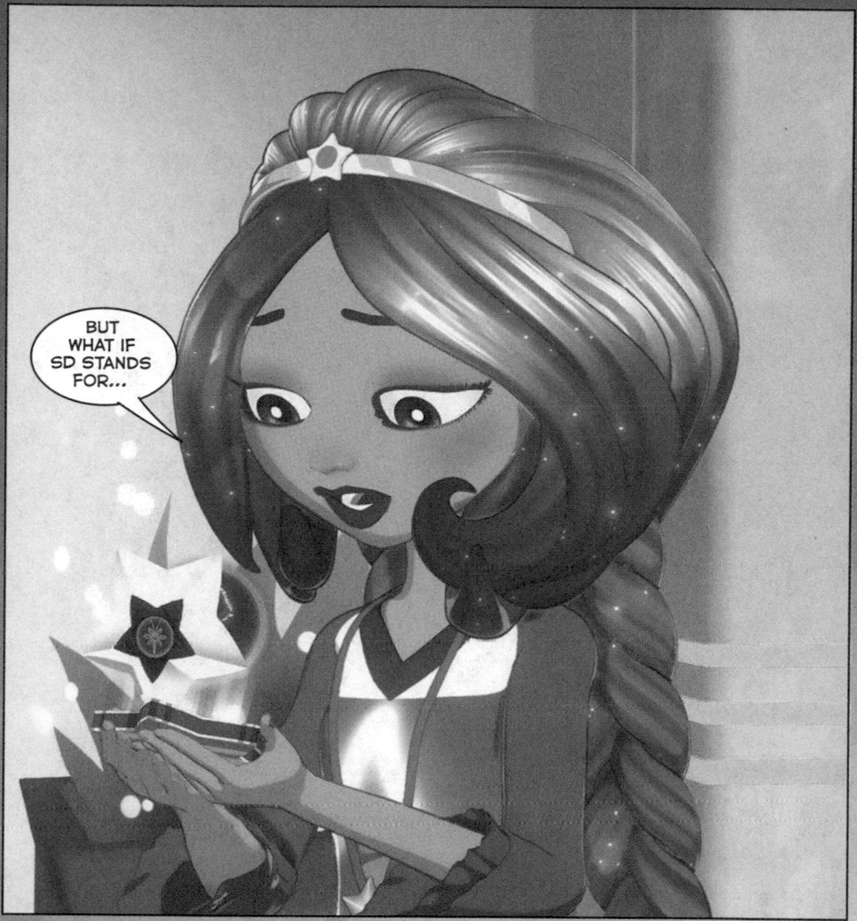
BUT WHAT IF SD STANDS FOR...

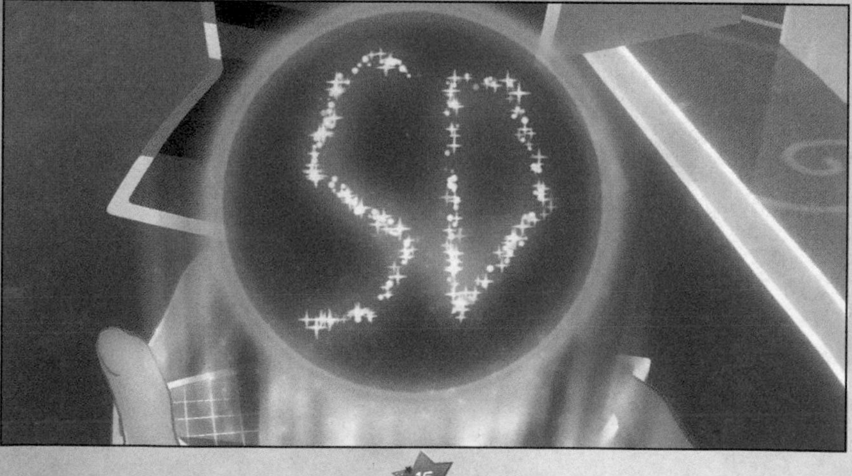
SD

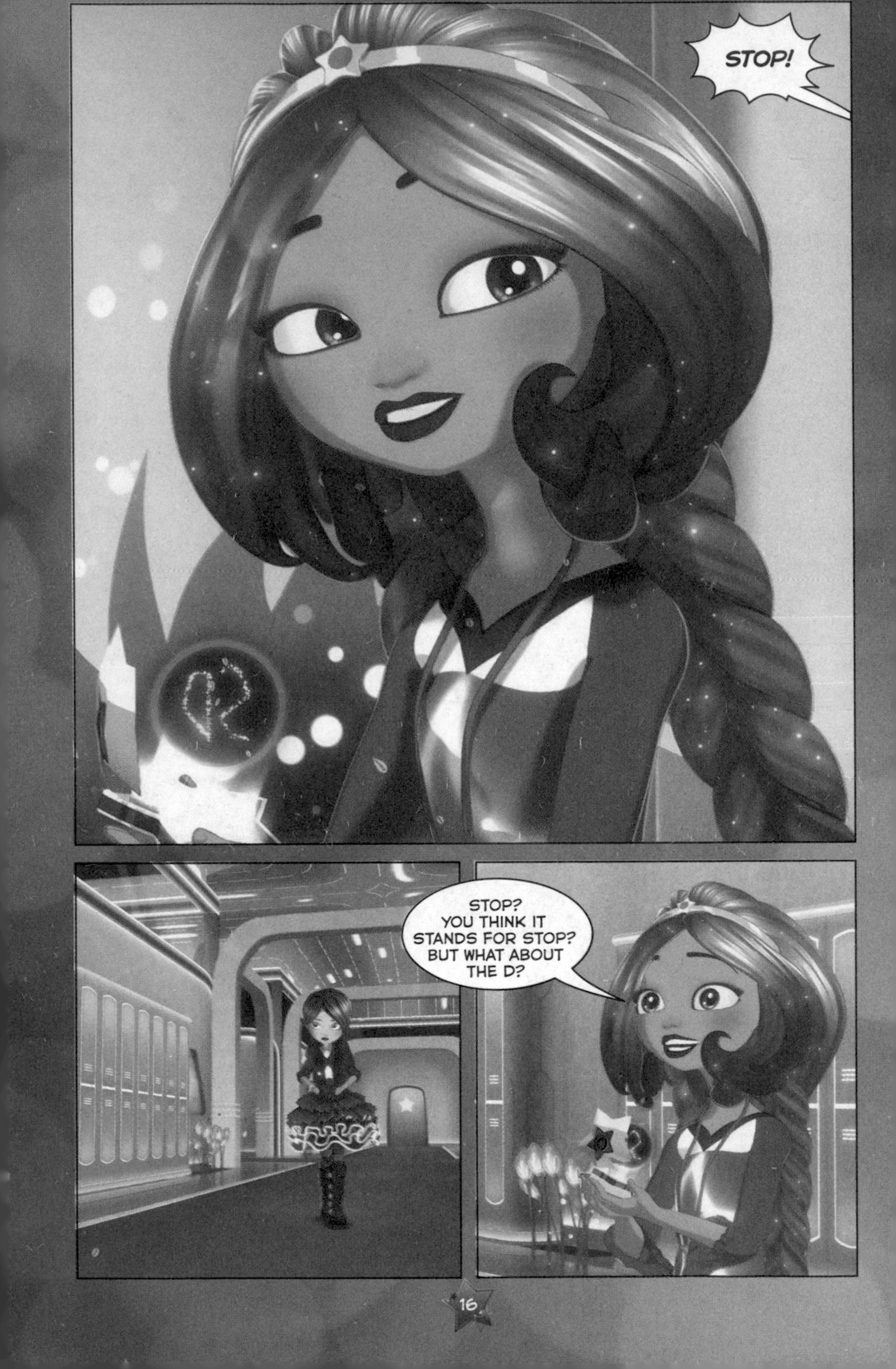
STOP!
STOP? YOU THINK IT STANDS FOR STOP? BUT WHAT ABOUT THE D?

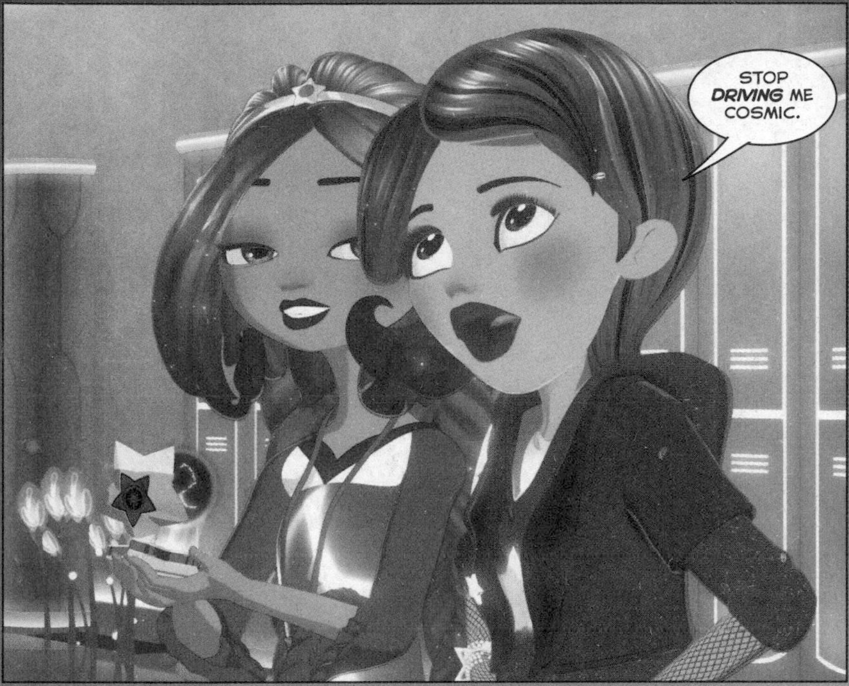
STOP DRIVING ME COSMIC.

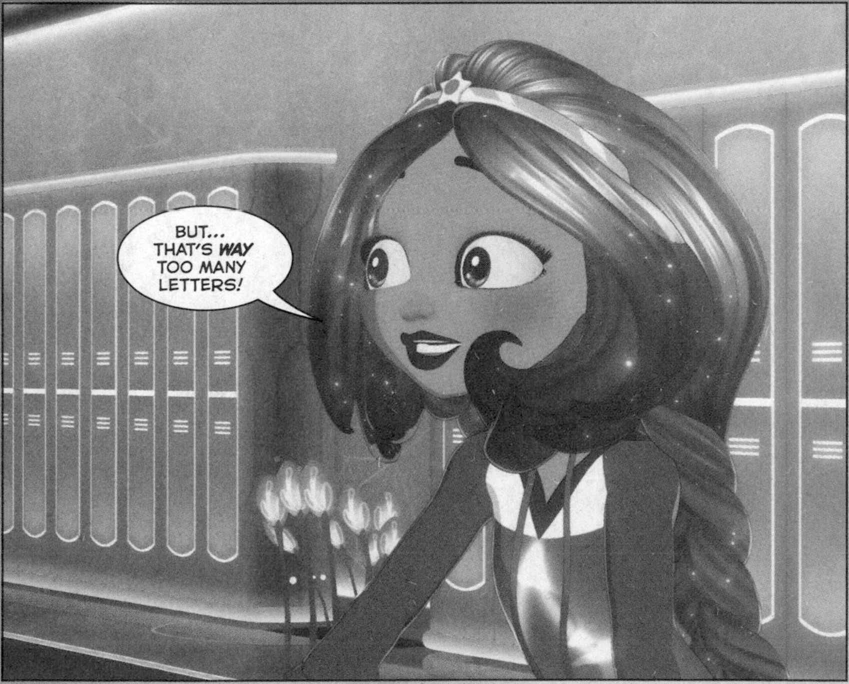
BUT... THAT'S WAY TOO MANY LETTERS!

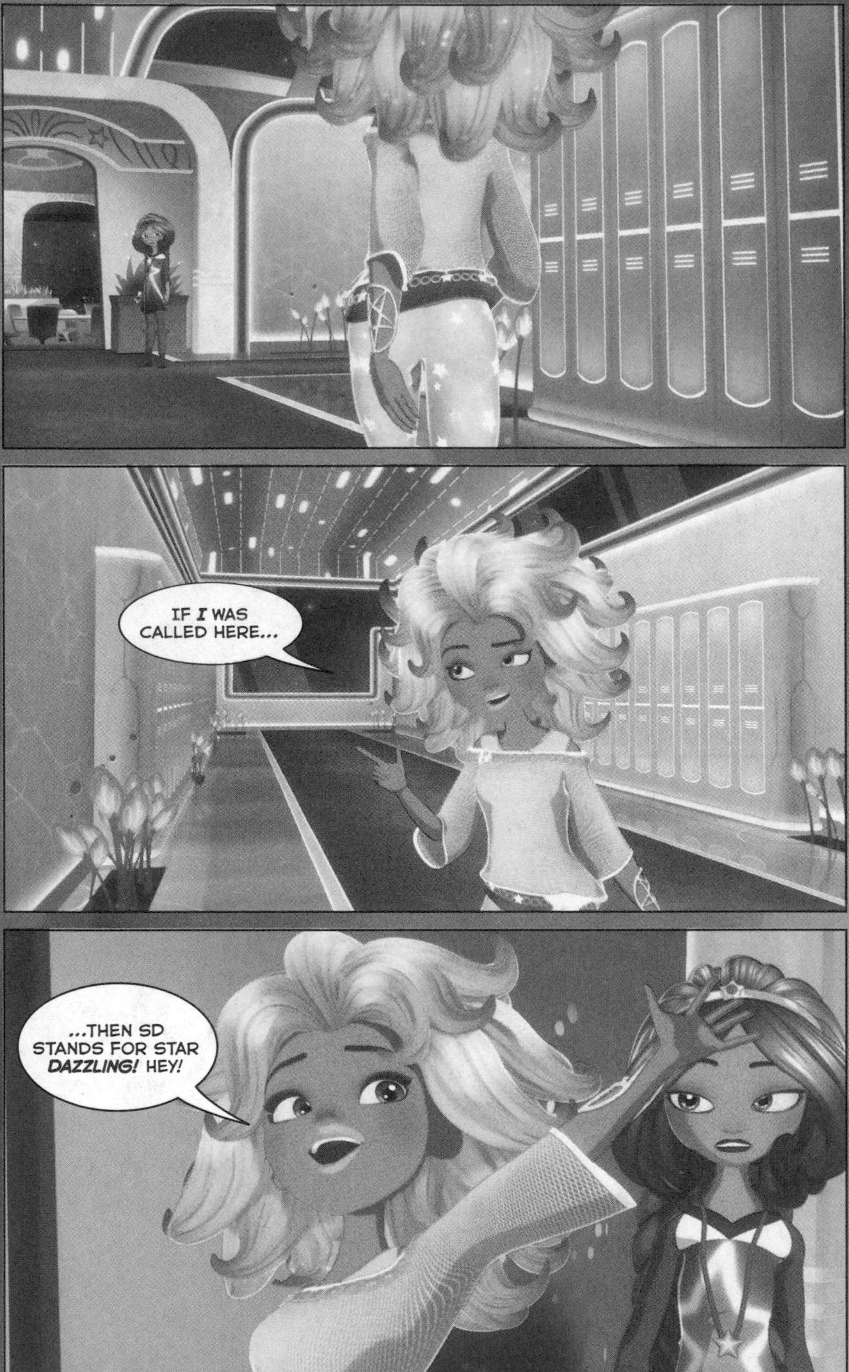
IF *I* WAS CALLED HERE...
...THEN SD STANDS FOR STAR *DAZZLING!* HEY!

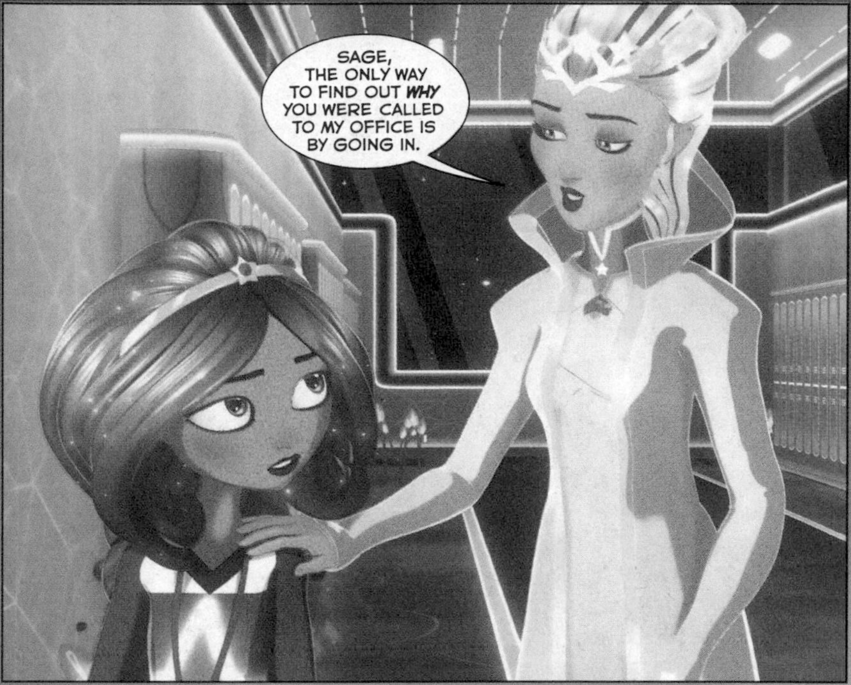
SAGE, THE ONLY WAY TO FIND OUT *WHY* YOU WERE CALLED TO MY OFFICE IS BY GOING IN.

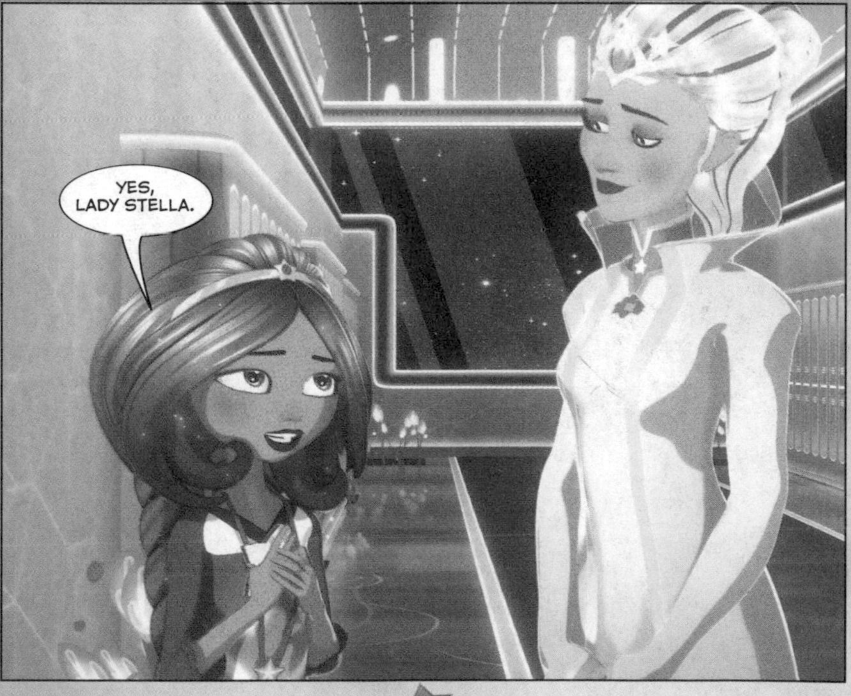
YES, LADY STELLA.

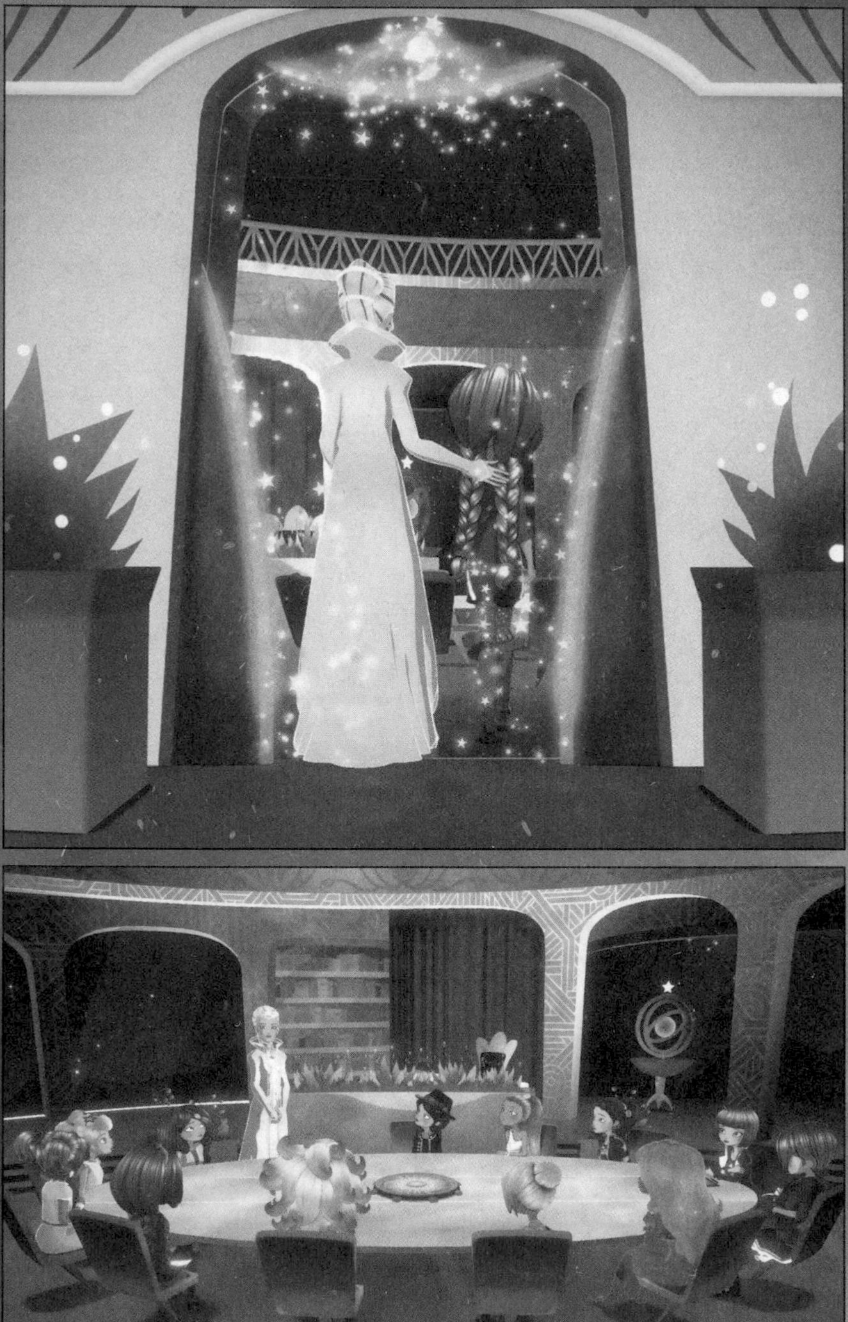

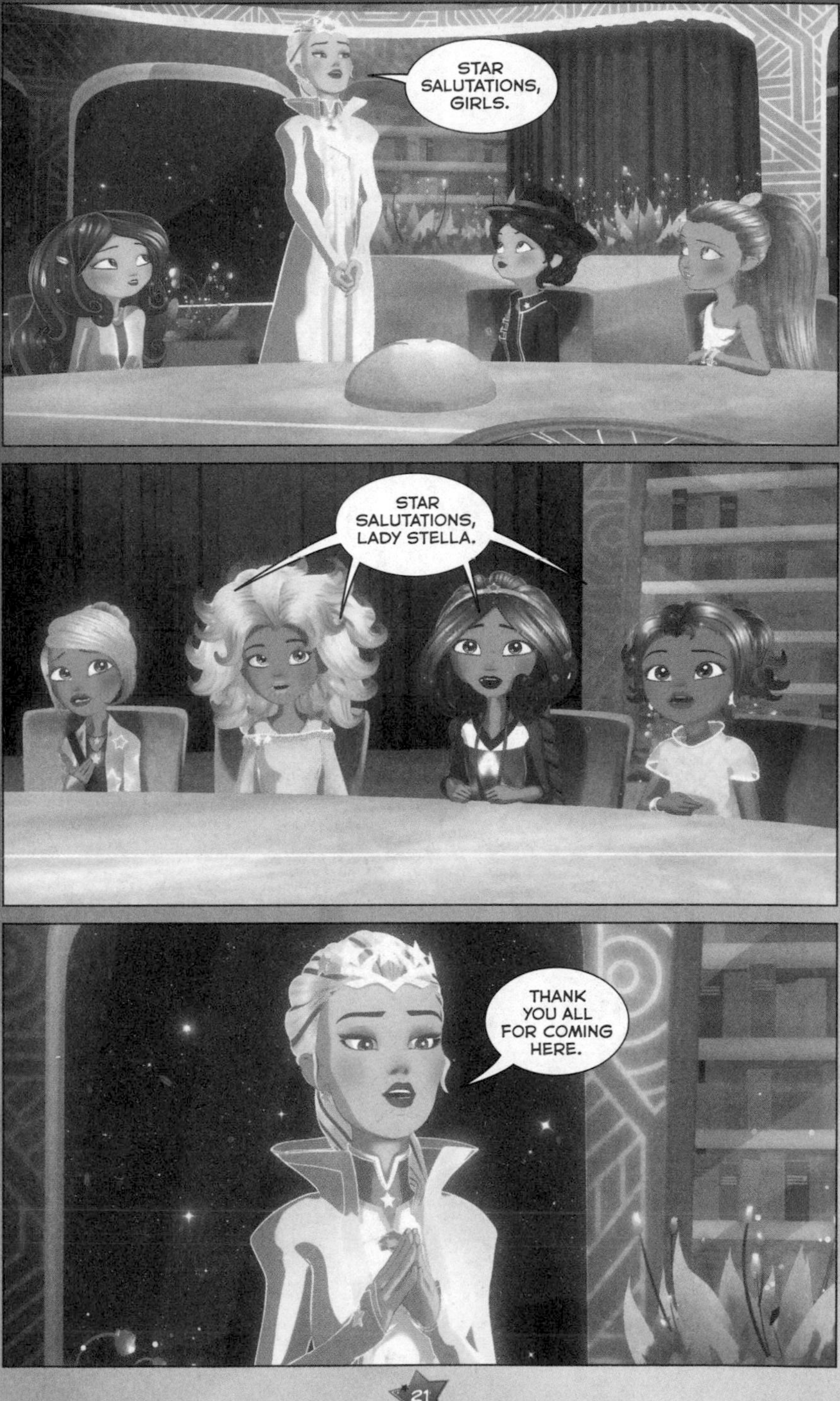
STAR SALUTATIONS, GIRLS.
STAR SALUTATIONS, LADY STELLA.
THANK YOU ALL FOR COMING HERE.

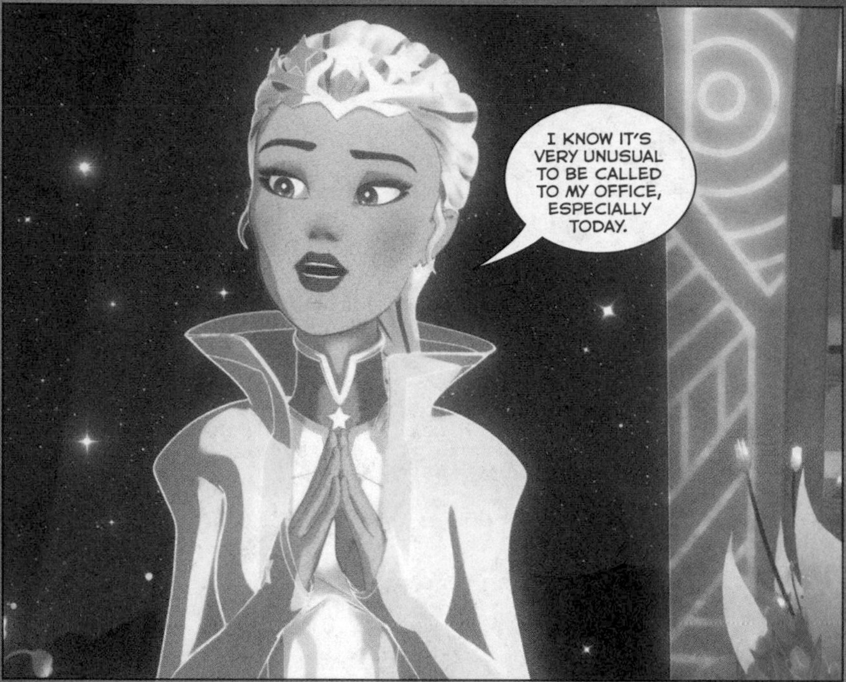
I KNOW IT'S VERY UNUSUAL TO BE CALLED TO MY OFFICE, ESPECIALLY TODAY.

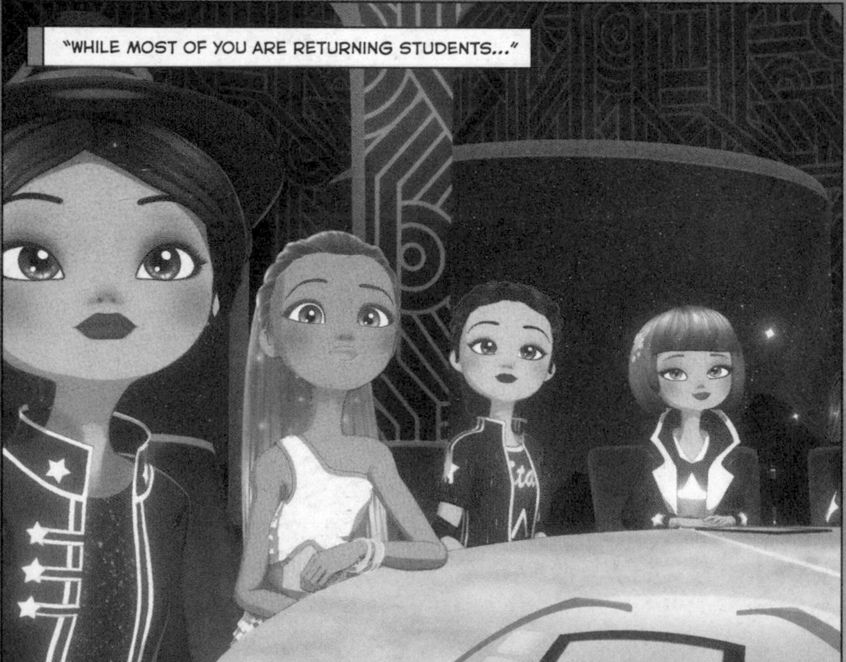
"WHILE MOST OF YOU ARE RETURNING STUDENTS..."

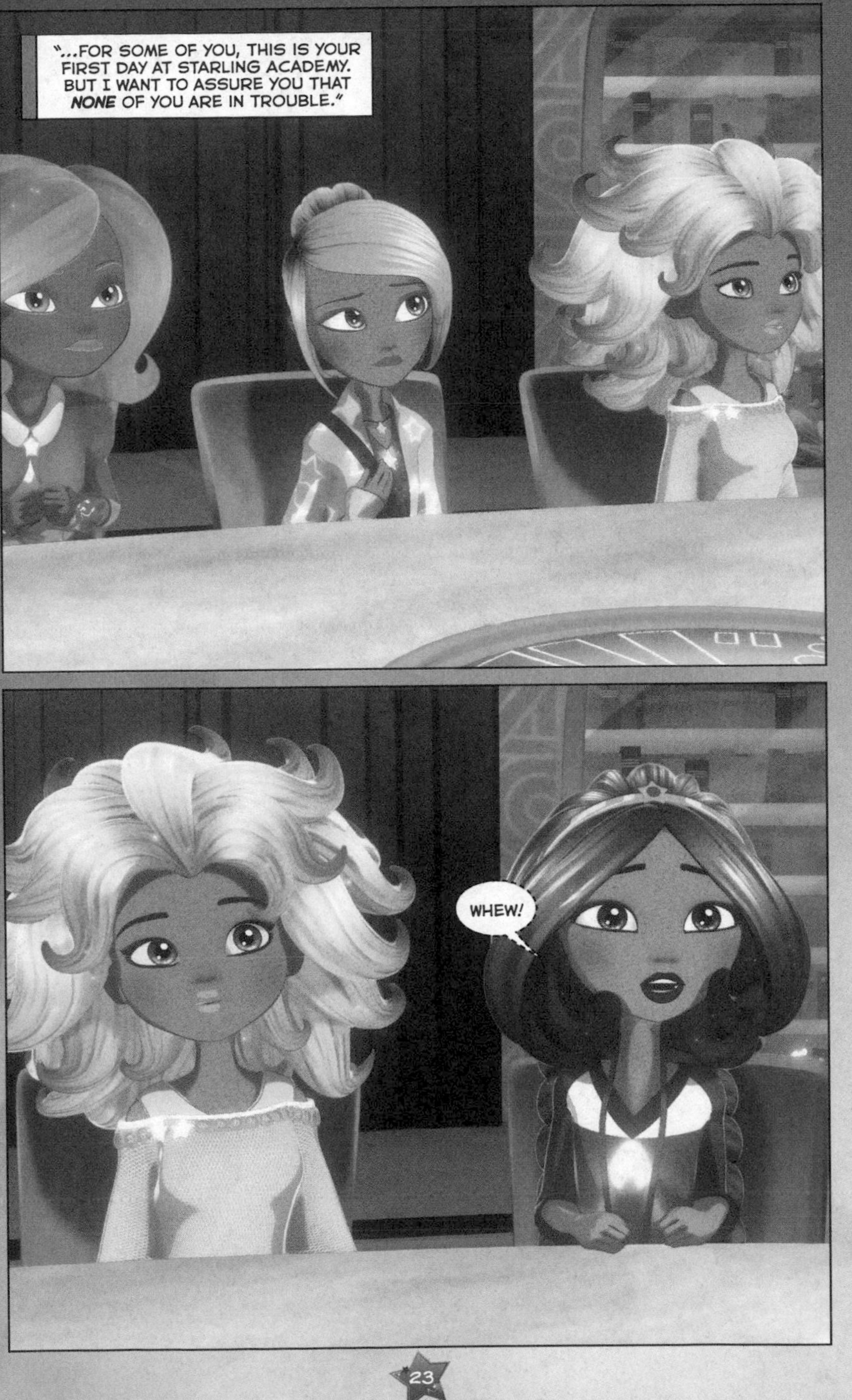
"...FOR SOME OF YOU, THIS IS YOUR FIRST DAY AT STARLING ACADEMY. BUT I WANT TO ASSURE YOU THAT *NONE* OF YOU ARE IN TROUBLE."
WHEW!

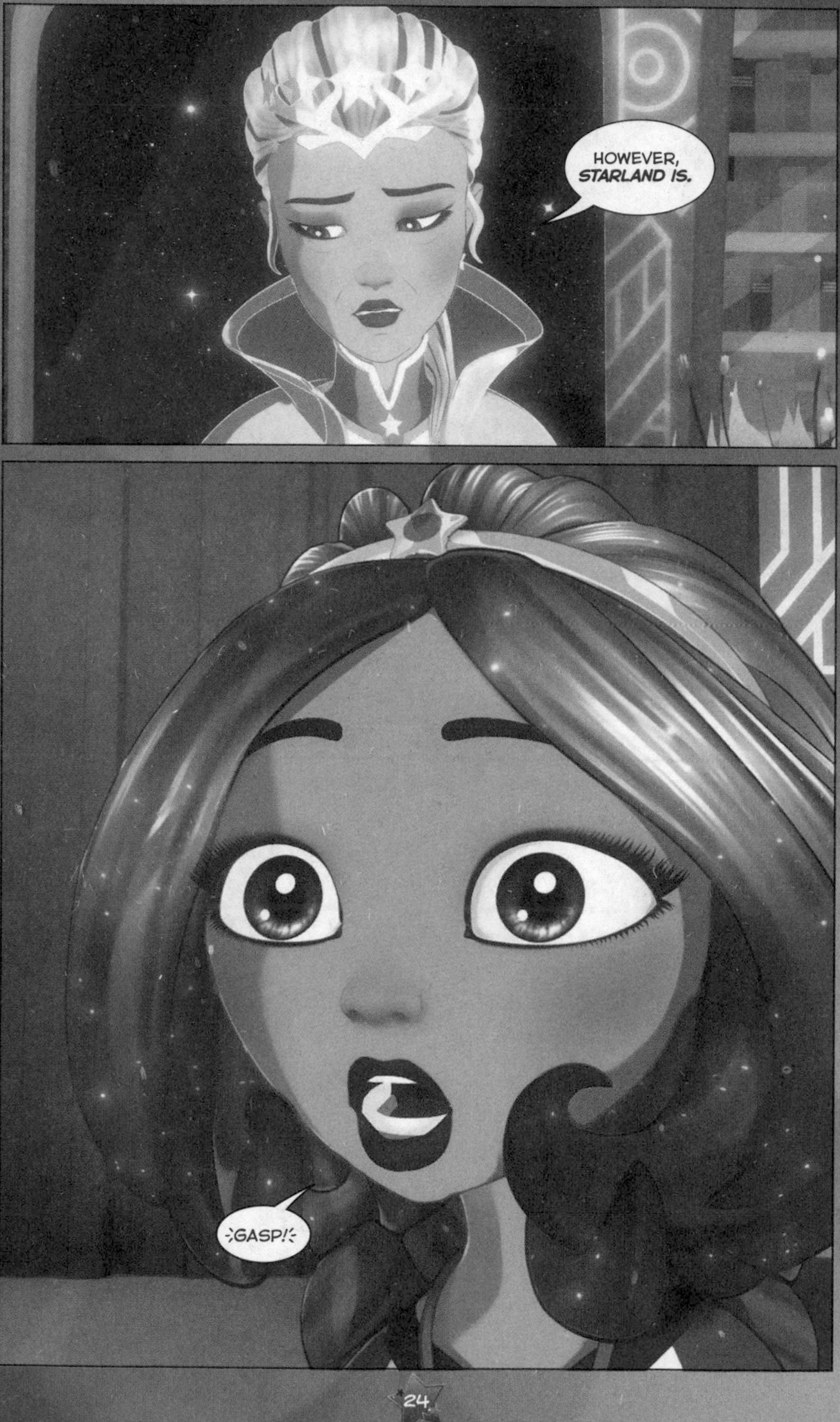
HOWEVER, STARLAND IS.
GASP!

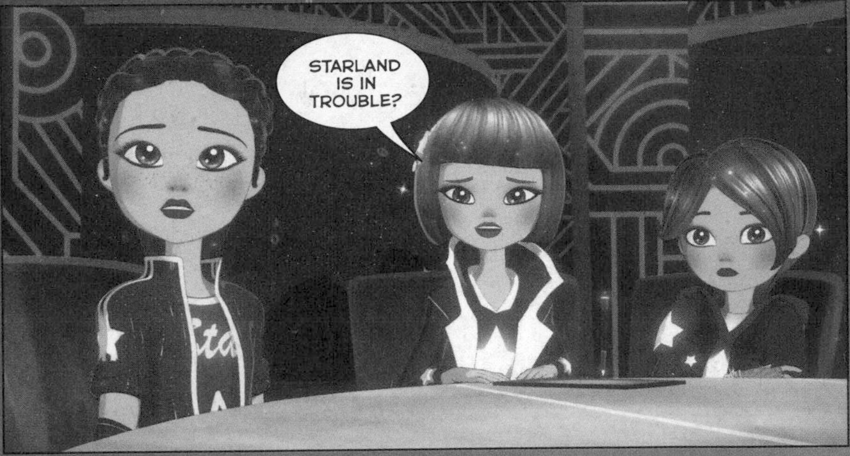
STARLAND IS IN TROUBLE?

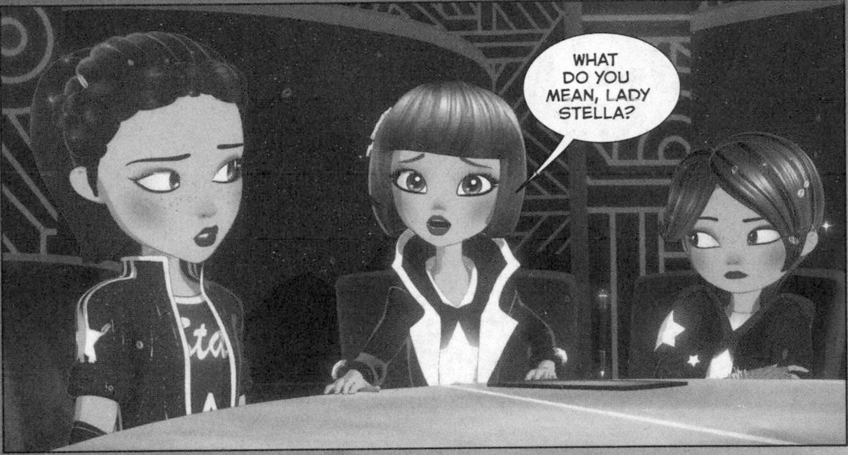
WHAT DO YOU MEAN, LADY STELLA?

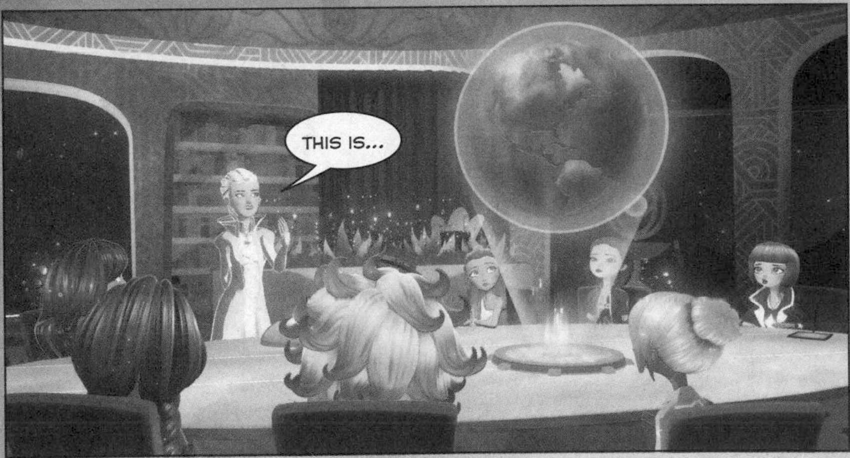
THIS IS...

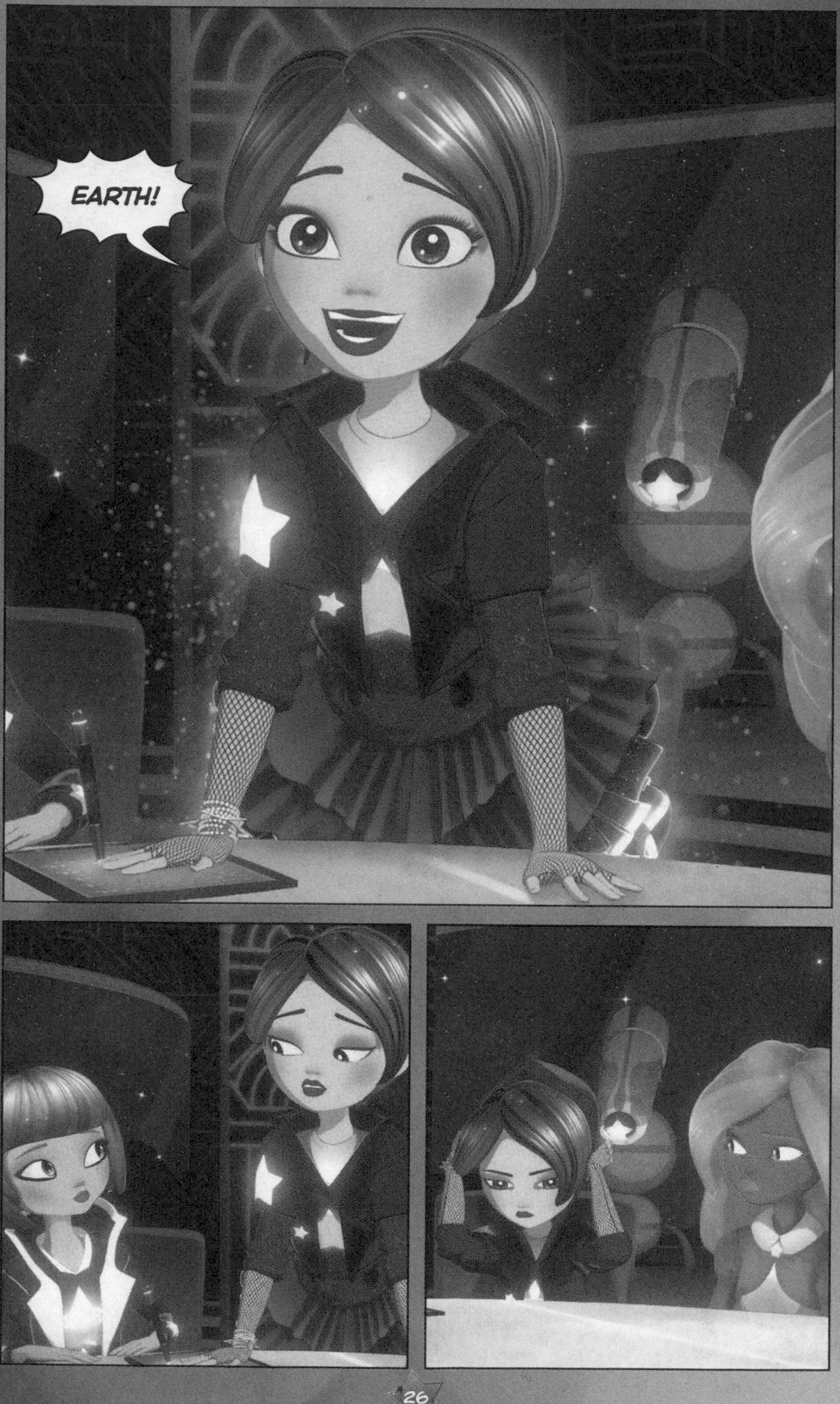
EARTH!

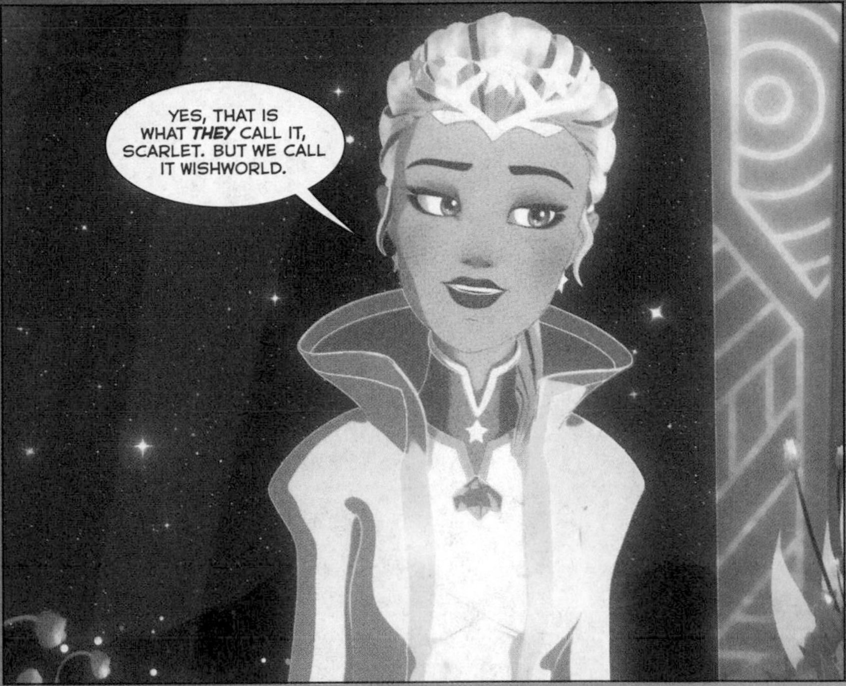
YES, THAT IS WHAT *THEY* CALL IT, SCARLET. BUT WE CALL IT WISHWORLD.

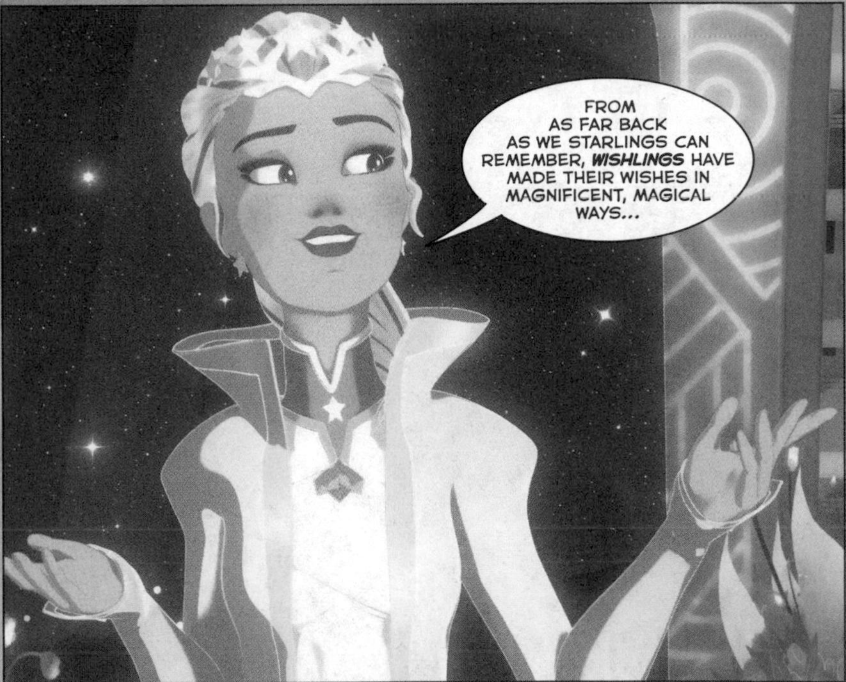
FROM AS FAR BACK AS WE STARLINGS CAN REMEMBER, *WISHLINGS* HAVE MADE THEIR WISHES IN MAGNIFICENT, MAGICAL WAYS...

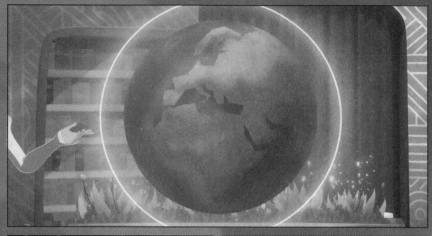

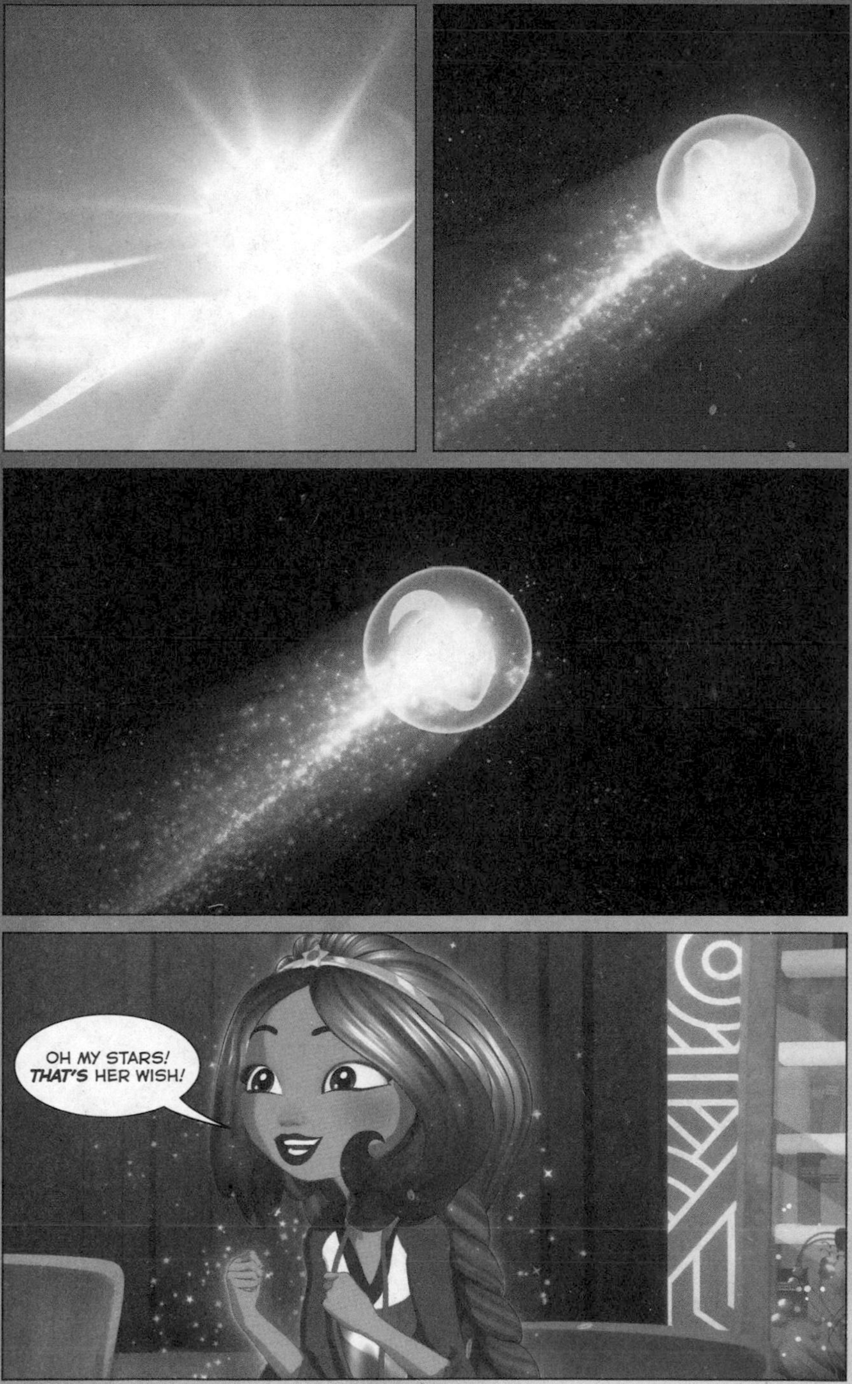
OH MY STARS! THAT'S HER WISH!

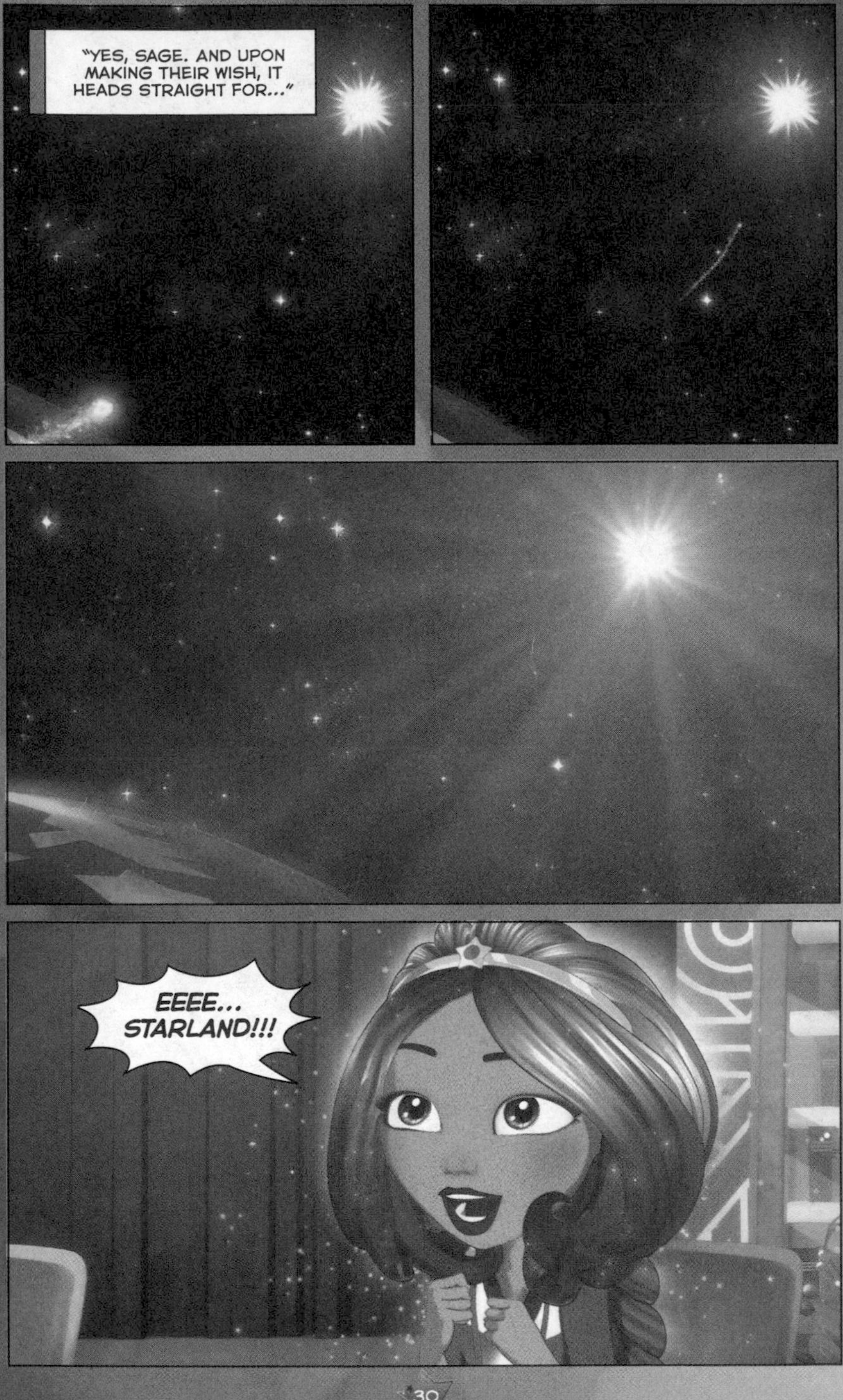
"YES, SAGE. AND UPON MAKING THEIR WISH, IT HEADS STRAIGHT FOR..."
EEEE... STARLAND!!!

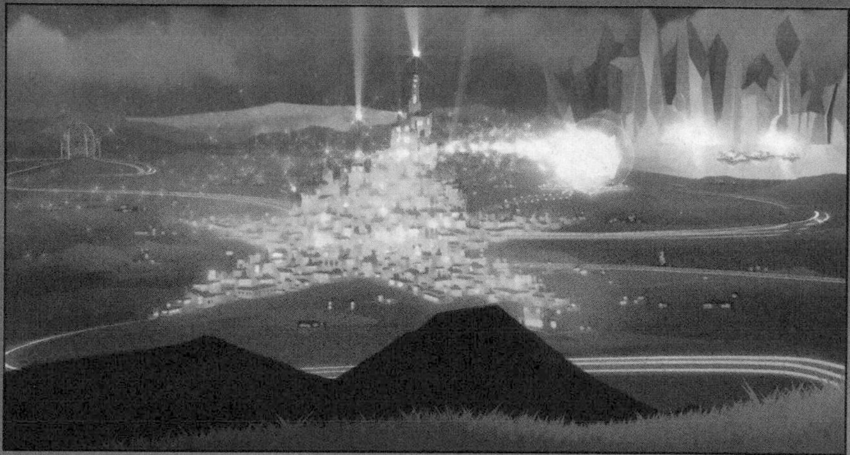

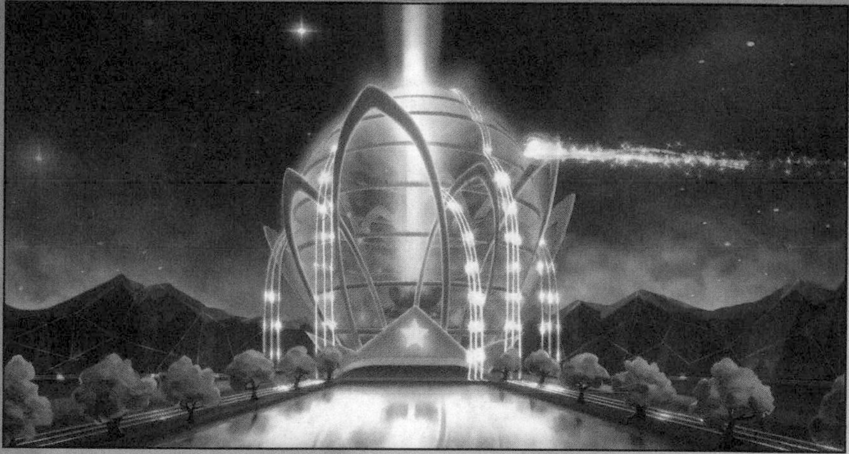

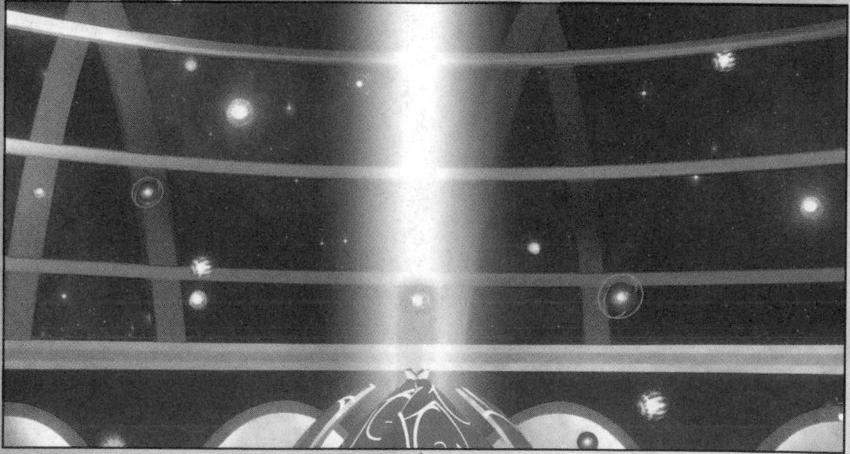

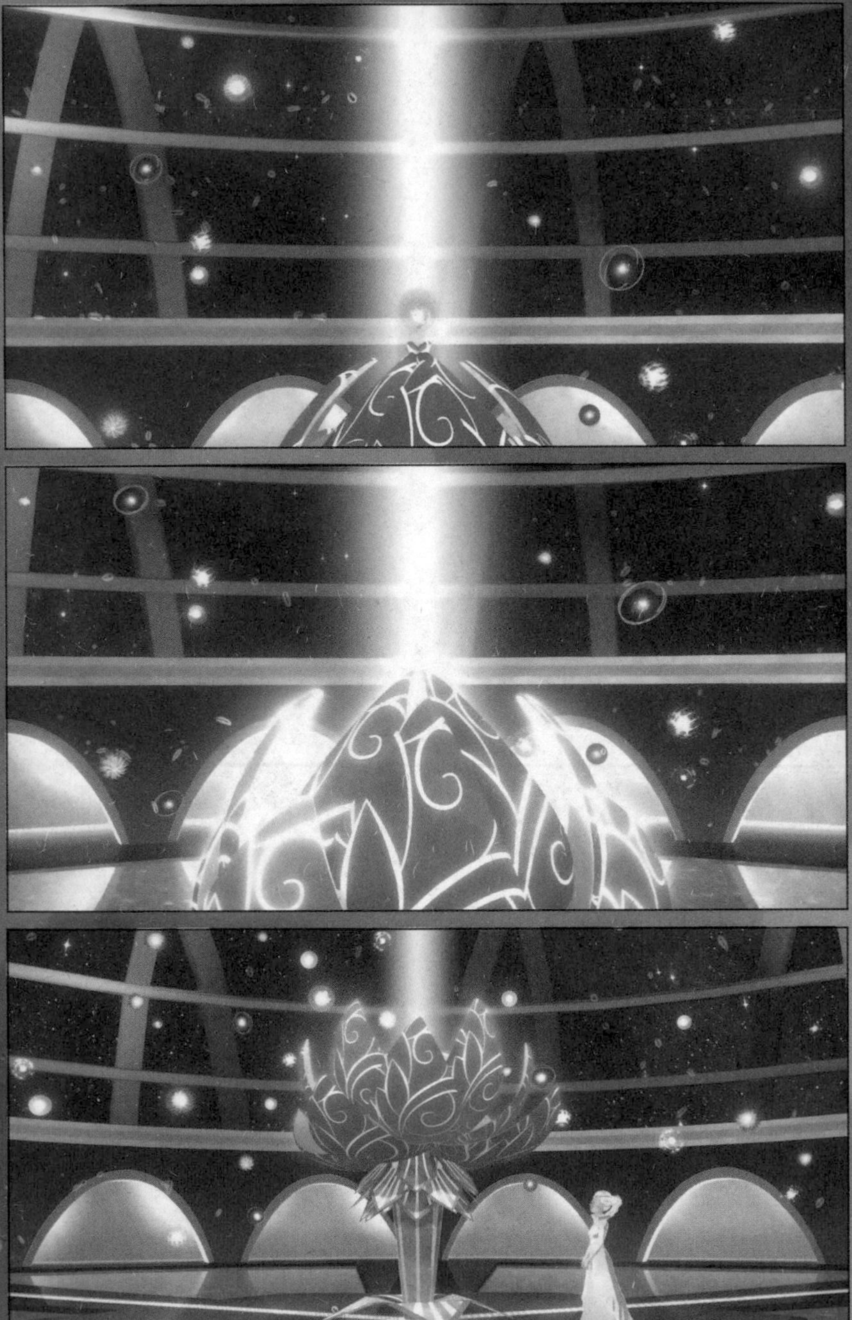

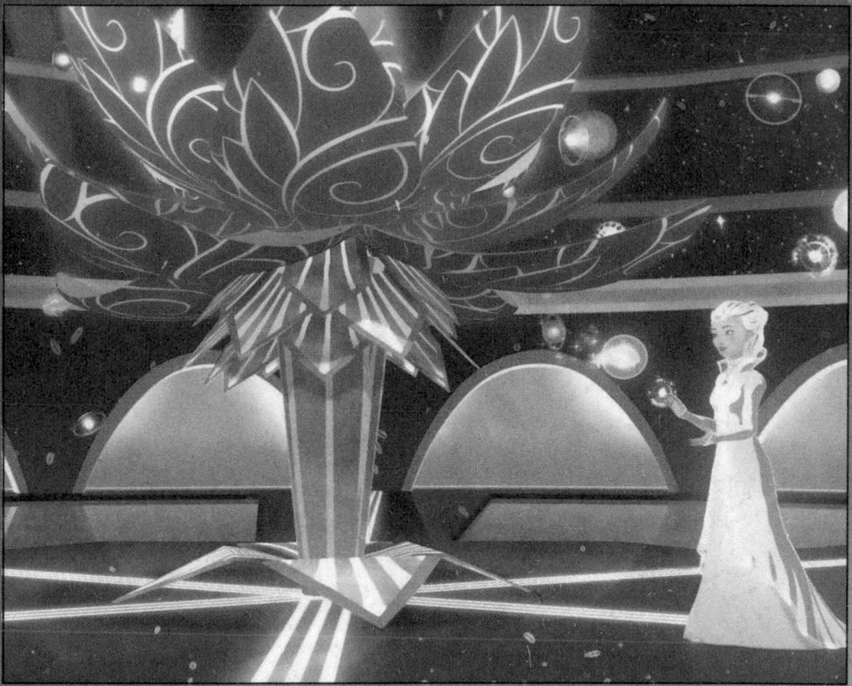

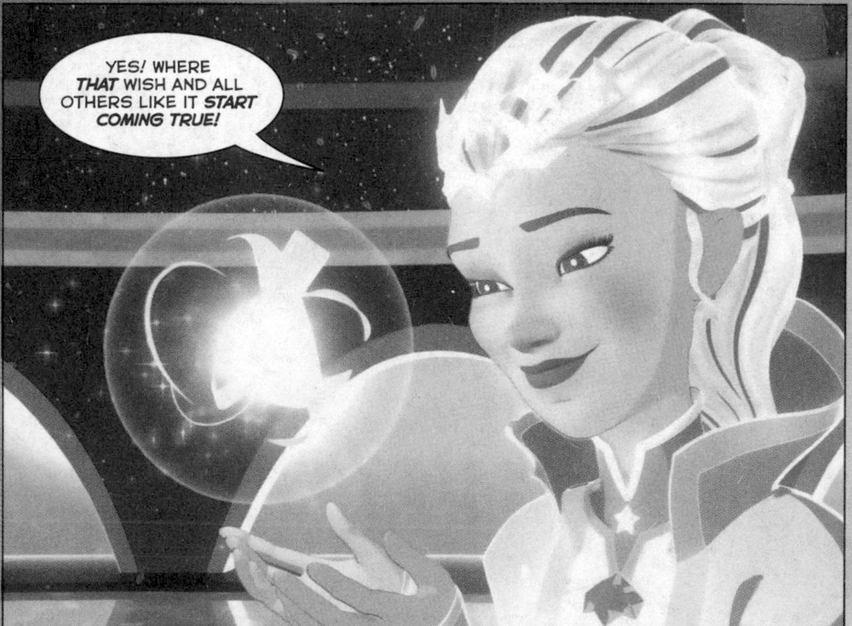
YES! WHERE *THAT* WISH AND ALL OTHERS LIKE IT *START COMING TRUE!*

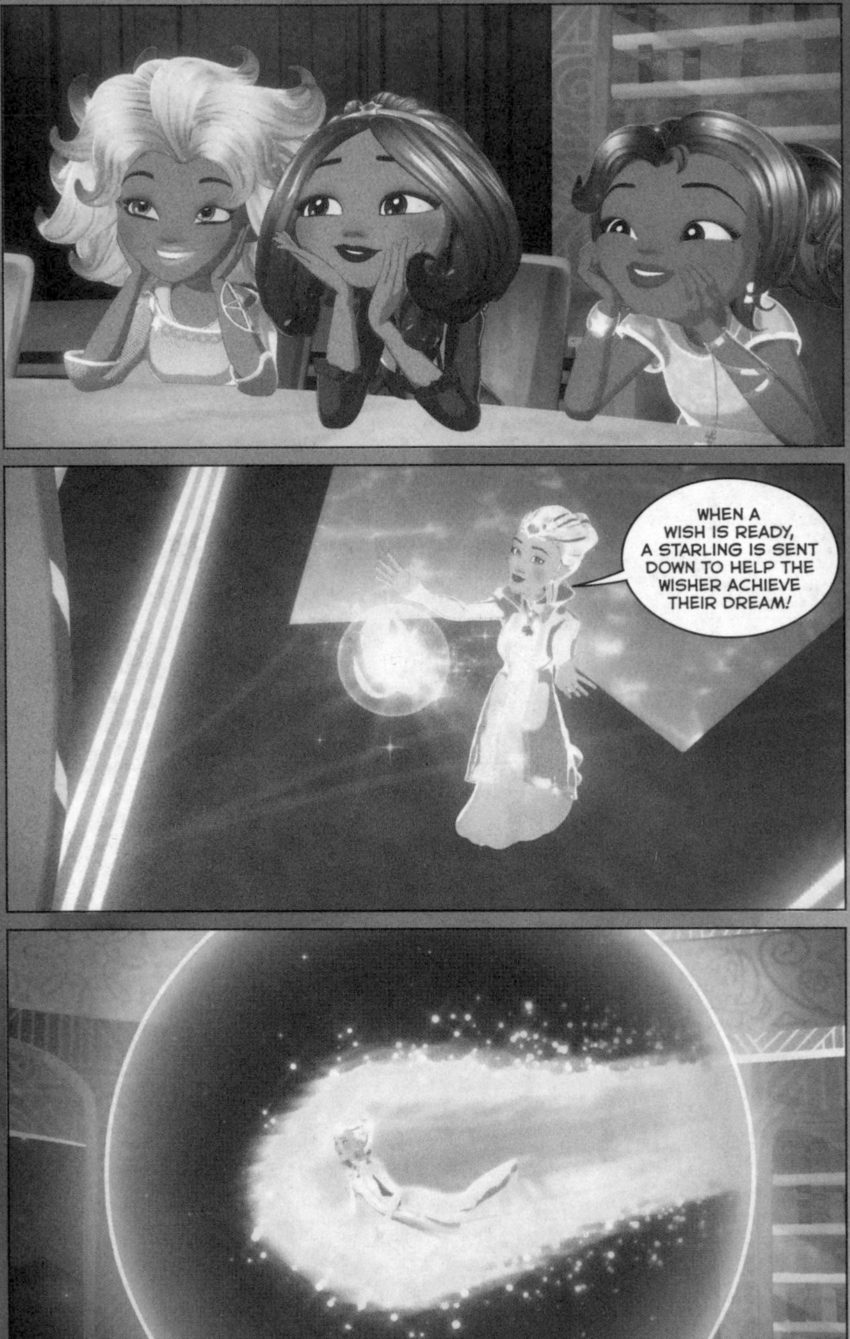
WHEN A WISH IS READY, A STARLING IS SENT DOWN TO HELP THE WISHER ACHIEVE THEIR DREAM!

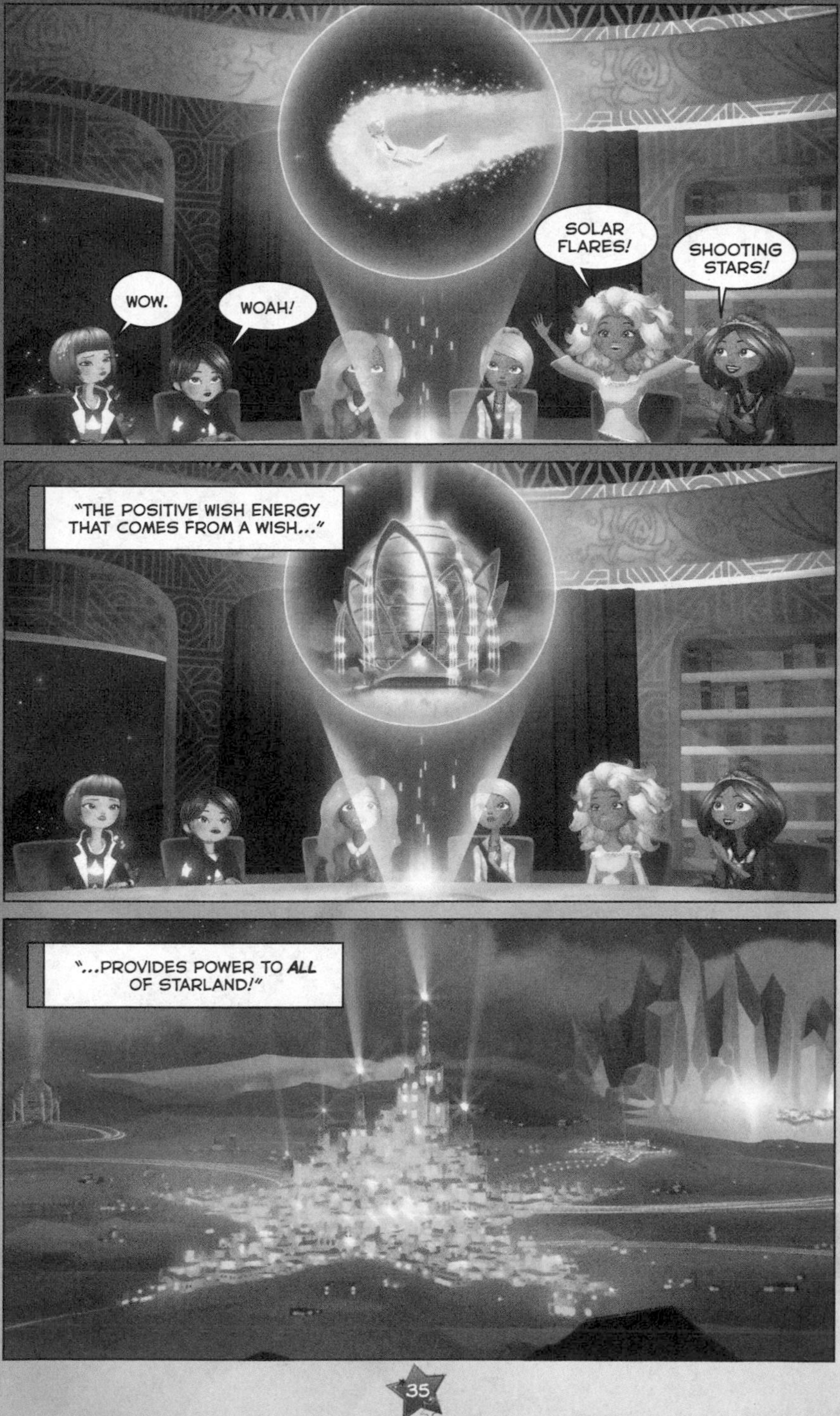
WOW.
WOAH!
SOLAR FLARES!
SHOOTING STARS!
"THE POSITIVE WISH ENERGY THAT COMES FROM A WISH..."
"...PROVIDES POWER TO *ALL* OF STARLAND!"

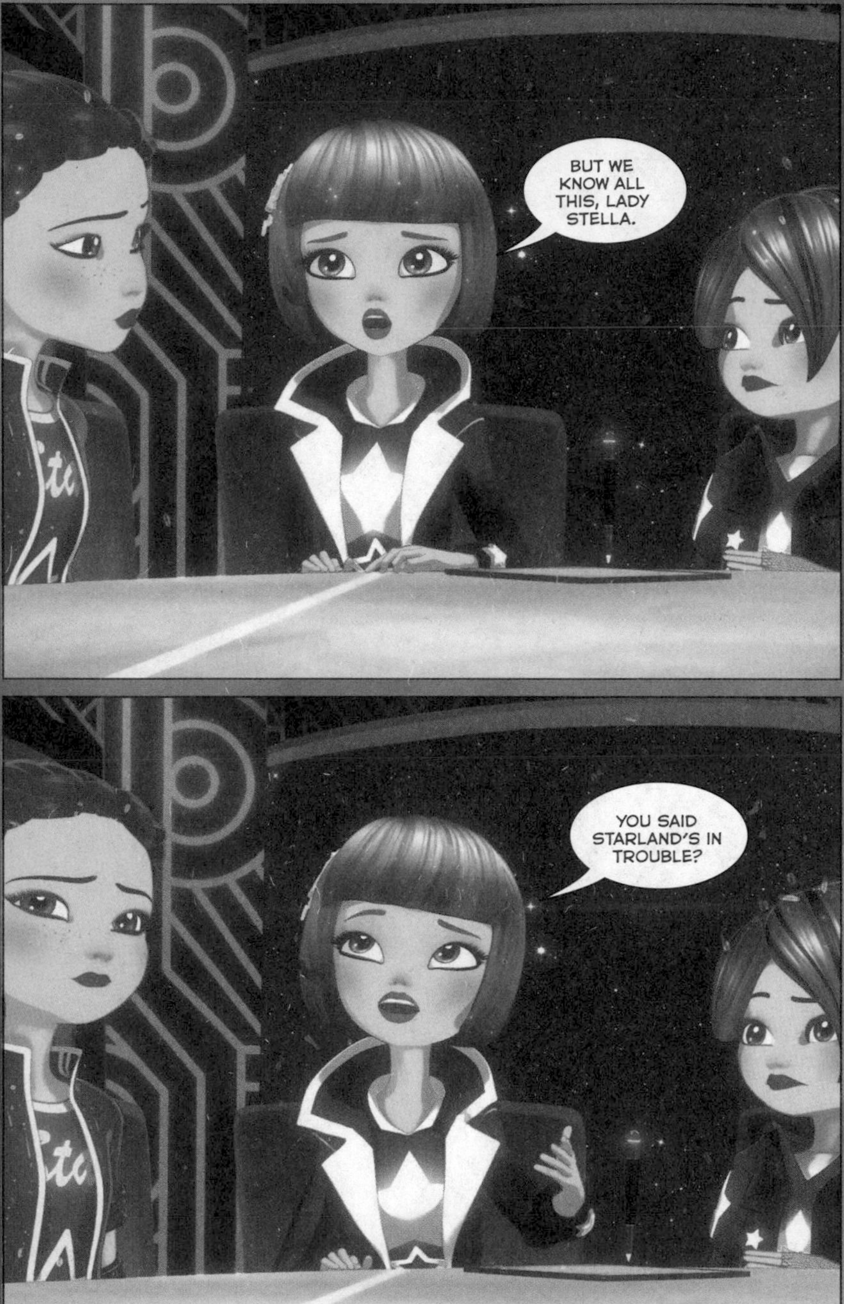
BUT WE KNOW ALL THIS, LADY STELLA.
YOU SAID STARLAND'S IN TROUBLE?

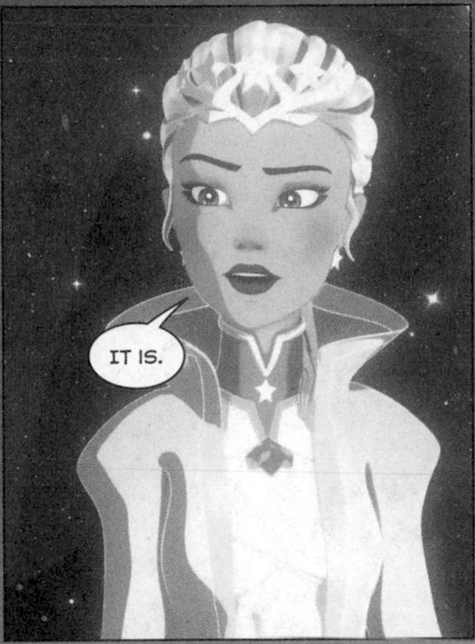
IT IS.

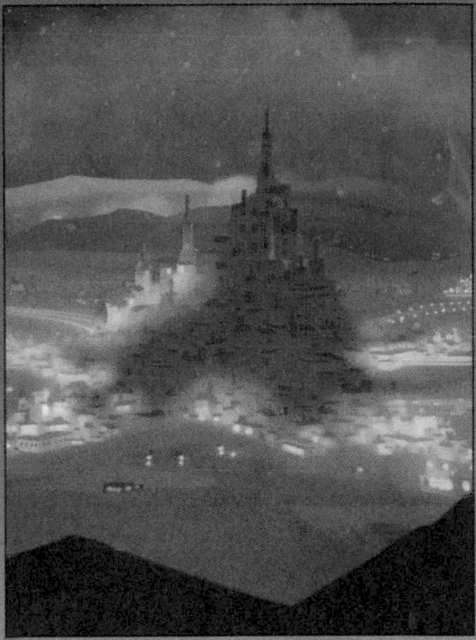

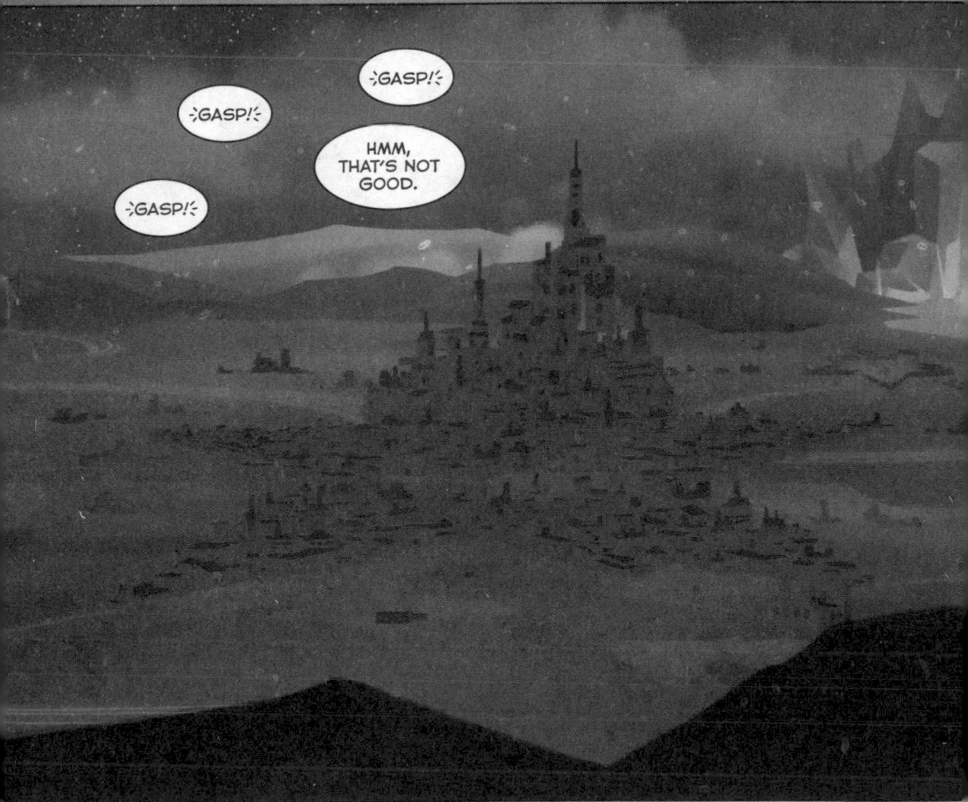
GASP!
GASP!
HMM, THAT'S NOT GOOD.
GASP!

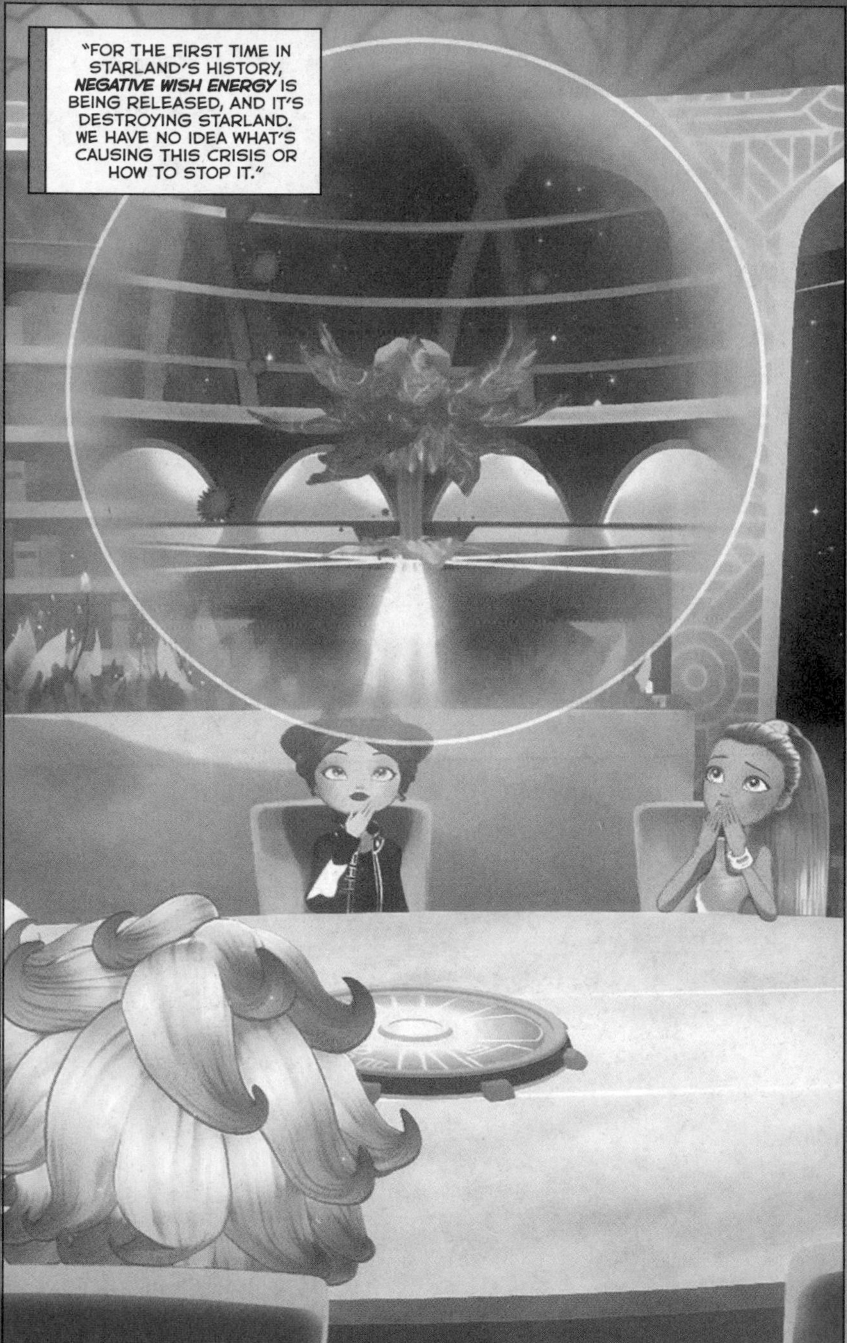
"FOR THE FIRST TIME IN STARLAND'S HISTORY, ***NEGATIVE WISH ENERGY*** IS BEING RELEASED, AND IT'S DESTROYING STARLAND. WE HAVE NO IDEA WHAT'S CAUSING THIS CRISIS OR HOW TO STOP IT."

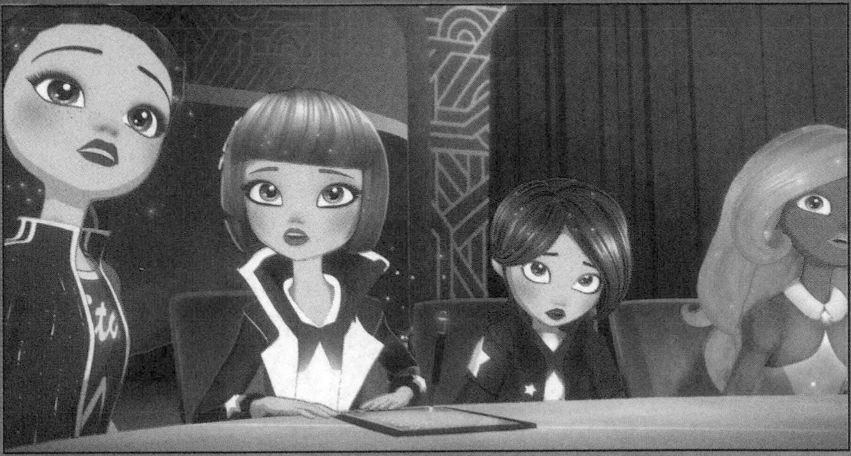

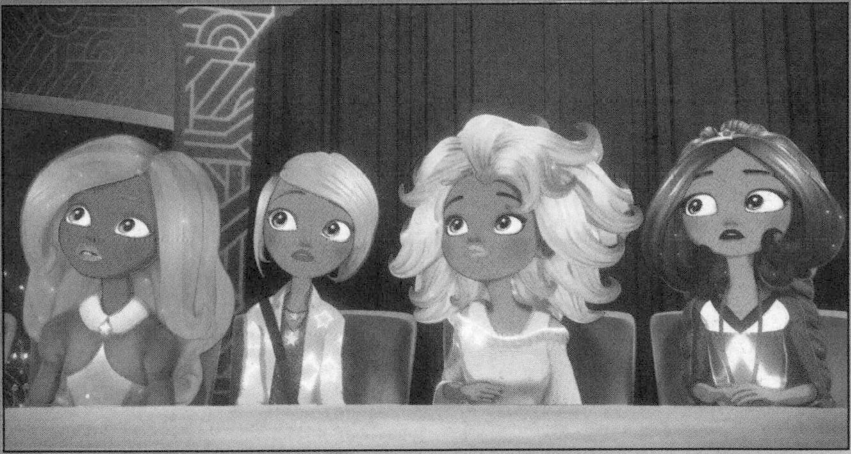

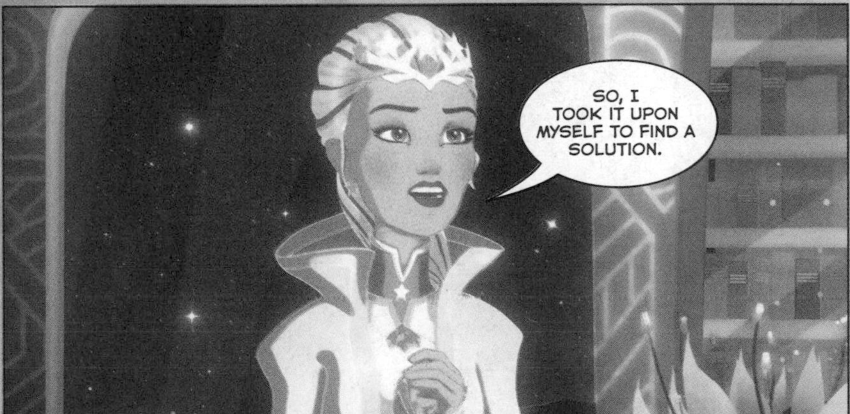
SO, I TOOK IT UPON MYSELF TO FIND A SOLUTION.

"SEARCHING IN THE ILLUMINATION LIBRARY, I FOUND AN ARCHAIC AND LONG-FORGOTTEN TOME. WITHIN ITS PAGES WAS AN ANCIENT *ORACLE* WHICH SPOKE OF..."

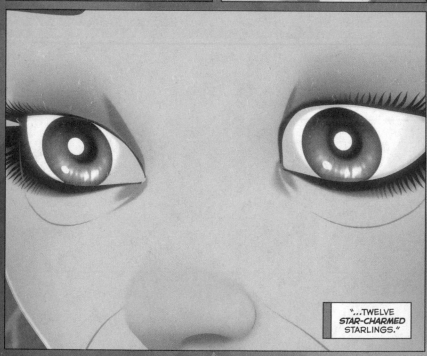

"...TWELVE *STAR-CHARMED* STARLINGS."

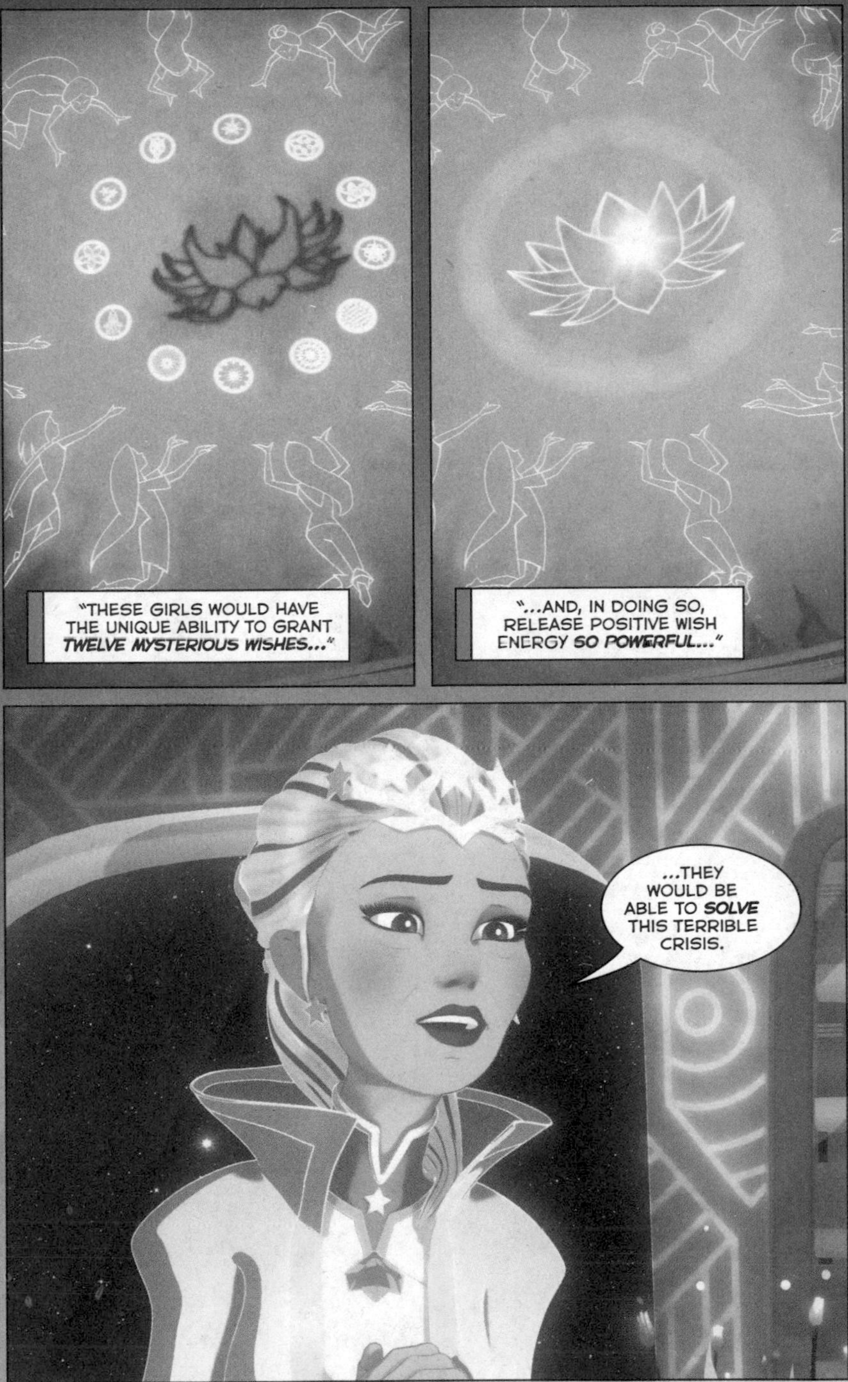
"THESE GIRLS WOULD HAVE THE UNIQUE ABILITY TO GRANT *TWELVE MYSTERIOUS WISHES...*"
"...AND, IN DOING SO, RELEASE POSITIVE WISH ENERGY *SO POWERFUL...*"
...THEY WOULD BE ABLE TO *SOLVE* THIS TERRIBLE CRISIS.

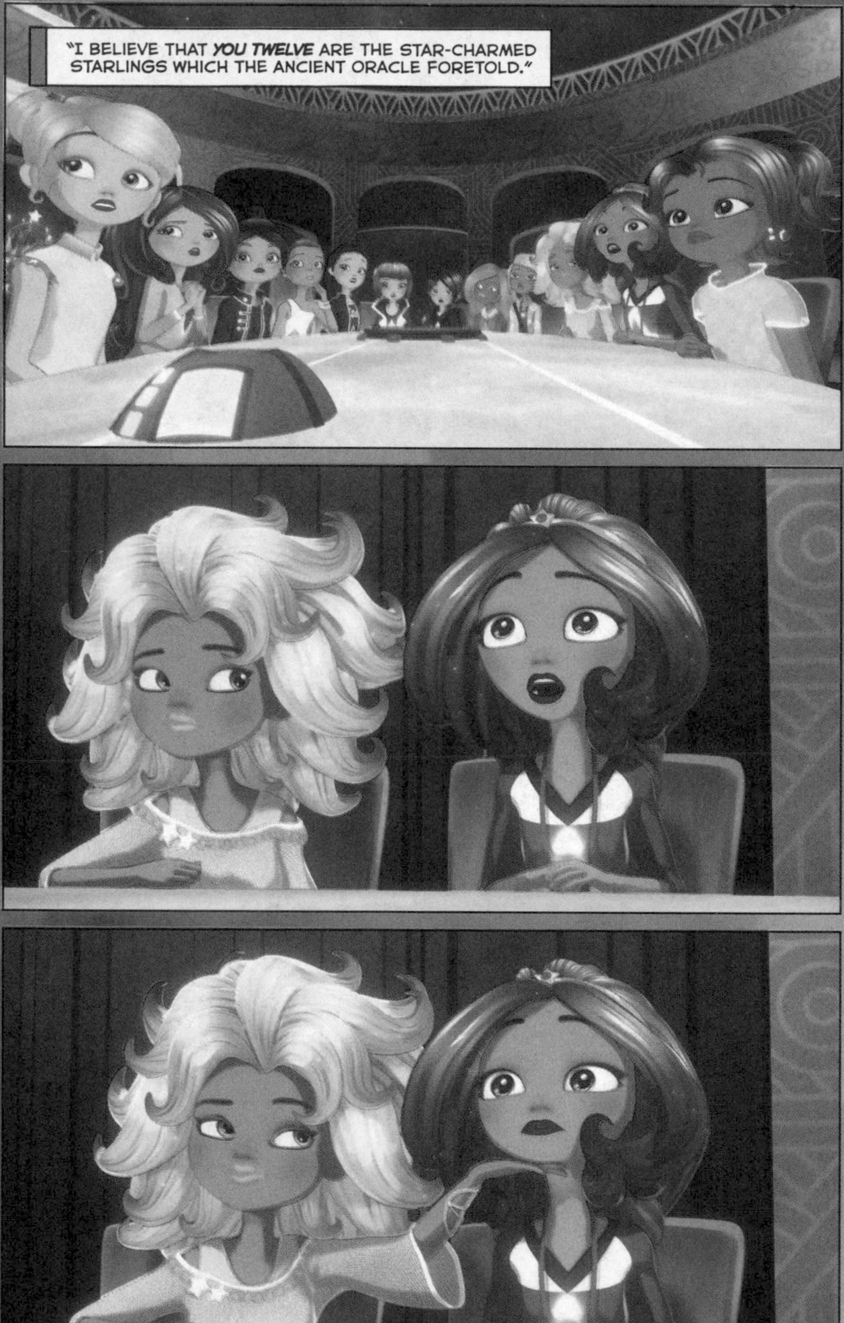
"I BELIEVE THAT *YOU TWELVE* ARE THE STAR-CHARMED STARLINGS WHICH THE ANCIENT ORACLE FORETOLD."

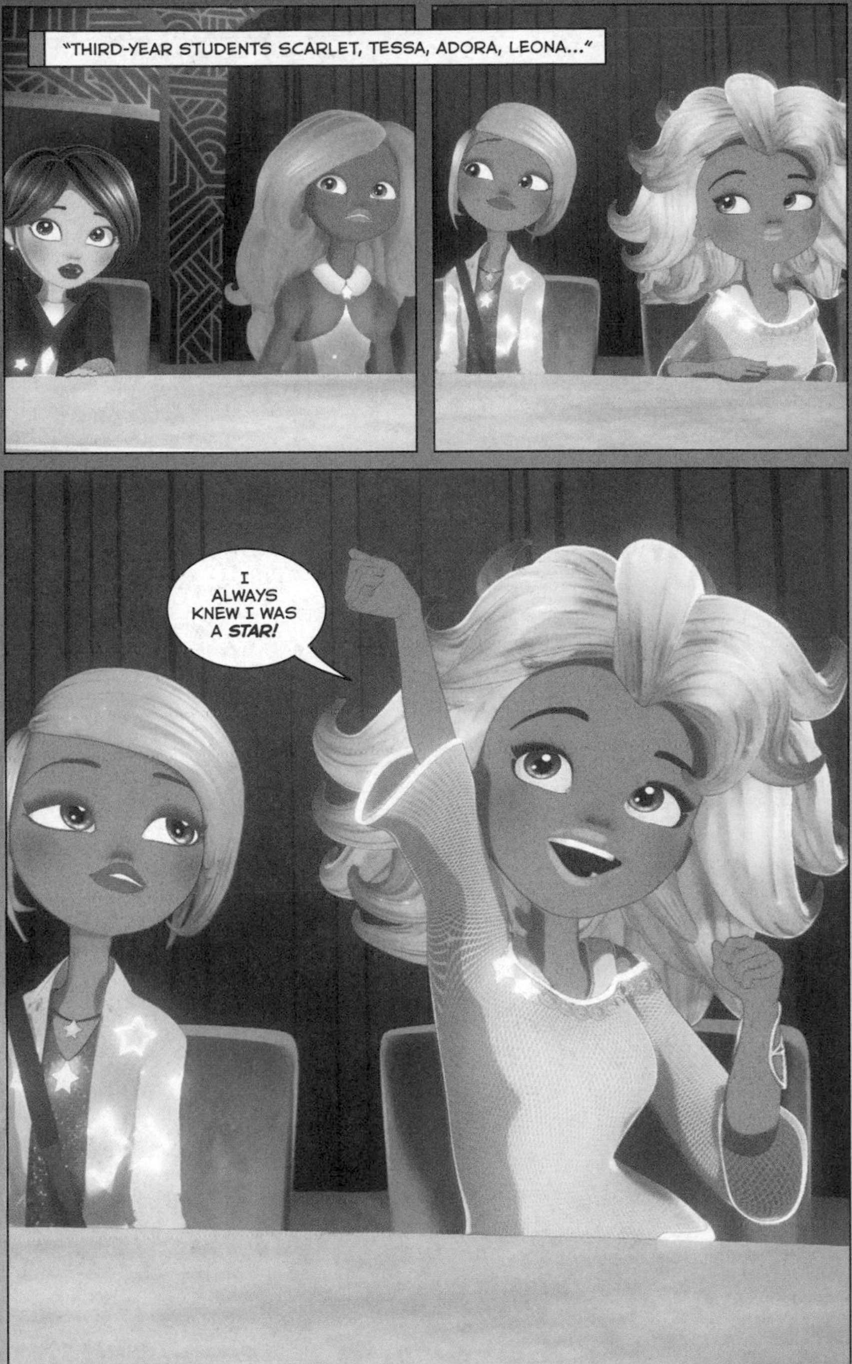
"THIRD-YEAR STUDENTS SCARLET, TESSA, ADORA, LEONA..."
I ALWAYS KNEW I WAS A *STAR!*

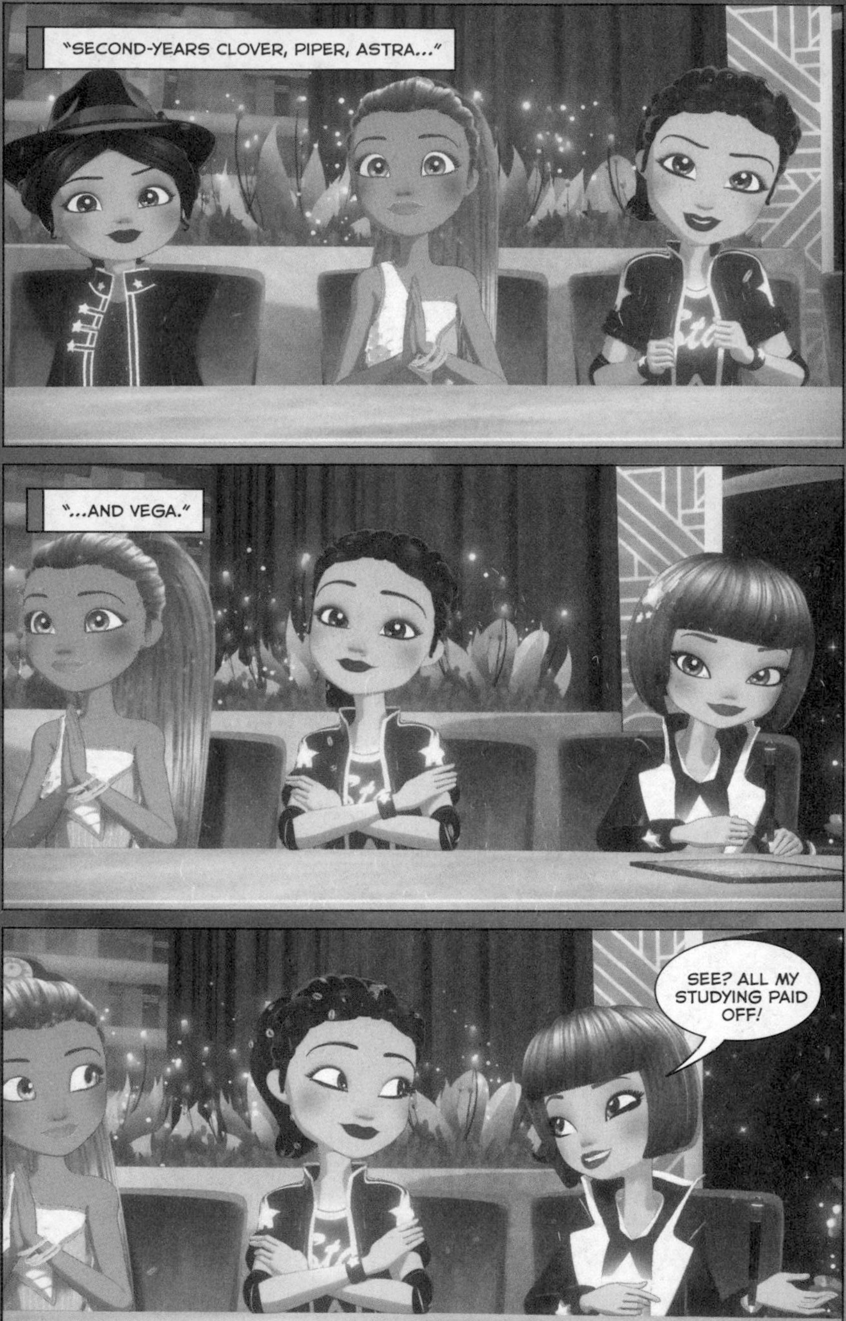
"SECOND-YEARS CLOVER, PIPER, ASTRA..."
"...AND VEGA."
SEE? ALL MY STUDYING PAID OFF!

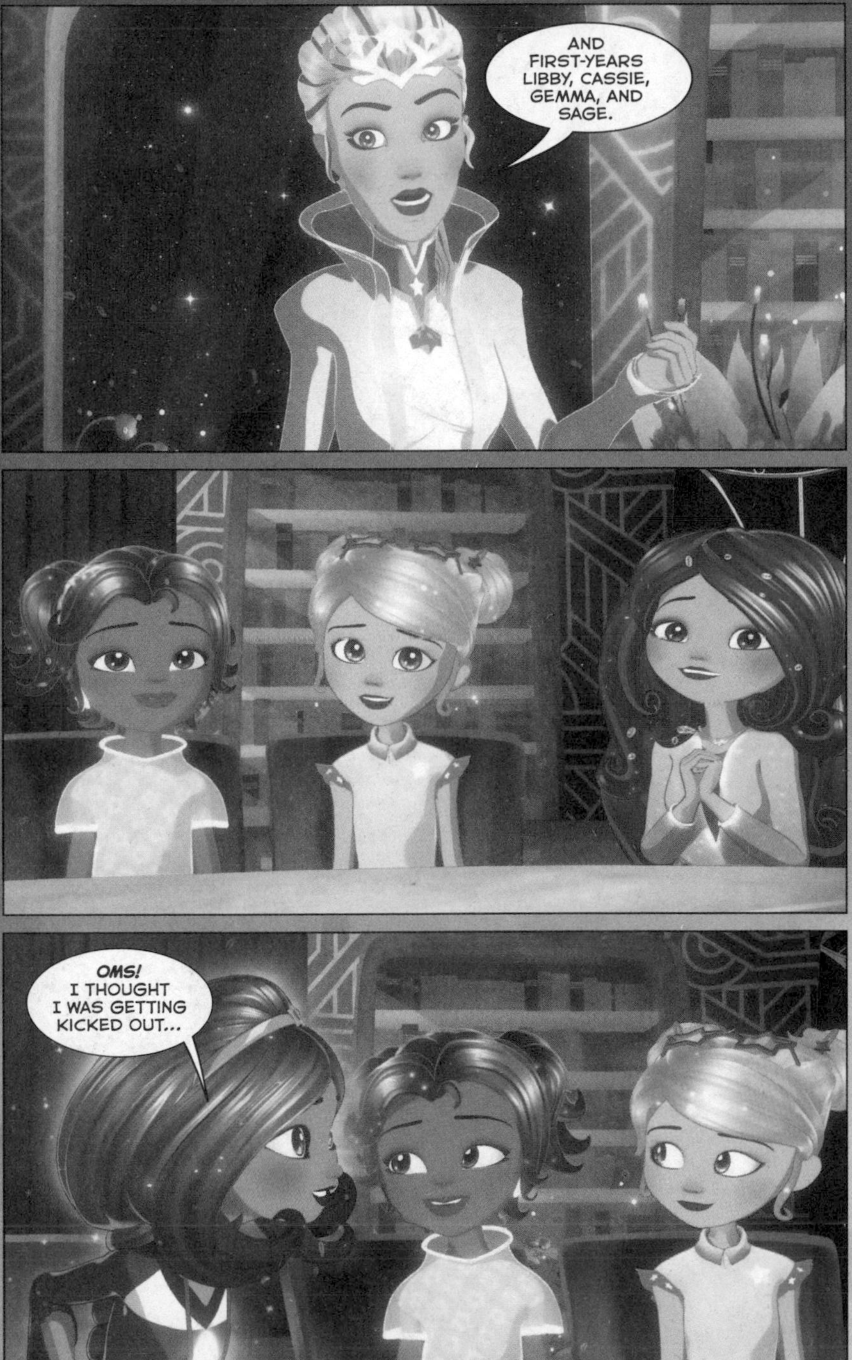
AND FIRST-YEARS LIBBY, CASSIE, GEMMA, AND SAGE.
OMS! I THOUGHT I WAS GETTING KICKED OUT...

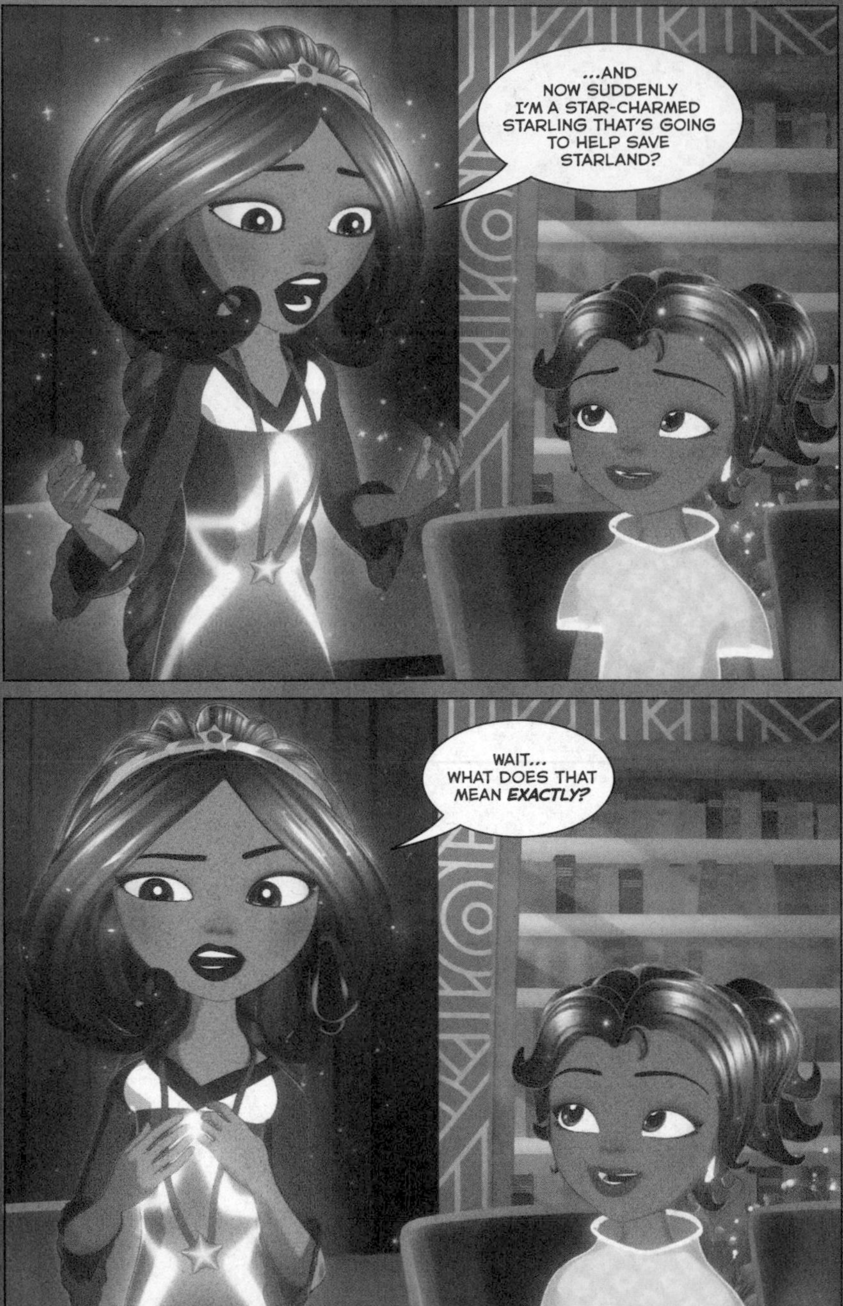
...AND NOW SUDDENLY I'M A STAR-CHARMED STARLING THAT'S GOING TO HELP SAVE STARLAND?
WAIT... WHAT DOES THAT MEAN *EXACTLY?*

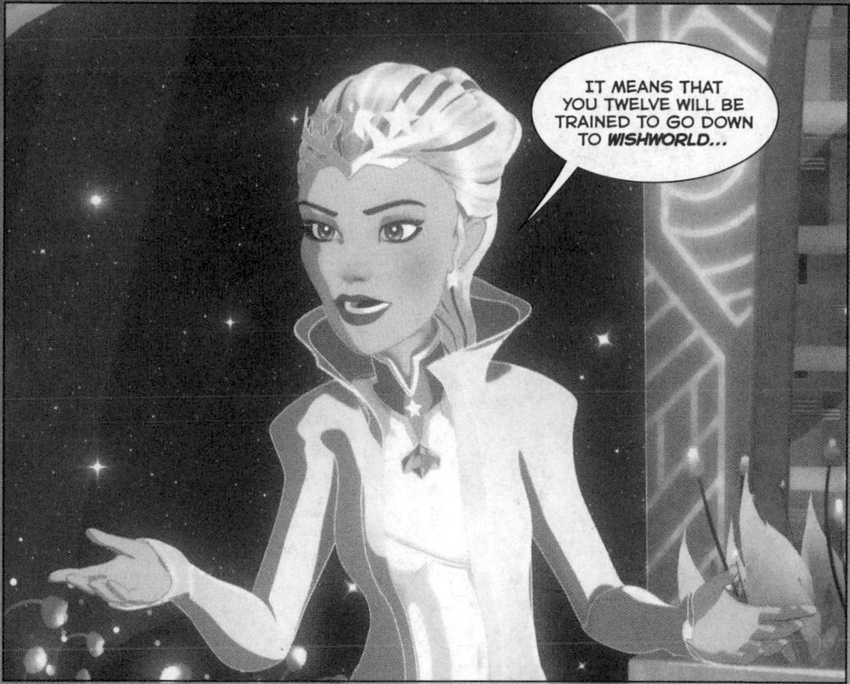
IT MEANS THAT YOU TWELVE WILL BE TRAINED TO GO DOWN TO *WISHWORLD...*

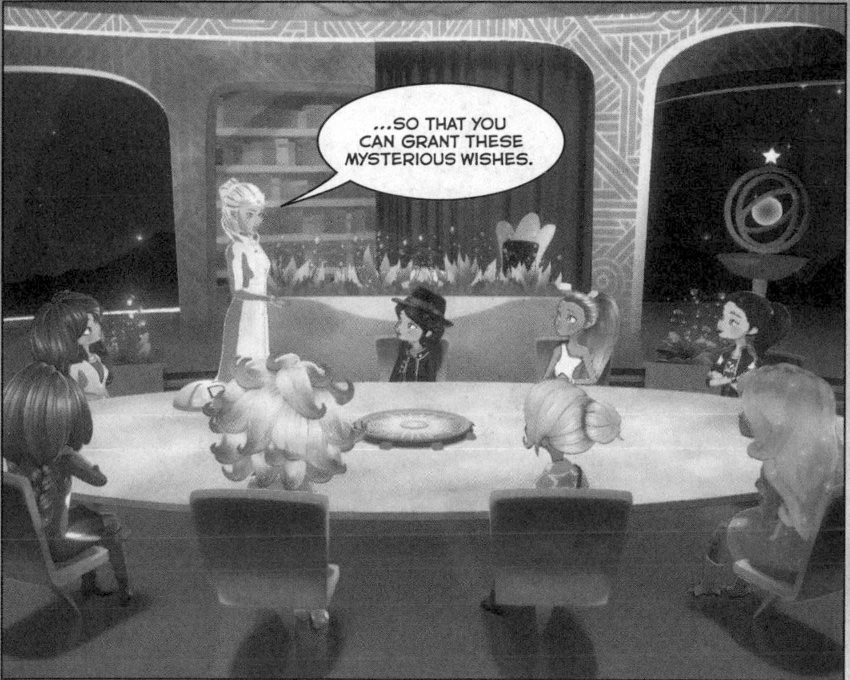
...SO THAT YOU CAN GRANT THESE MYSTERIOUS WISHES.

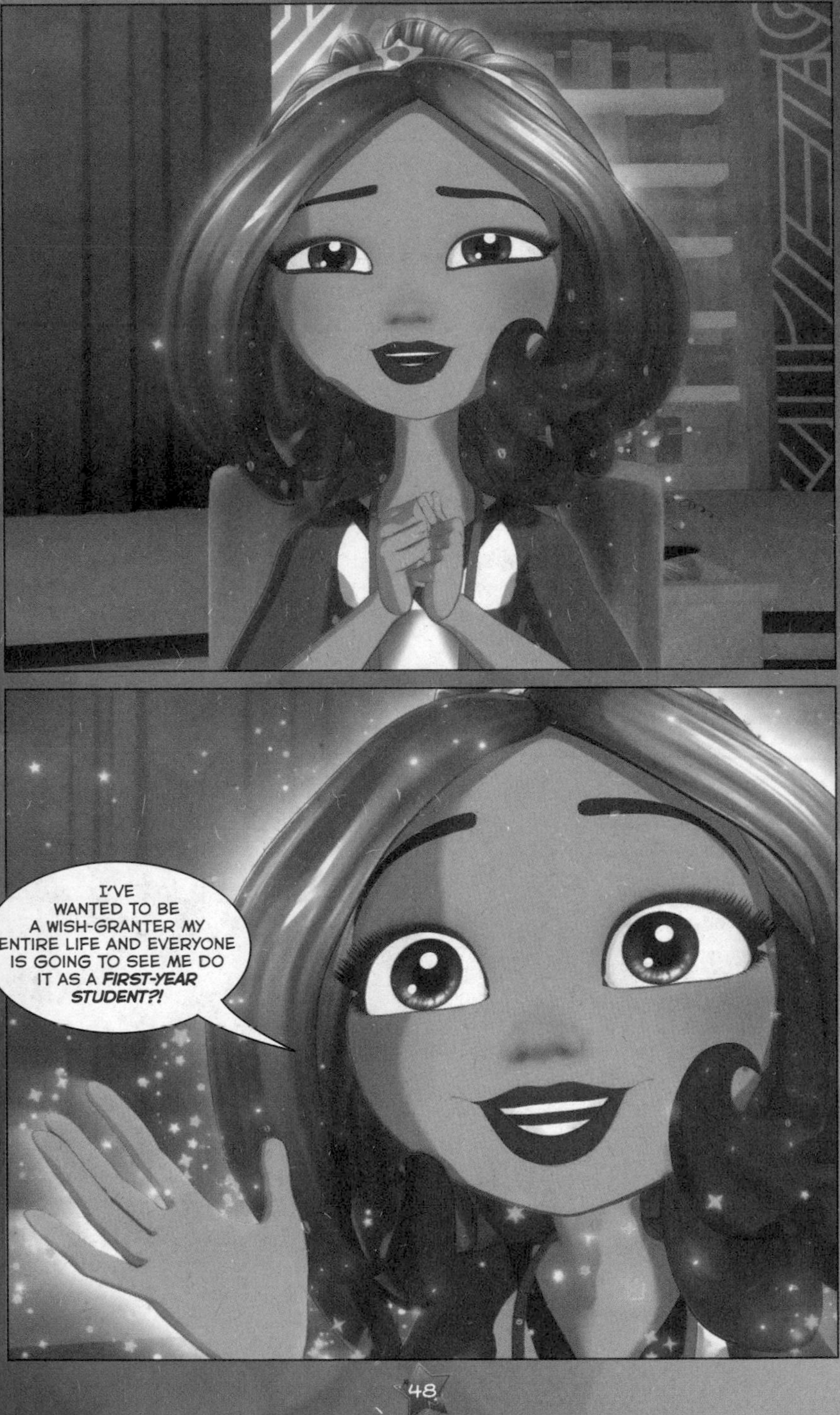
I'VE WANTED TO BE A WISH-GRANTER MY ENTIRE LIFE AND EVERYONE IS GOING TO SEE ME DO IT AS A *FIRST-YEAR STUDENT?!*

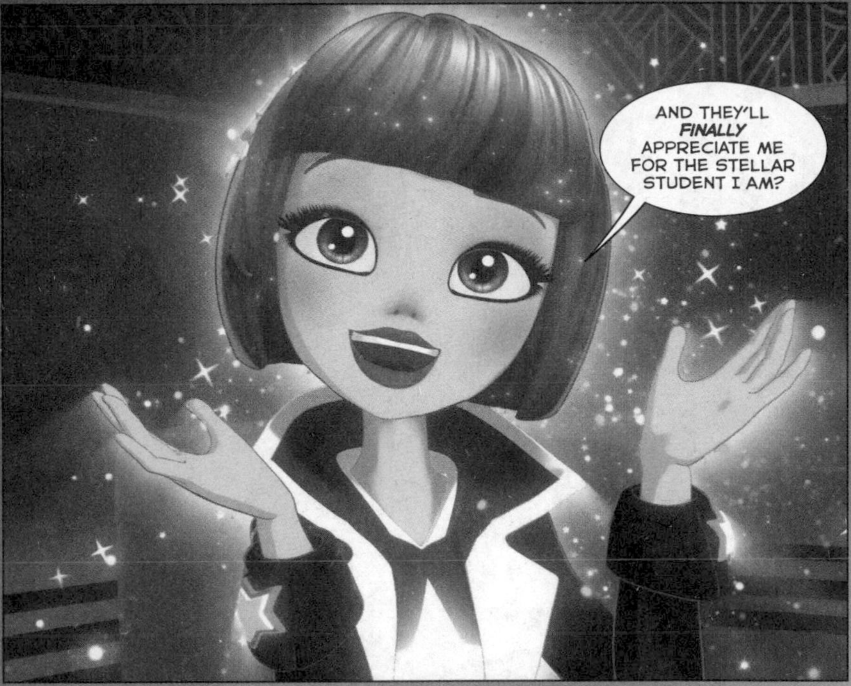
AND THEY'LL ***FINALLY*** APPRECIATE ME FOR THE STELLAR STUDENT I AM?

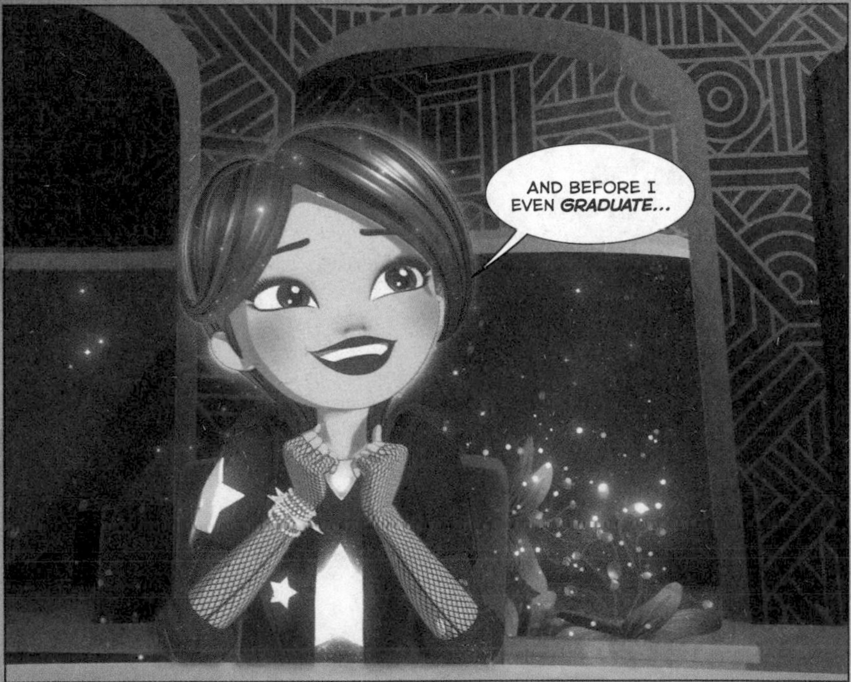
AND BEFORE I EVEN ***GRADUATE...***

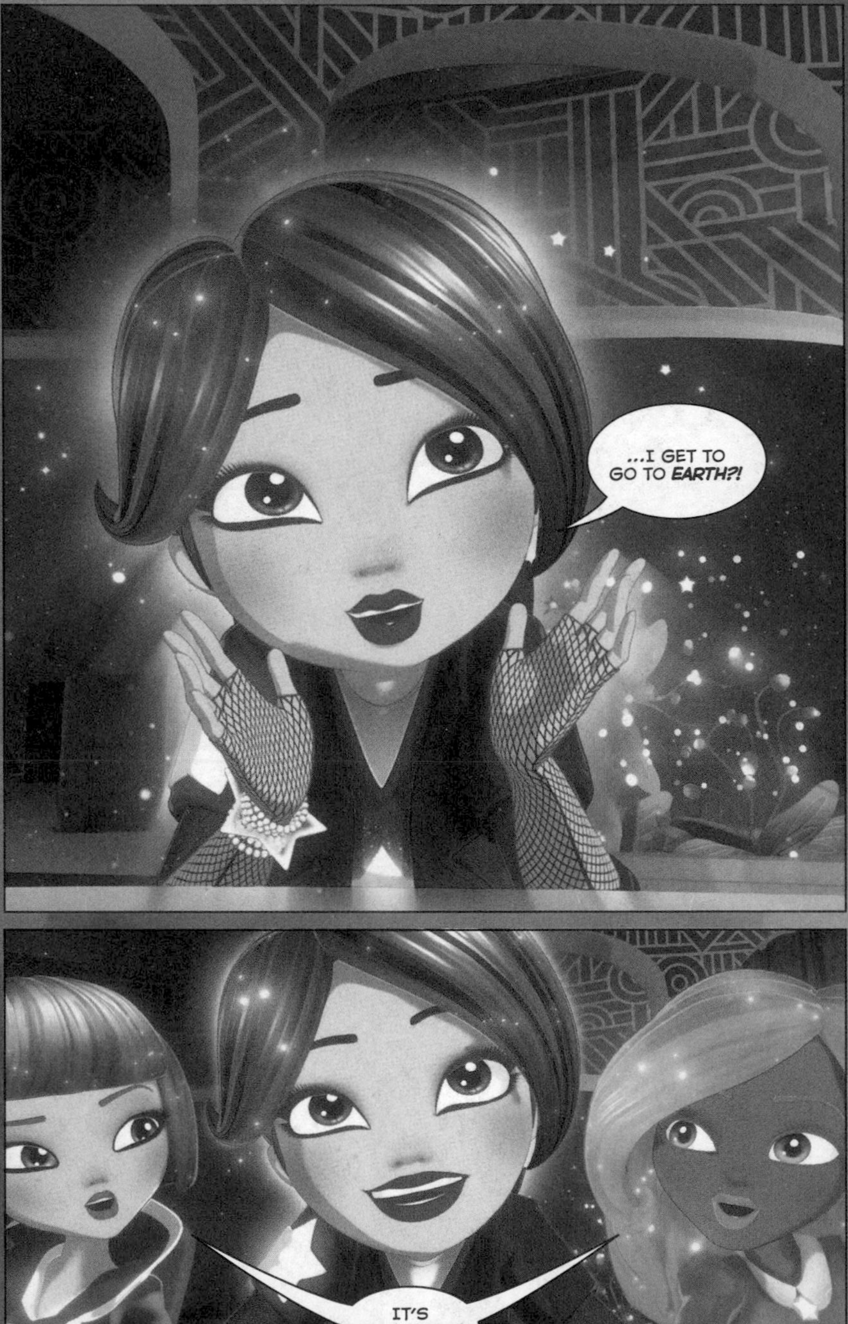
...I GET TO GO TO EARTH?!
IT'S WISHWORLD!

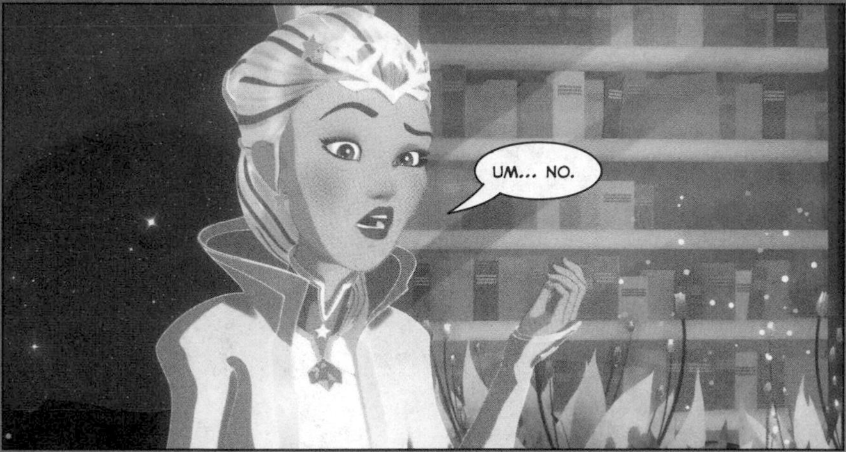
UM... NO.

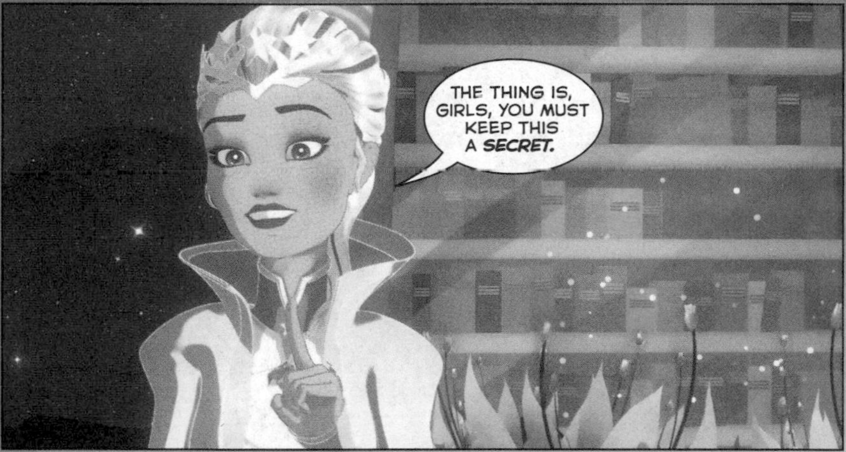
THE THING IS, GIRLS, YOU MUST KEEP THIS A ***SECRET.***

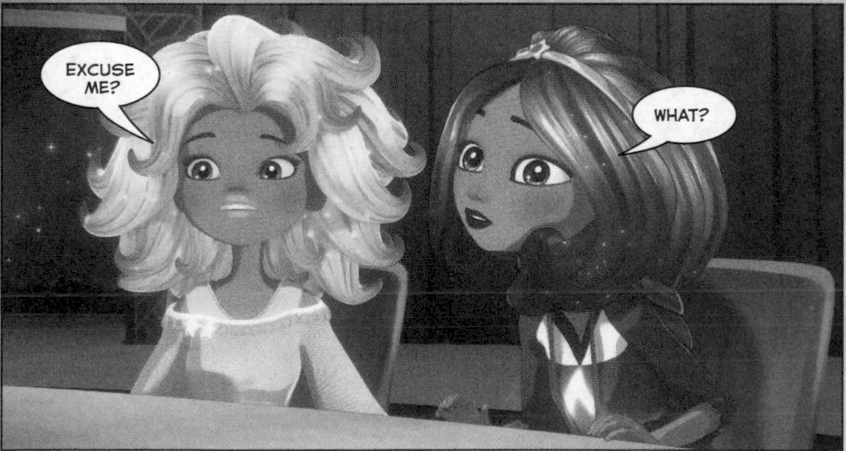
EXCUSE ME?
WHAT?

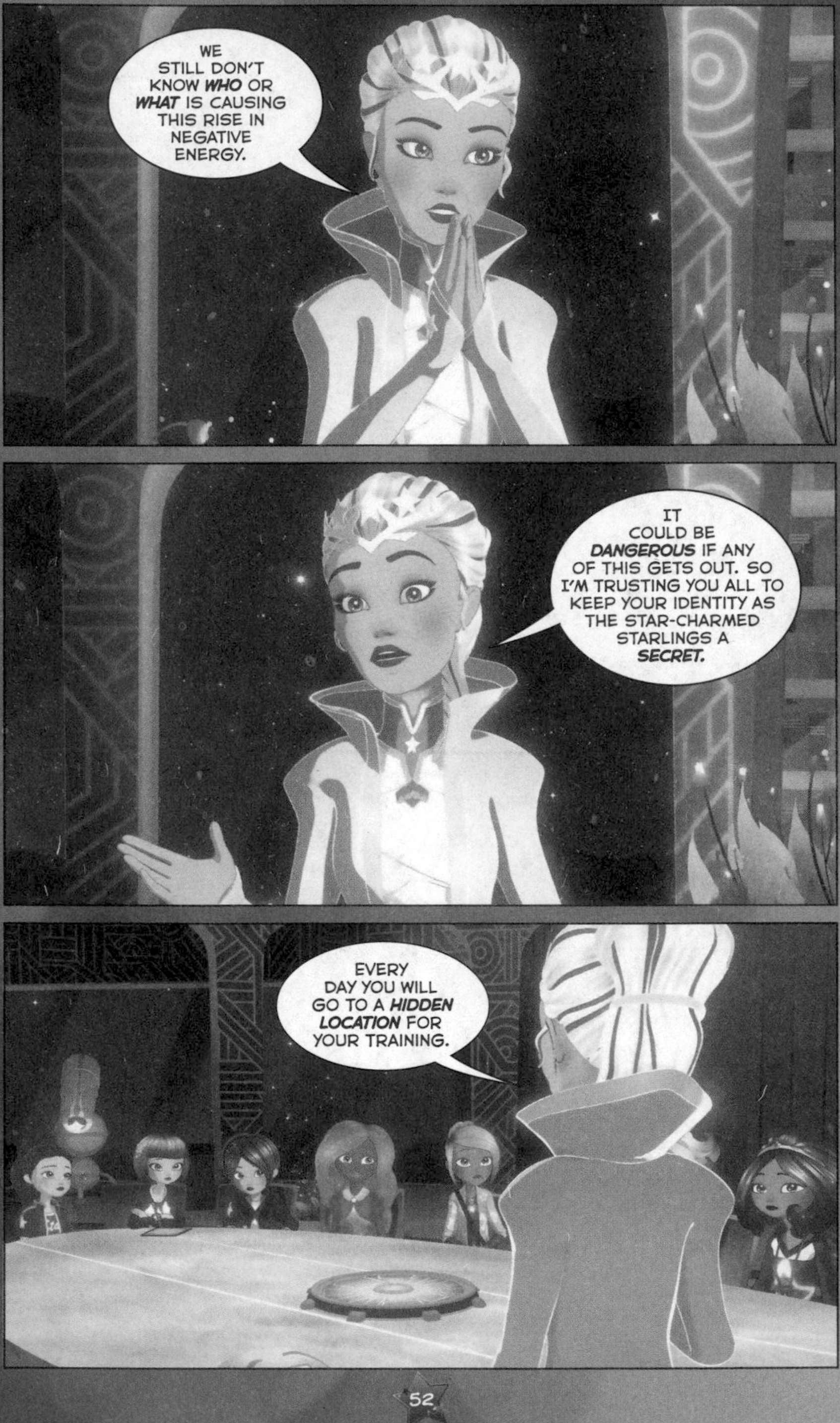
WE STILL DON'T KNOW **WHO** OR **WHAT** IS CAUSING THIS RISE IN NEGATIVE ENERGY.
IT COULD BE **DANGEROUS** IF ANY OF THIS GETS OUT. SO I'M TRUSTING YOU ALL TO KEEP YOUR IDENTITY AS THE STAR-CHARMED STARLINGS A **SECRET.**
EVERY DAY YOU WILL GO TO A **HIDDEN LOCATION** FOR YOUR TRAINING.

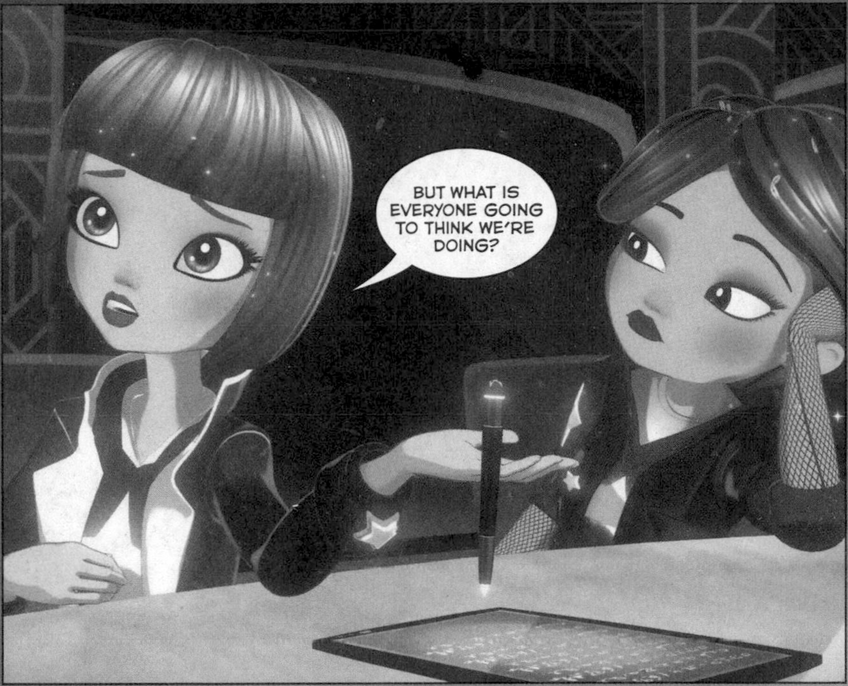
BUT WHAT IS EVERYONE GOING TO THINK WE'RE DOING?

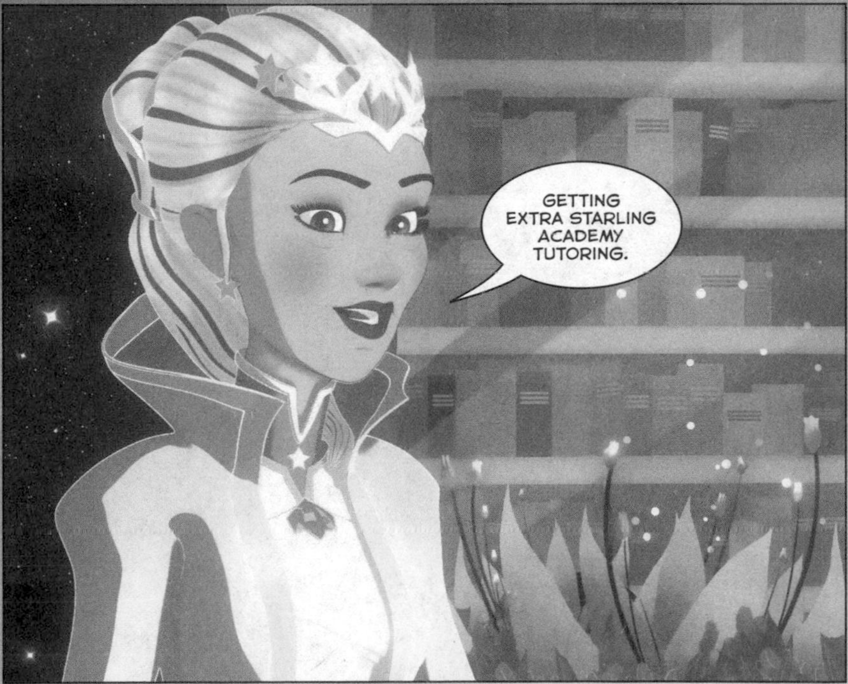
GETTING EXTRA STARLING ACADEMY TUTORING.

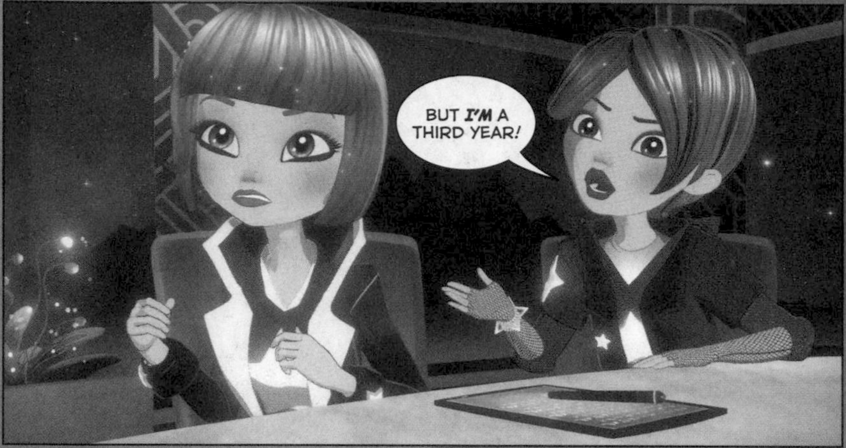
BUT ***I'M*** A THIRD YEAR!

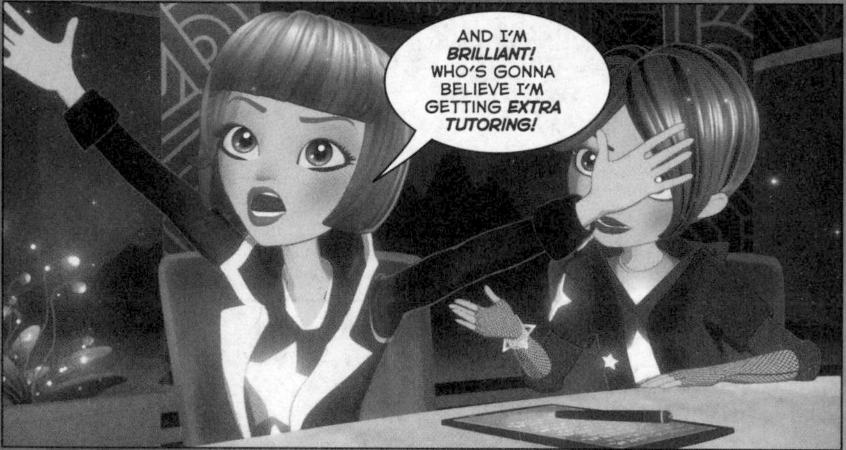
AND I'M ***BRILLIANT!*** WHO'S GONNA BELIEVE I'M GETTING ***EXTRA TUTORING!***

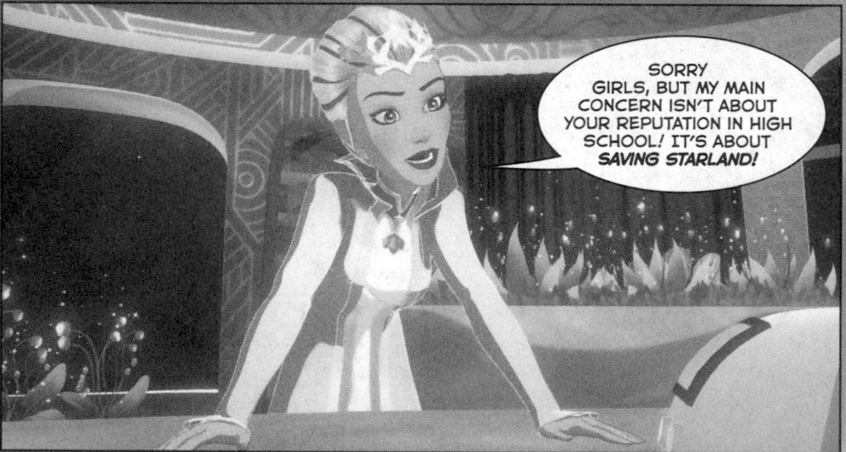
SORRY GIRLS, BUT MY MAIN CONCERN ISN'T ABOUT YOUR REPUTATION IN HIGH SCHOOL! IT'S ABOUT ***SAVING STARLAND!***

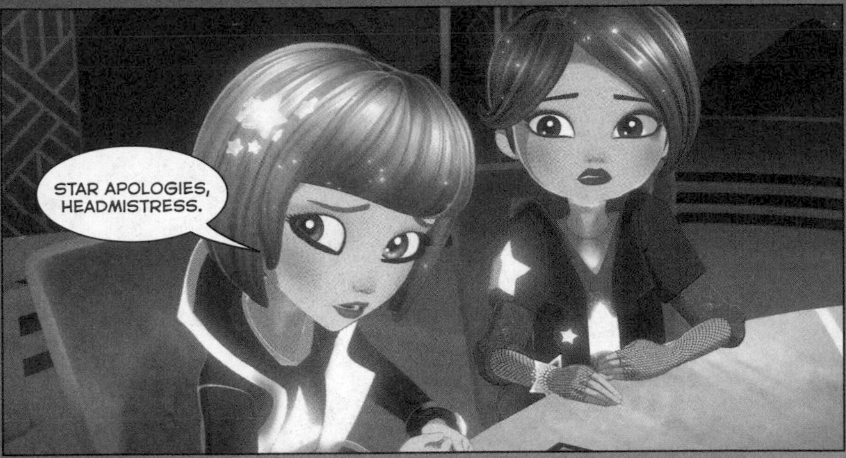
STAR APOLOGIES, HEADMISTRESS.

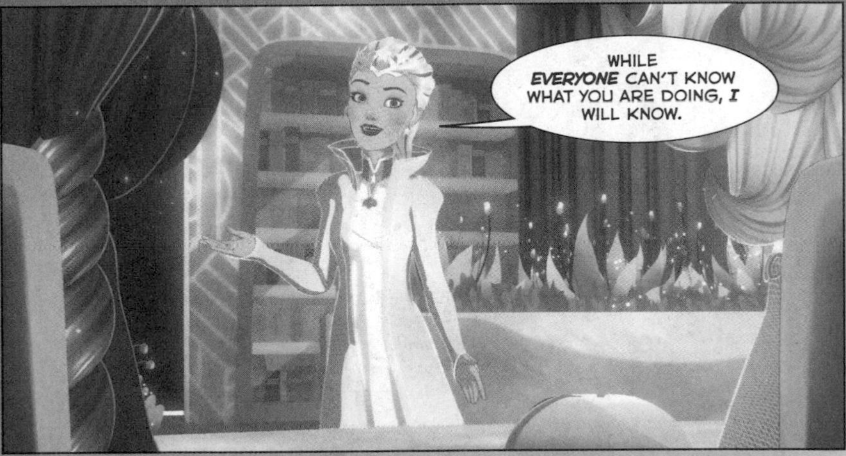
WHILE *EVERYONE* CAN'T KNOW WHAT YOU ARE DOING, *I* WILL KNOW.

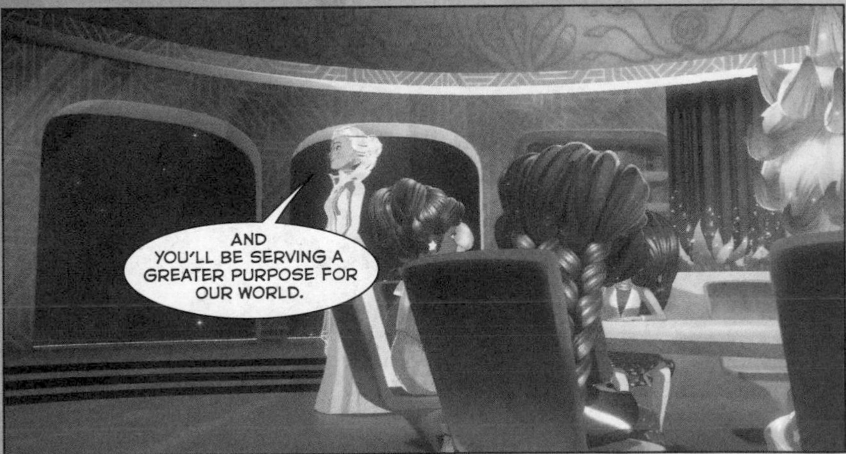
AND YOU'LL BE SERVING A GREATER PURPOSE FOR OUR WORLD.

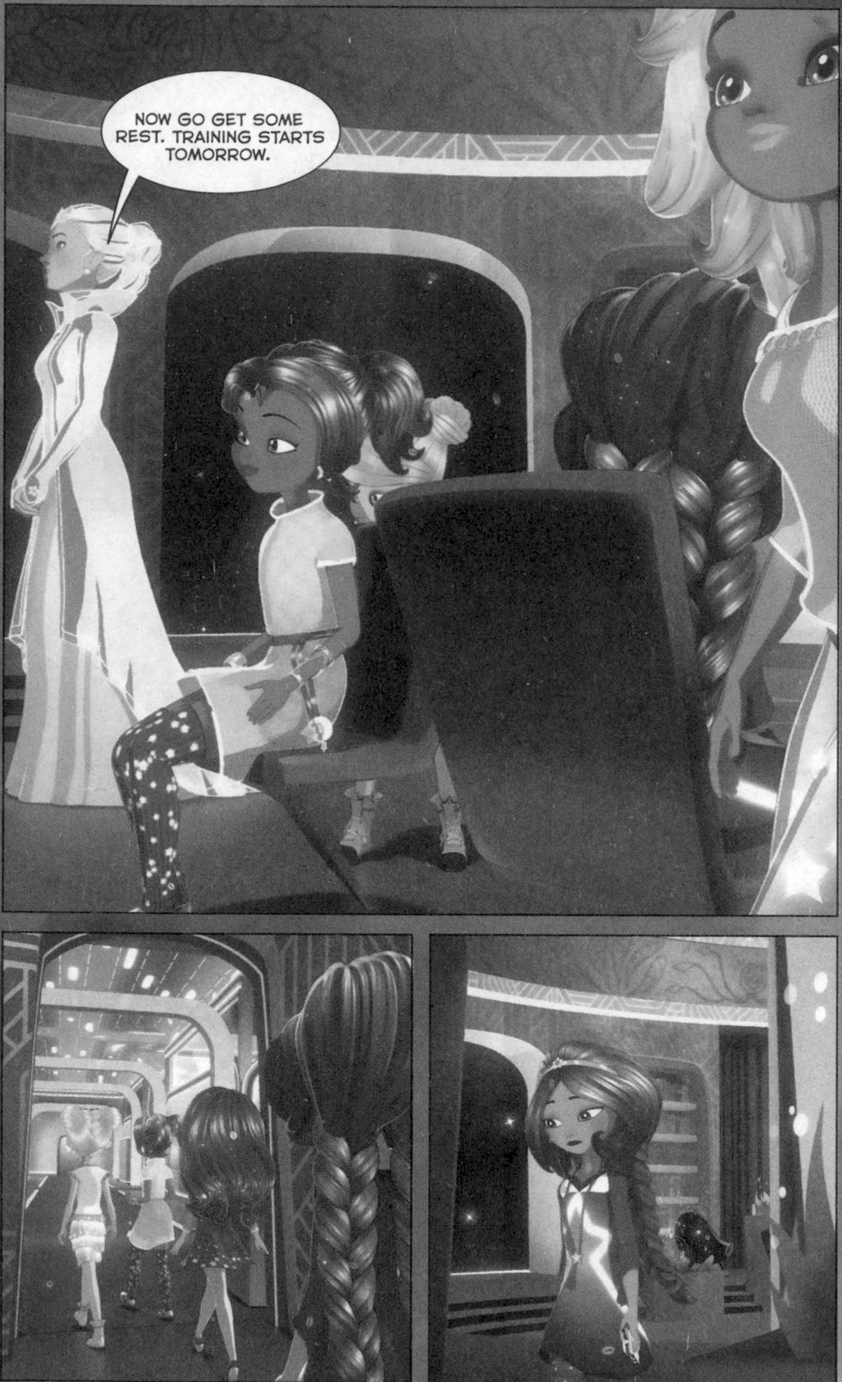
NOW GO GET SOME REST. TRAINING STARTS TOMORROW.

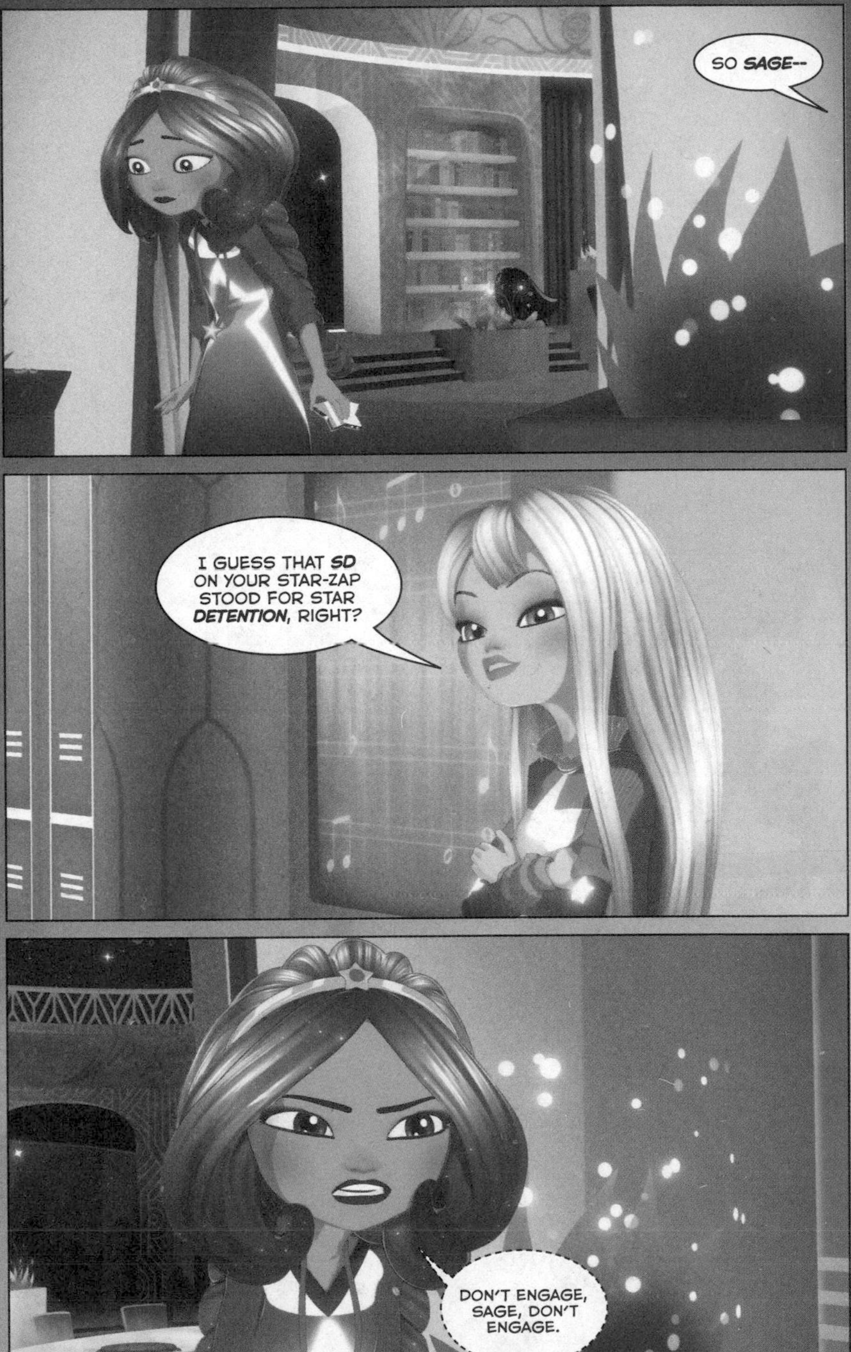
SO **SAGE**--
I GUESS THAT **SD** ON YOUR STAR-ZAP STOOD FOR STAR ***DETENTION***, RIGHT?
DON'T ENGAGE, SAGE, DON'T ENGAGE.

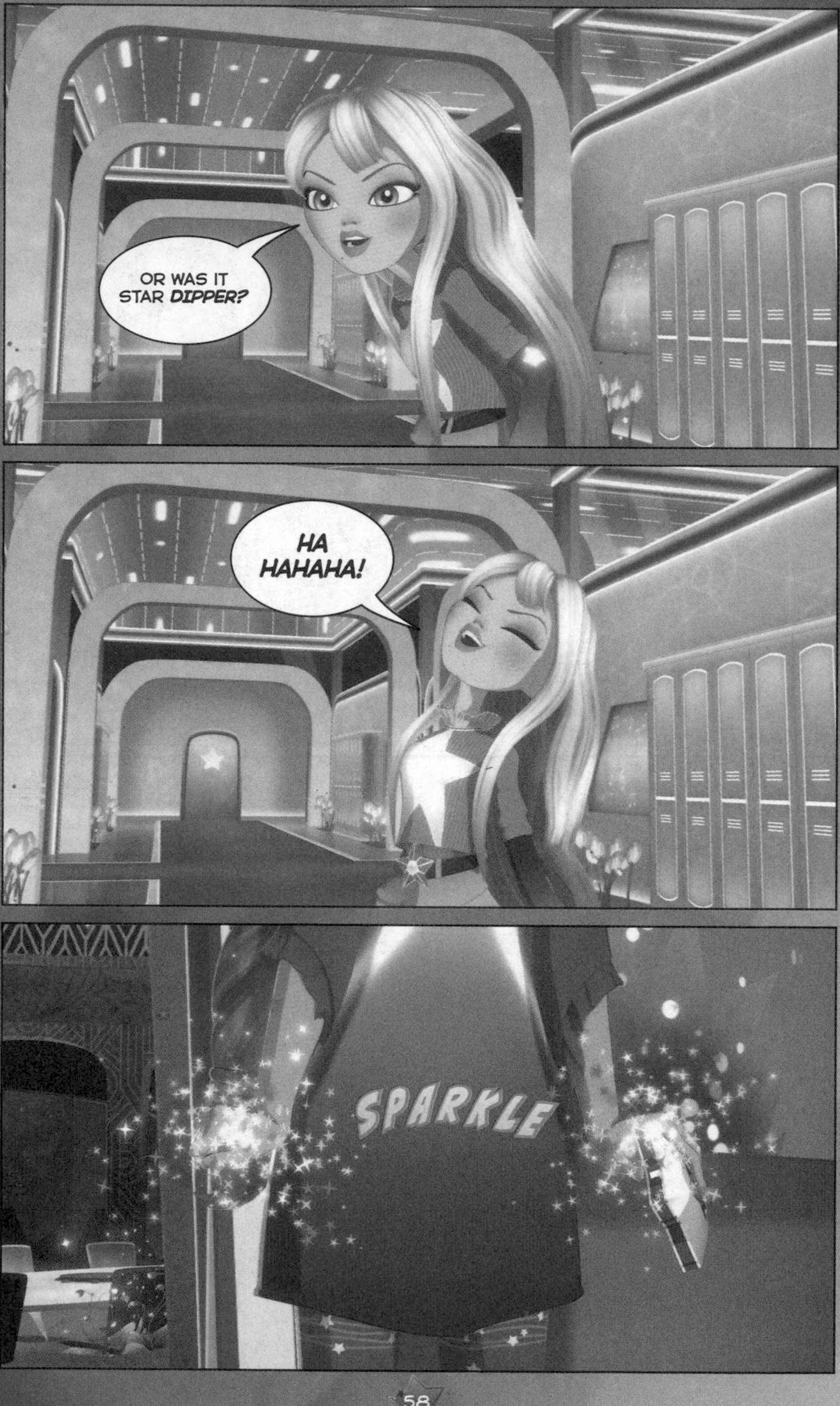
OR WAS IT STAR DIPPER?
HA HAHAHA!
SPARKLE

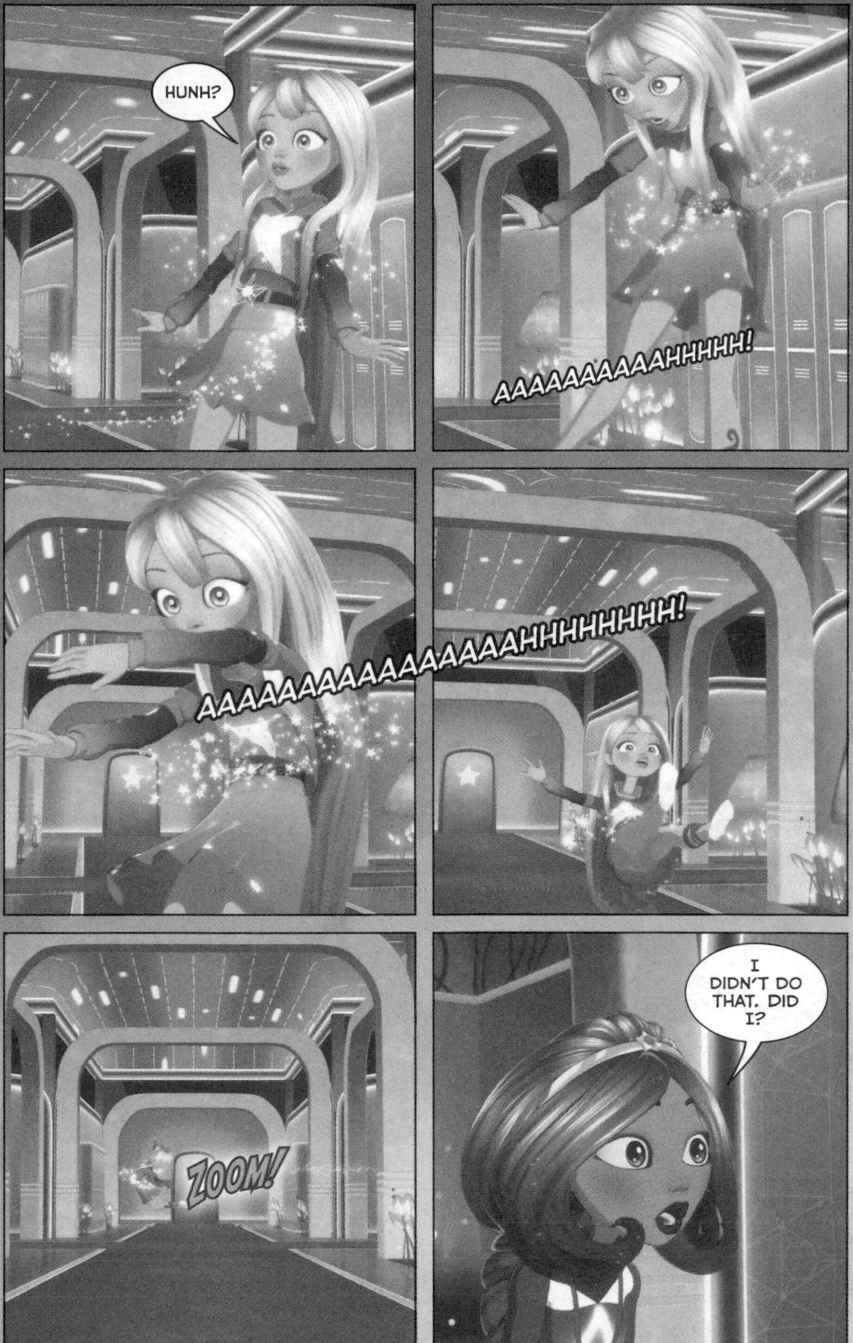
HUNH?
AAAAAAAAAAHHHHH!
AAAAAAAAAAAAAAAAAAHHHHHHHH!
ZOOM!
I DIDN'T DO THAT. DID I?

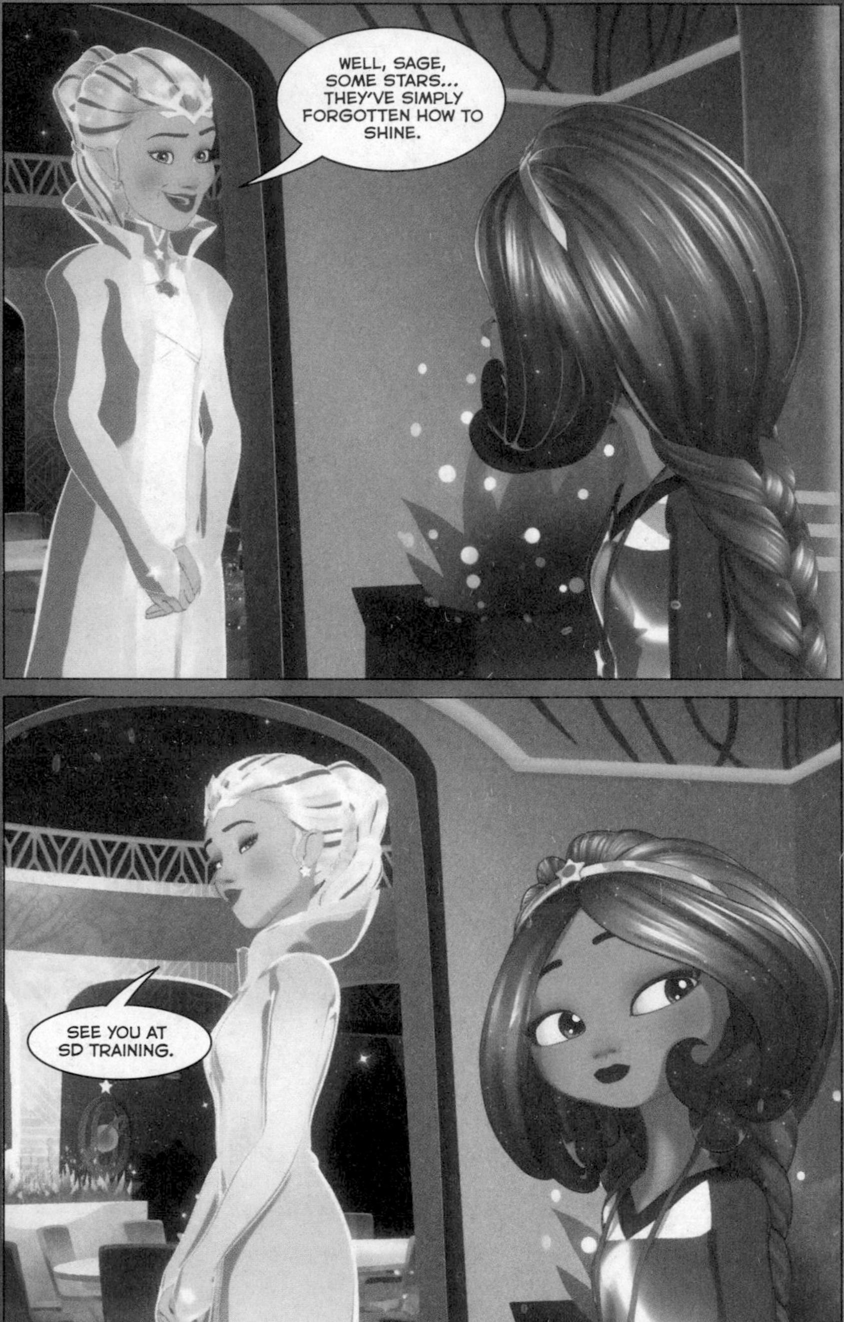
WELL, SAGE, SOME STARS... THEY'VE SIMPLY FORGOTTEN HOW TO SHINE.
SEE YOU AT SD TRAINING.

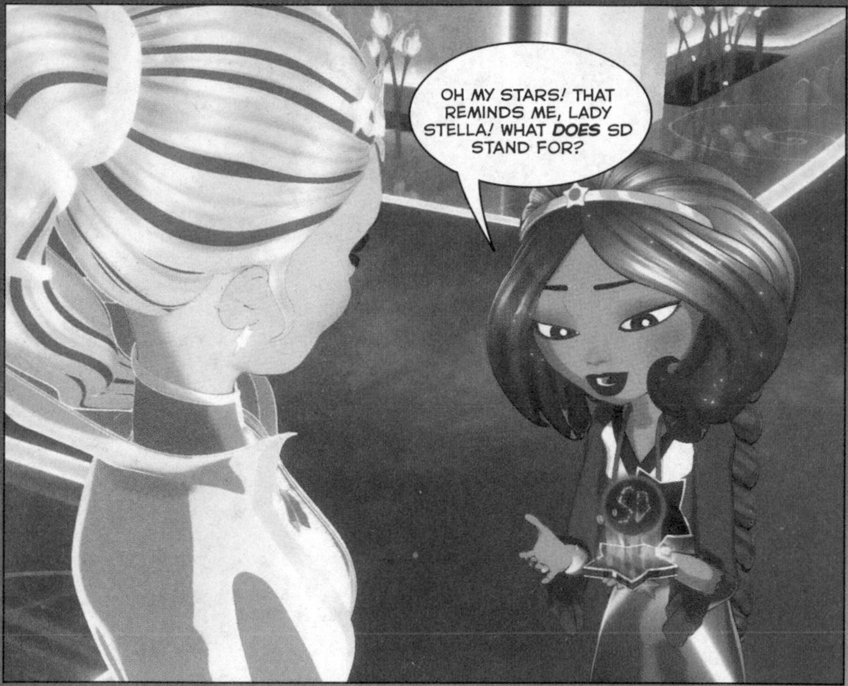
OH MY STARS! THAT REMINDS ME, LADY STELLA! WHAT **DOES** SD STAND FOR?
SD

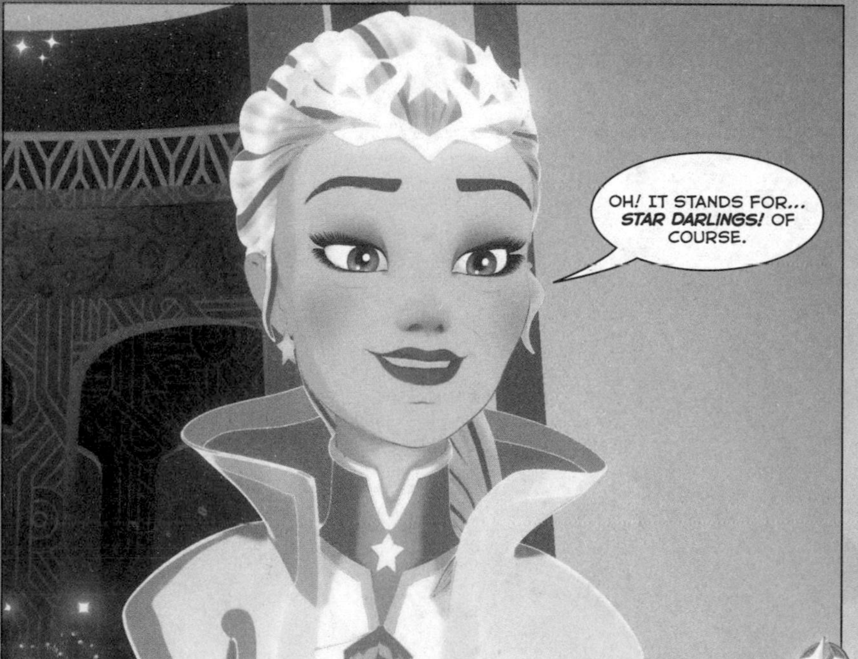
OH! IT STANDS FOR... ***STAR DARLINGS!*** OF COURSE.
END

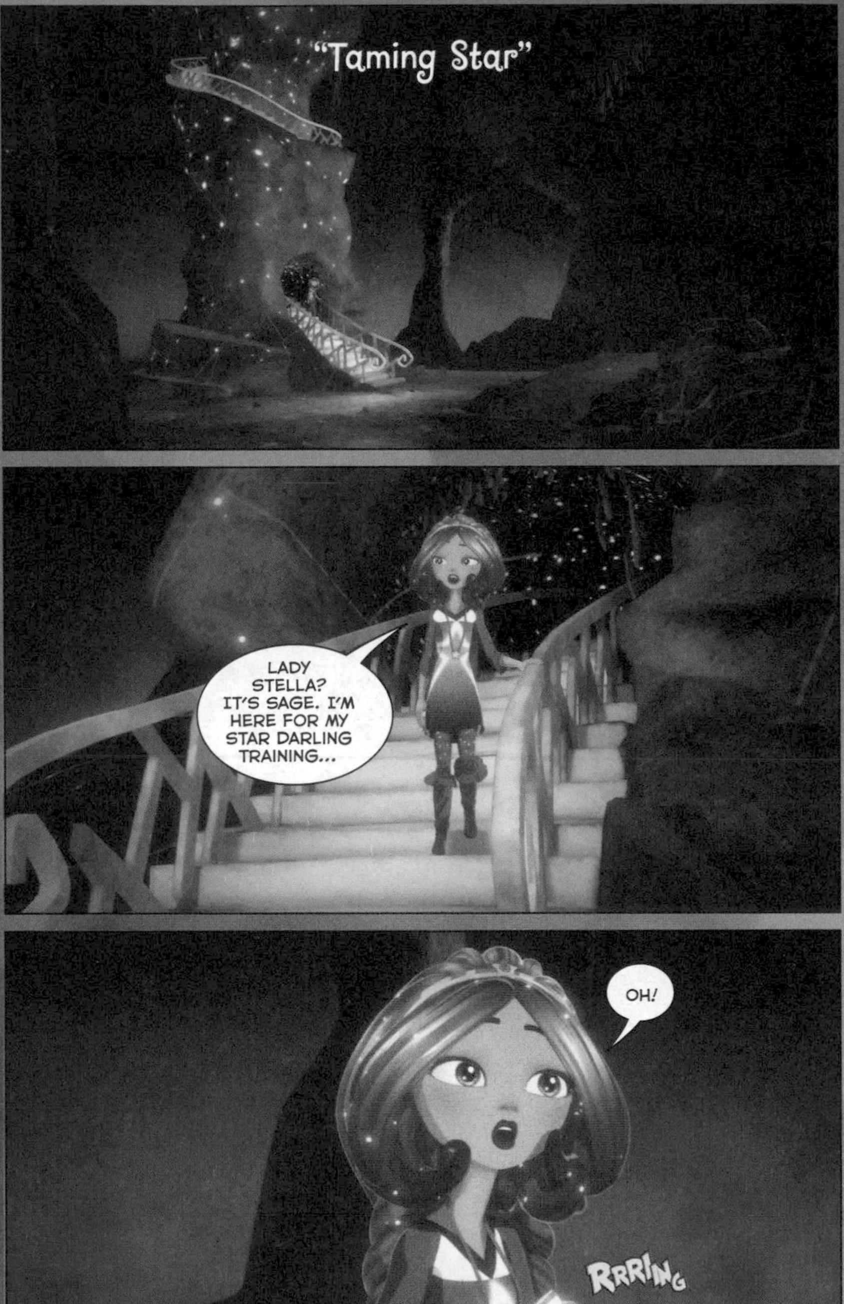
"Taming Star"
LADY STELLA? IT'S SAGE. I'M HERE FOR MY STAR DARLING TRAINING...
OH!
RRRIING

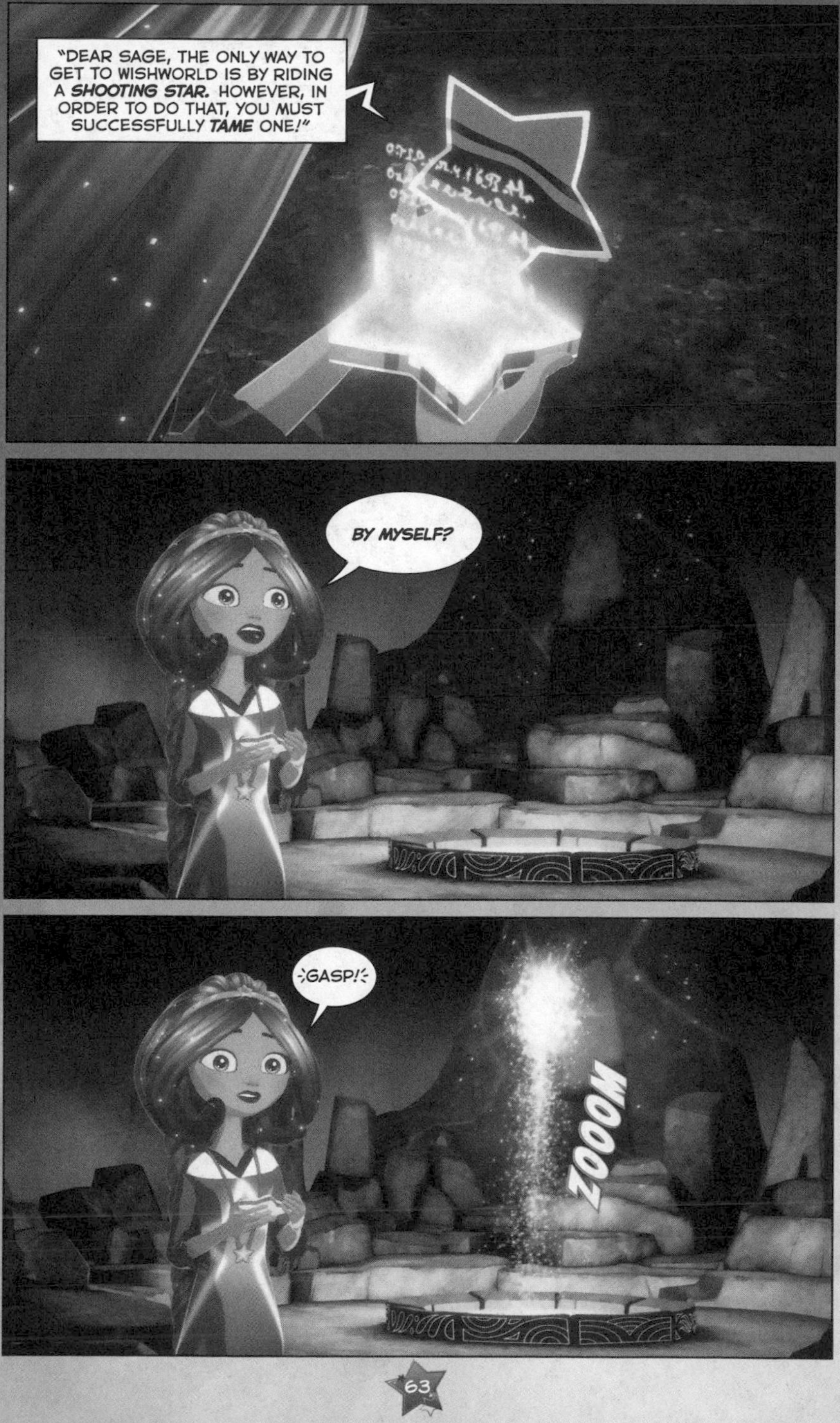
"DEAR SAGE, THE ONLY WAY TO GET TO WISHWORLD IS BY RIDING A SHOOTING STAR. HOWEVER, IN ORDER TO DO THAT, YOU MUST SUCCESSFULLY TAME ONE!"
BY MYSELF?
GASP!
ZOOOM

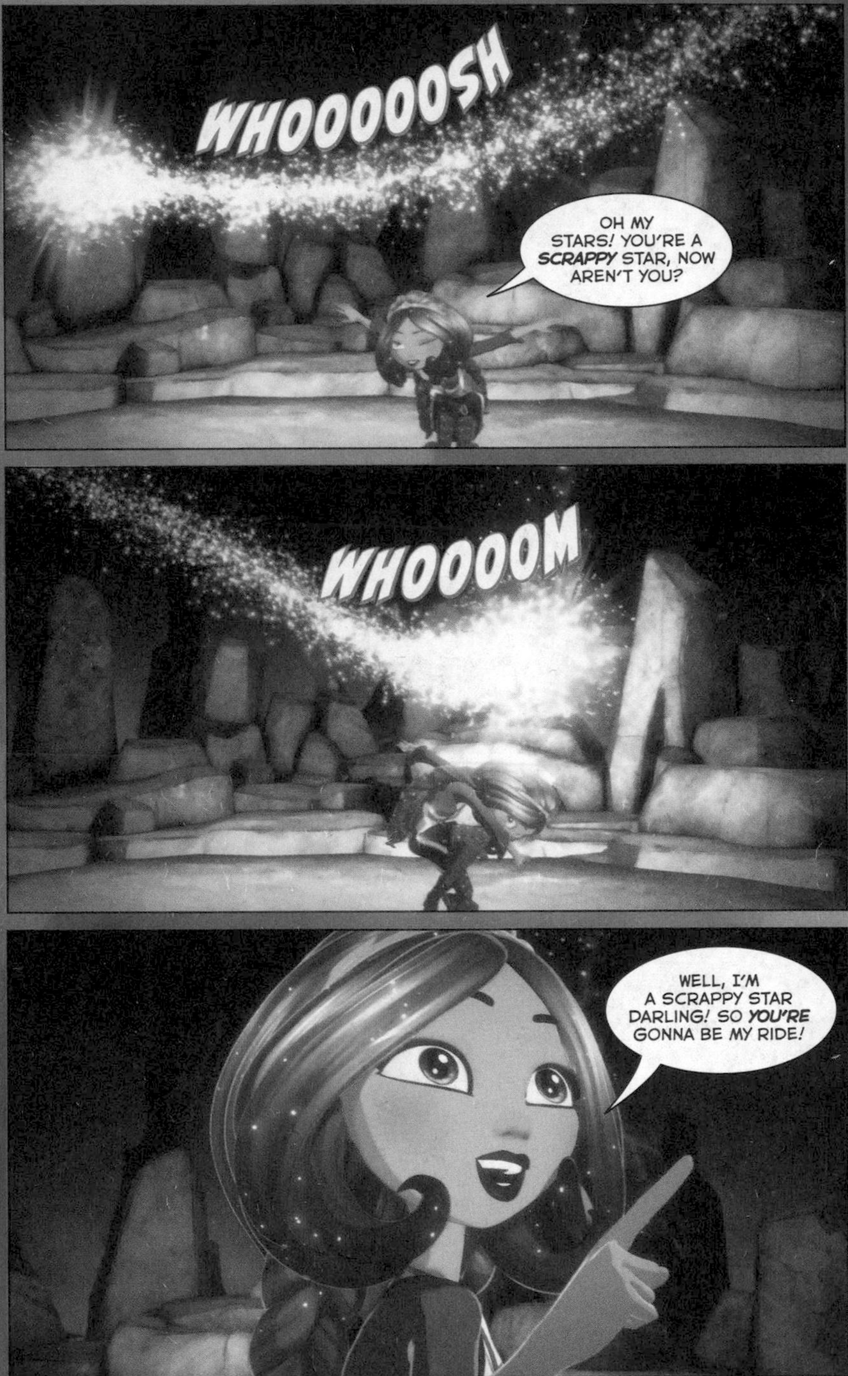
WHOOOOOSH
OH MY STARS! YOU'RE A *SCRAPPY* STAR, NOW AREN'T YOU?
WHOOOOM
WELL, I'M A SCRAPPY STAR DARLING! SO *YOU'RE* GONNA BE MY RIDE!

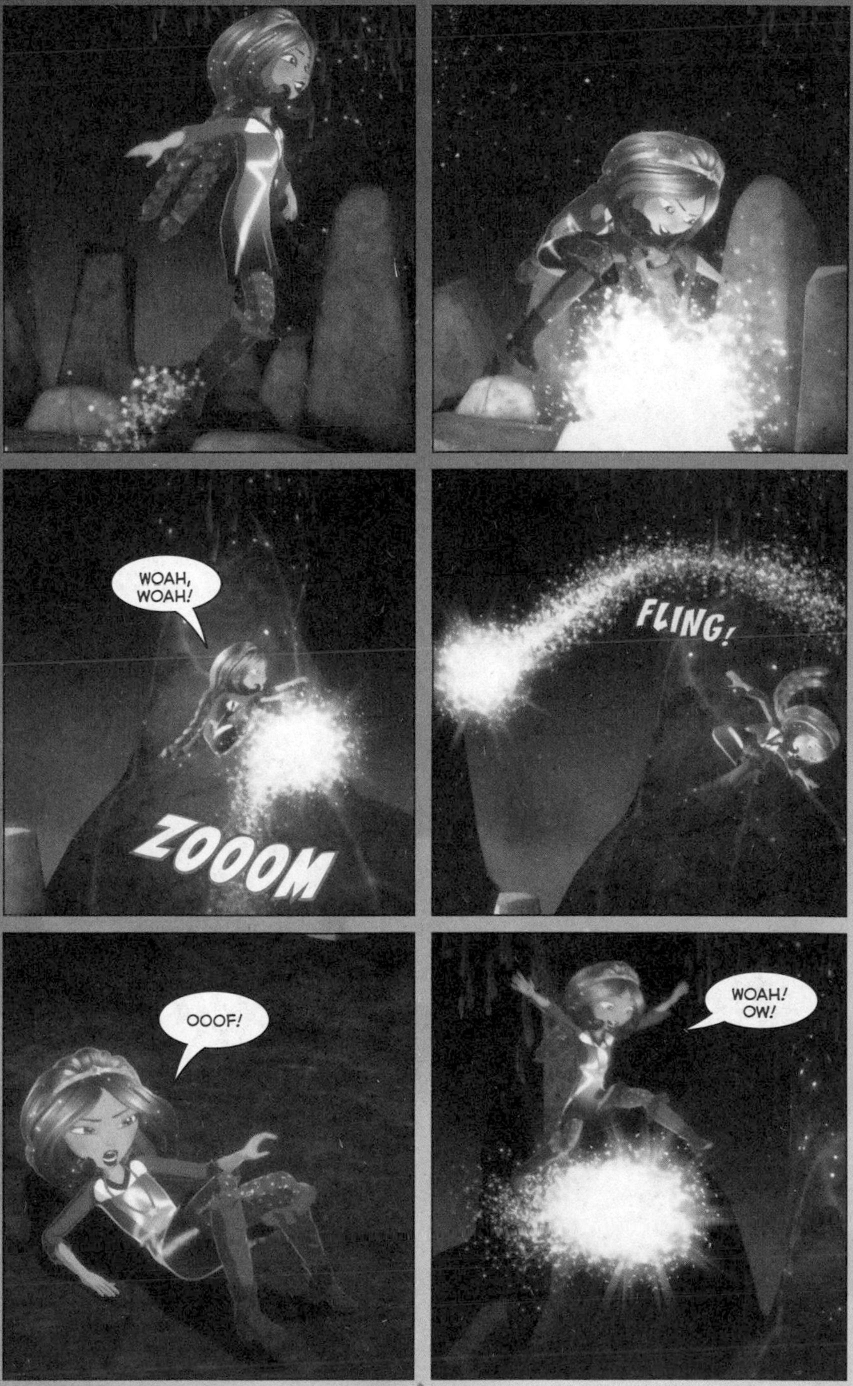
WOAH, WOAH!
ZOOOM
FLING!
OOOF!
WOAH! OW!

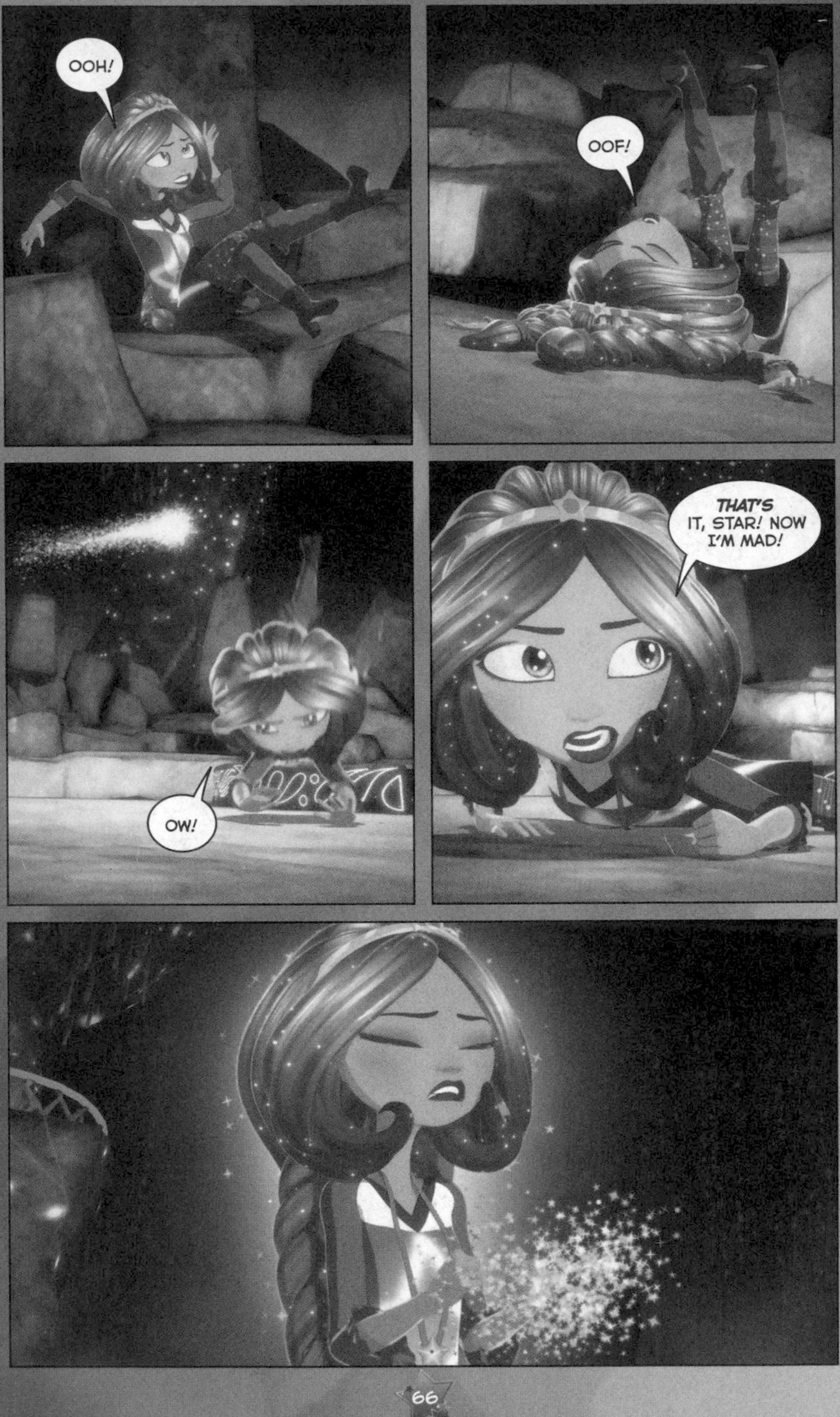
OOH!
OOF!
OW!
THAT'S IT, STAR! NOW I'M MAD!

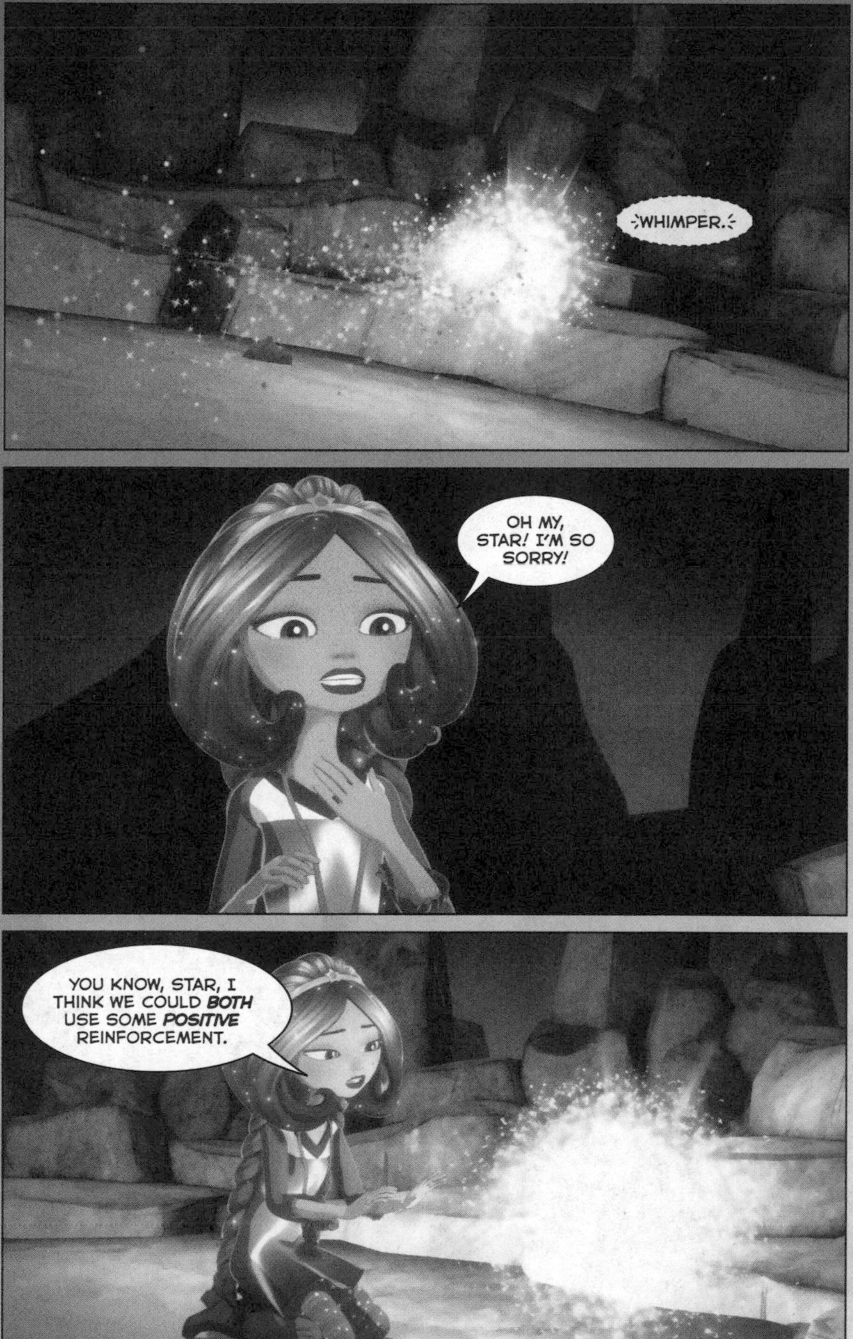
WHIMPER.
OH MY, STAR! I'M SO SORRY!
YOU KNOW, STAR, I THINK WE COULD *BOTH* USE SOME *POSITIVE* REINFORCEMENT.

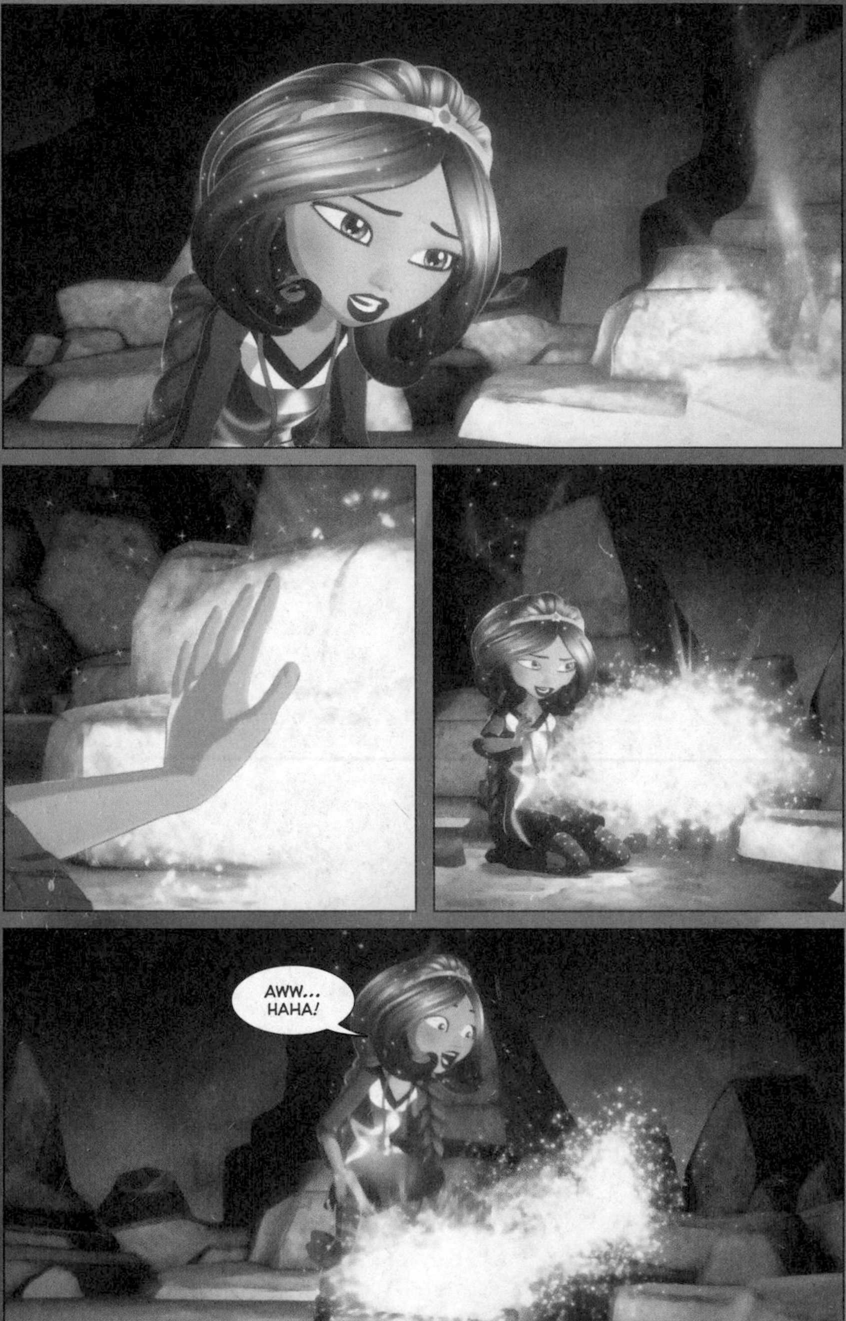
AWW...
HAHA!

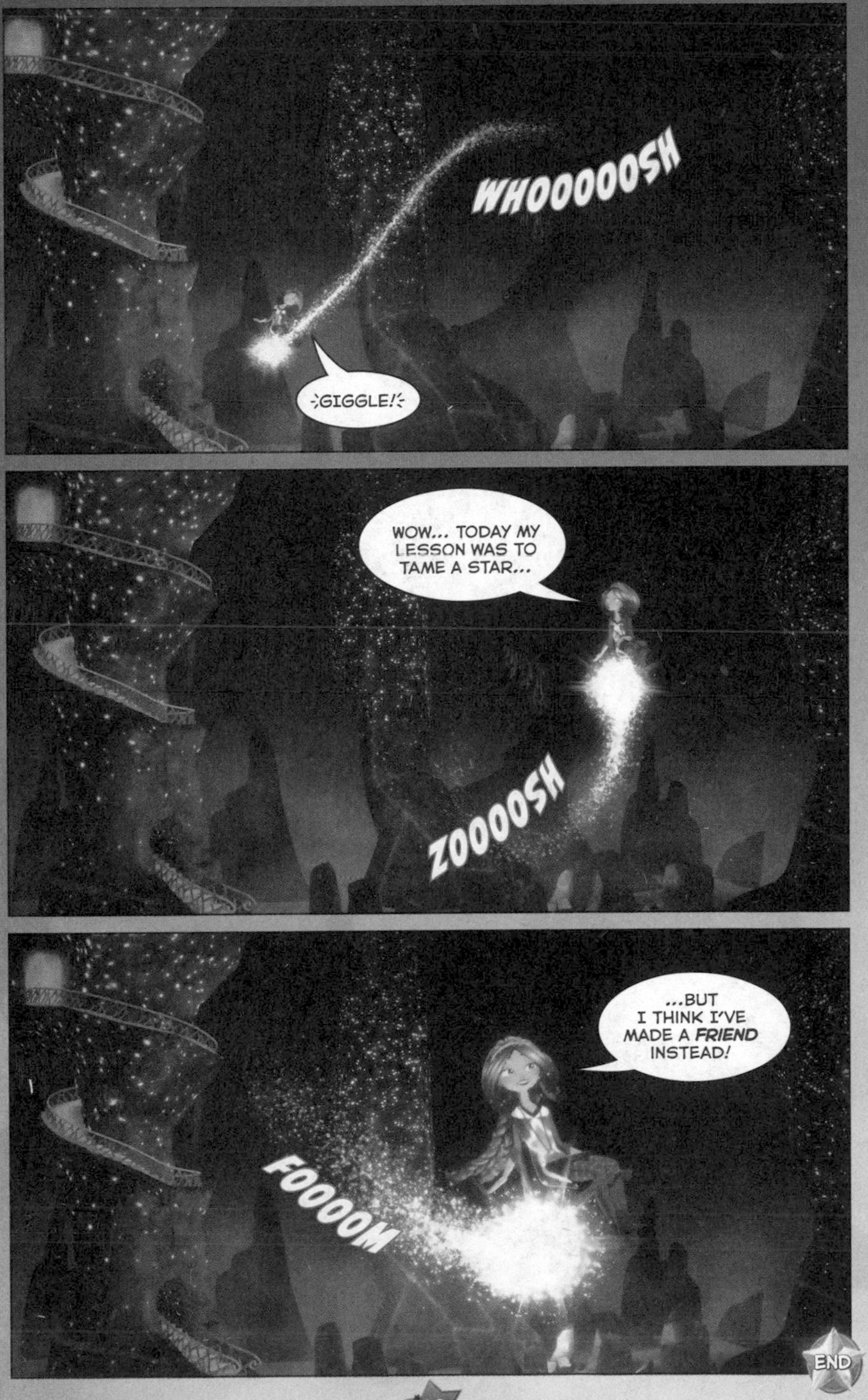
WHOOOOOSH
GIGGLE!
WOW... TODAY MY LESSON WAS TO TAME A STAR...
ZOOOOSH
...BUT I THINK I'VE MADE A FRIEND INSTEAD!
FOOOOM
END

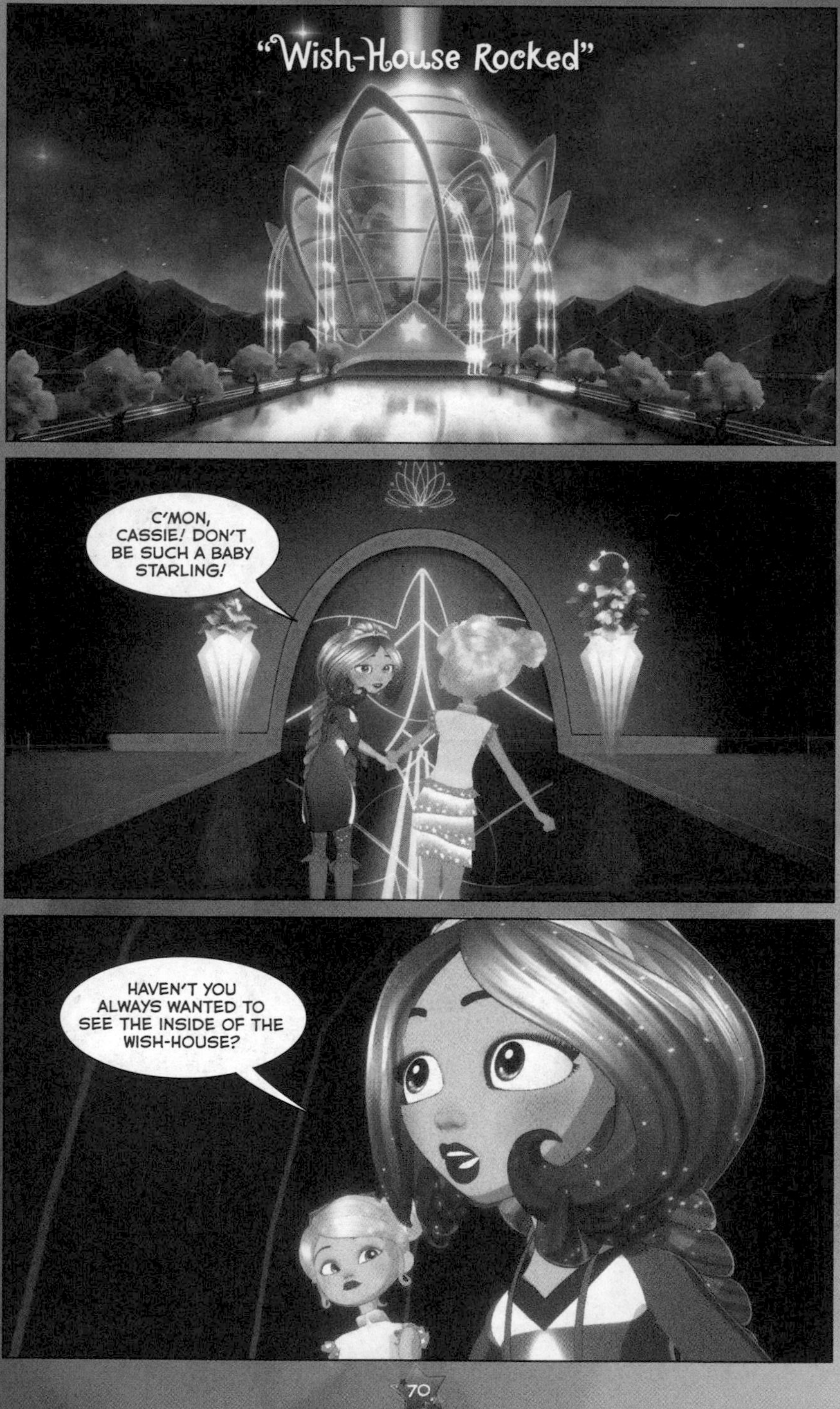
"Wish-House Rocked"
C'MON, CASSIE! DON'T BE SUCH A BABY STARLING!
HAVEN'T YOU ALWAYS WANTED TO SEE THE INSIDE OF THE WISH-HOUSE?

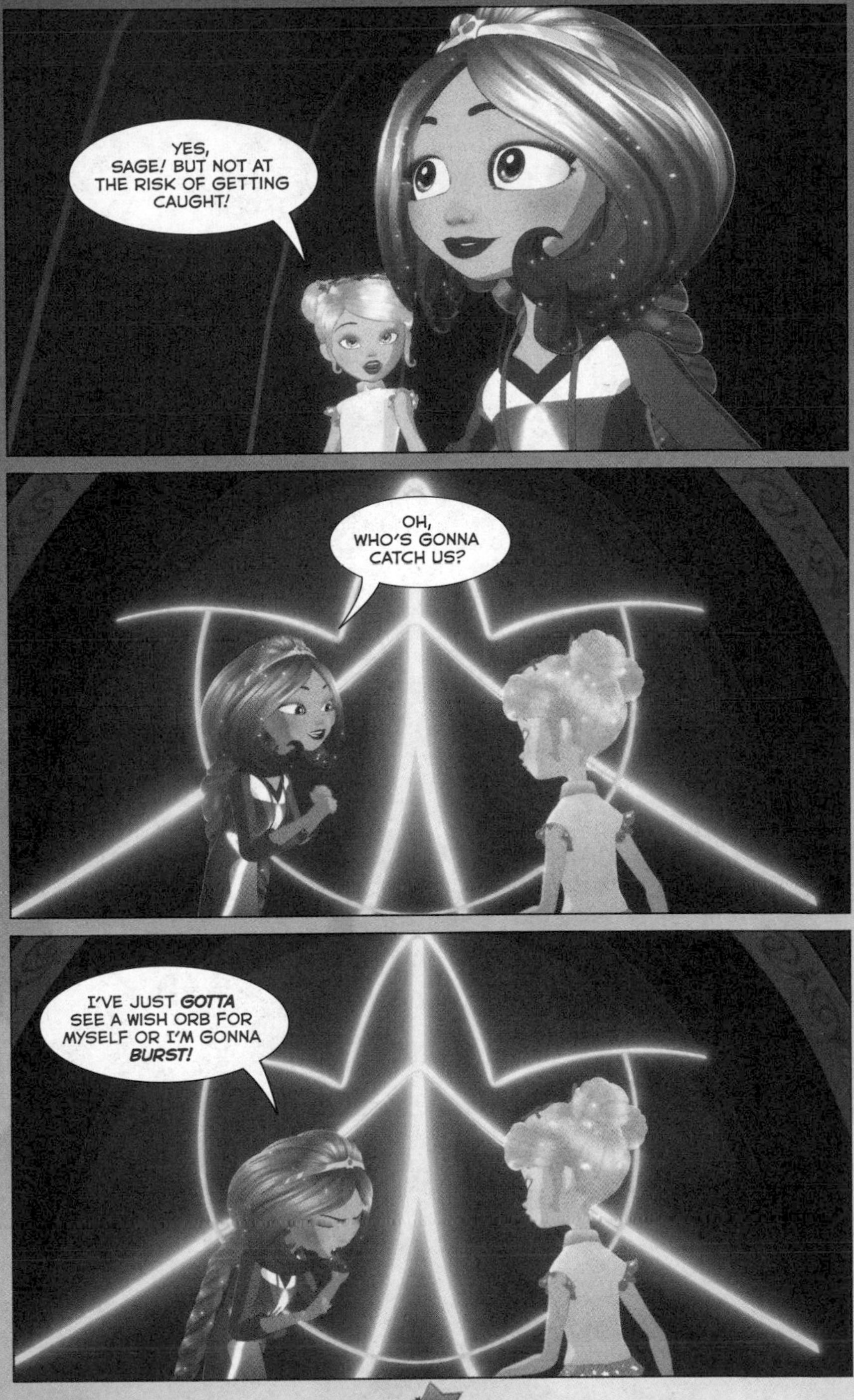
YES, SAGE! BUT NOT AT THE RISK OF GETTING CAUGHT!
OH, WHO'S GONNA CATCH US?
I'VE JUST *GOTTA* SEE A WISH ORB FOR MYSELF OR I'M GONNA *BURST!*

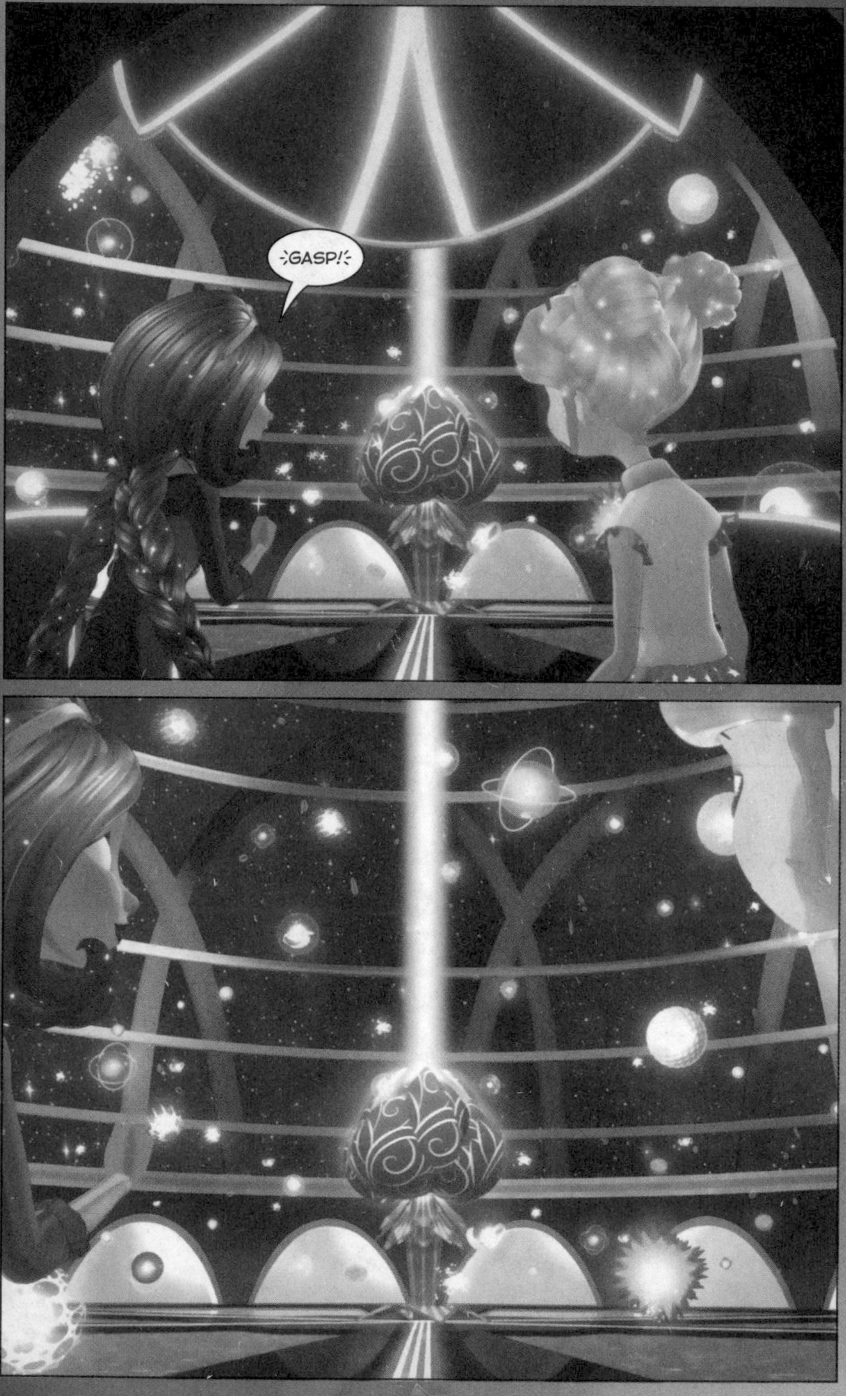
GASP!

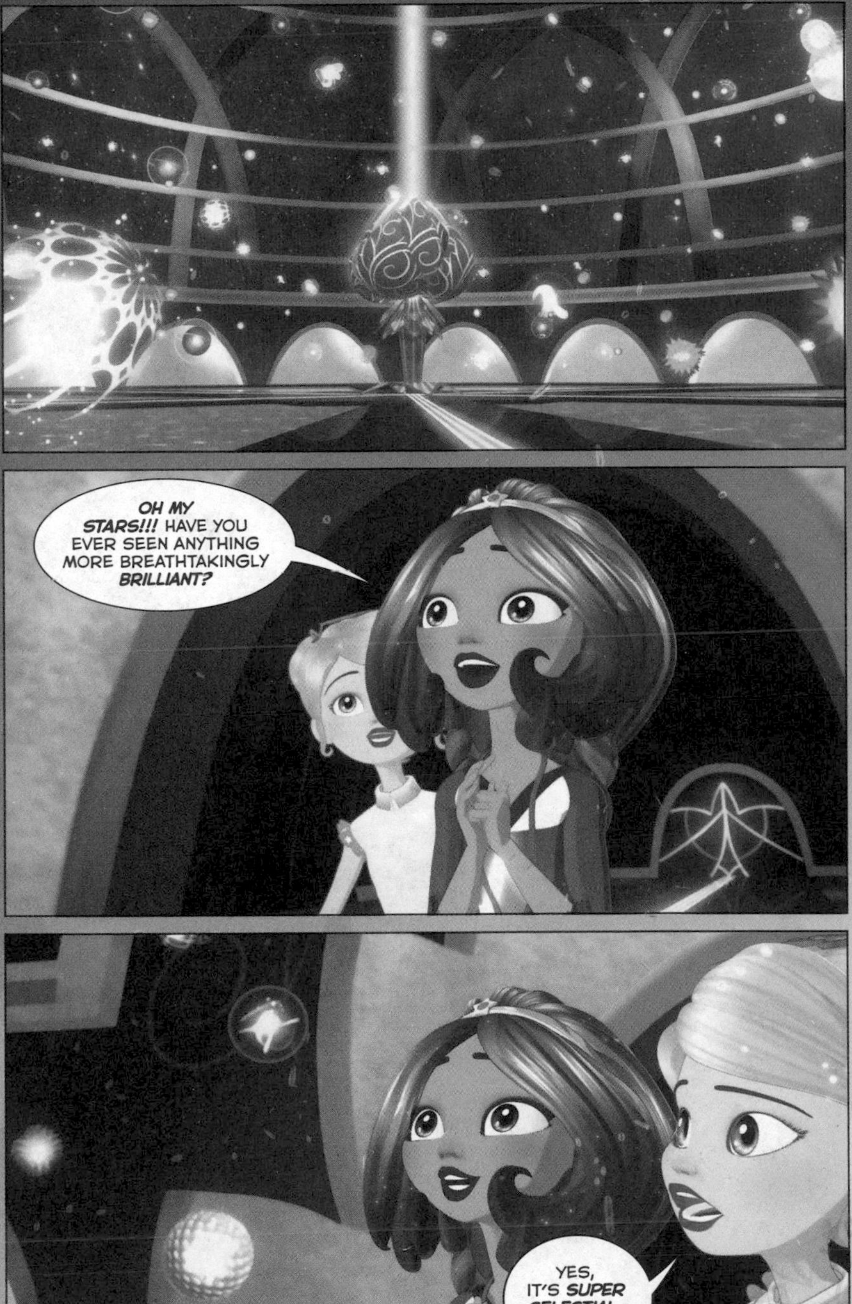
OH MY STARS!!! HAVE YOU EVER SEEN ANYTHING MORE BREATHTAKINGLY BRILLIANT?
YES, IT'S SUPER CELESTIAL. C'MON!

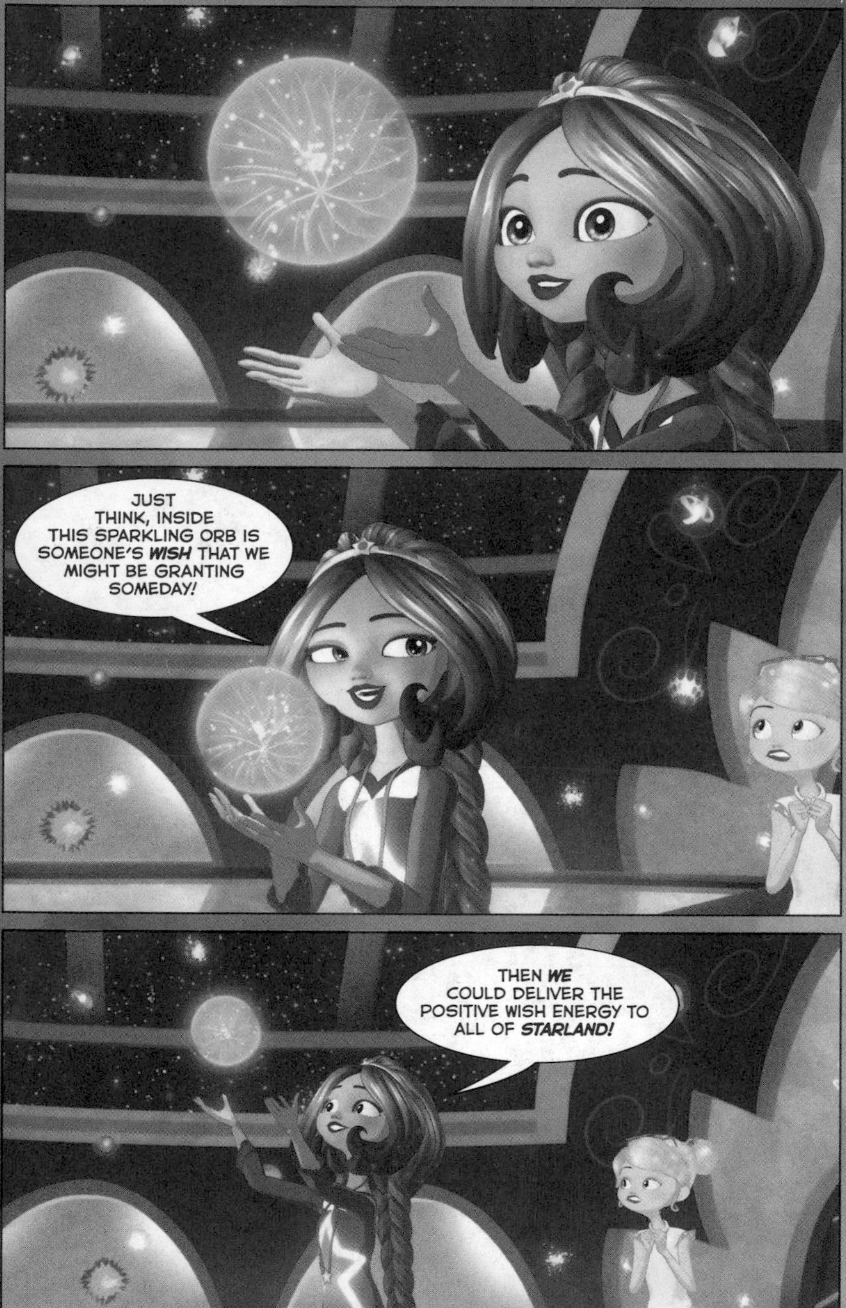
JUST THINK, INSIDE THIS SPARKLING ORB IS SOMEONE'S **WISH** THAT WE MIGHT BE GRANTING SOMEDAY!
THEN **WE** COULD DELIVER THE POSITIVE WISH ENERGY TO ALL OF **STARLAND!**

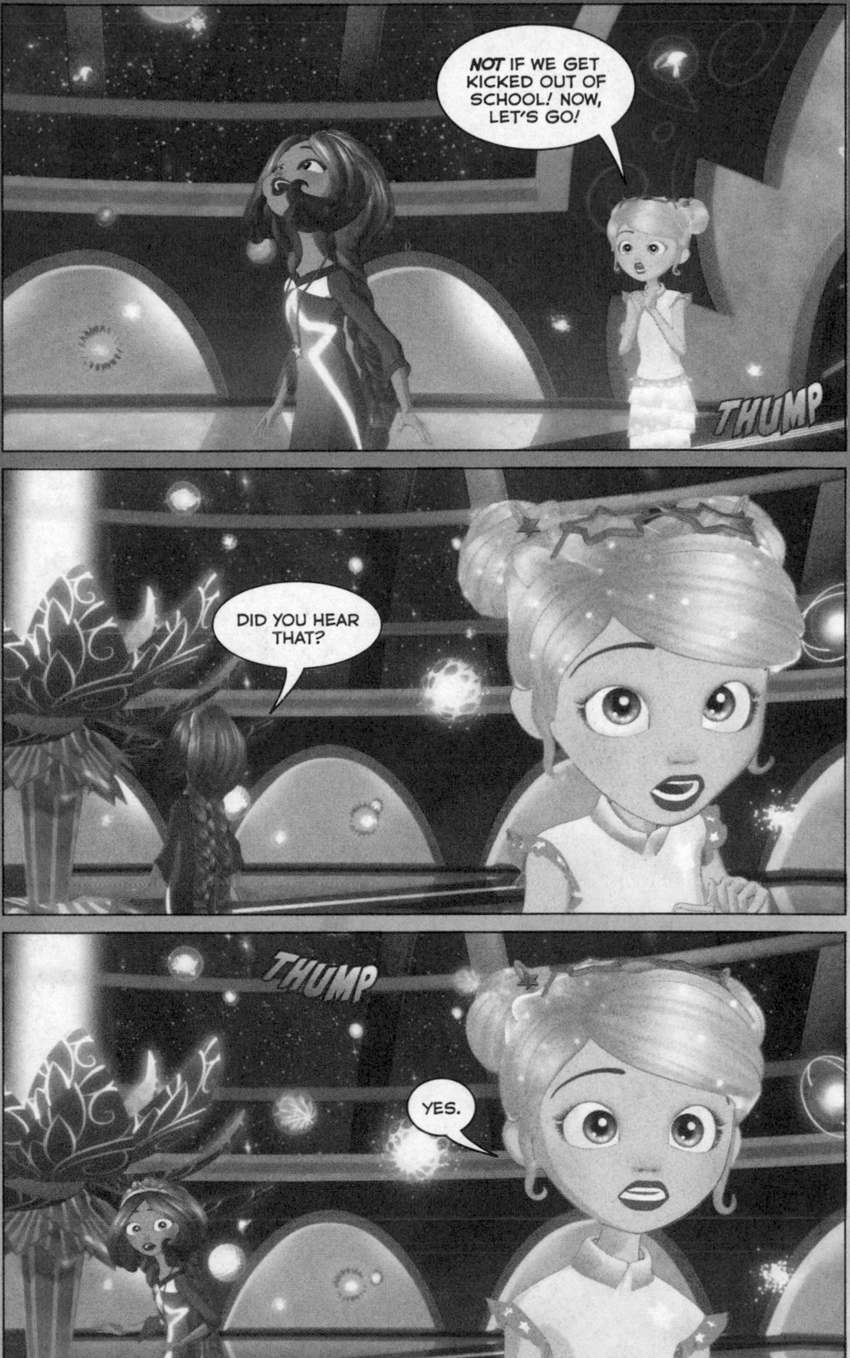
NOT IF WE GET KICKED OUT OF SCHOOL! NOW, LET'S GO!
THUMP
DID YOU HEAR THAT?
THUMP
YES.

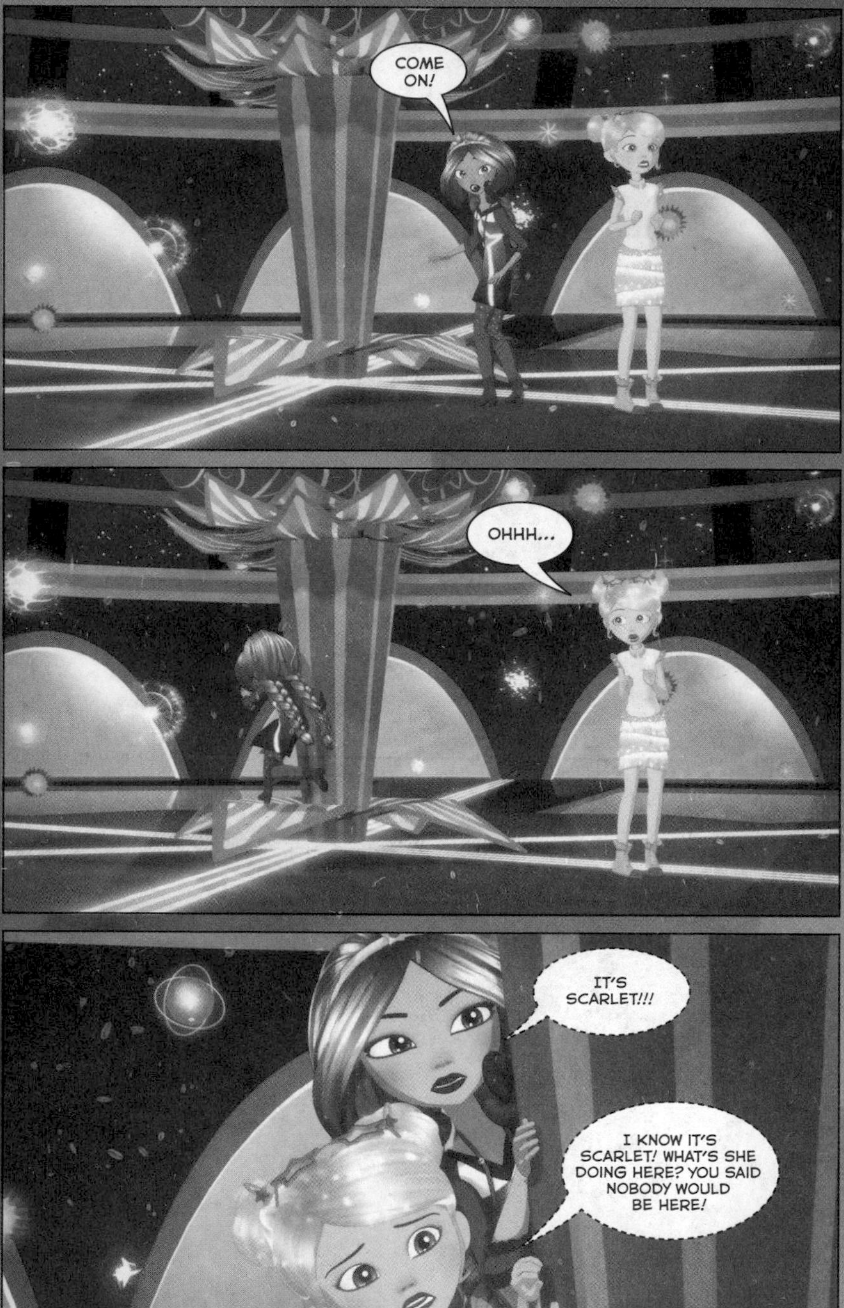
COME ON!
OHHH...
IT'S SCARLET!!!
I KNOW IT'S SCARLET! WHAT'S SHE DOING HERE? YOU SAID NOBODY WOULD BE HERE!

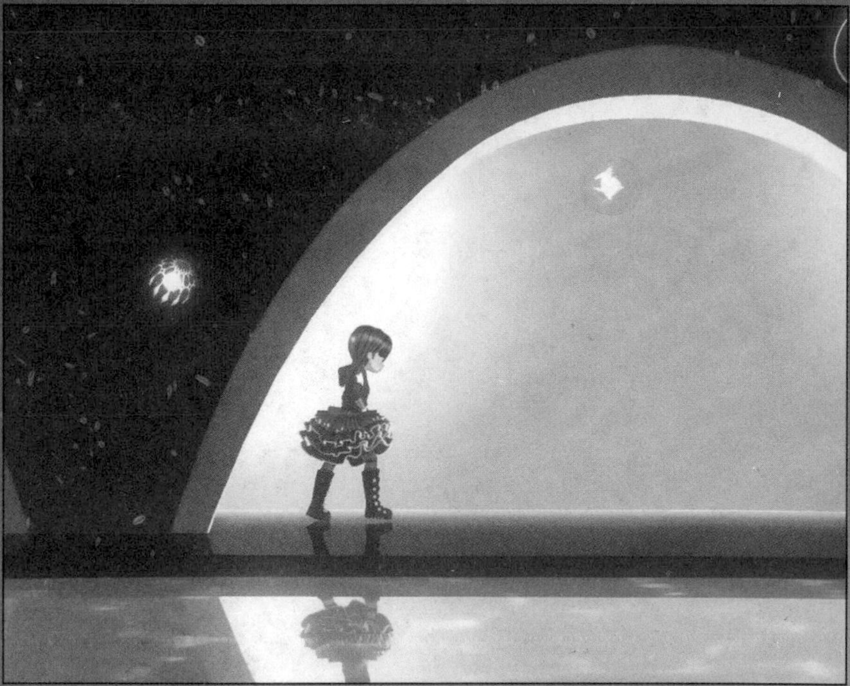

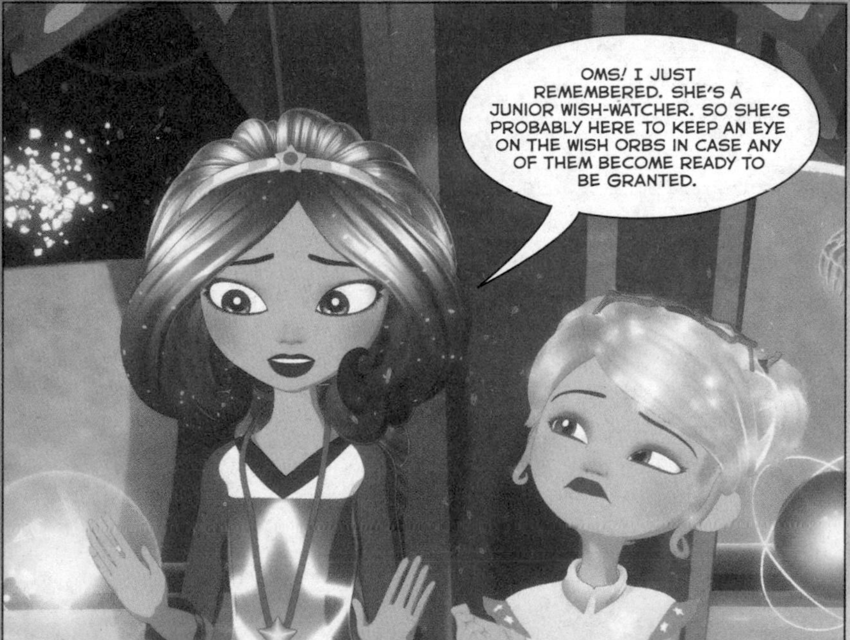
OMS! I JUST REMEMBERED. SHE'S A JUNIOR WISH-WATCHER. SO SHE'S PROBABLY HERE TO KEEP AN EYE ON THE WISH ORBS IN CASE ANY OF THEM BECOME READY TO BE GRANTED.

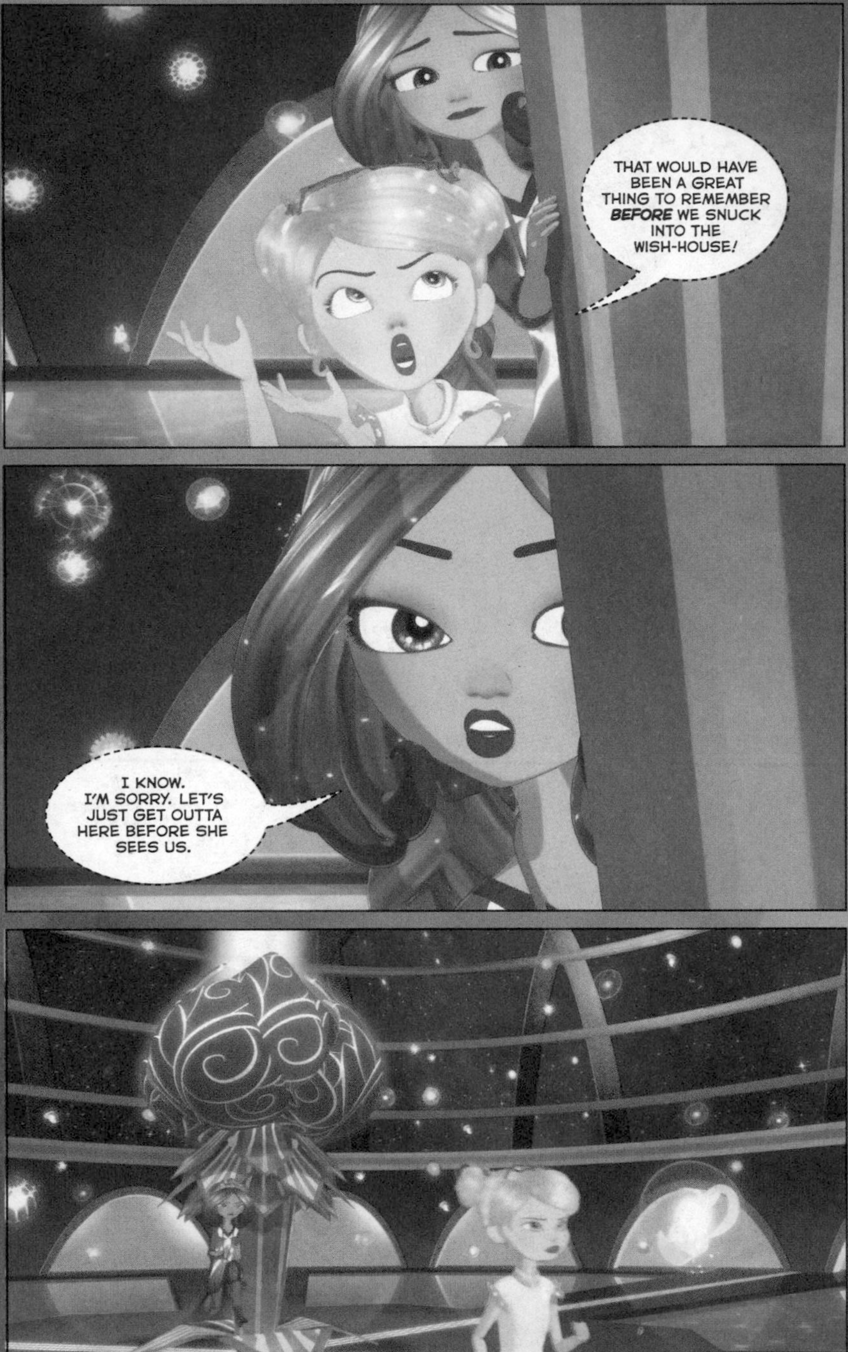
THAT WOULD HAVE BEEN A GREAT THING TO REMEMBER *BEFORE* WE SNUCK INTO THE WISH-HOUSE!
I KNOW. I'M SORRY. LET'S JUST GET OUTTA HERE BEFORE SHE SEES US.

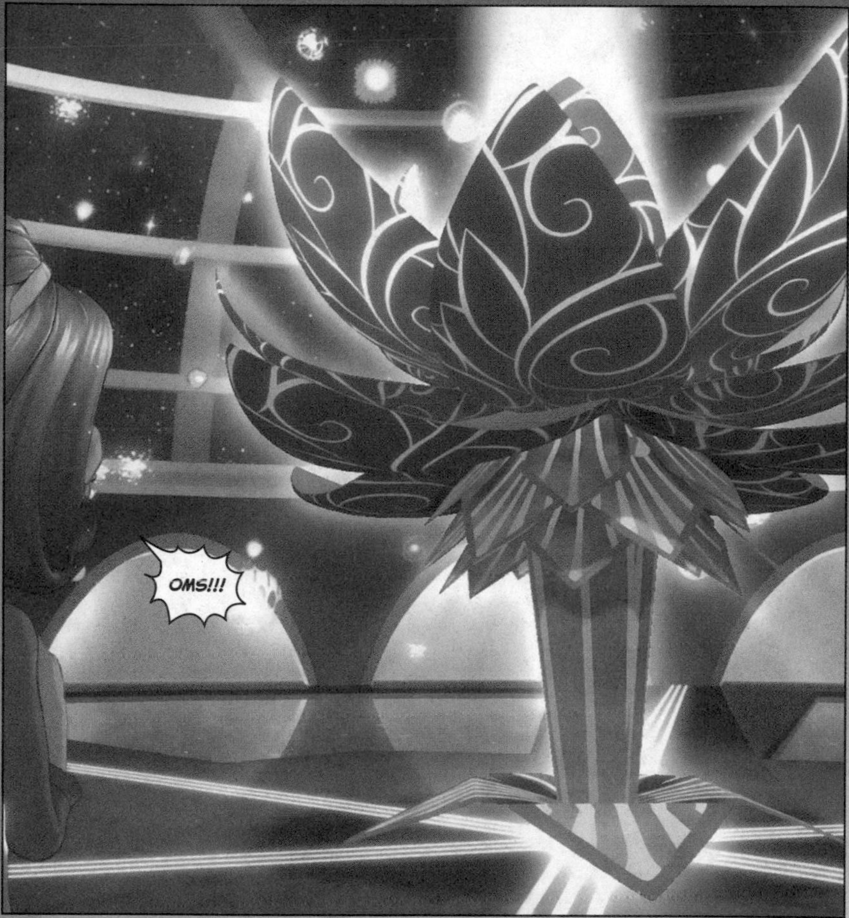
OMS!!!

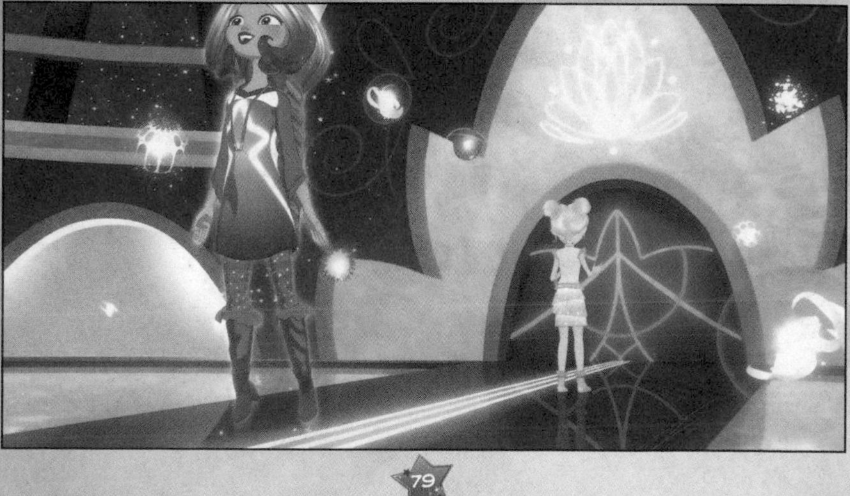

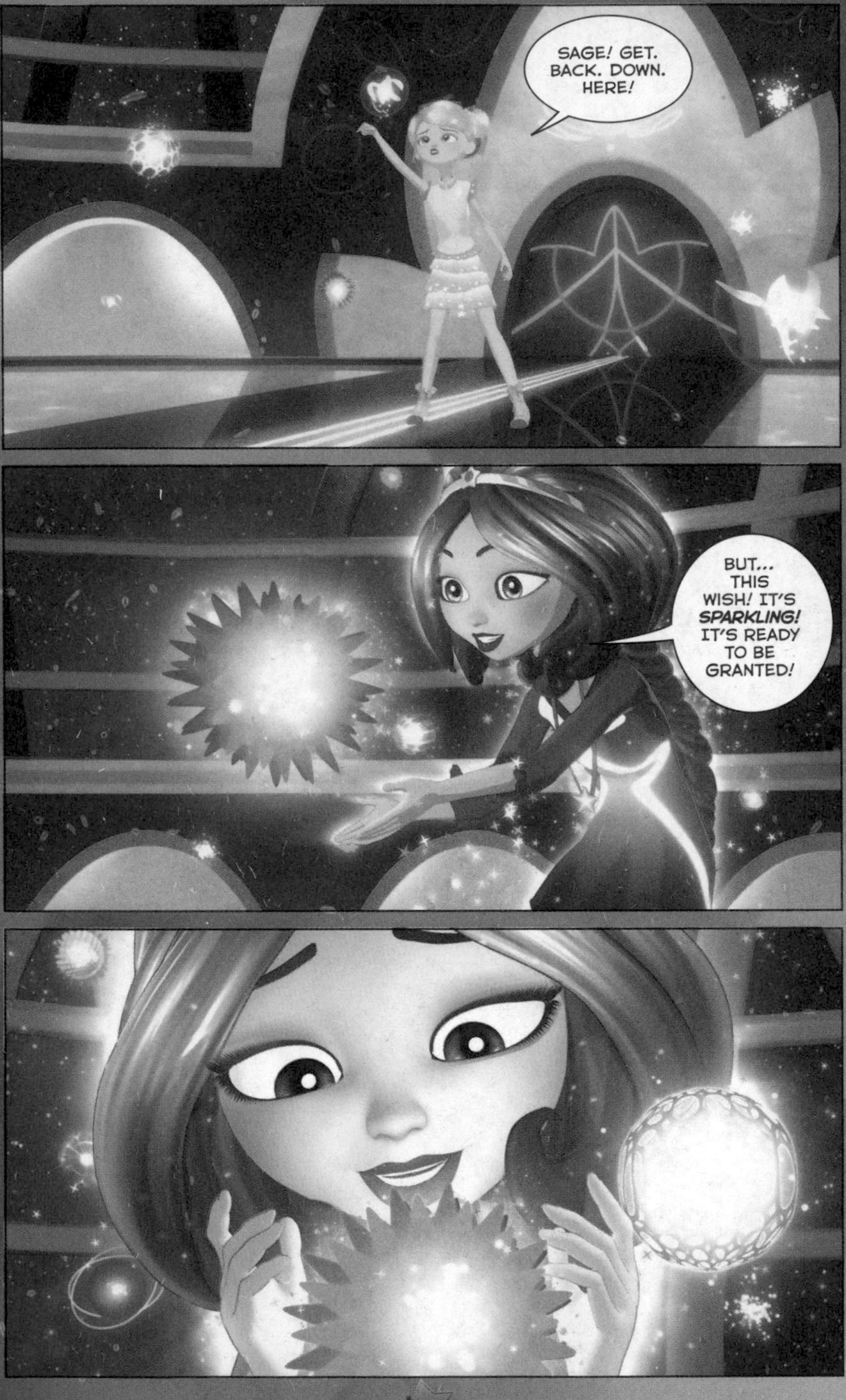
SAGE! GET. BACK. DOWN. HERE!
BUT... THIS WISH! IT'S *SPARKLING!* IT'S READY TO BE GRANTED!

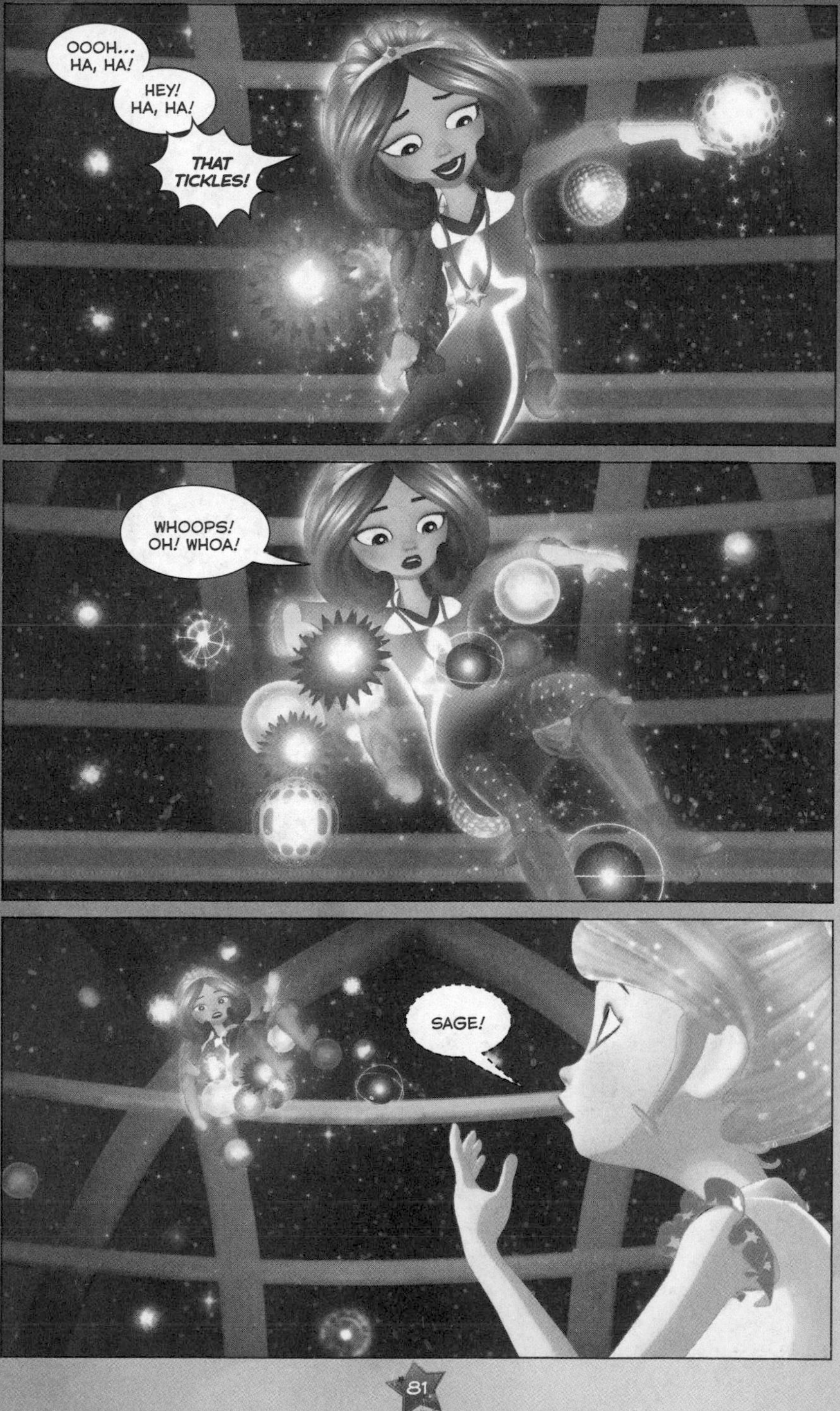
OOOH... HA, HA!
HEY! HA, HA!
THAT TICKLES!
WHOOPS! OH! WHOA!
SAGE!

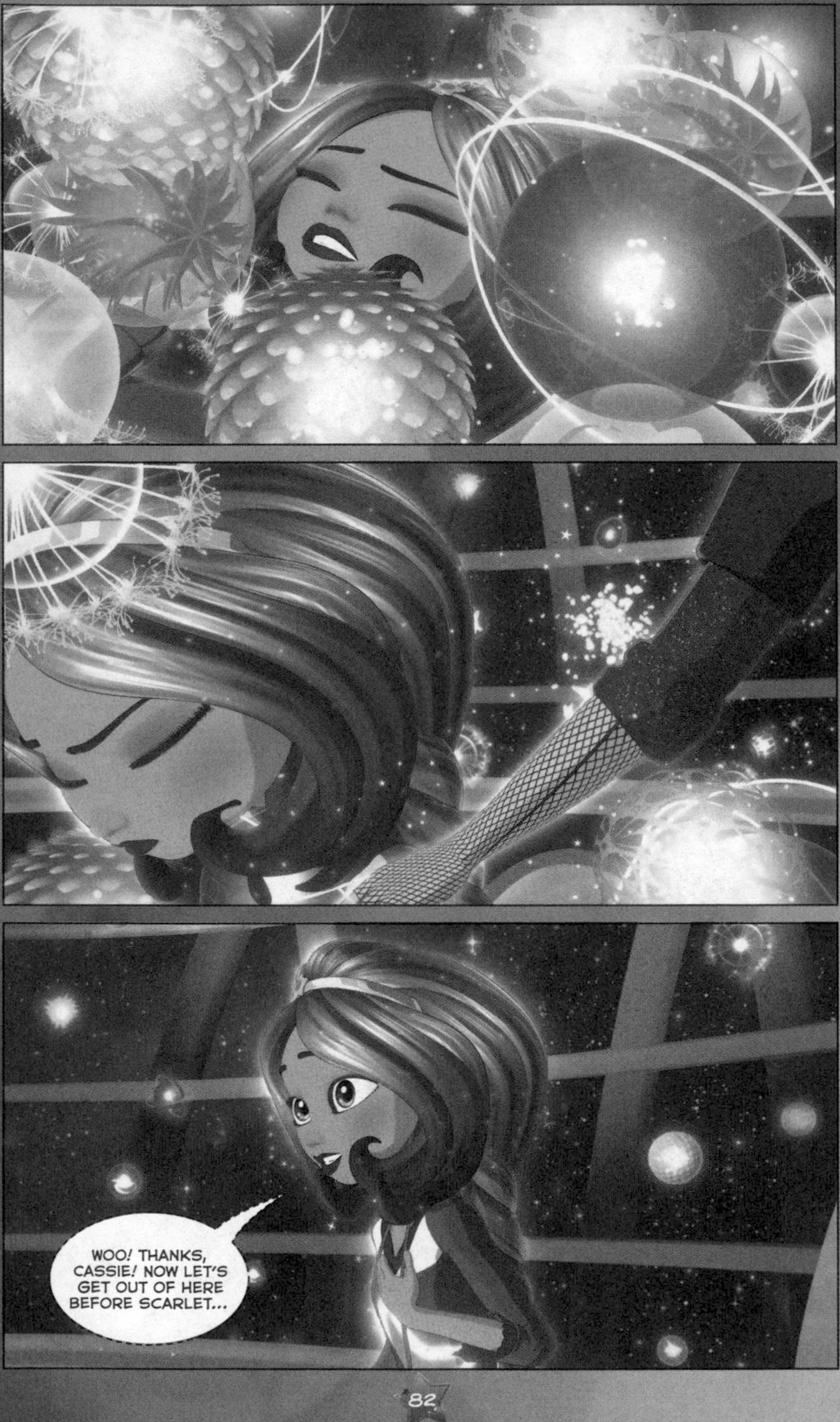
WOO! THANKS, CASSIE! NOW LET'S GET OUT OF HERE BEFORE SCARLET...

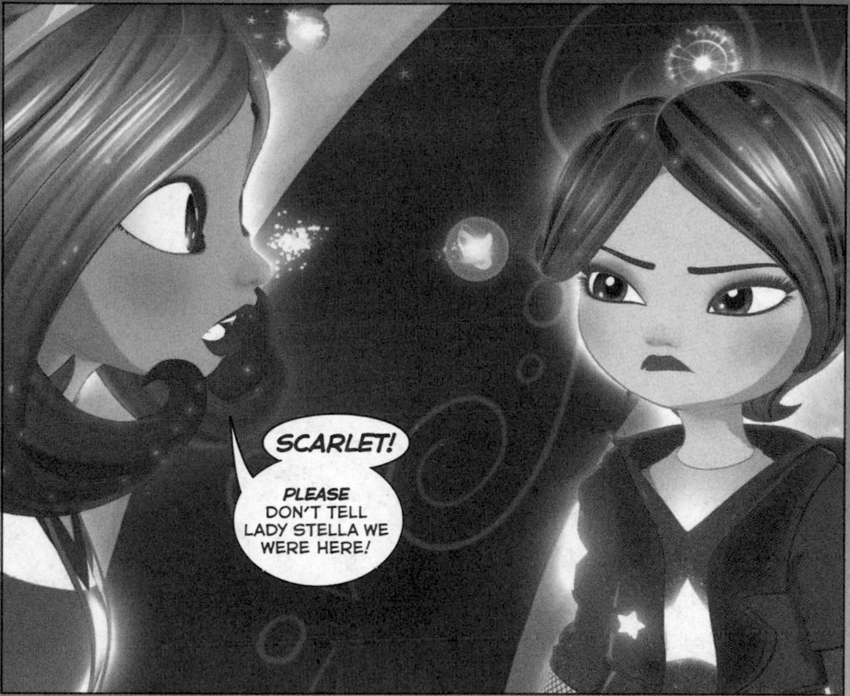
SCARLET!
PLEASE DON'T TELL LADY STELLA WE WERE HERE!

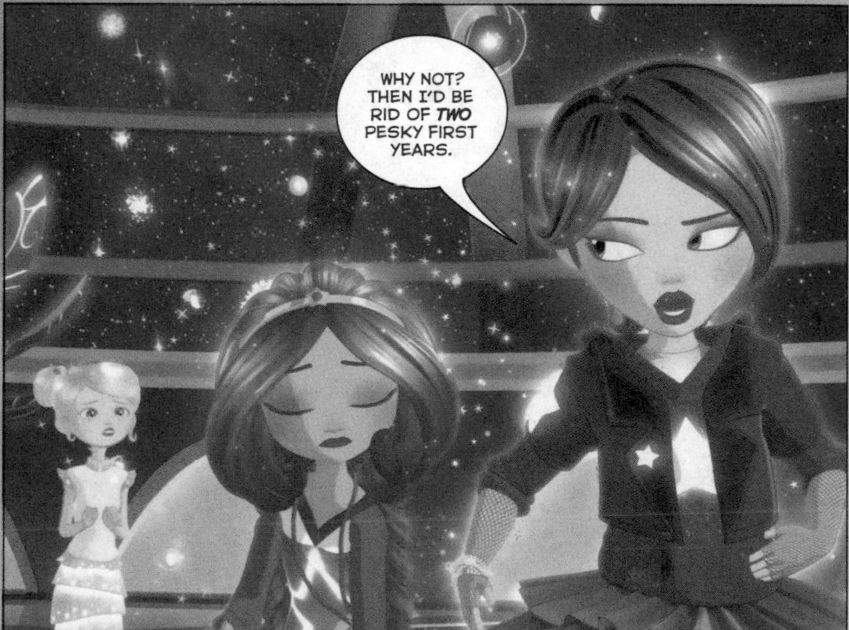
WHY NOT? THEN I'D BE RID OF TWO PESKY FIRST YEARS.

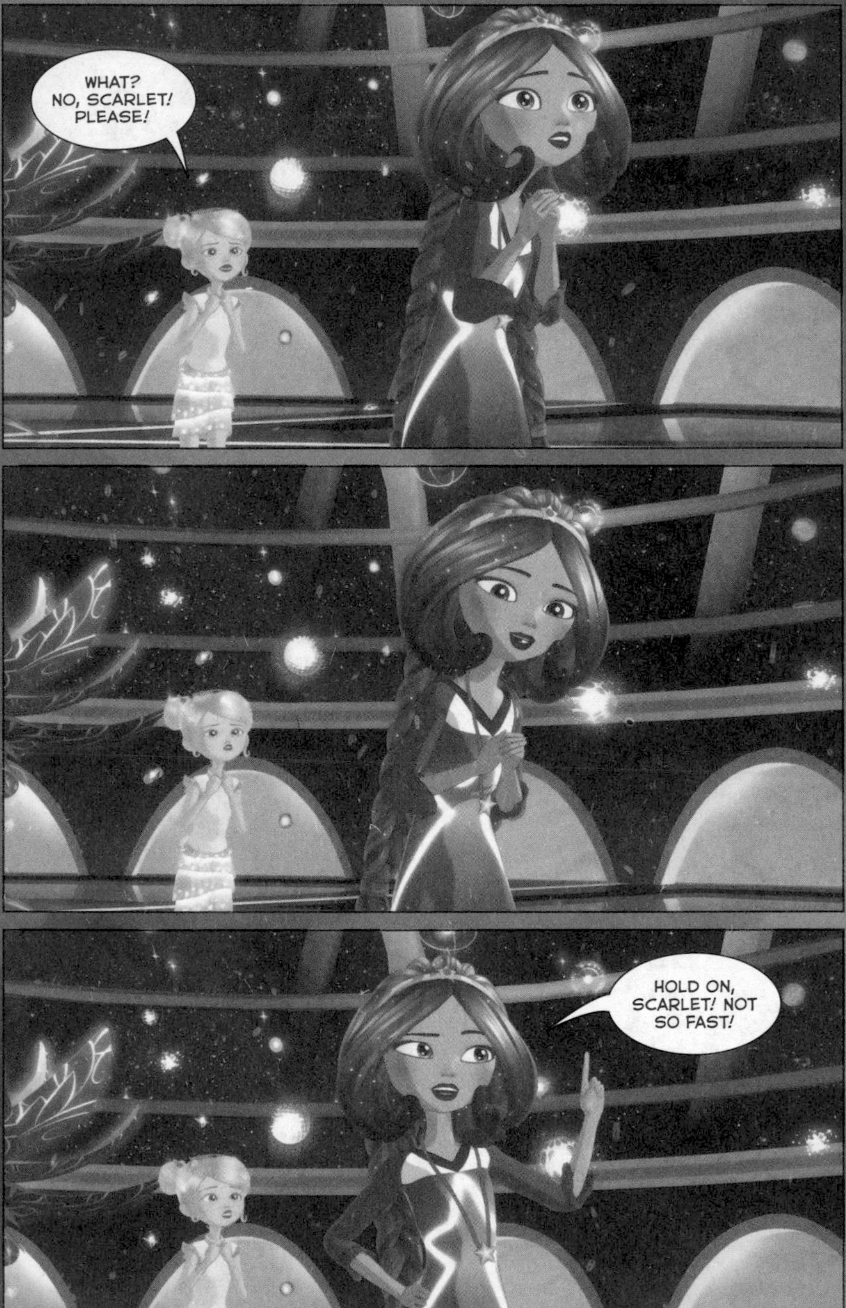
WHAT? NO, SCARLET! PLEASE!
HOLD ON, SCARLET! NOT SO FAST!

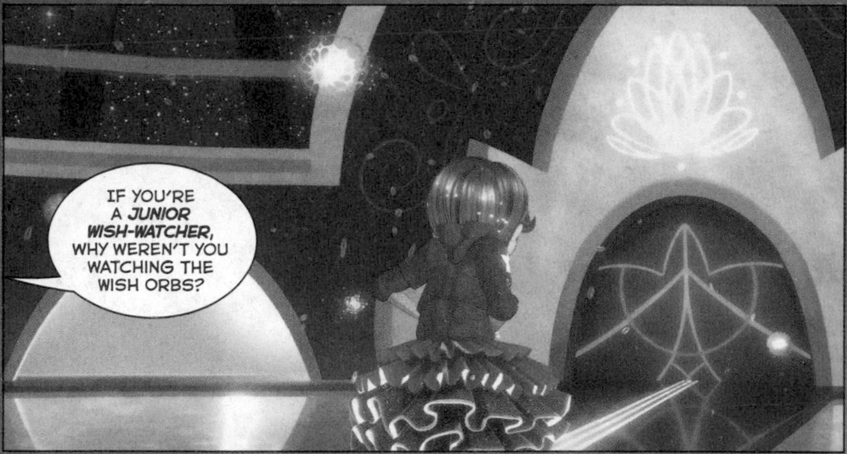
IF YOU'RE A *JUNIOR WISH-WATCHER,* WHY WEREN'T YOU WATCHING THE WISH ORBS?

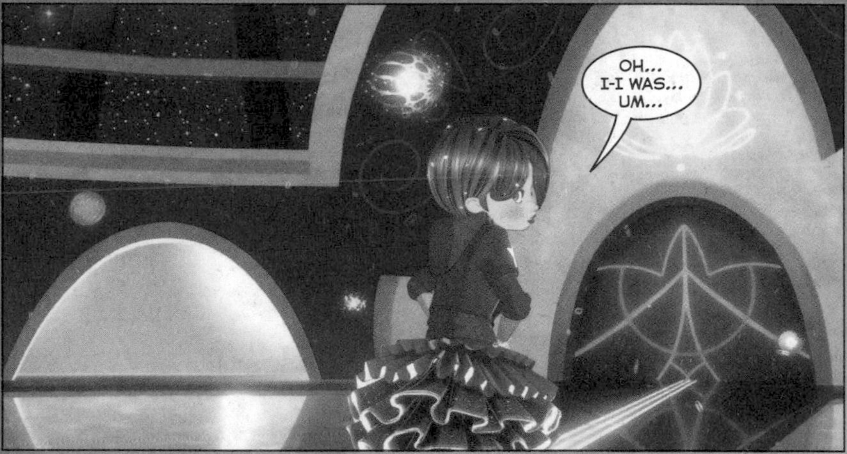
OH... I-I WAS... UM...

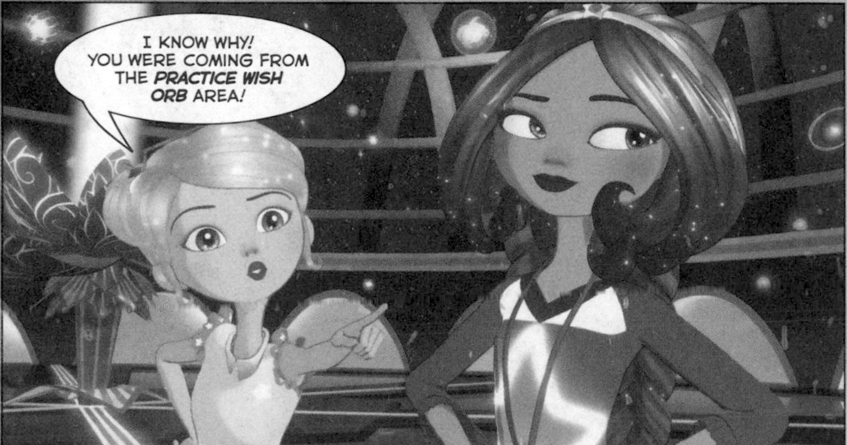
I KNOW WHY! YOU WERE COMING FROM THE *PRACTICE WISH ORB* AREA!

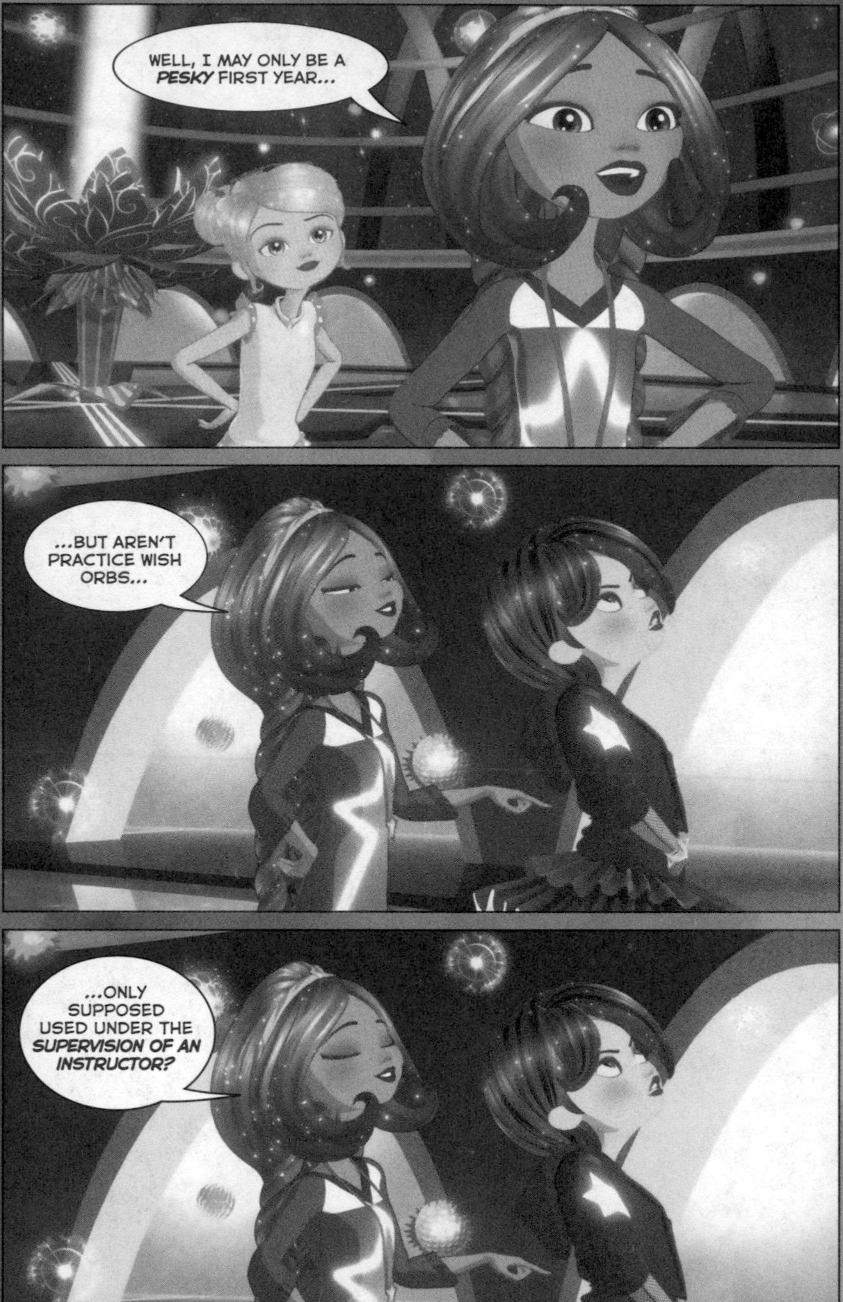
WELL, I MAY ONLY BE A *PESKY* FIRST YEAR...
...BUT AREN'T PRACTICE WISH ORBS...
...ONLY SUPPOSED USED UNDER THE *SUPERVISION OF AN INSTRUCTOR?*

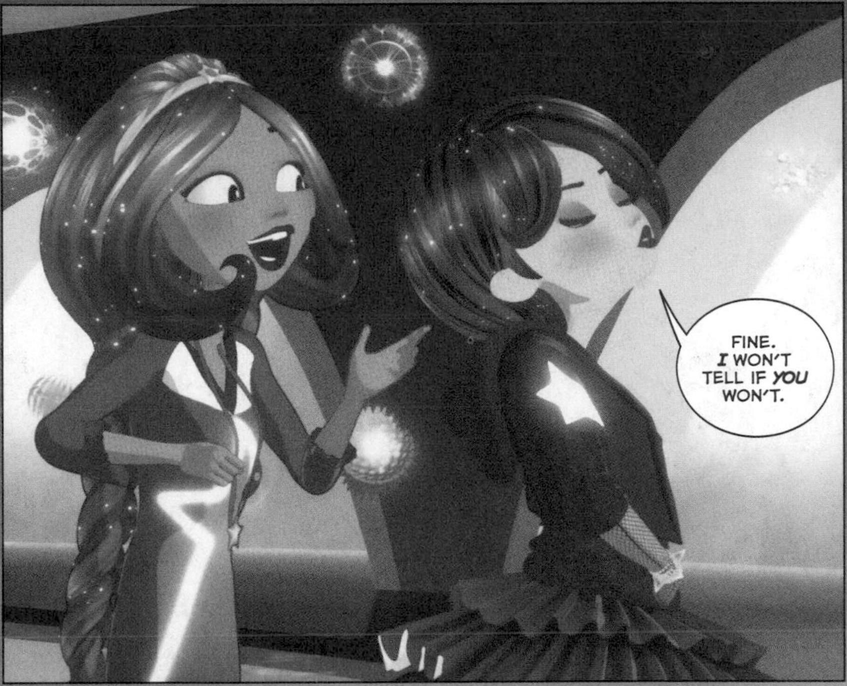
FINE. *I* WON'T TELL IF *YOU* WON'T.

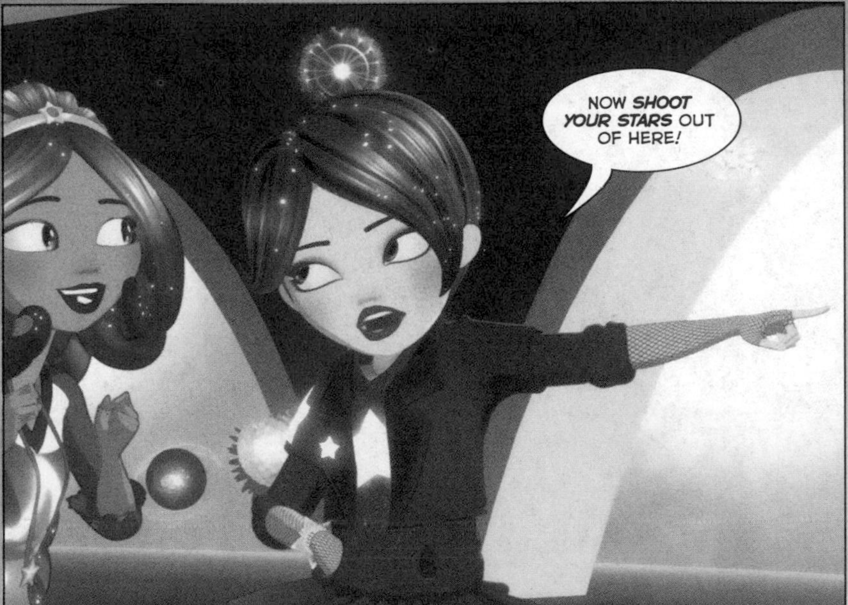
NOW ***SHOOT YOUR STARS*** OUT OF HERE!

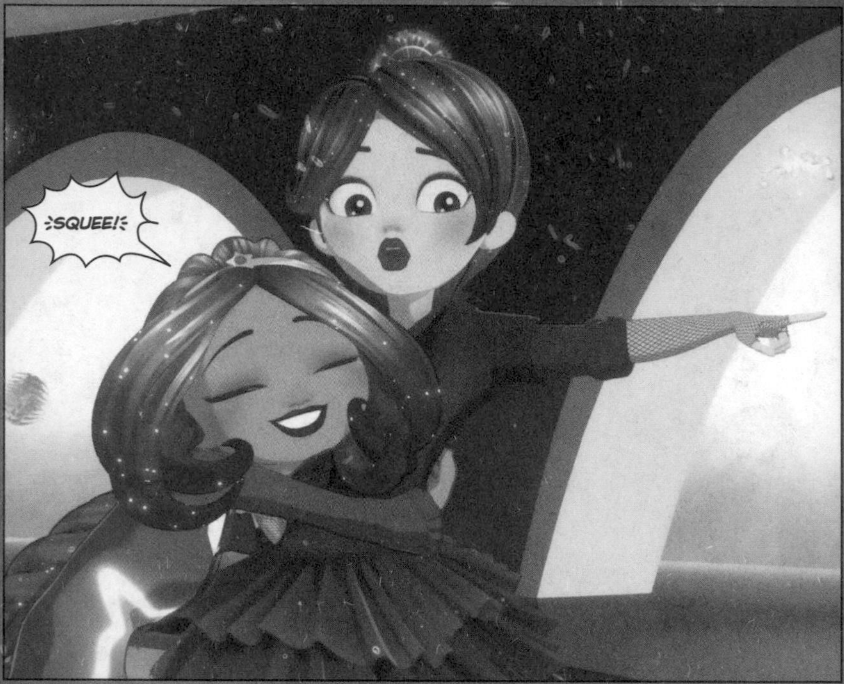
SQUEE!

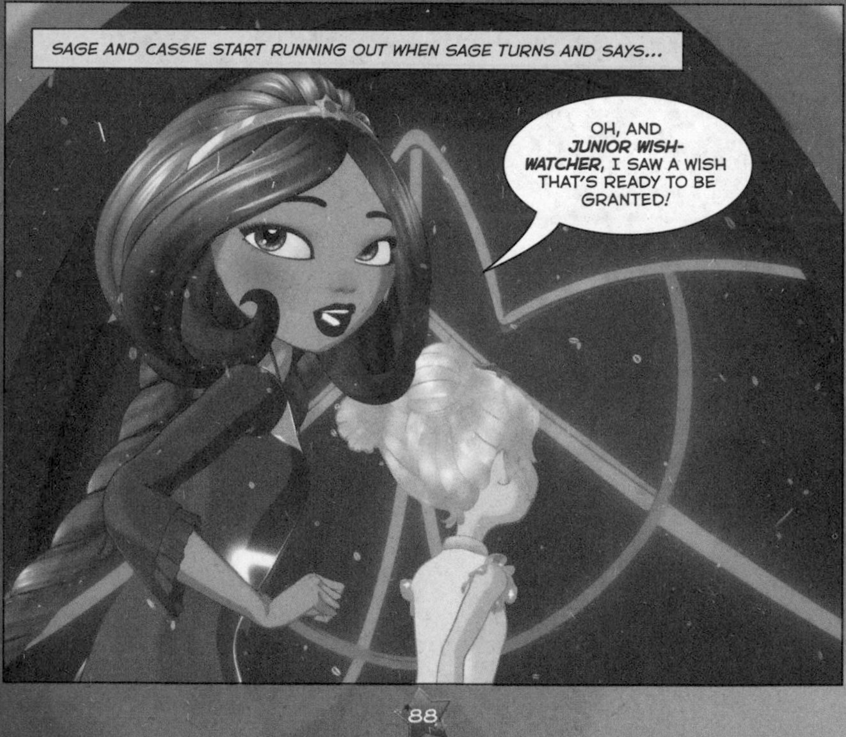
SAGE AND CASSIE START RUNNING OUT WHEN SAGE TURNS AND SAYS...
OH, AND *JUNIOR WISH-WATCHER*, I SAW A WISH THAT'S READY TO BE GRANTED!

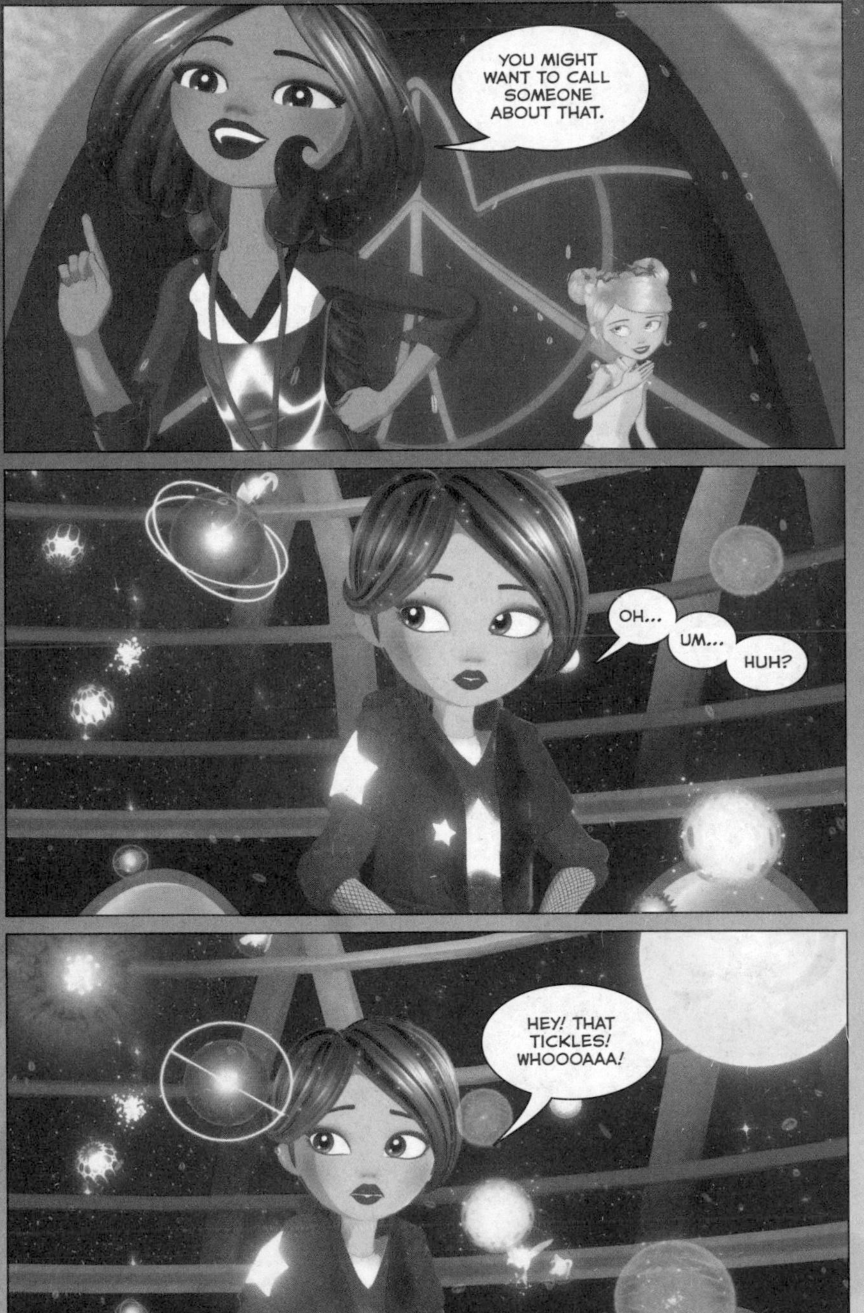
YOU MIGHT WANT TO CALL SOMEONE ABOUT THAT.
OH...
UM...
HUH?
HEY! THAT TICKLES! WHOOOAAA!
END

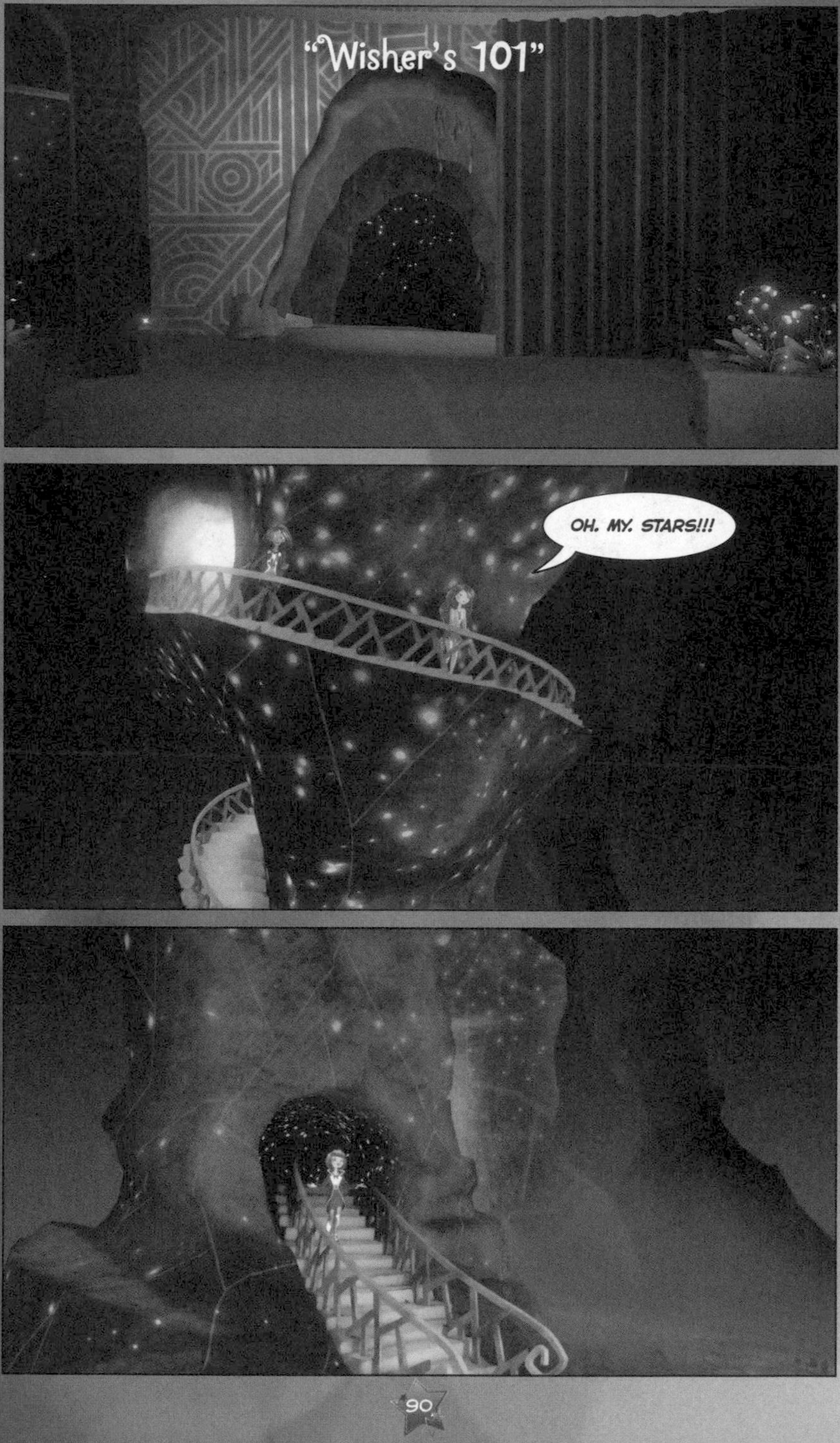
"Wisher's 101"
OH. MY. STARS!!!

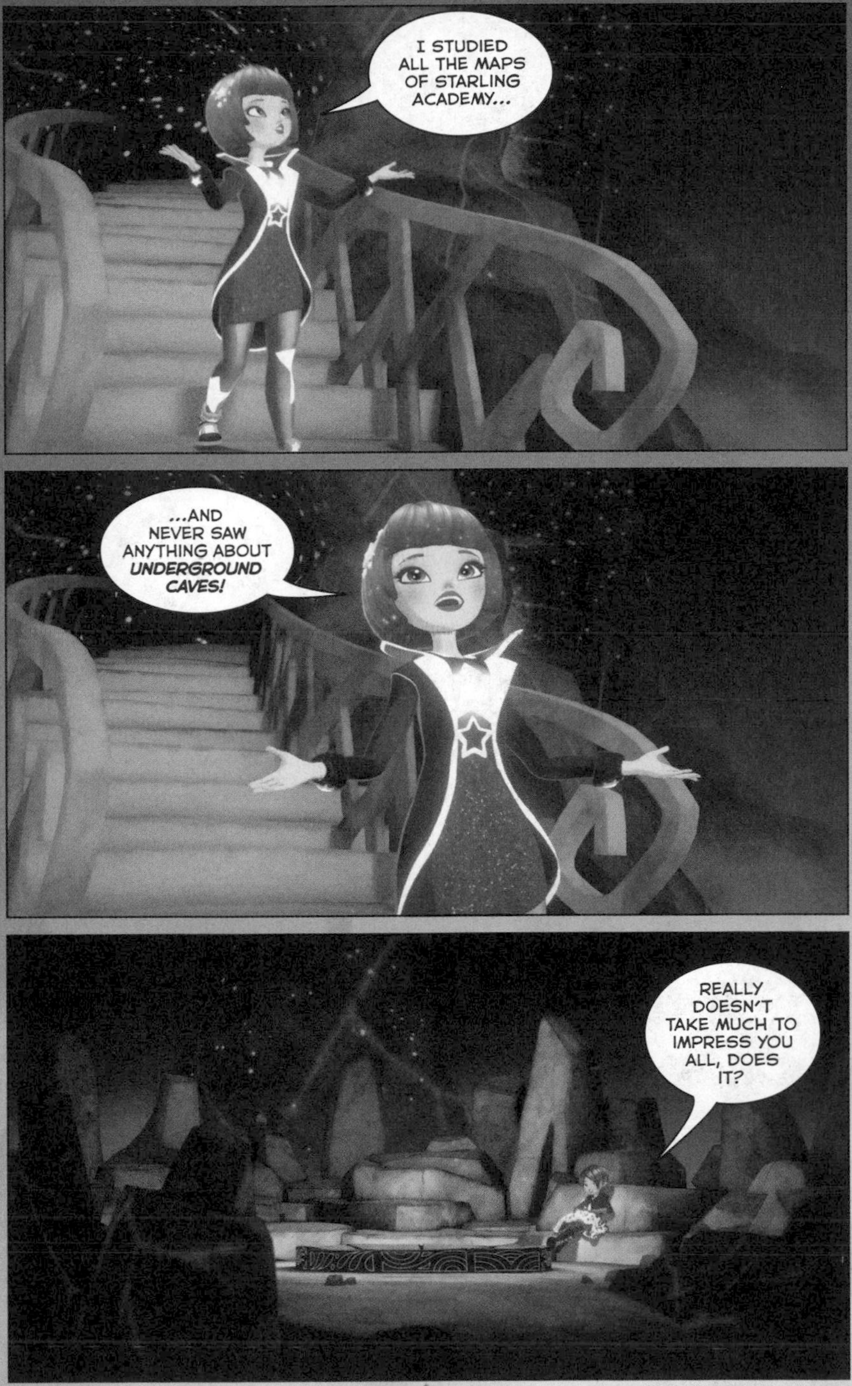
I STUDIED ALL THE MAPS OF STARLING ACADEMY...
...AND NEVER SAW ANYTHING ABOUT *UNDERGROUND CAVES!*
REALLY DOESN'T TAKE MUCH TO IMPRESS YOU ALL, DOES IT?

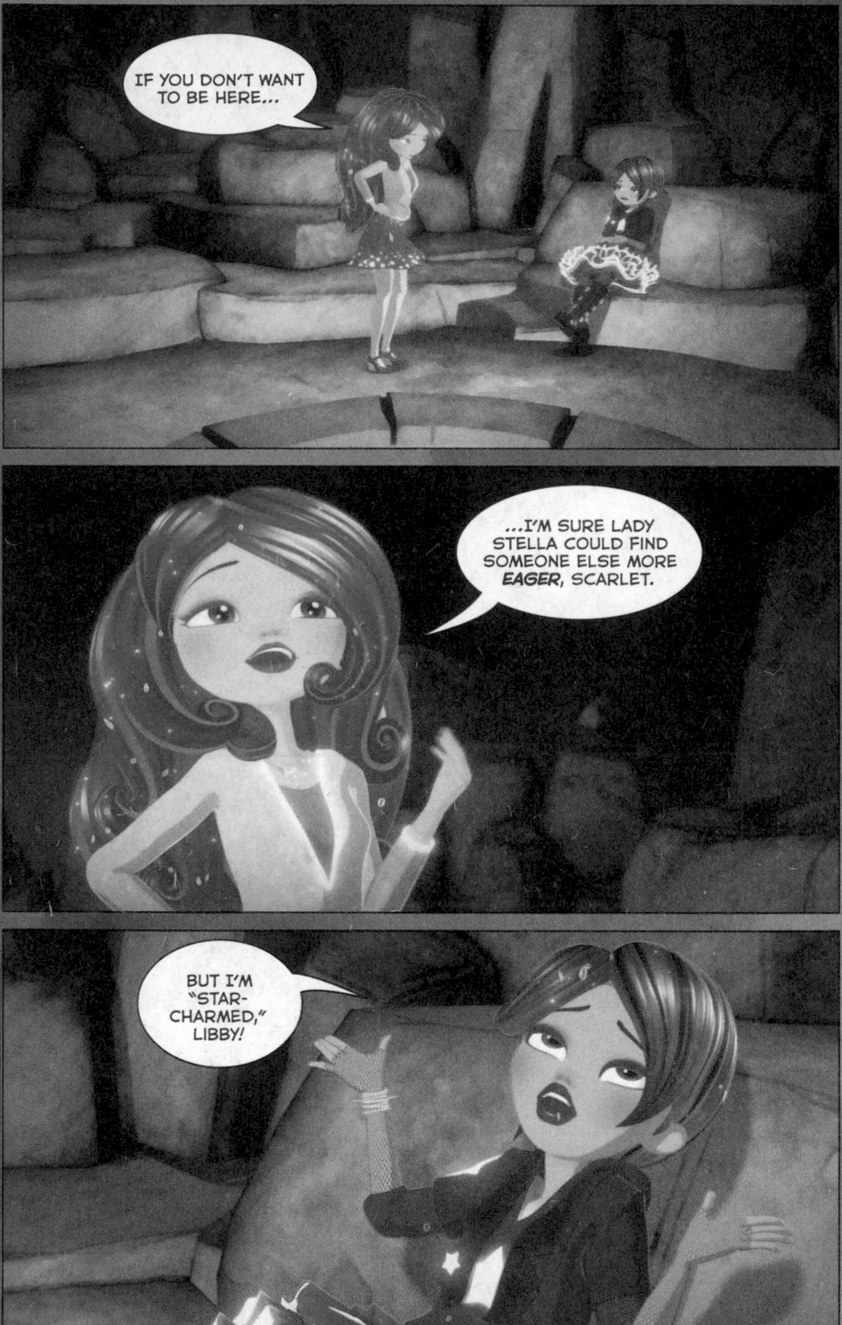
IF YOU DON'T WANT TO BE HERE...
...I'M SURE LADY STELLA COULD FIND SOMEONE ELSE MORE **EAGER**, SCARLET.
BUT I'M "STAR-CHARMED," LIBBY!

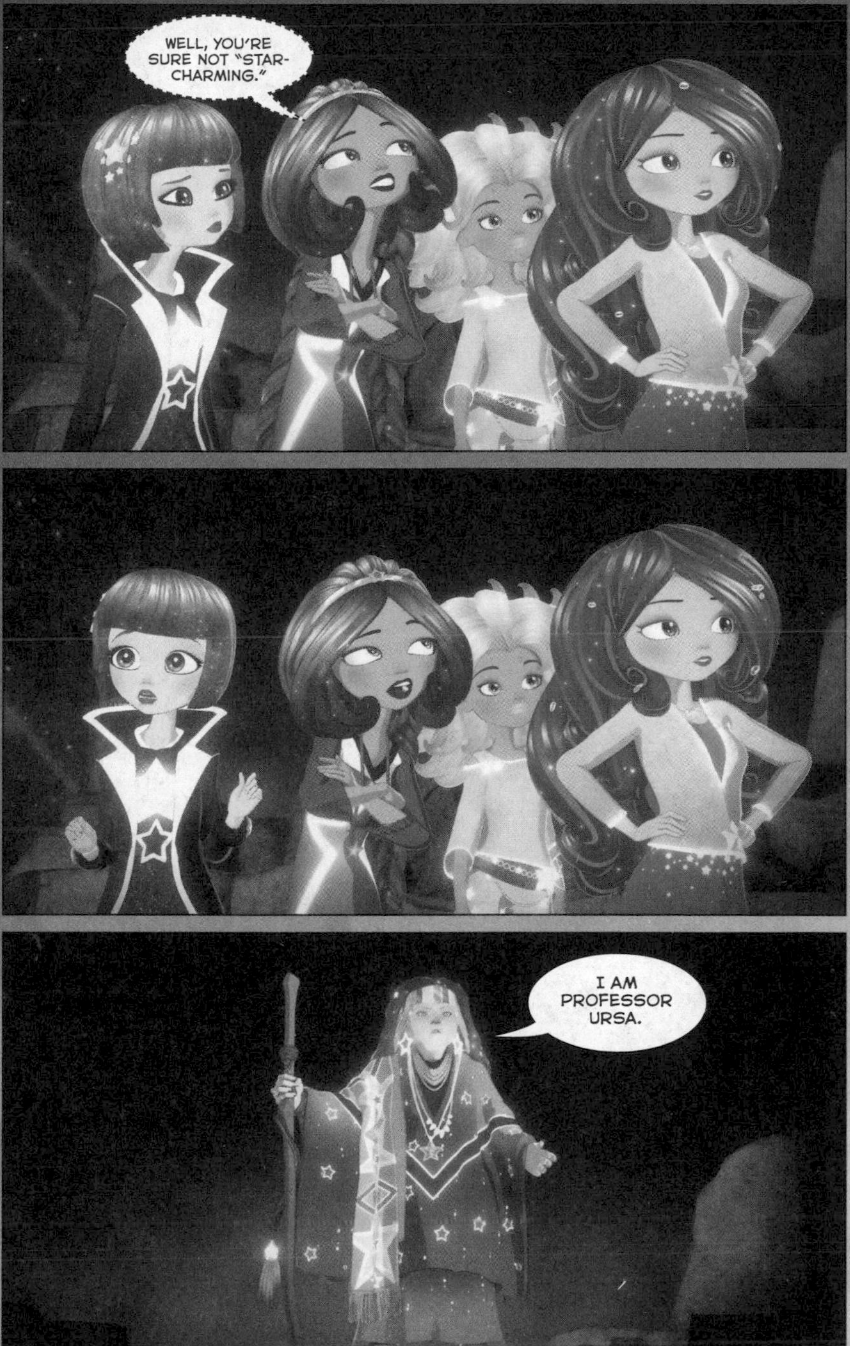
WELL, YOU'RE SURE NOT "STAR-CHARMING."
I AM PROFESSOR URSA.

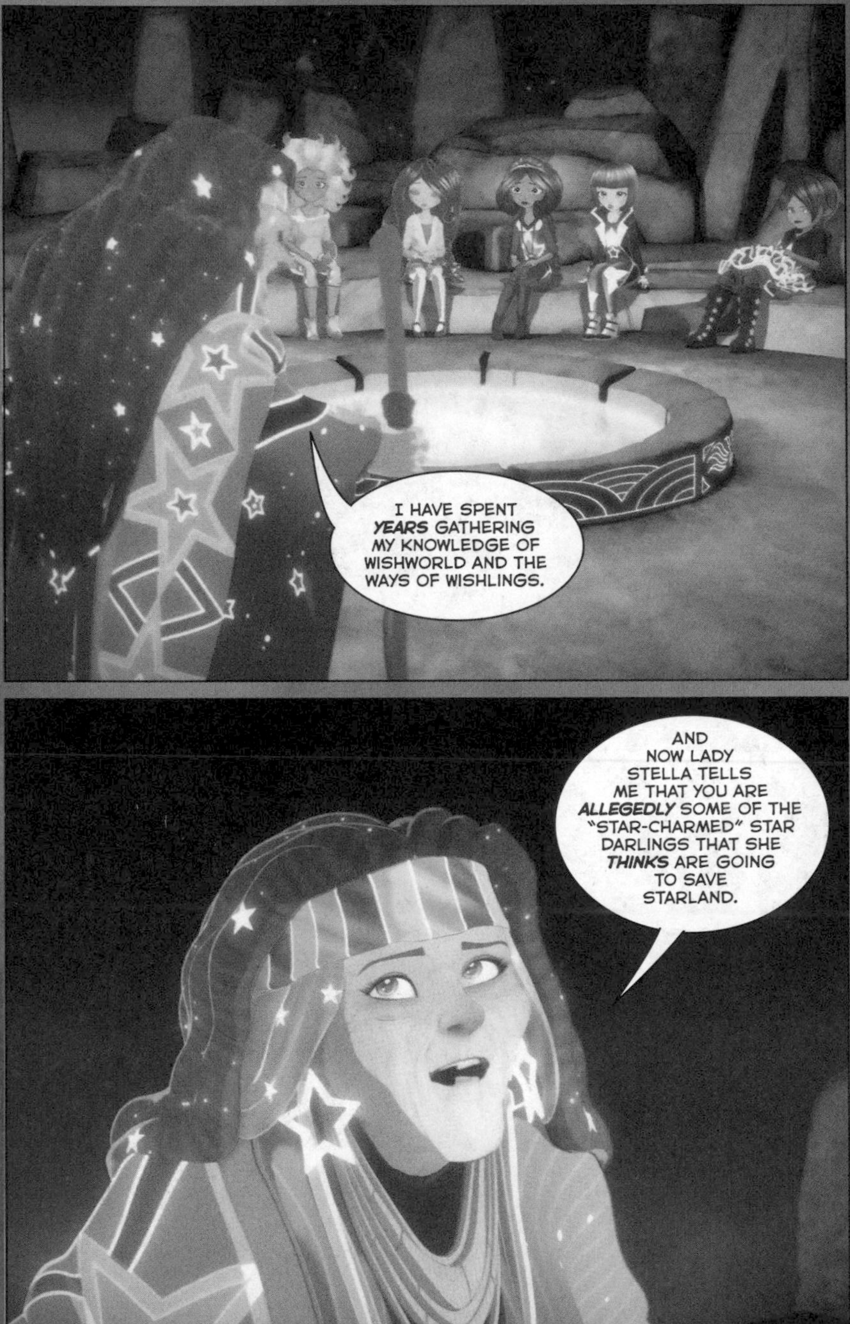
I HAVE SPENT YEARS GATHERING MY KNOWLEDGE OF WISHWORLD AND THE WAYS OF WISHLINGS.
AND NOW LADY STELLA TELLS ME THAT YOU ARE ALLEGEDLY SOME OF THE "STAR-CHARMED" STAR DARLINGS THAT SHE THINKS ARE GOING TO SAVE STARLAND.

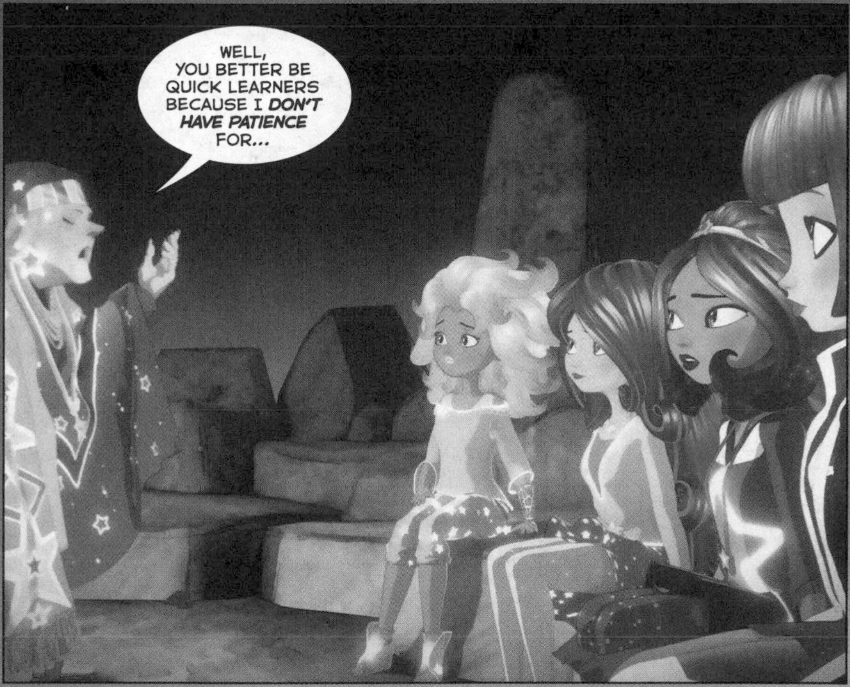
WELL, YOU BETTER BE QUICK LEARNERS BECAUSE I *DON'T HAVE PATIENCE* FOR...

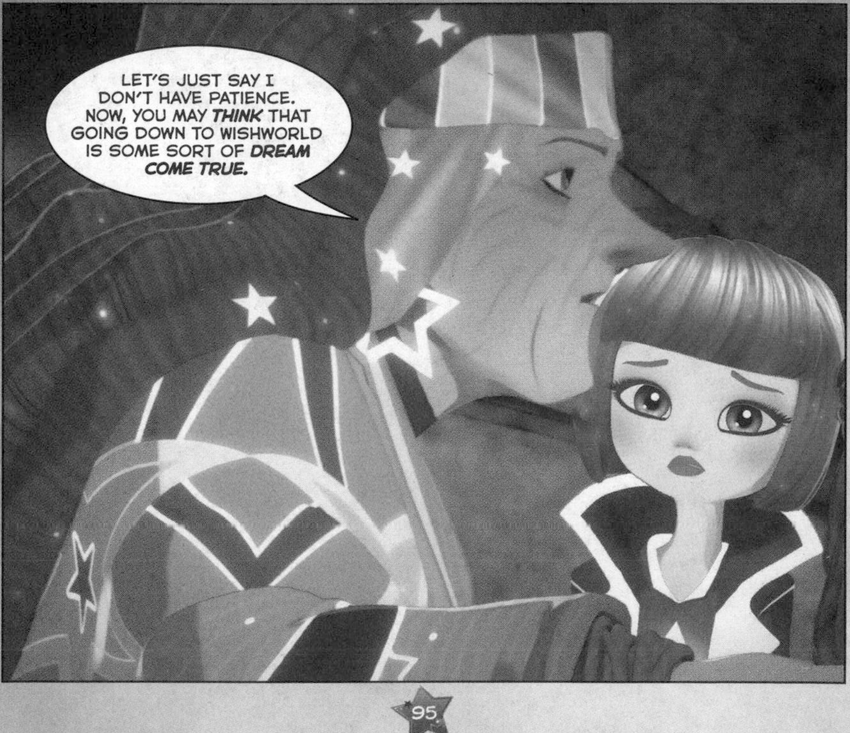
LET'S JUST SAY I DON'T HAVE PATIENCE. NOW, YOU MAY *THINK* THAT GOING DOWN TO WISHWORLD IS SOME SORT OF *DREAM COME TRUE.*

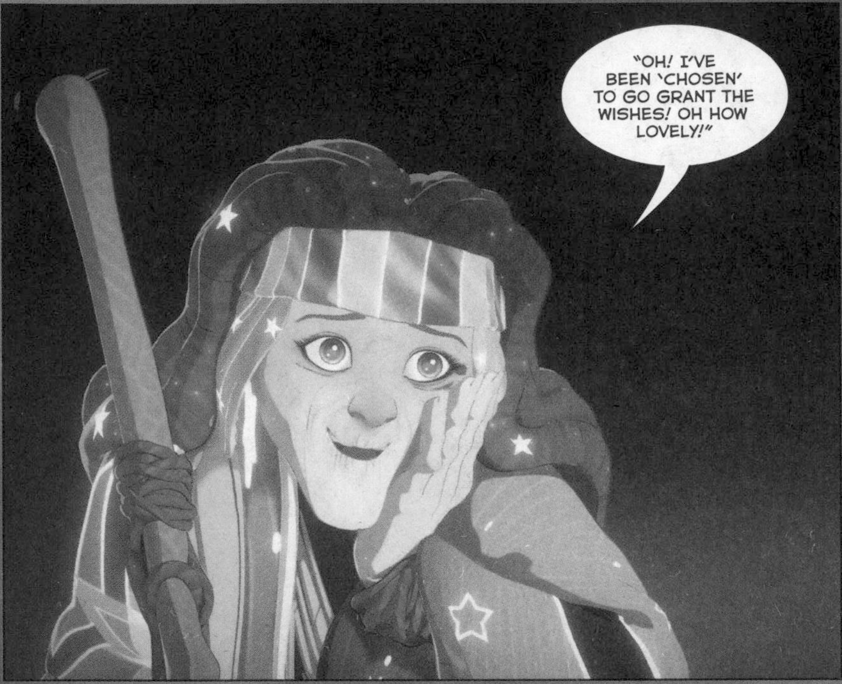
"OH! I'VE BEEN 'CHOSEN' TO GO GRANT THE WISHES! OH HOW LOVELY!"
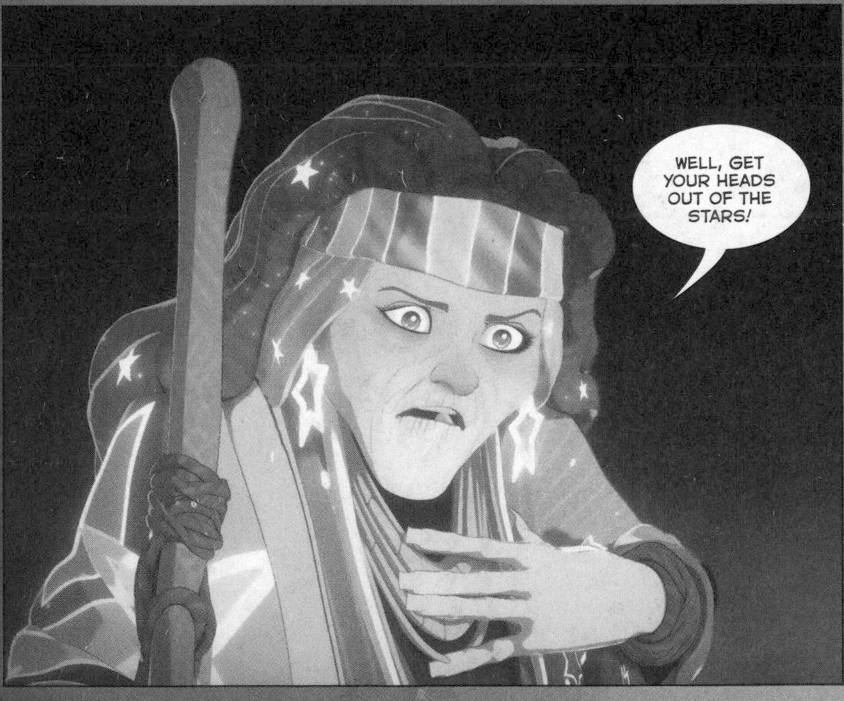
WELL, GET YOUR HEADS OUT OF THE STARS!

WISHERS ARE
WEIRDOS!

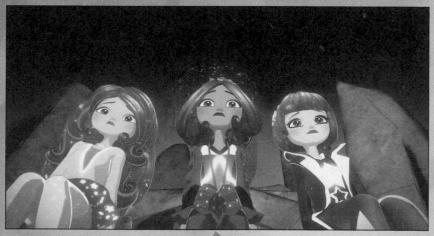

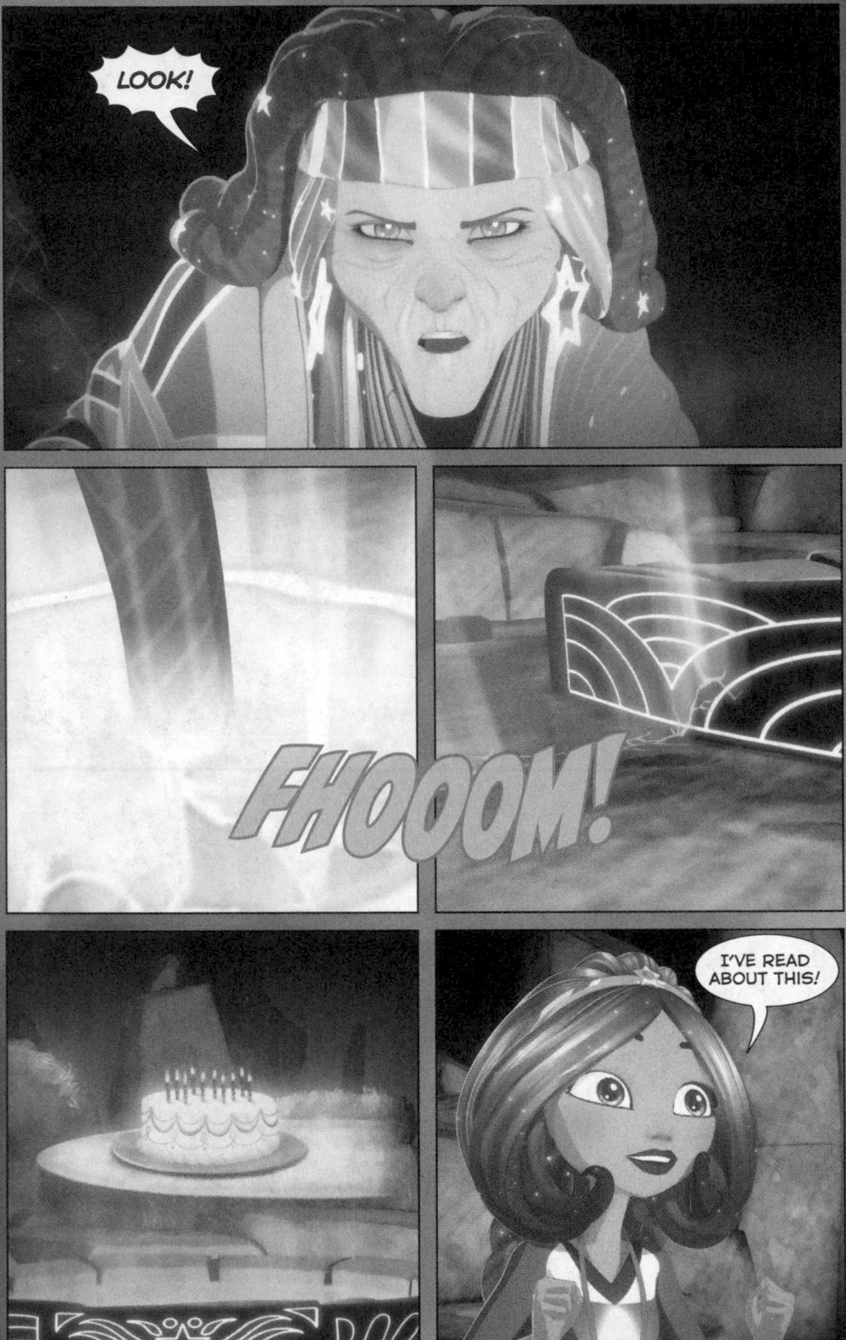
LOOK!
FHOOOM!
I'VE READ ABOUT THIS!

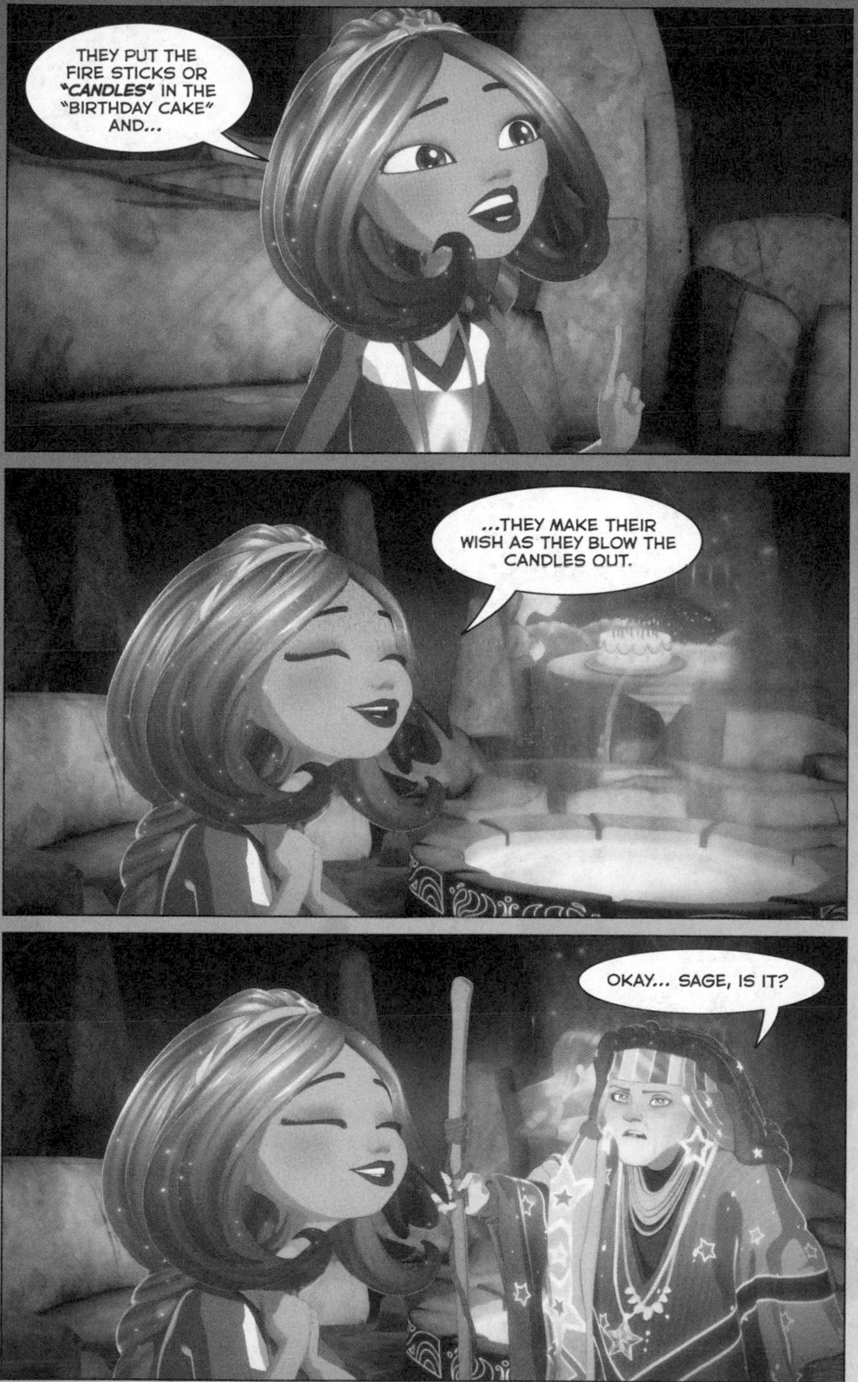
THEY PUT THE FIRE STICKS OR "CANDLES" IN THE "BIRTHDAY CAKE" AND...
...THEY MAKE THEIR WISH AS THEY BLOW THE CANDLES OUT.
OKAY... SAGE, IS IT?

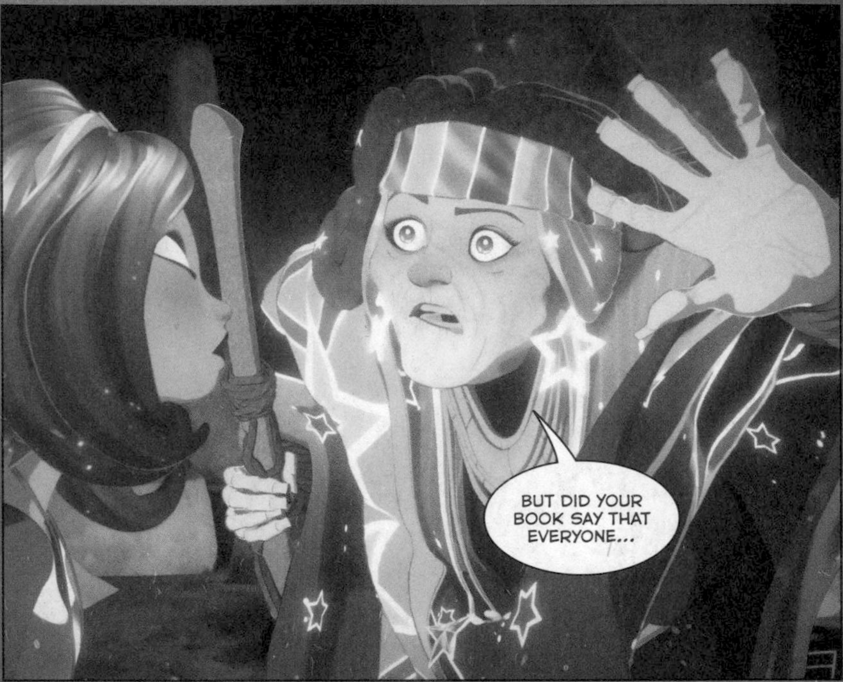
BUT DID YOUR BOOK SAY THAT EVERYONE...

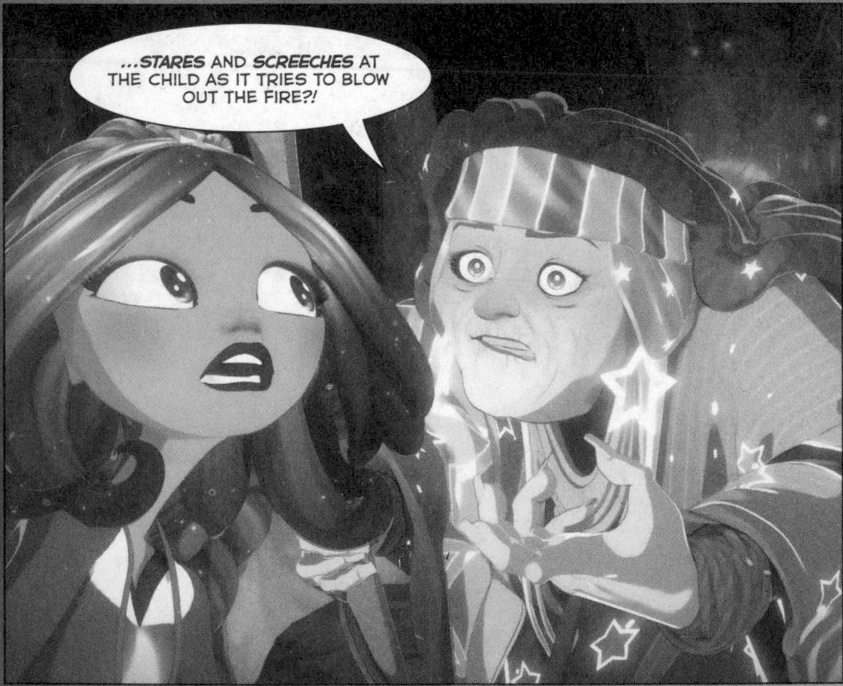
...STARES AND SCREECHES AT THE CHILD AS IT TRIES TO BLOW OUT THE FIRE?!

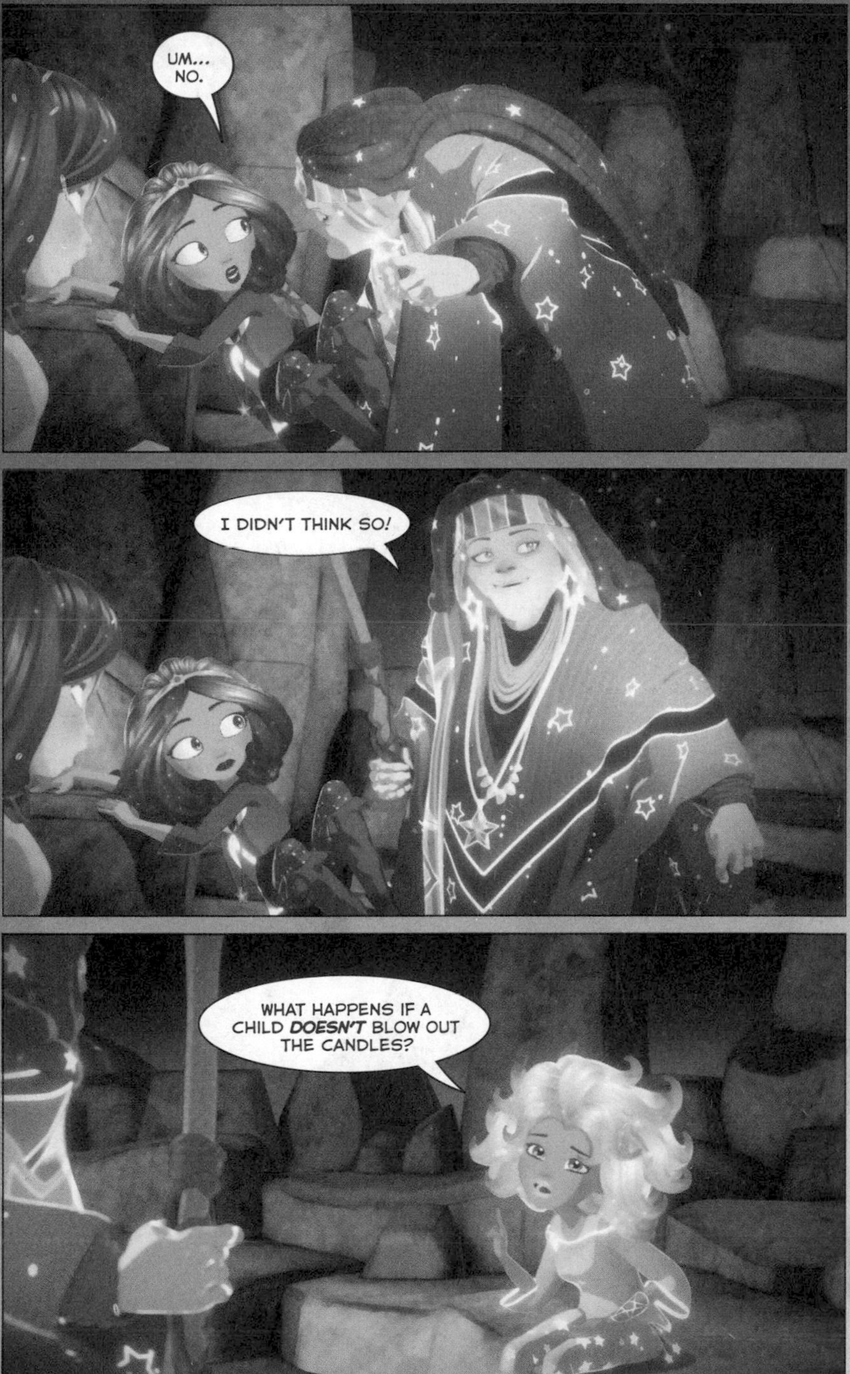
UM... NO.
I DIDN'T THINK SO!
WHAT HAPPENS IF A CHILD DOESN'T BLOW OUT THE CANDLES?

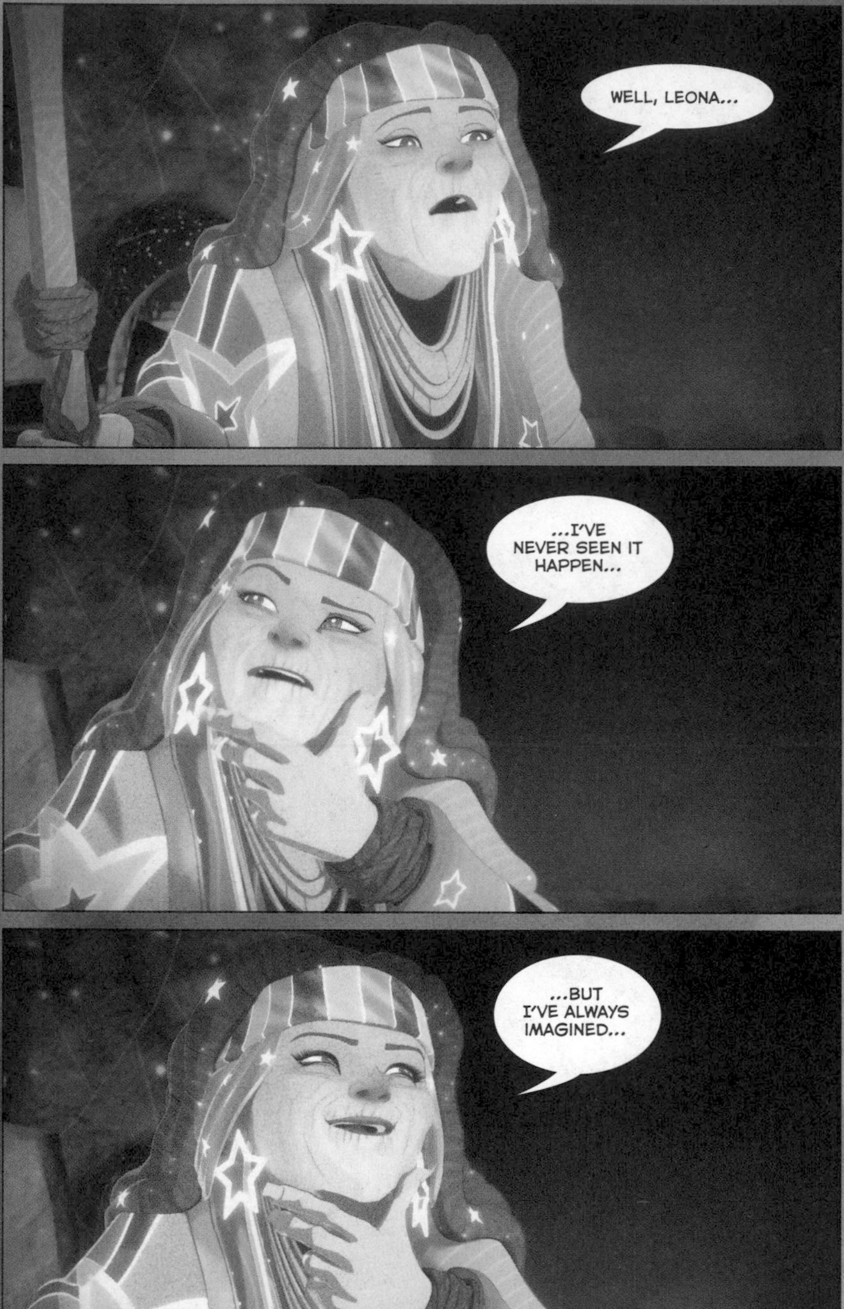
WELL, LEONA...
...I'VE NEVER SEEN IT HAPPEN...
...BUT I'VE ALWAYS IMAGINED...

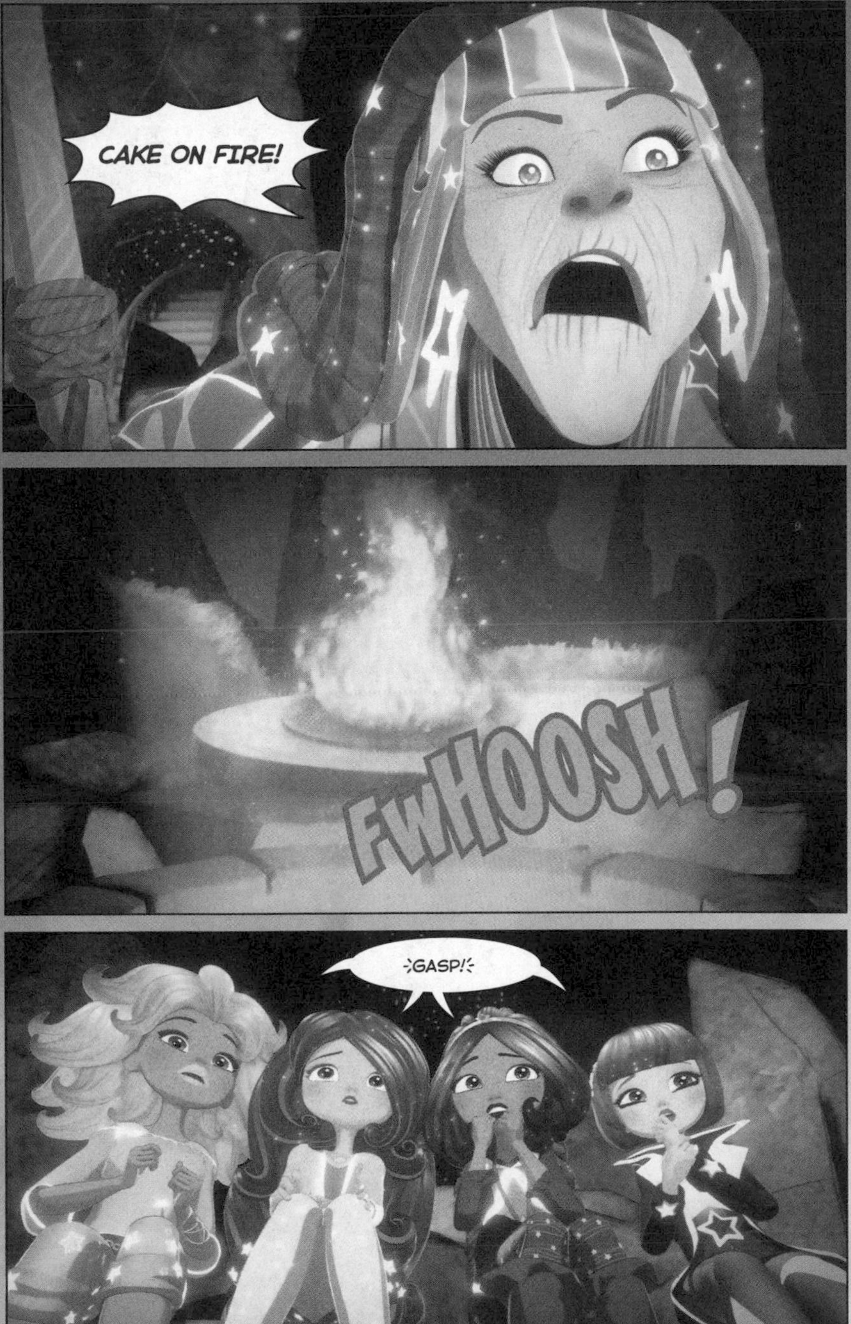
CAKE ON FIRE!
FWHOOSH!
-GASP!-

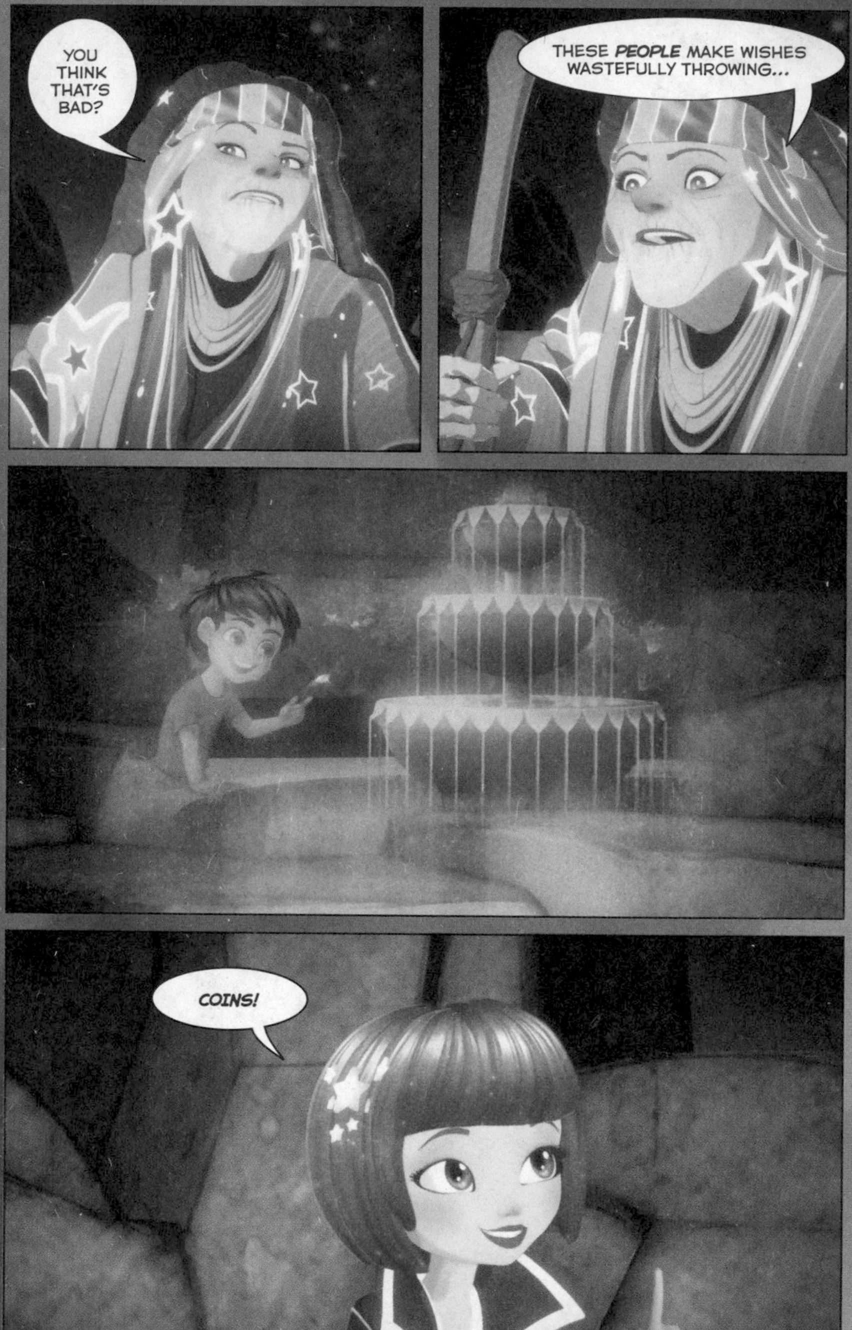
YOU THINK THAT'S BAD?
THESE *PEOPLE* MAKE WISHES WASTEFULLY THROWING...
COINS!

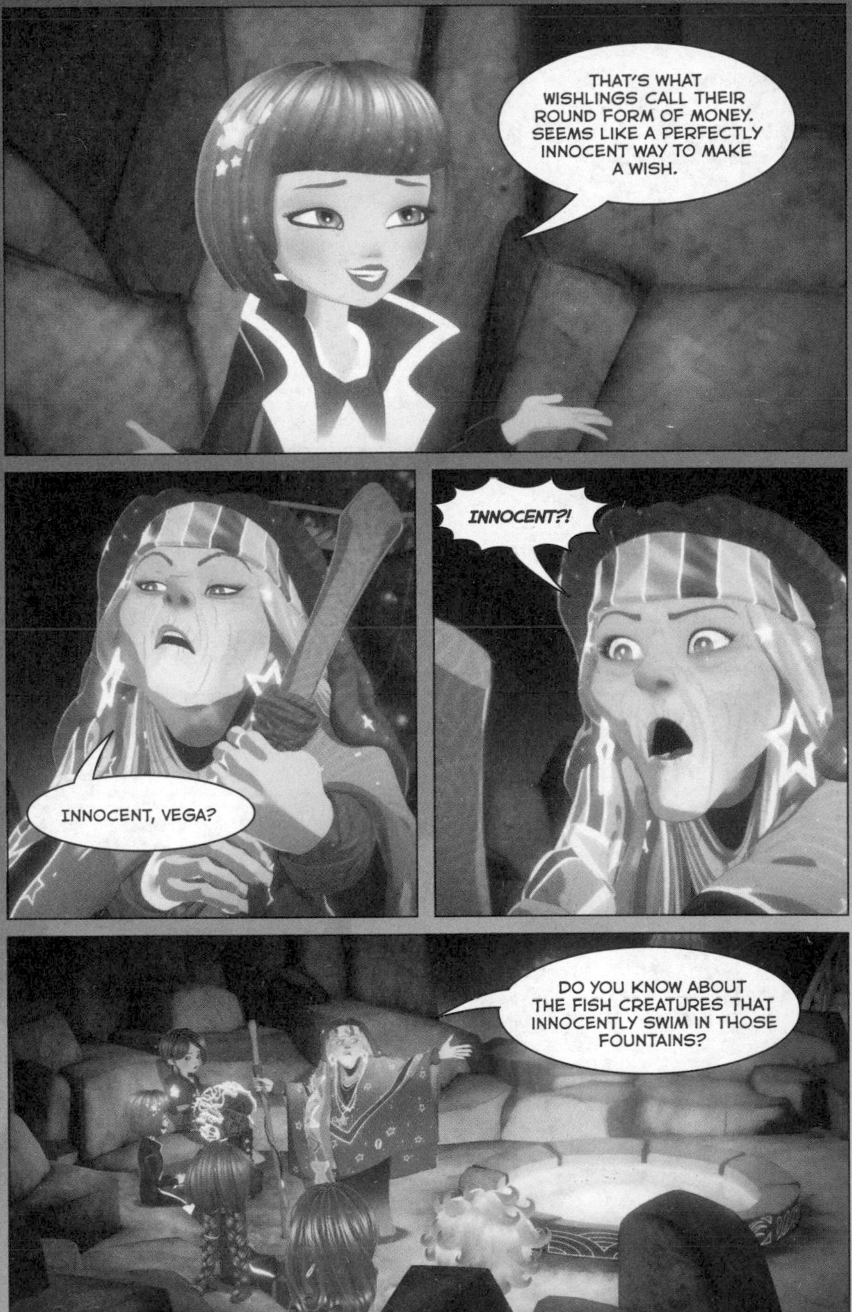
THAT'S WHAT WISHLINGS CALL THEIR ROUND FORM OF MONEY. SEEMS LIKE A PERFECTLY INNOCENT WAY TO MAKE A WISH.
INNOCENT, VEGA?
INNOCENT?!
DO YOU KNOW ABOUT THE FISH CREATURES THAT INNOCENTLY SWIM IN THOSE FOUNTAINS?

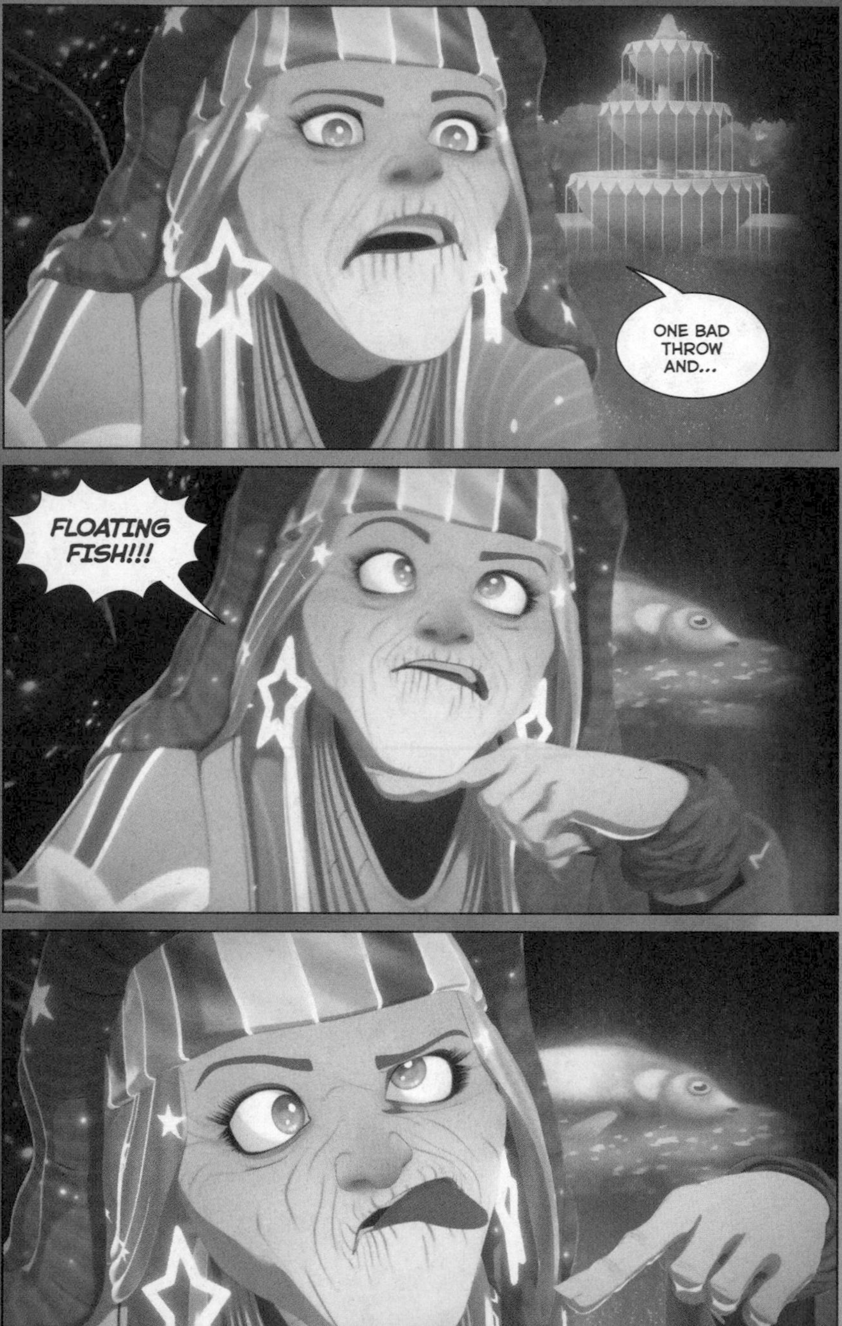
ONE BAD THROW AND...
FLOATING FISH!!!

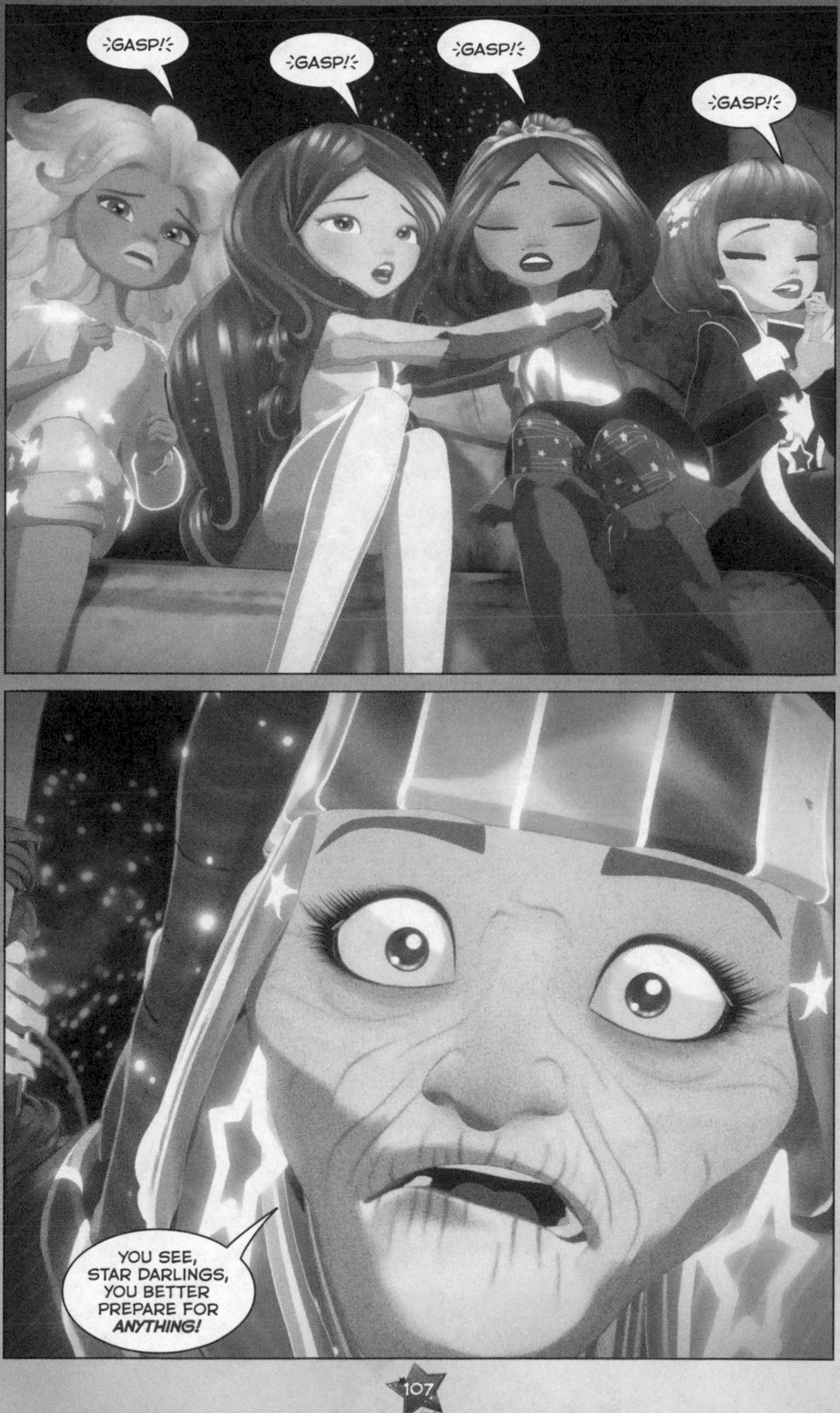
GASP!
GASP!
GASP!
GASP!
YOU SEE, STAR DARLINGS, YOU BETTER PREPARE FOR *ANYTHING!*

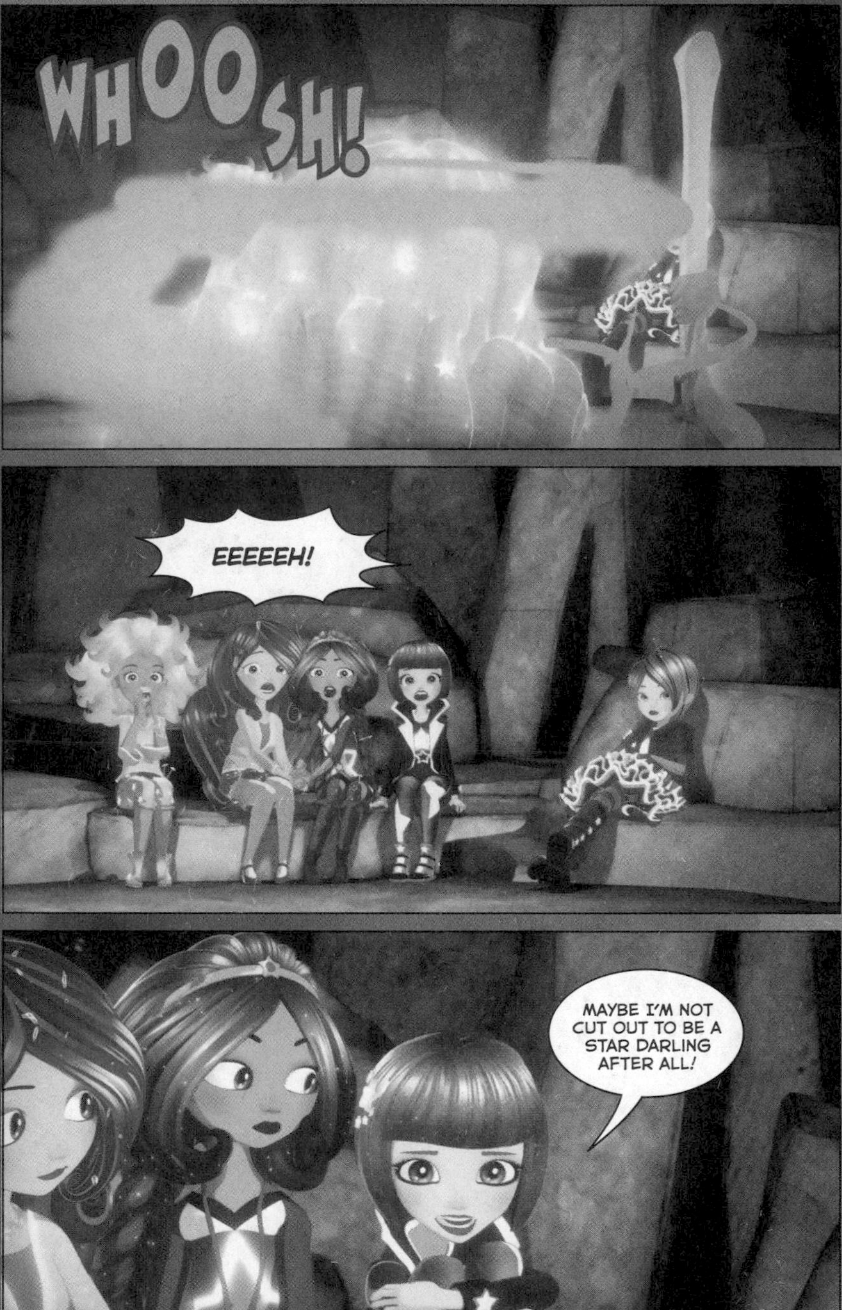
WHOOSH!
EEEEEH!
MAYBE I'M NOT CUT OUT TO BE A STAR DARLING AFTER ALL!

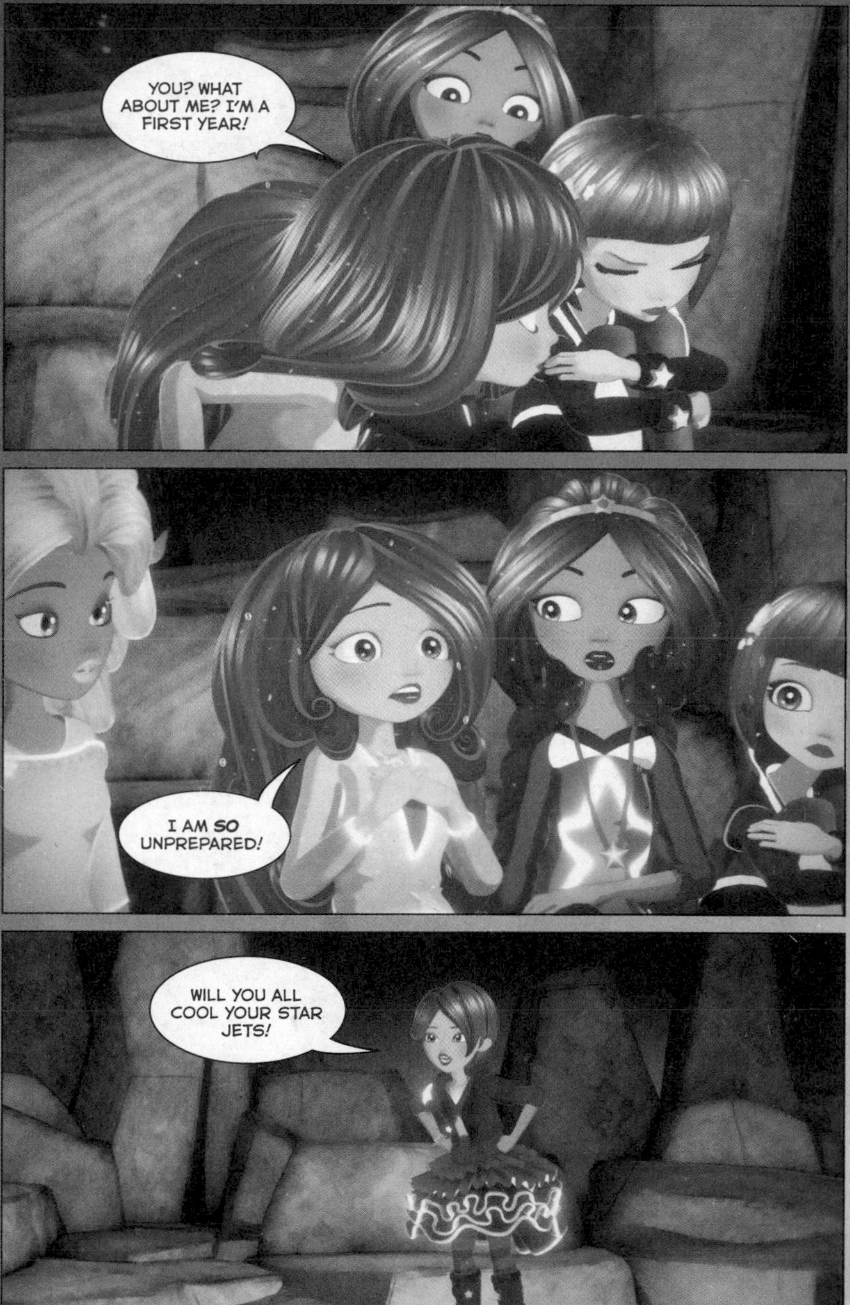
YOU? WHAT ABOUT ME? I'M A FIRST YEAR!
I AM **SO** UNPREPARED!
WILL YOU ALL COOL YOUR STAR JETS!

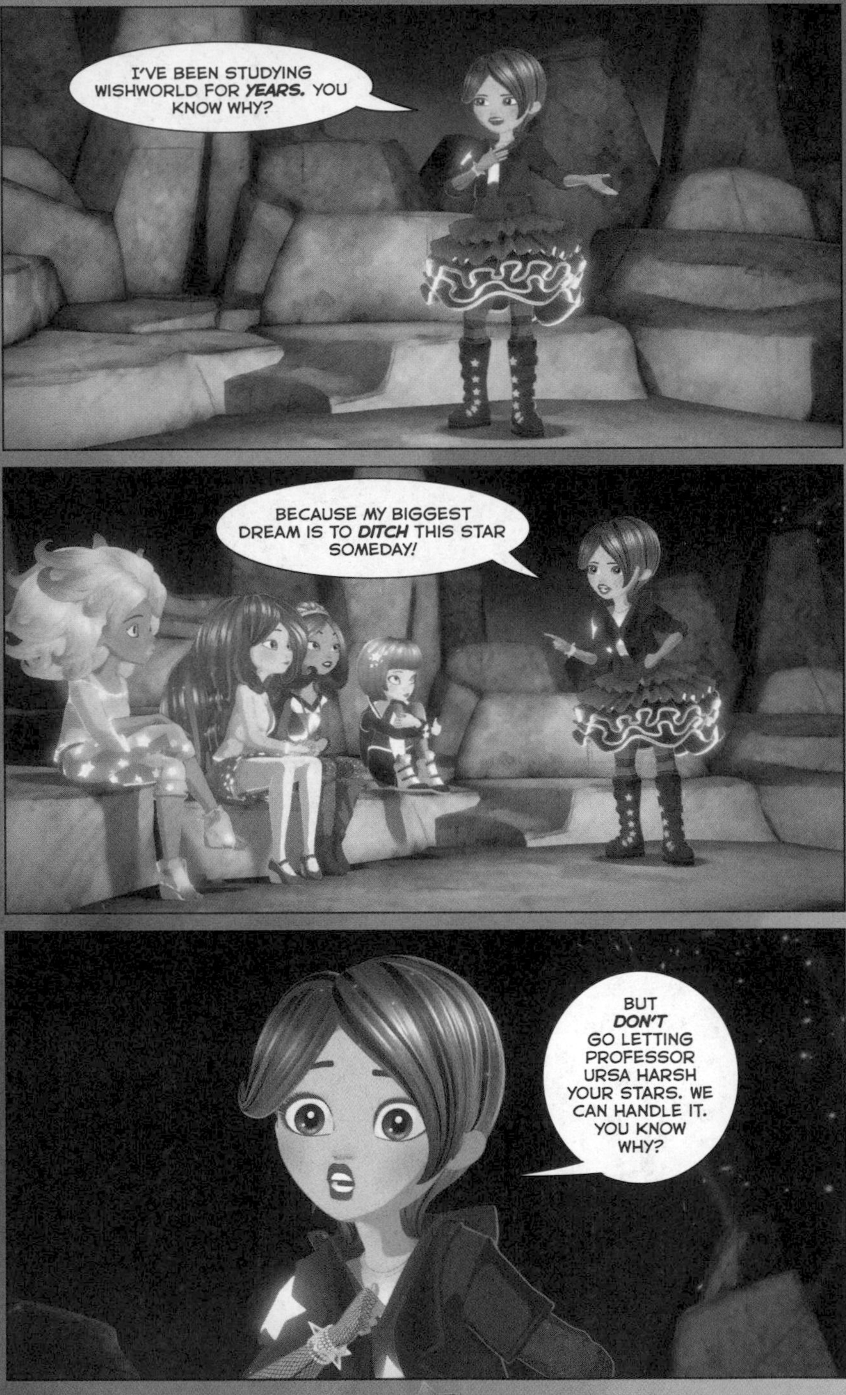
I'VE BEEN STUDYING WISHWORLD FOR ***YEARS.*** YOU KNOW WHY?
BECAUSE MY BIGGEST DREAM IS TO ***DITCH*** THIS STAR SOMEDAY!
BUT ***DON'T*** GO LETTING PROFESSOR URSA HARSH YOUR STARS. WE CAN HANDLE IT. YOU KNOW WHY?

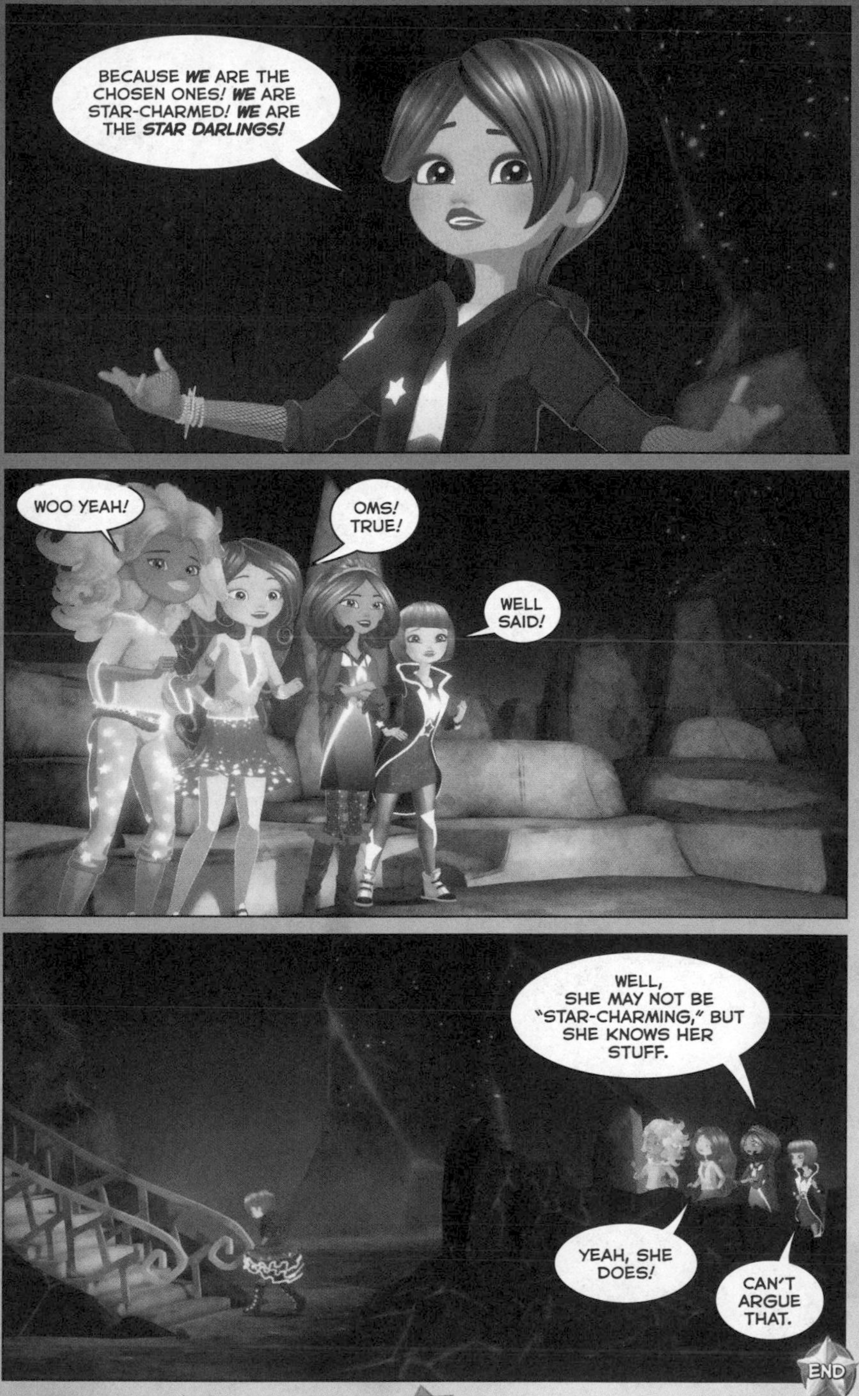
BECAUSE WE ARE THE CHOSEN ONES! WE ARE STAR-CHARMED! WE ARE THE STAR DARLINGS!
WOO YEAH!
OMS! TRUE!
WELL SAID!
WELL, SHE MAY NOT BE "STAR-CHARMING," BUT SHE KNOWS HER STUFF.
YEAH, SHE DOES!
CAN'T ARGUE THAT.
END

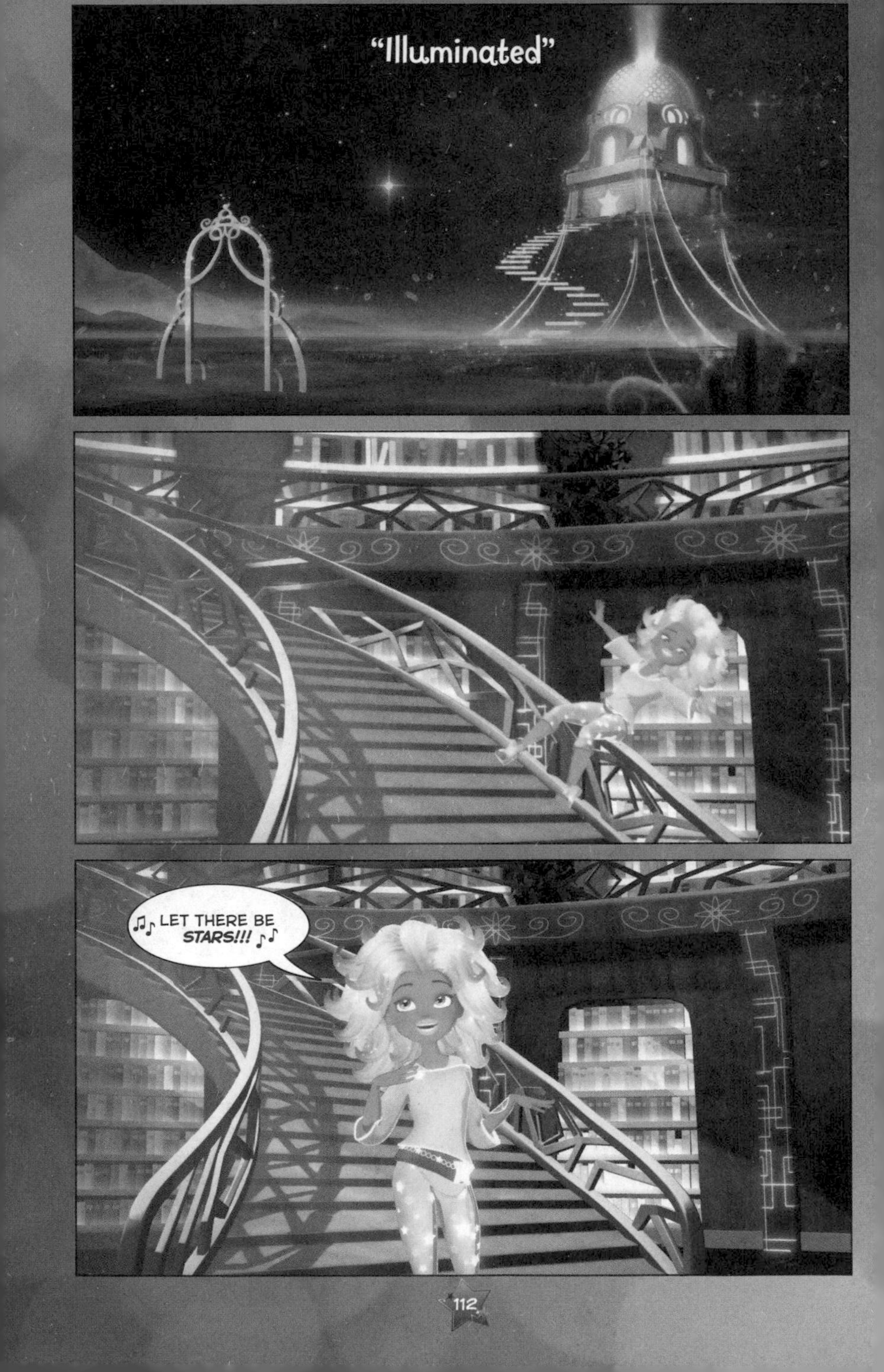
"Illuminated"
♫♪ LET THERE BE STARS!!! ♪♪

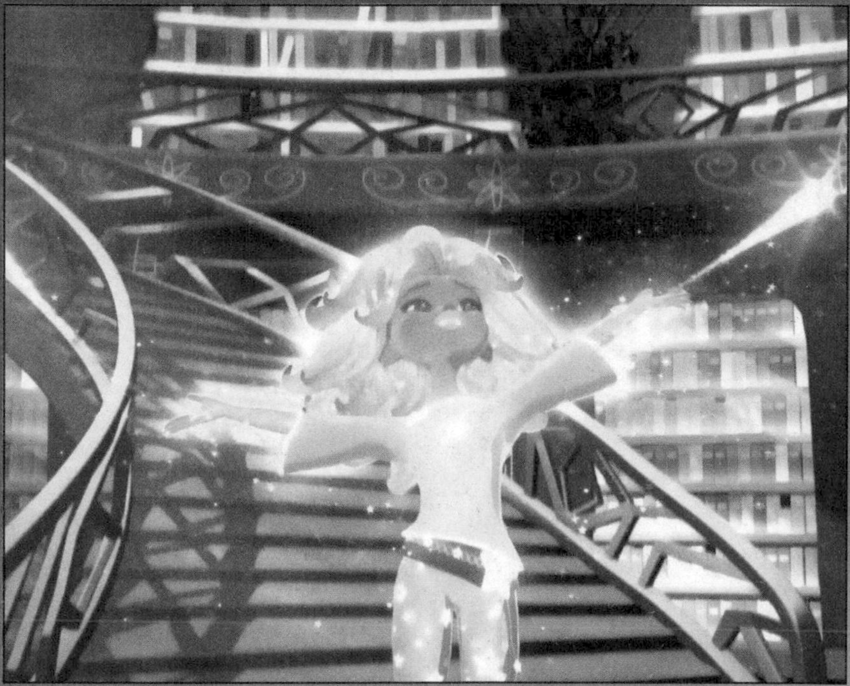

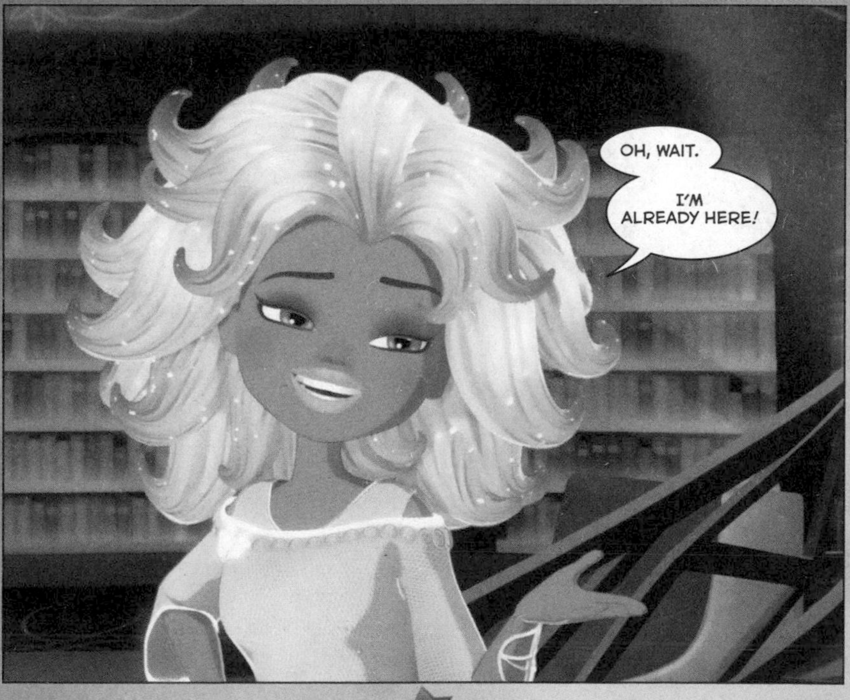
OH, WAIT.
I'M ALREADY HERE!

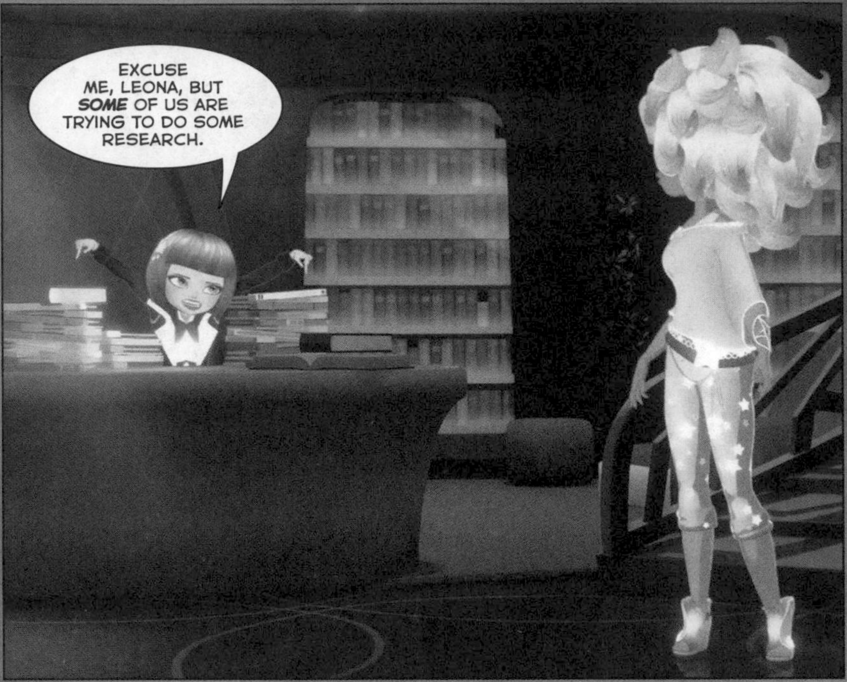
EXCUSE ME, LEONA, BUT SOME OF US ARE TRYING TO DO SOME RESEARCH.

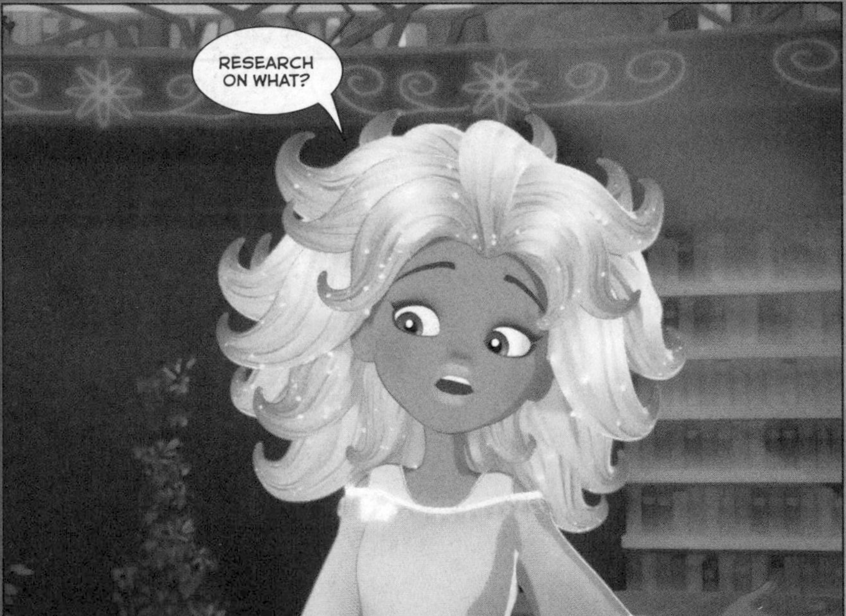
RESEARCH ON WHAT?

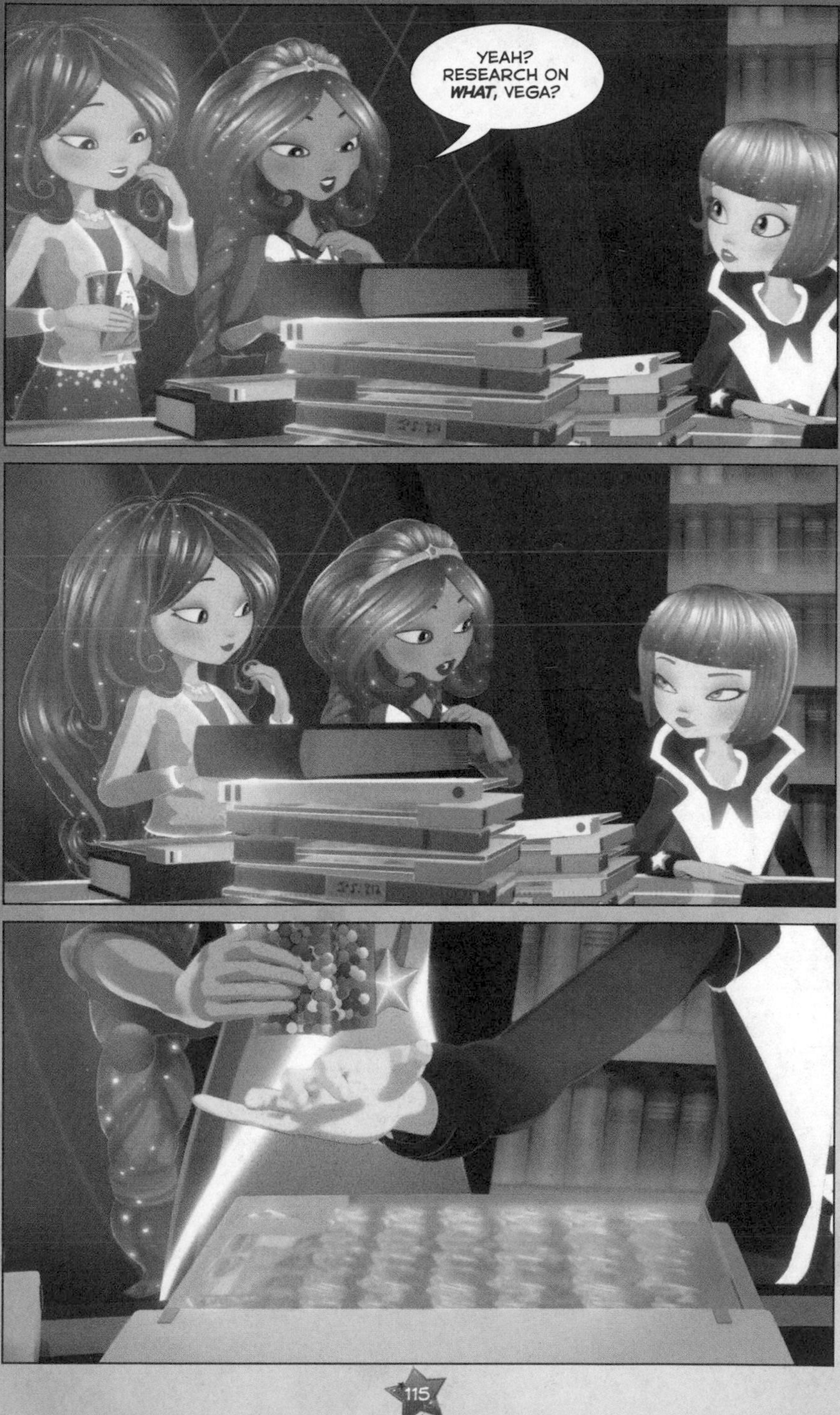
YEAH? RESEARCH ON *WHAT*, VEGA?

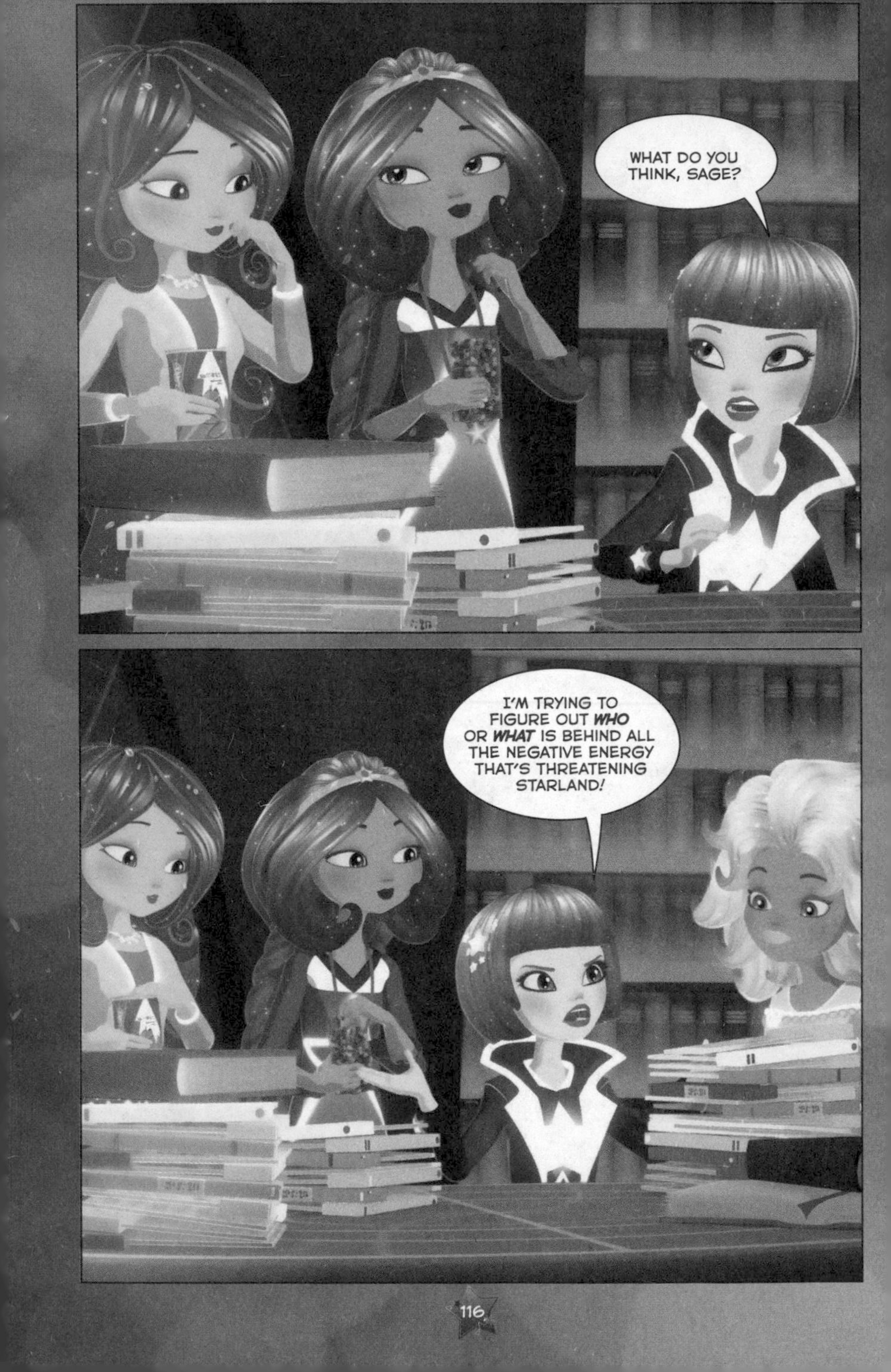
WHAT DO YOU THINK, SAGE?
I'M TRYING TO FIGURE OUT ***WHO*** OR ***WHAT*** IS BEHIND ALL THE NEGATIVE ENERGY THAT'S THREATENING STARLAND!

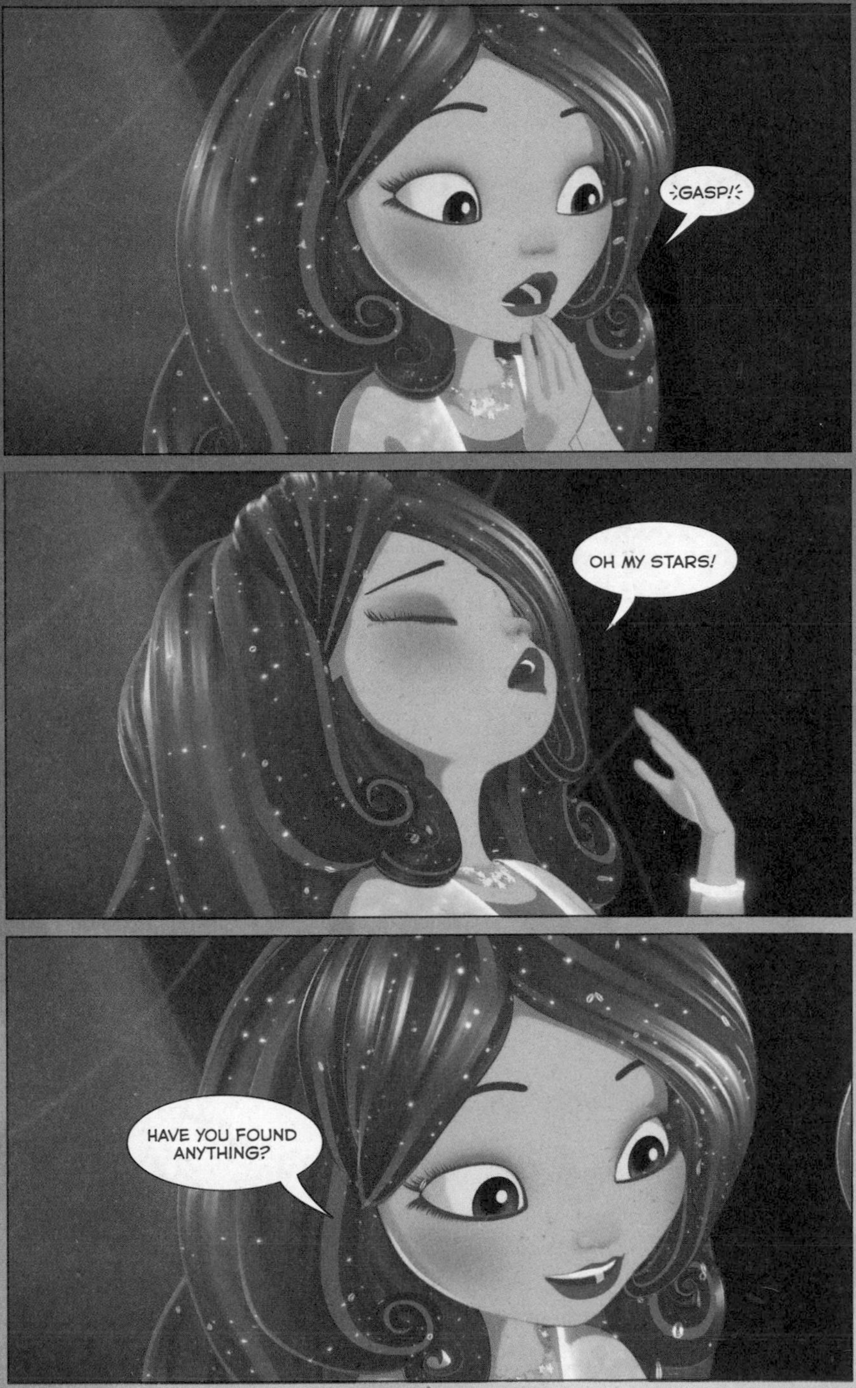
GASP!
OH MY STARS!
HAVE YOU FOUND ANYTHING?

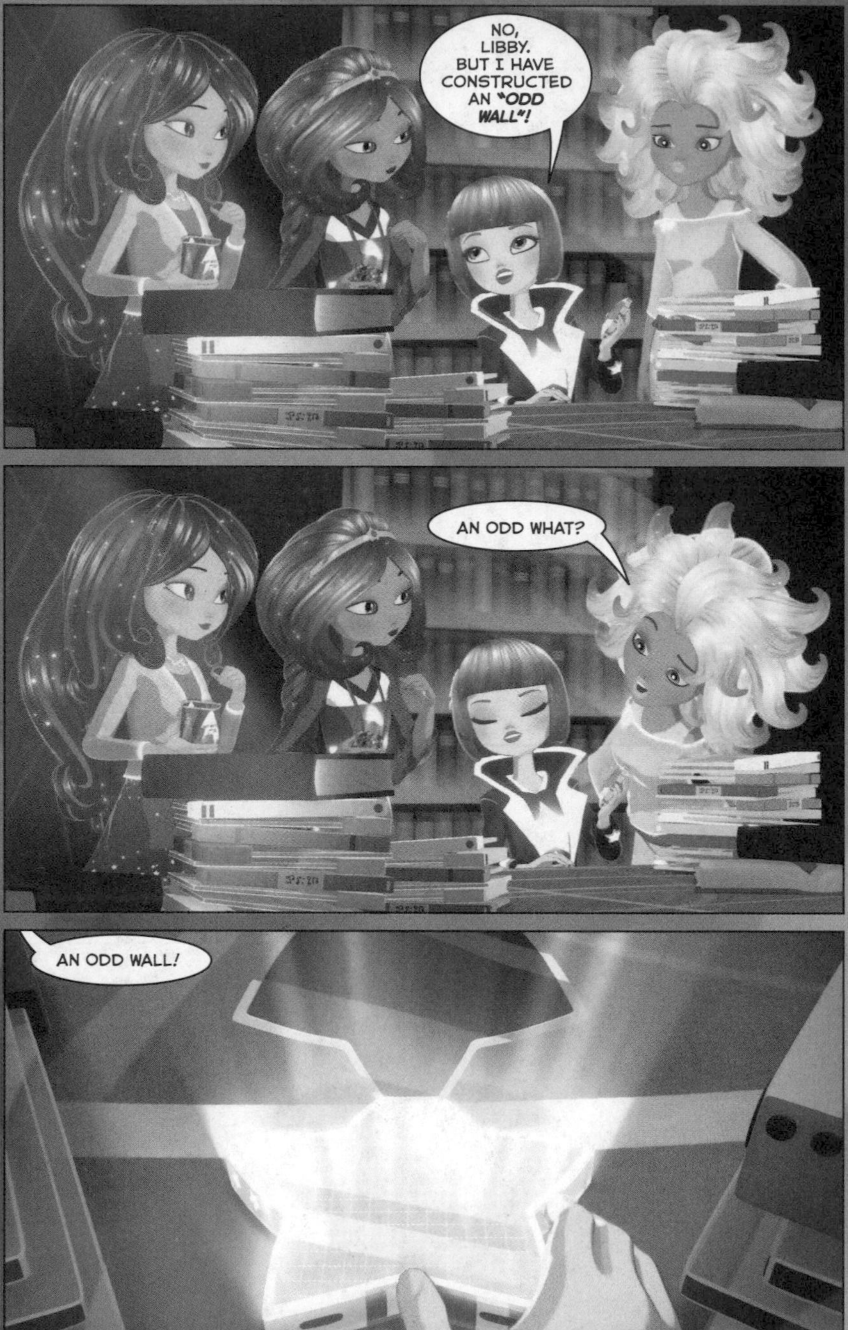
NO, LIBBY. BUT I HAVE CONSTRUCTED AN "ODD WALL"!
AN ODD WHAT?
AN ODD WALL!

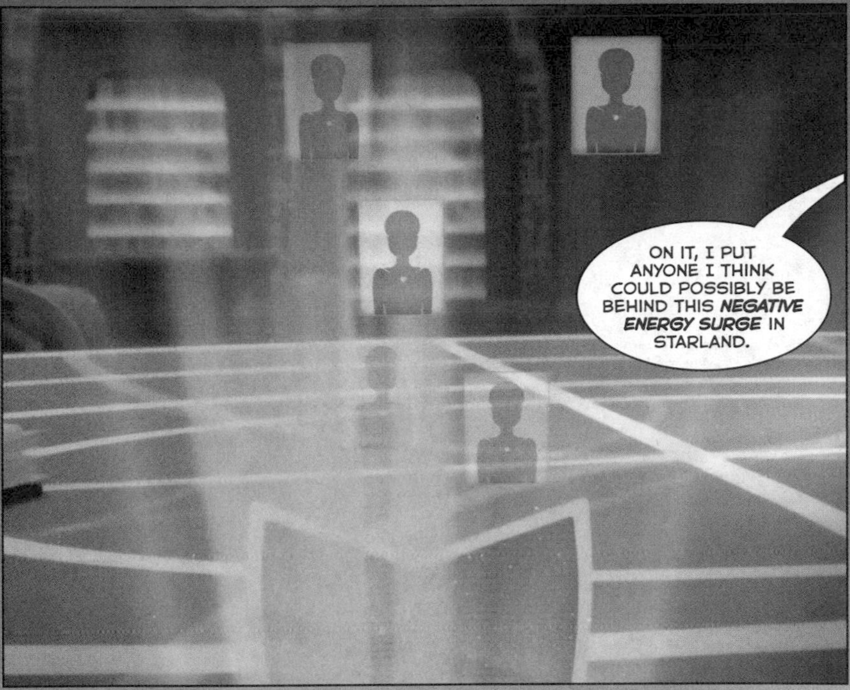
ON IT, I PUT ANYONE I THINK COULD POSSIBLY BE BEHIND THIS NEGATIVE ENERGY SURGE IN STARLAND.

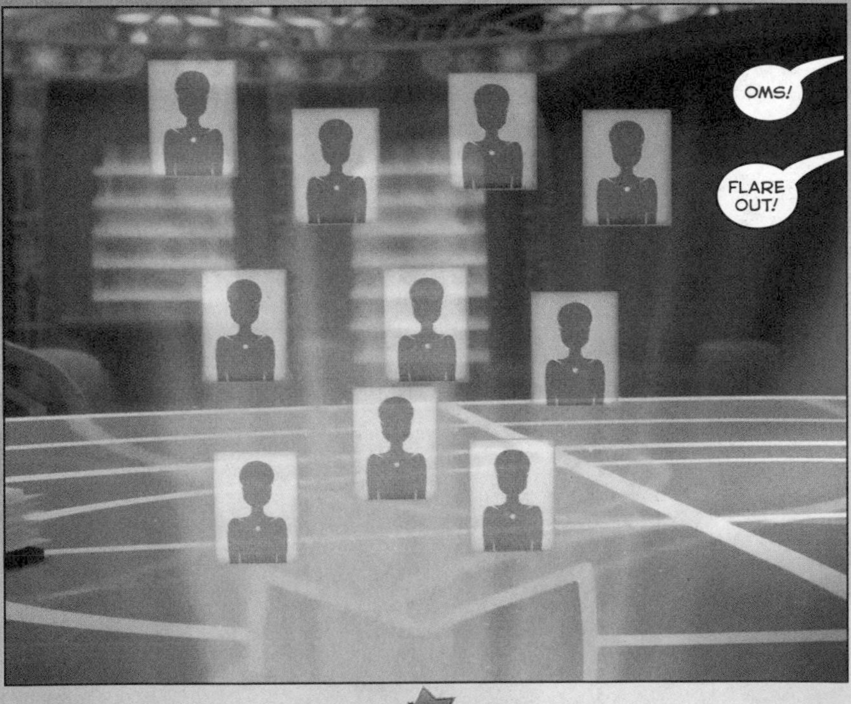
OMS!
FLARE OUT!

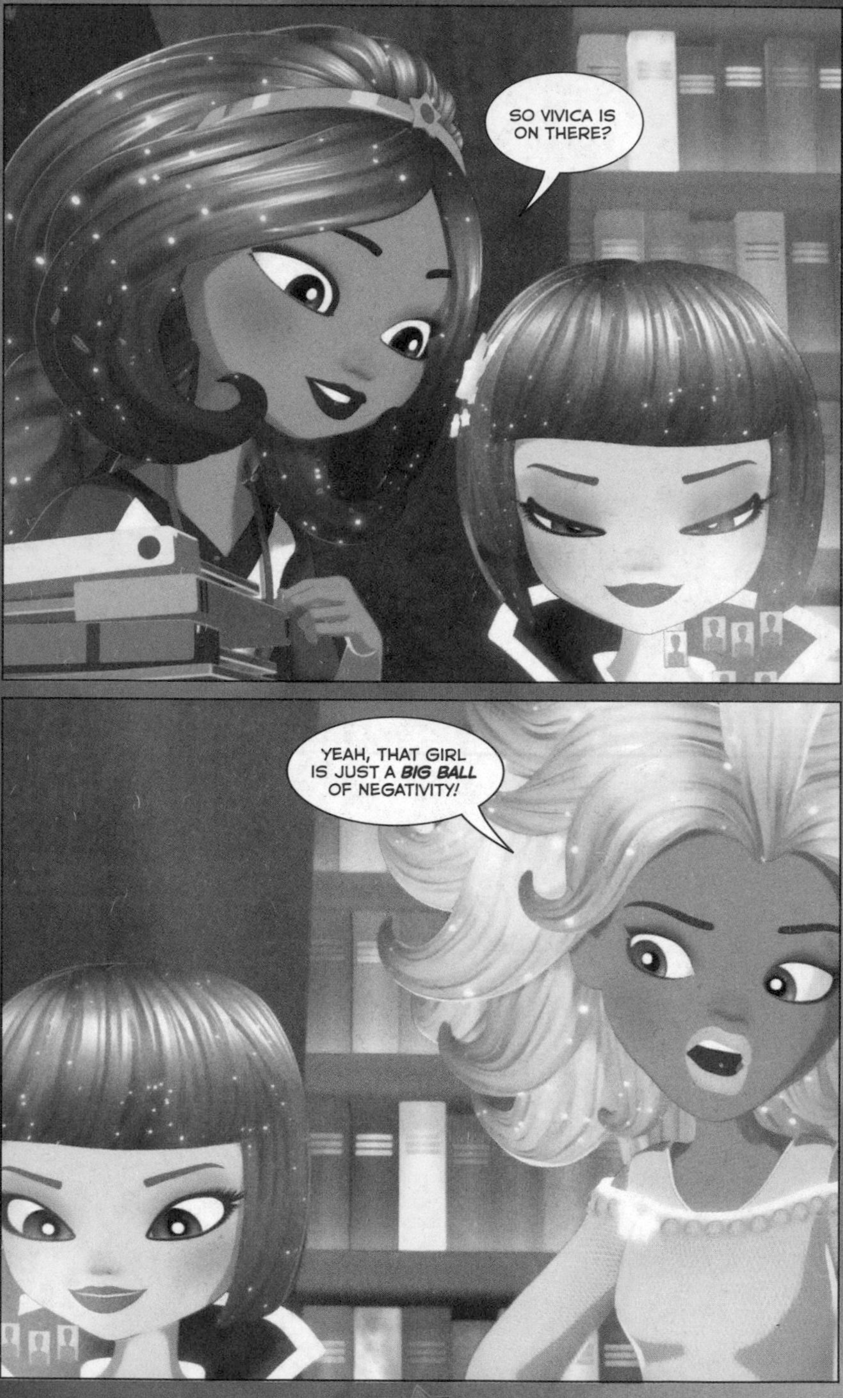
SO VIVICA IS ON THERE?
YEAH, THAT GIRL IS JUST A ***BIG BALL*** OF NEGATIVITY!

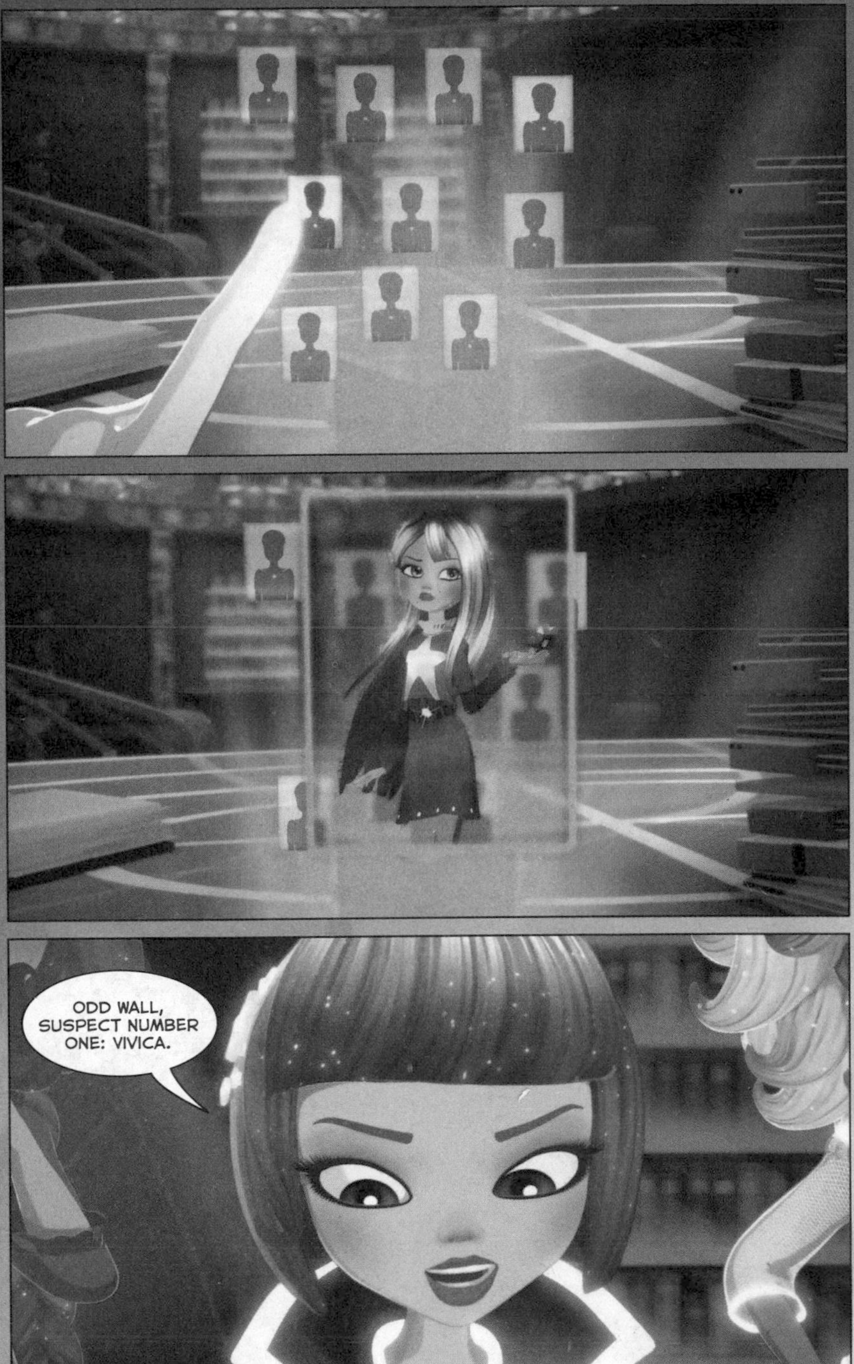
ODD WALL,
SUSPECT NUMBER
ONE: VIVICA.

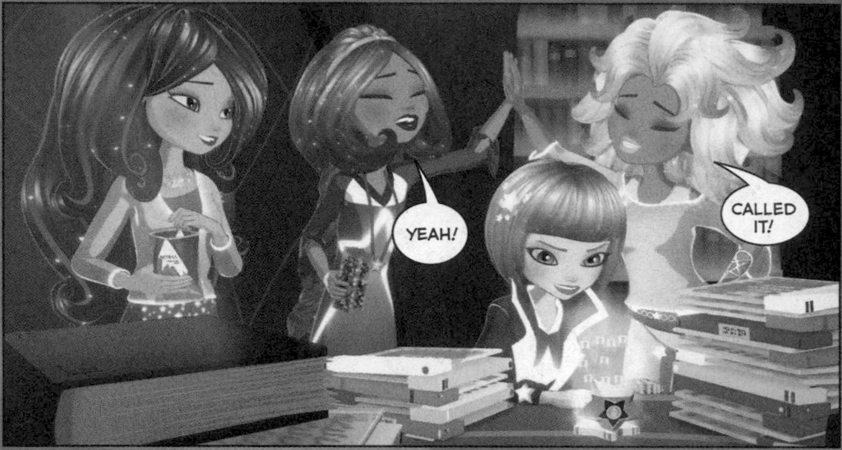
YEAH!
CALLED IT!

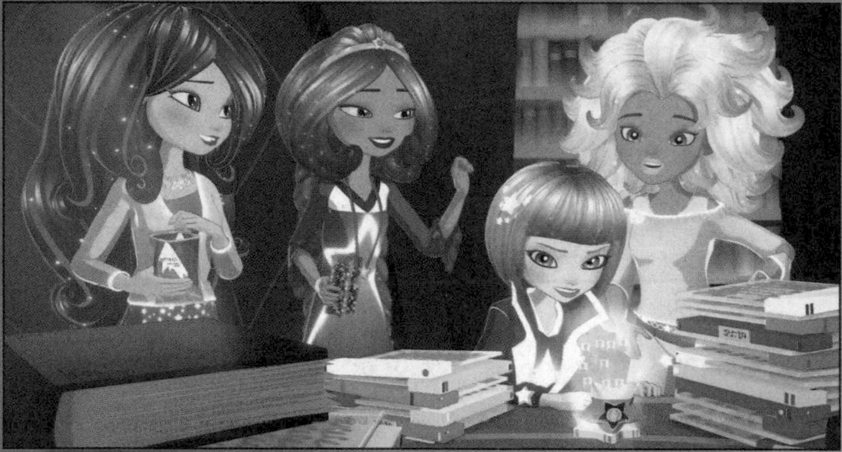

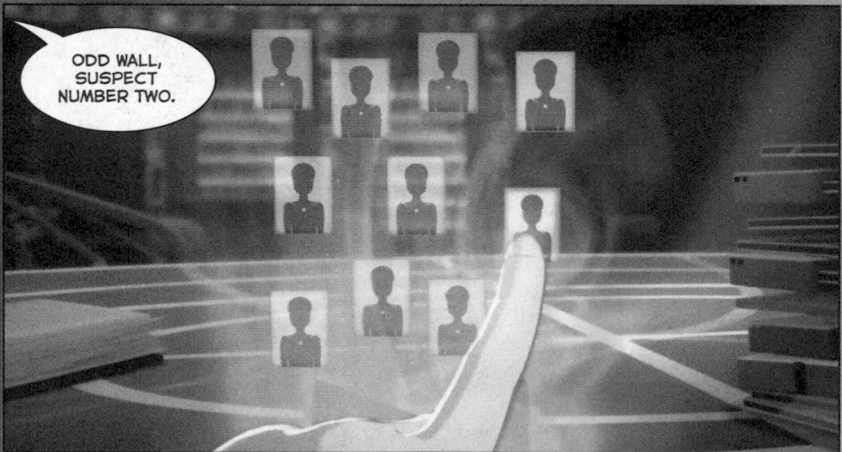
ODD WALL, SUSPECT NUMBER TWO.

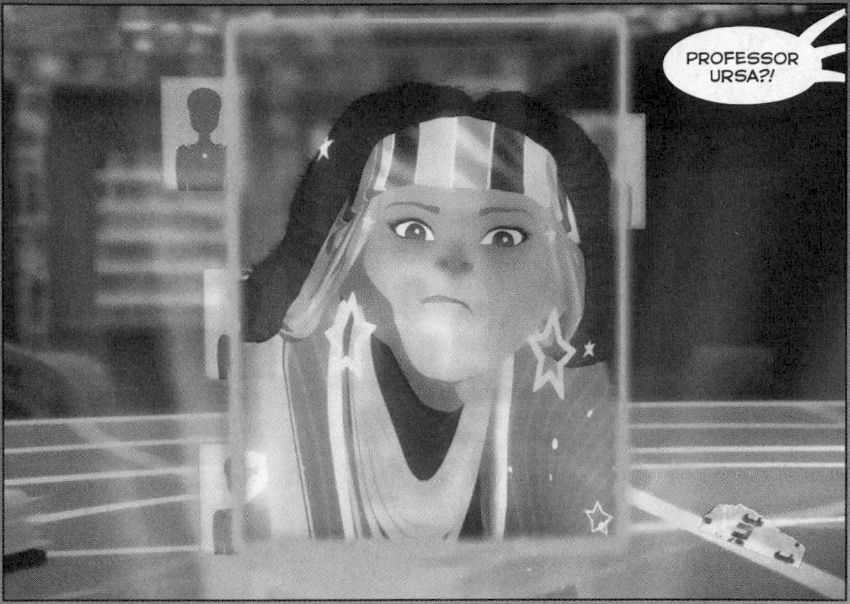
PROFESSOR URSA?!

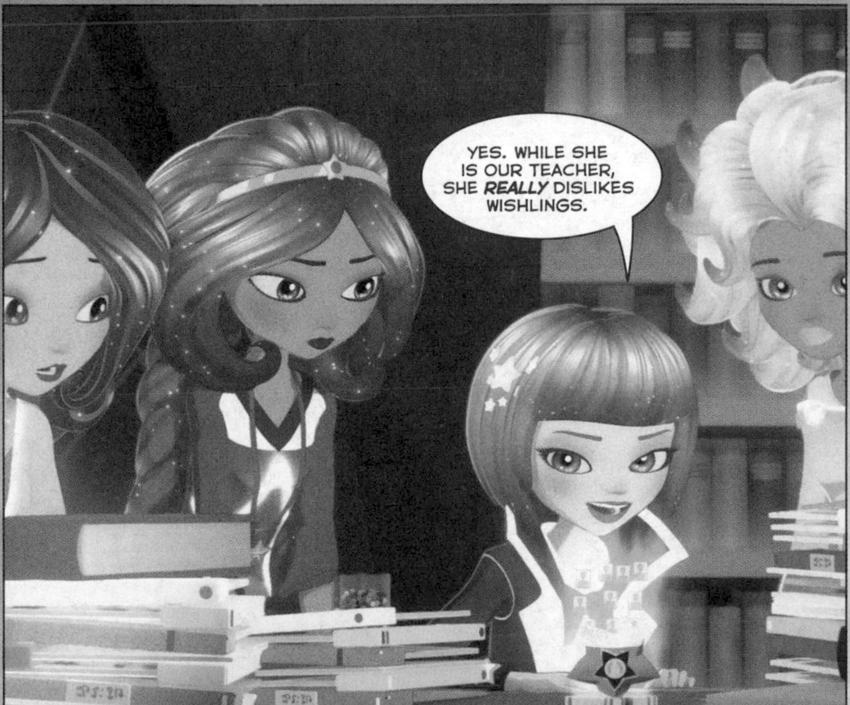
YES. WHILE SHE IS OUR TEACHER, SHE *REALLY* DISLIKES WISHLINGS.

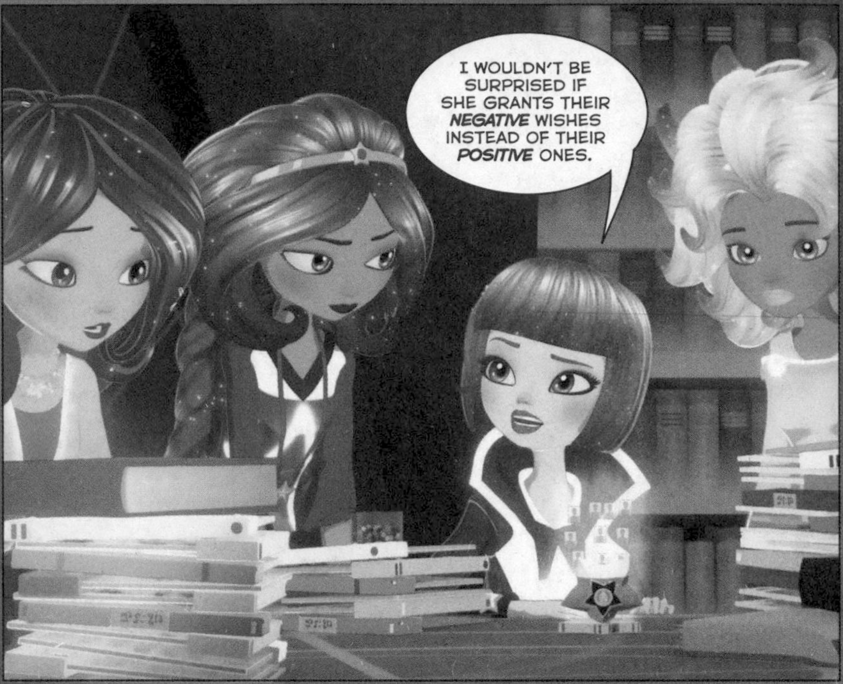
I WOULDN'T BE SURPRISED IF SHE GRANTS THEIR *NEGATIVE* WISHES INSTEAD OF THEIR *POSITIVE* ONES.

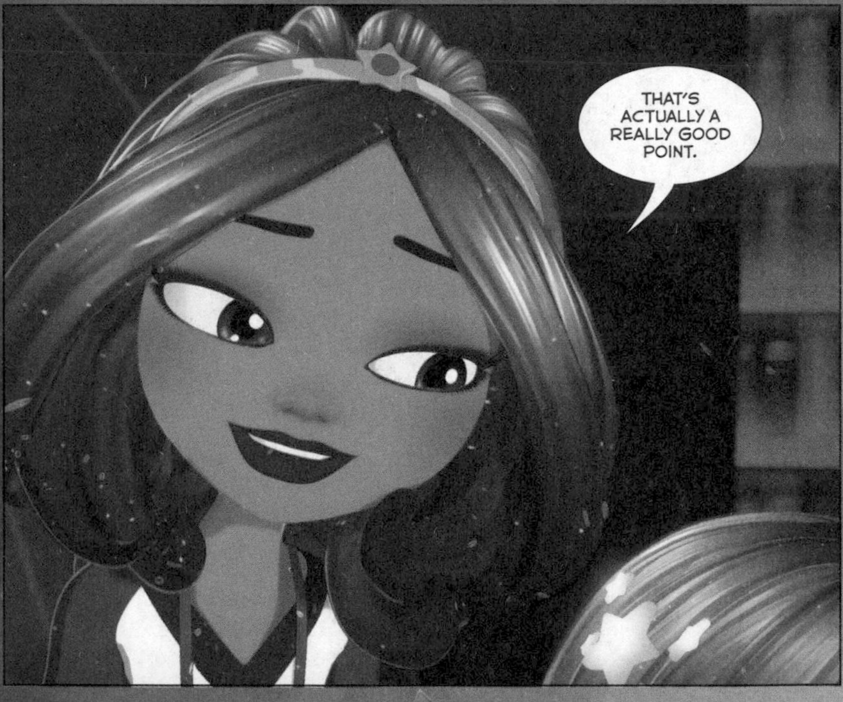
THAT'S ACTUALLY A REALLY GOOD POINT.

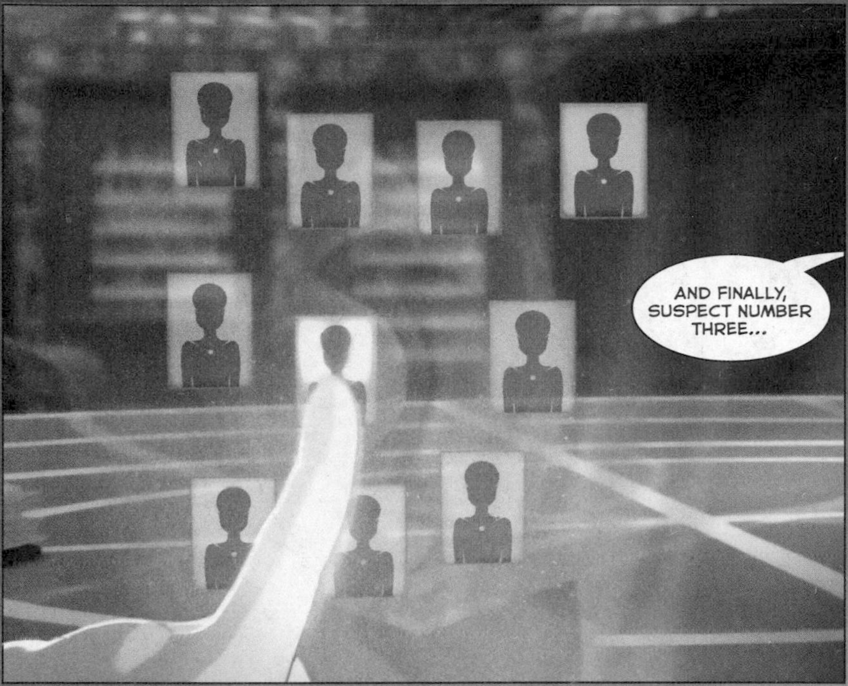
AND FINALLY, SUSPECT NUMBER THREE...

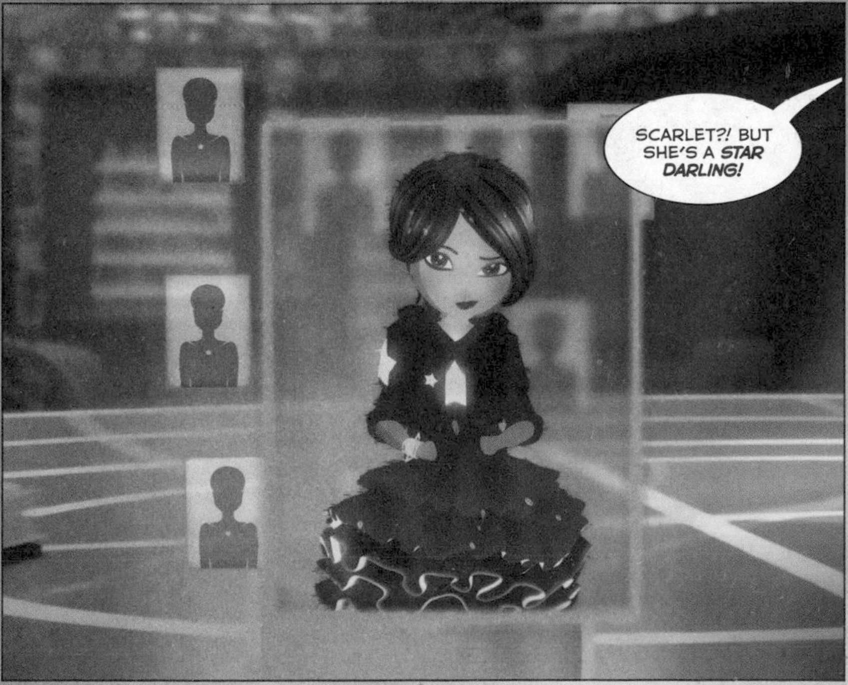
SCARLET?! BUT SHE'S A ***STAR DARLING!***

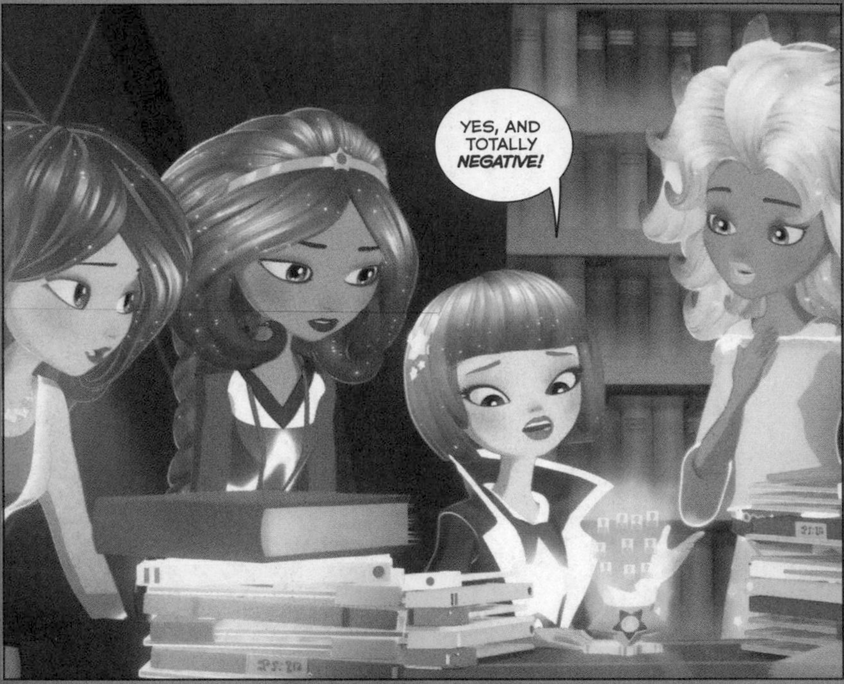
YES, AND TOTALLY *NEGATIVE!*

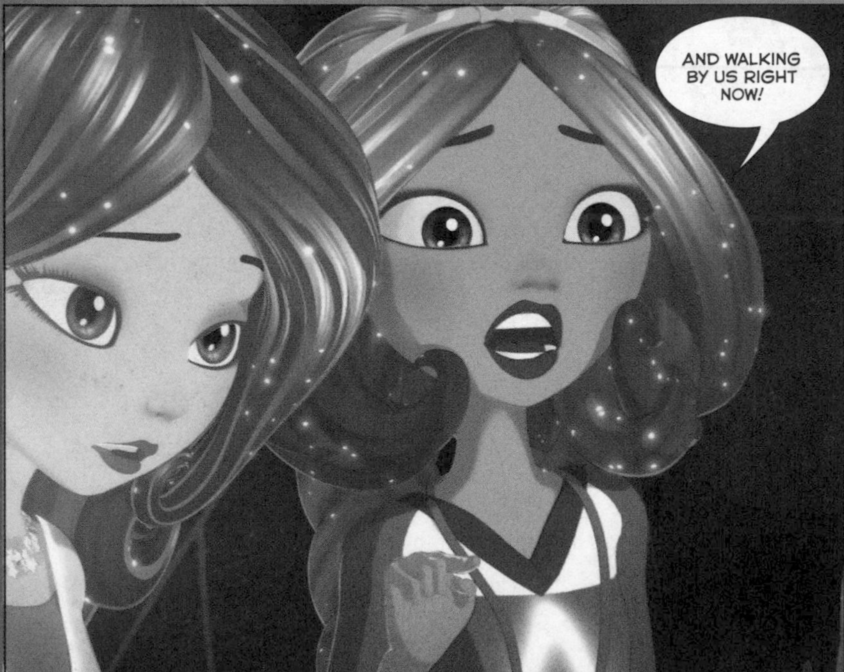
AND WALKING BY US RIGHT NOW!

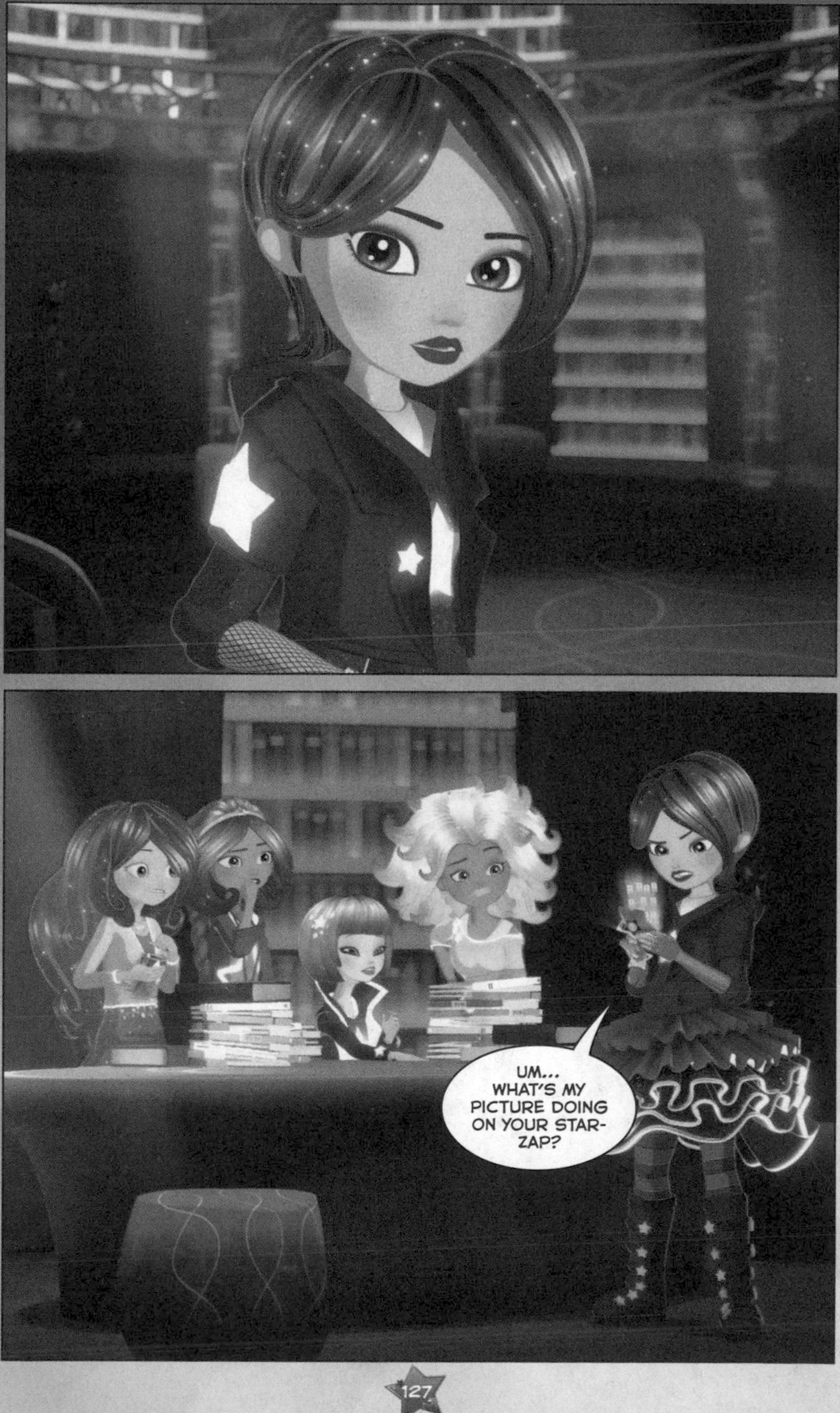
UM... WHAT'S MY PICTURE DOING ON YOUR STAR-ZAP?

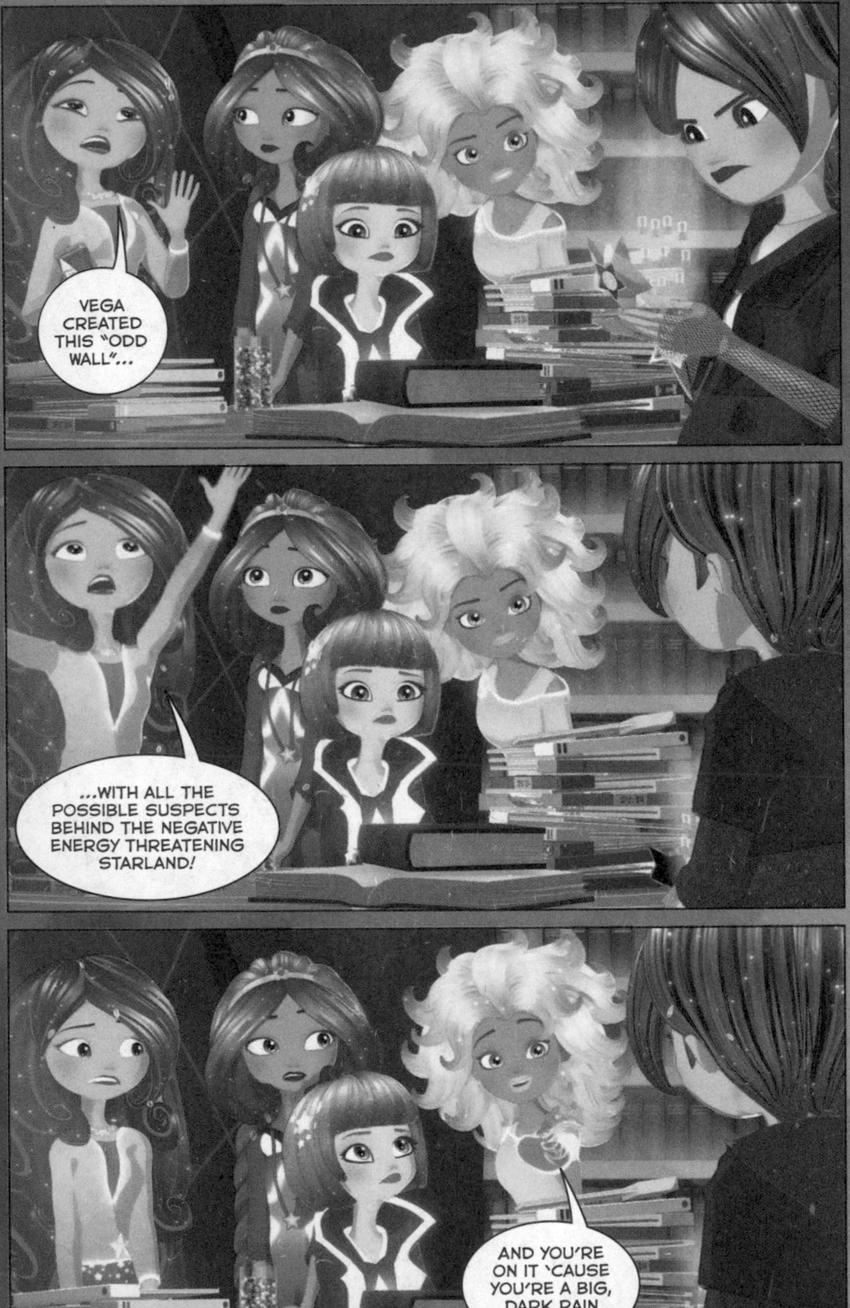
VEGA CREATED THIS "ODD WALL"...
...WITH ALL THE POSSIBLE SUSPECTS BEHIND THE NEGATIVE ENERGY THREATENING STARLAND!
AND YOU'RE ON IT 'CAUSE YOU'RE A BIG, DARK RAIN CLOUD.

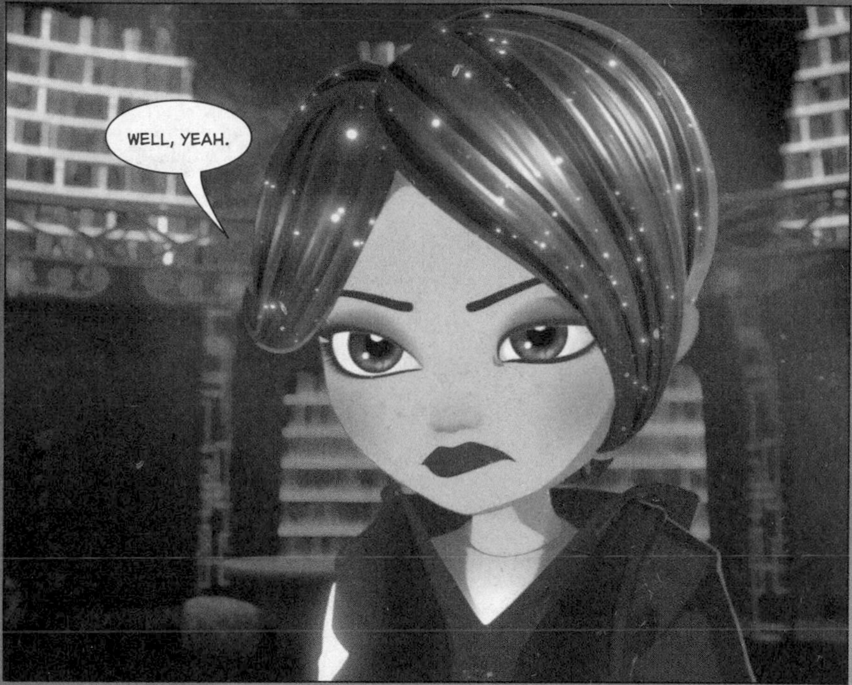
WELL, YEAH.

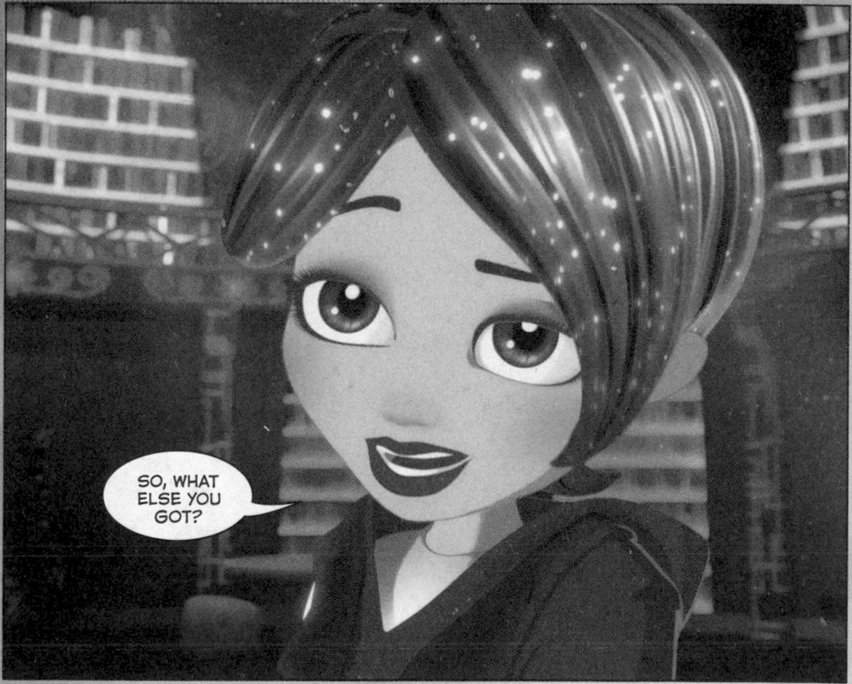
SO, WHAT ELSE YOU GOT?

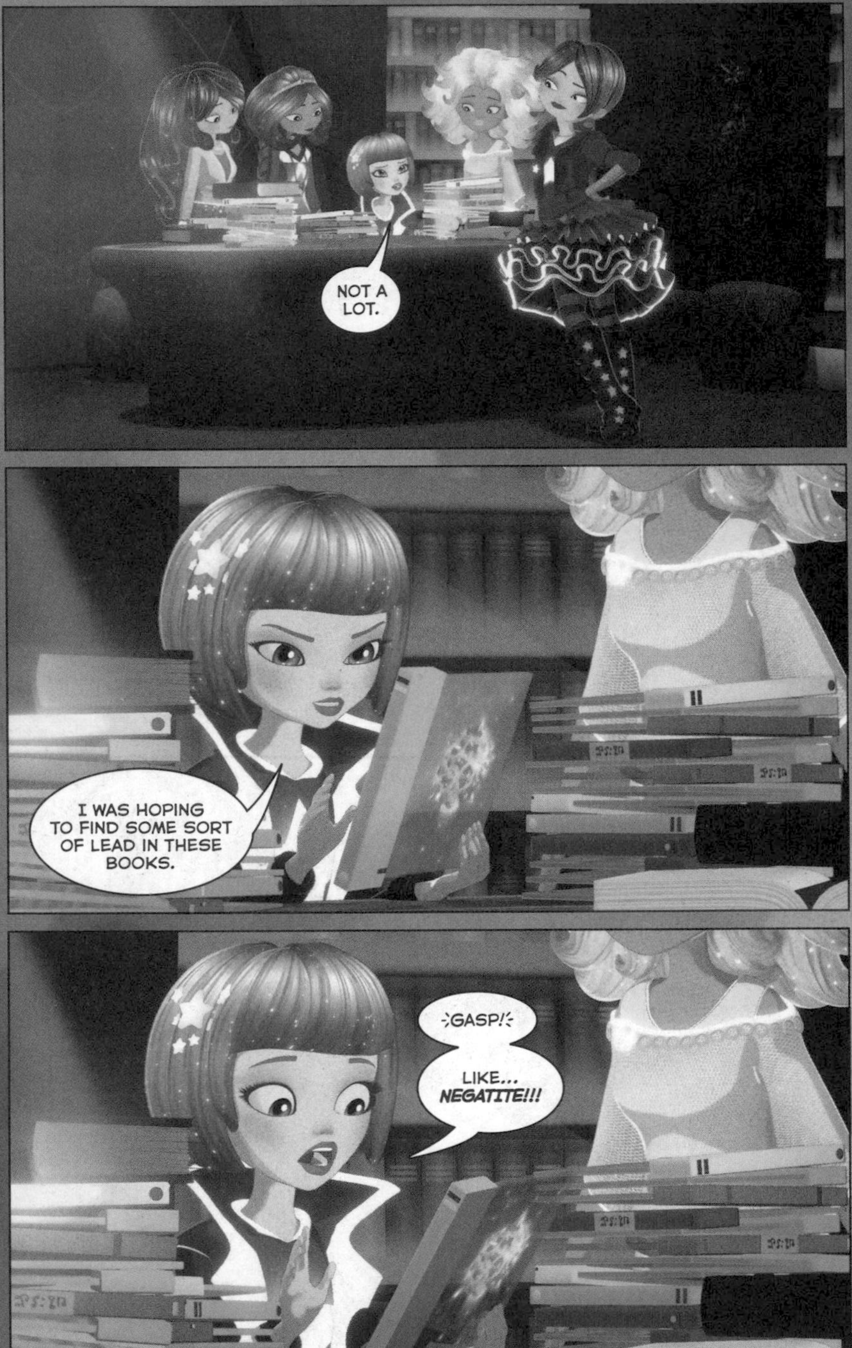
NOT A LOT.
I WAS HOPING TO FIND SOME SORT OF LEAD IN THESE BOOKS.
-GASP!-
LIKE... ***NEGATITE!!!***

NEGA-TITE? IS THAT SOME SORT OF NEGATIVE ELEMENT OR SOMETHING?

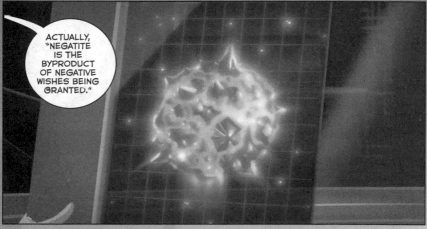

ACTUALLY, "NEGATITE IS THE BYPRODUCT OF NEGATIVE WISHES BEING GRANTED."

"SCIENTISTS HAVE THEORIZED THAT EXTREME AMOUNTS OF NEGATITE COULD **COUNTERACT** POSITIVE WISH ENERGY."

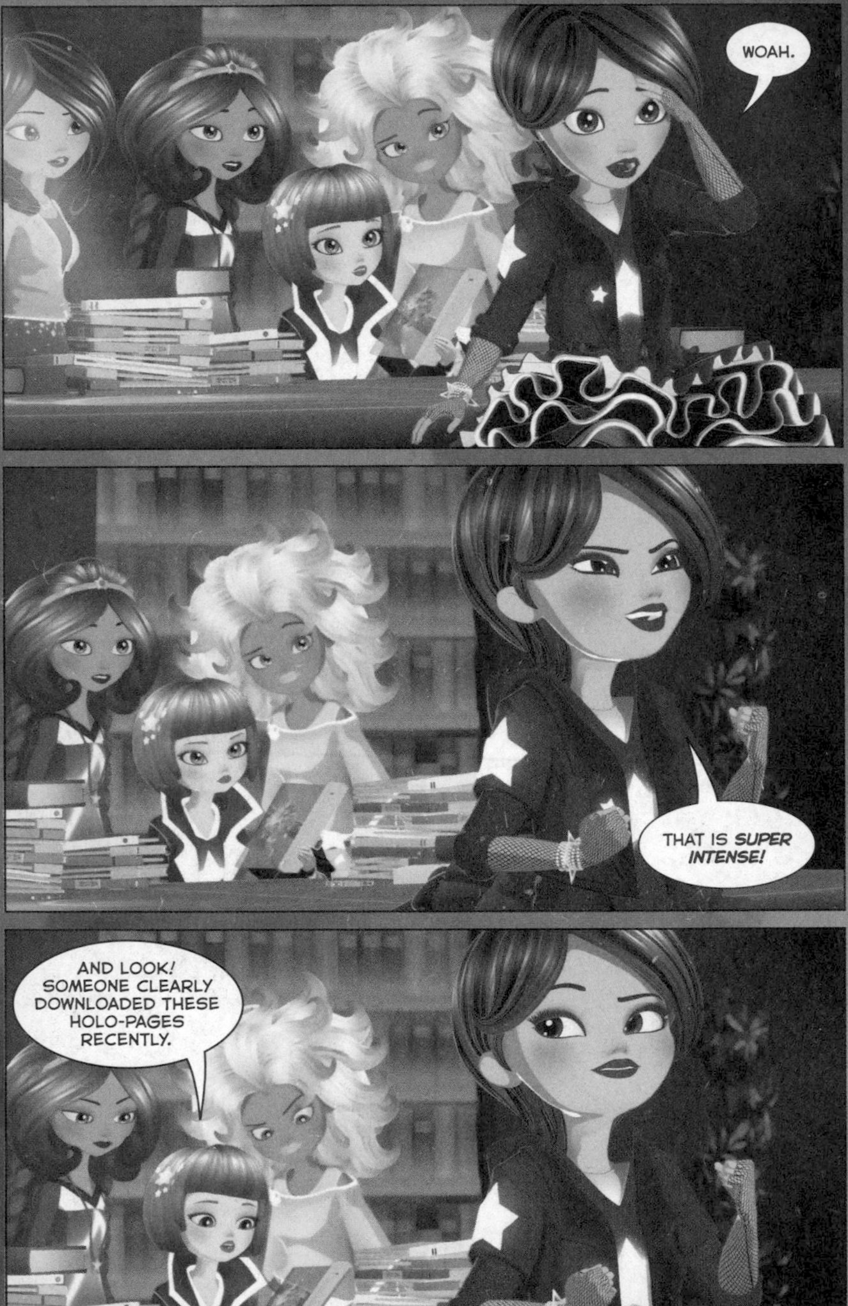
WOAH.
THAT IS SUPER INTENSE!
AND LOOK! SOMEONE CLEARLY DOWNLOADED THESE HOLO-PAGES RECENTLY.

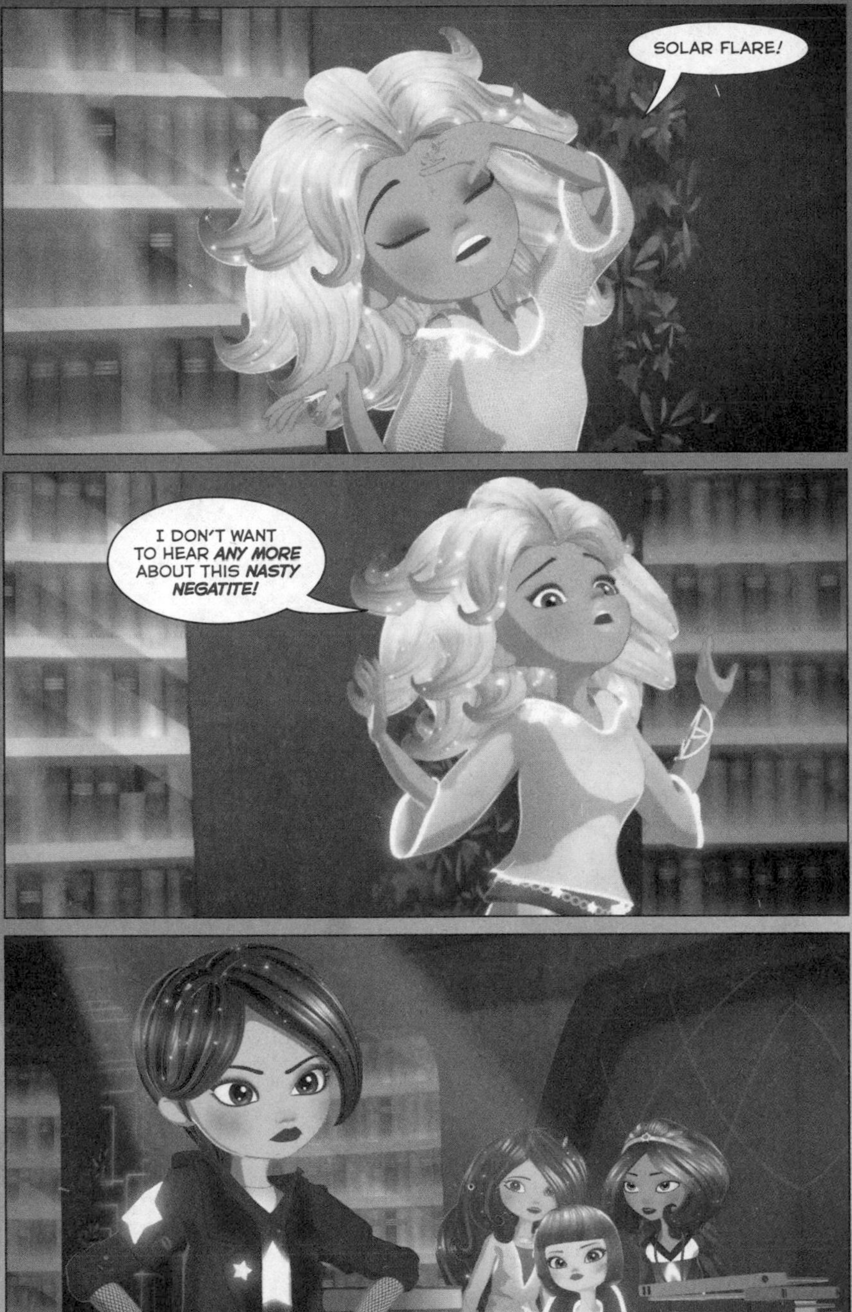
SOLAR FLARE!
I DON'T WANT TO HEAR ANY MORE ABOUT THIS NASTY NEGATITE!

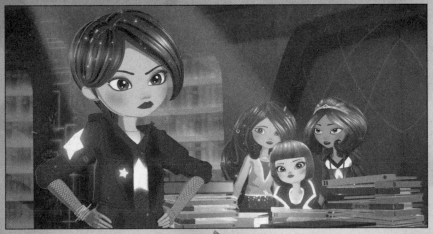

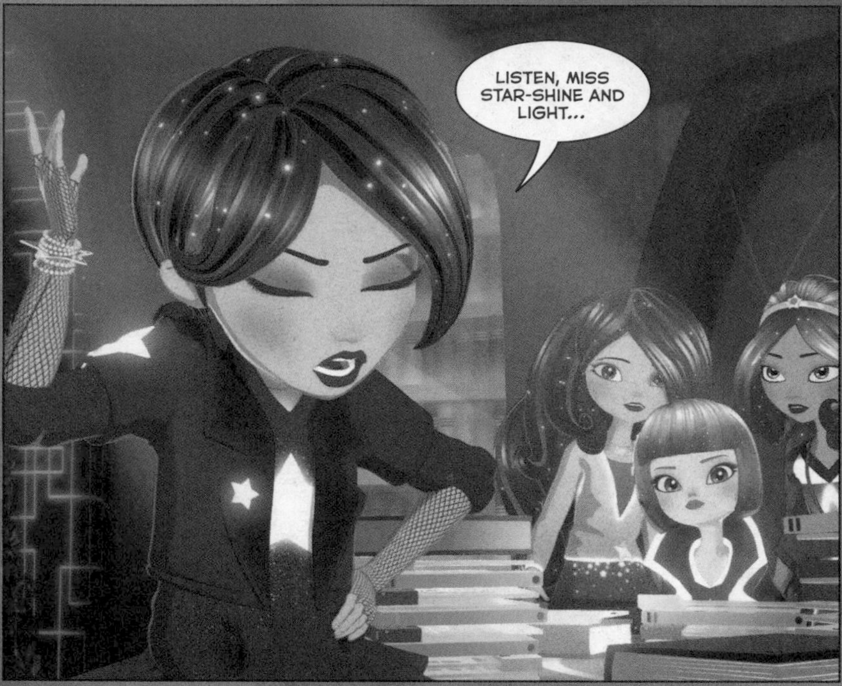
LISTEN, MISS STAR-SHINE AND LIGHT...

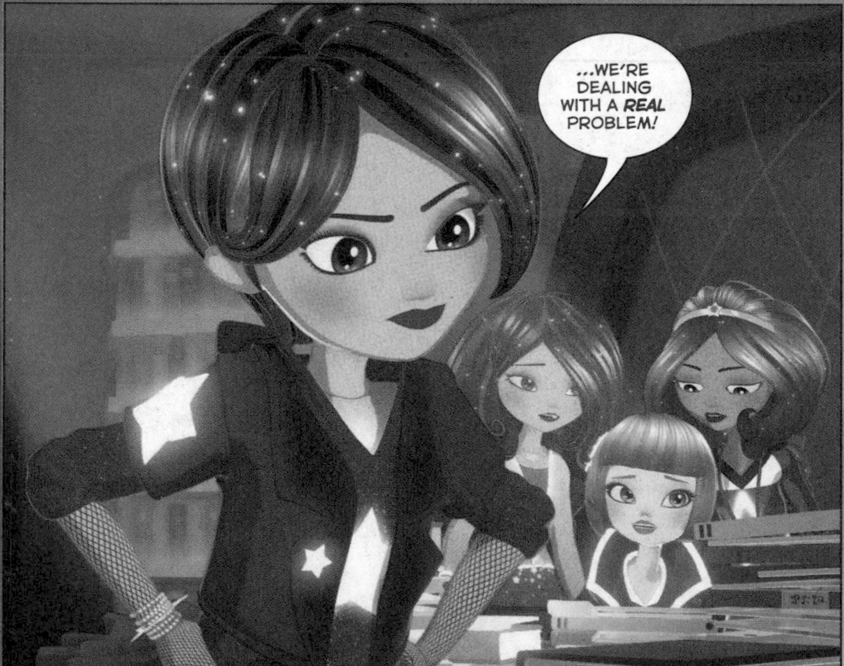
...WE'RE DEALING WITH A *REAL* PROBLEM!

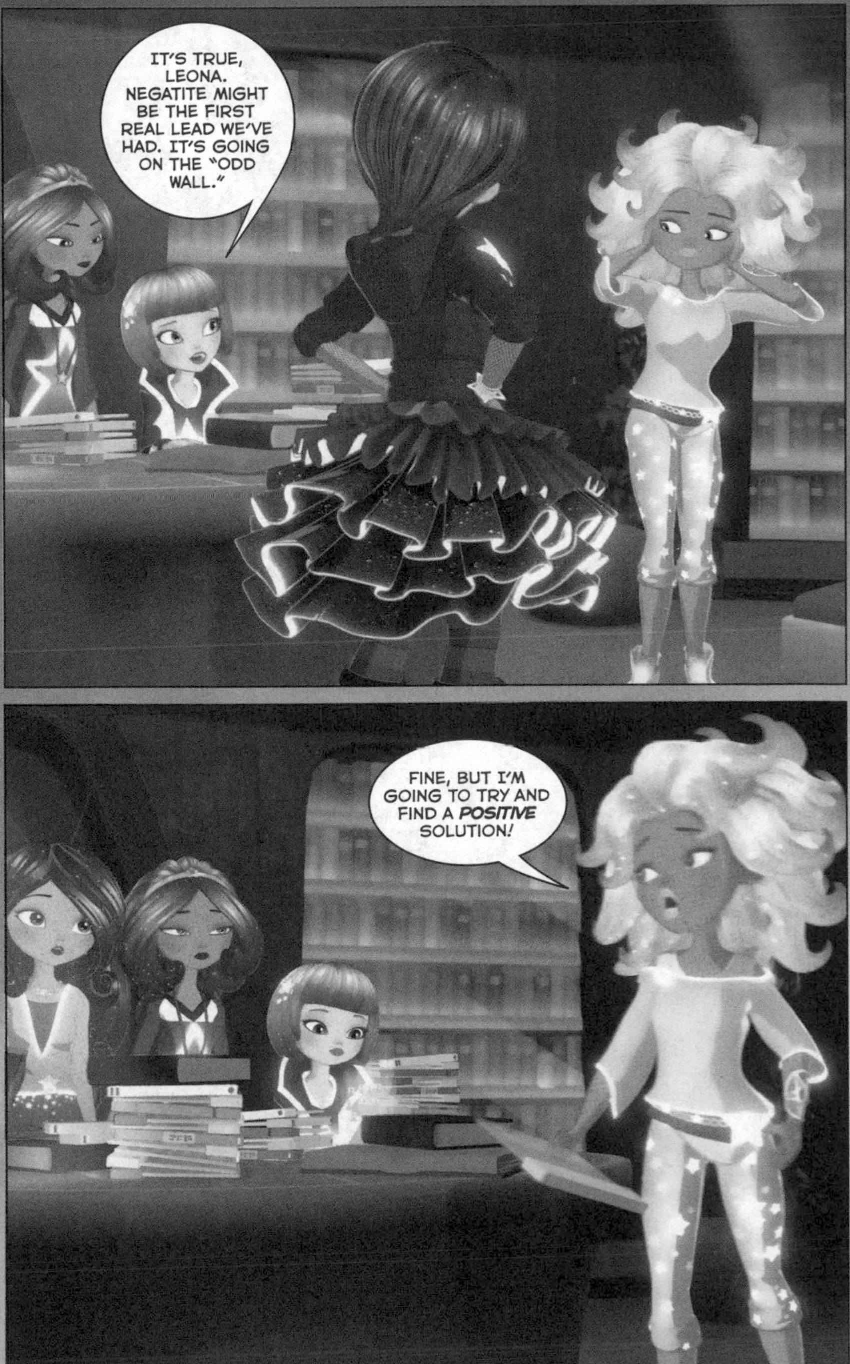
IT'S TRUE, LEONA. NEGATITE MIGHT BE THE FIRST REAL LEAD WE'VE HAD. IT'S GOING ON THE "ODD WALL."
FINE, BUT I'M GOING TO TRY AND FIND A ***POSITIVE*** SOLUTION!

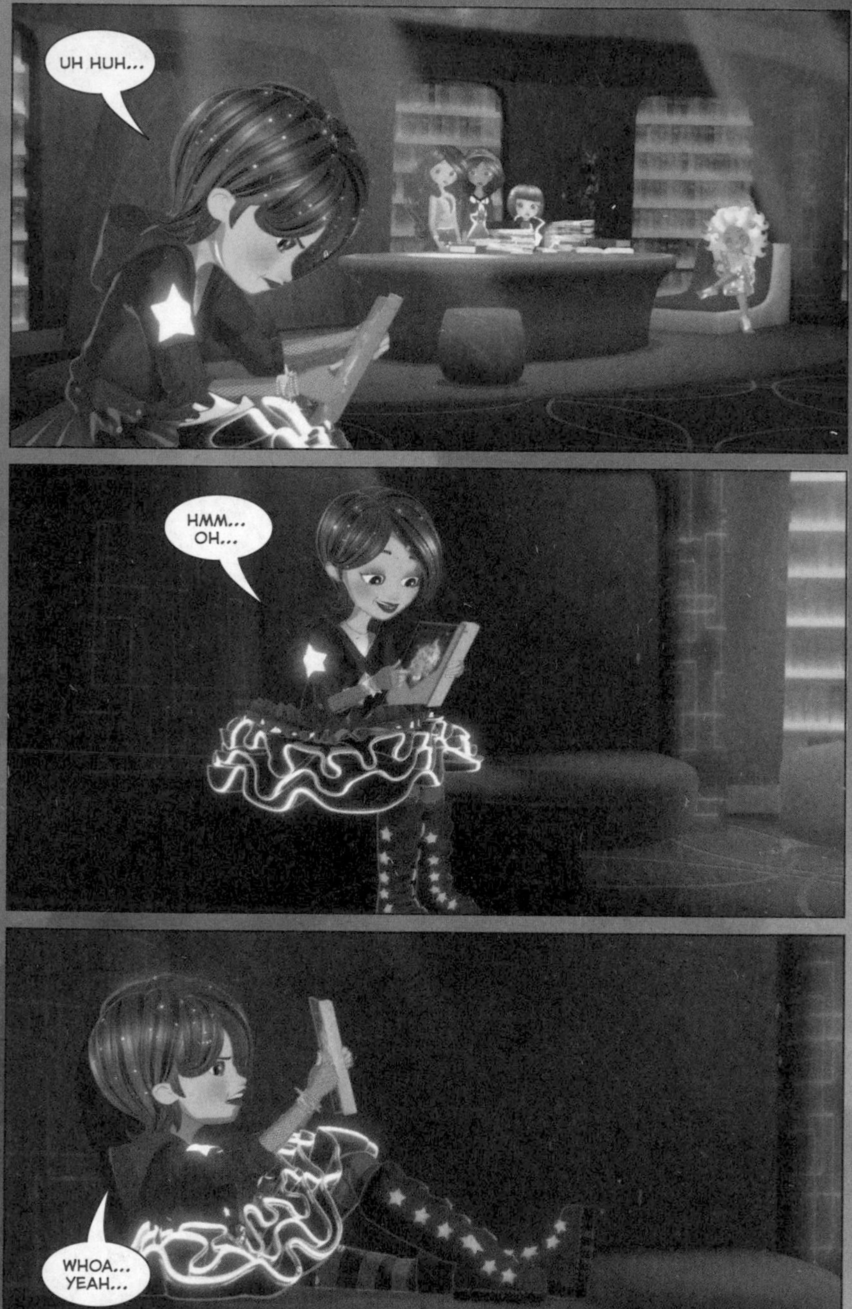
UH HUH...
HMM... OH...
WHOA... YEAH...

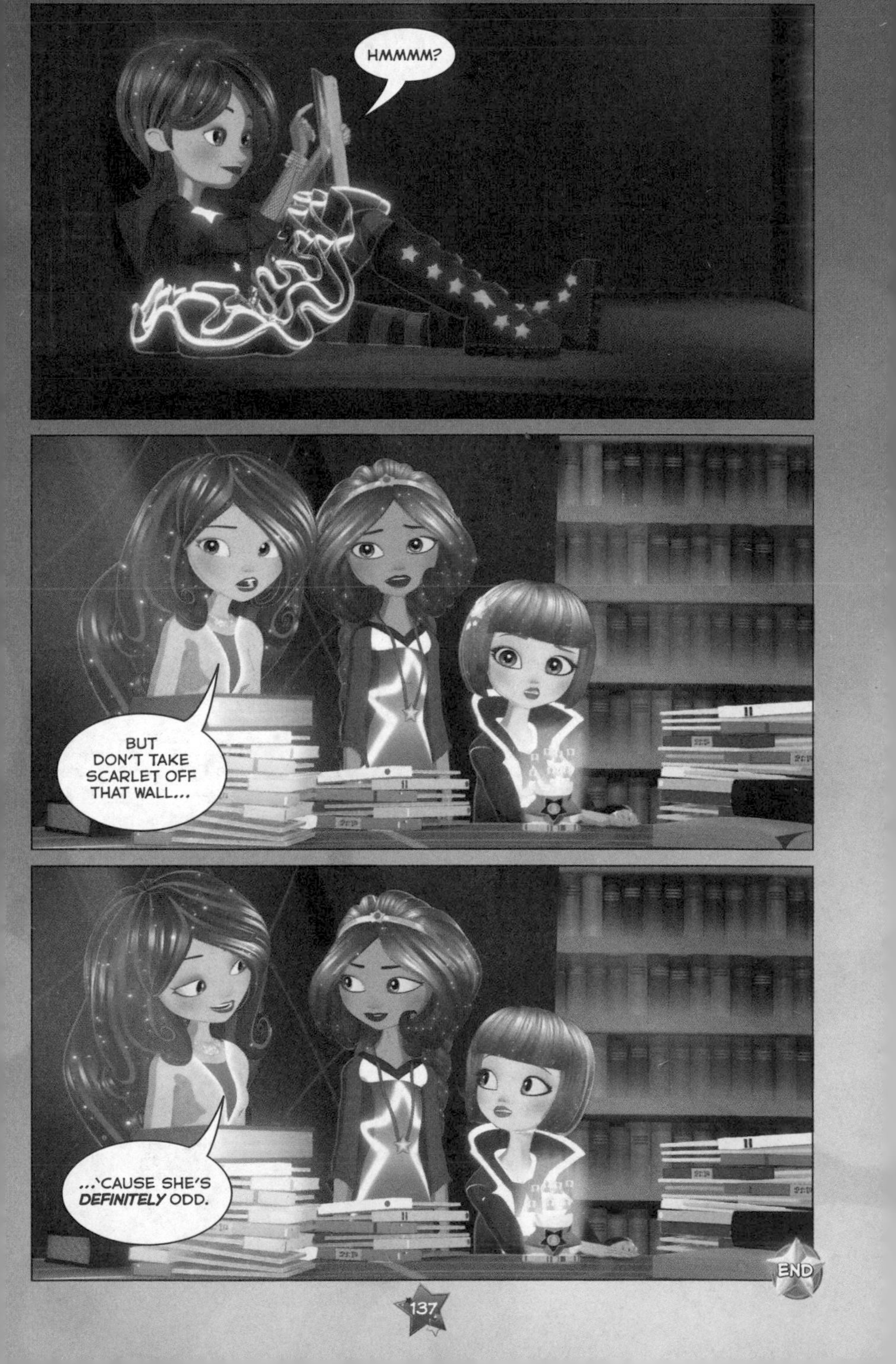
HMMMM?
BUT DON'T TAKE SCARLET OFF THAT WALL...
...'CAUSE SHE'S *DEFINITELY* ODD.
END

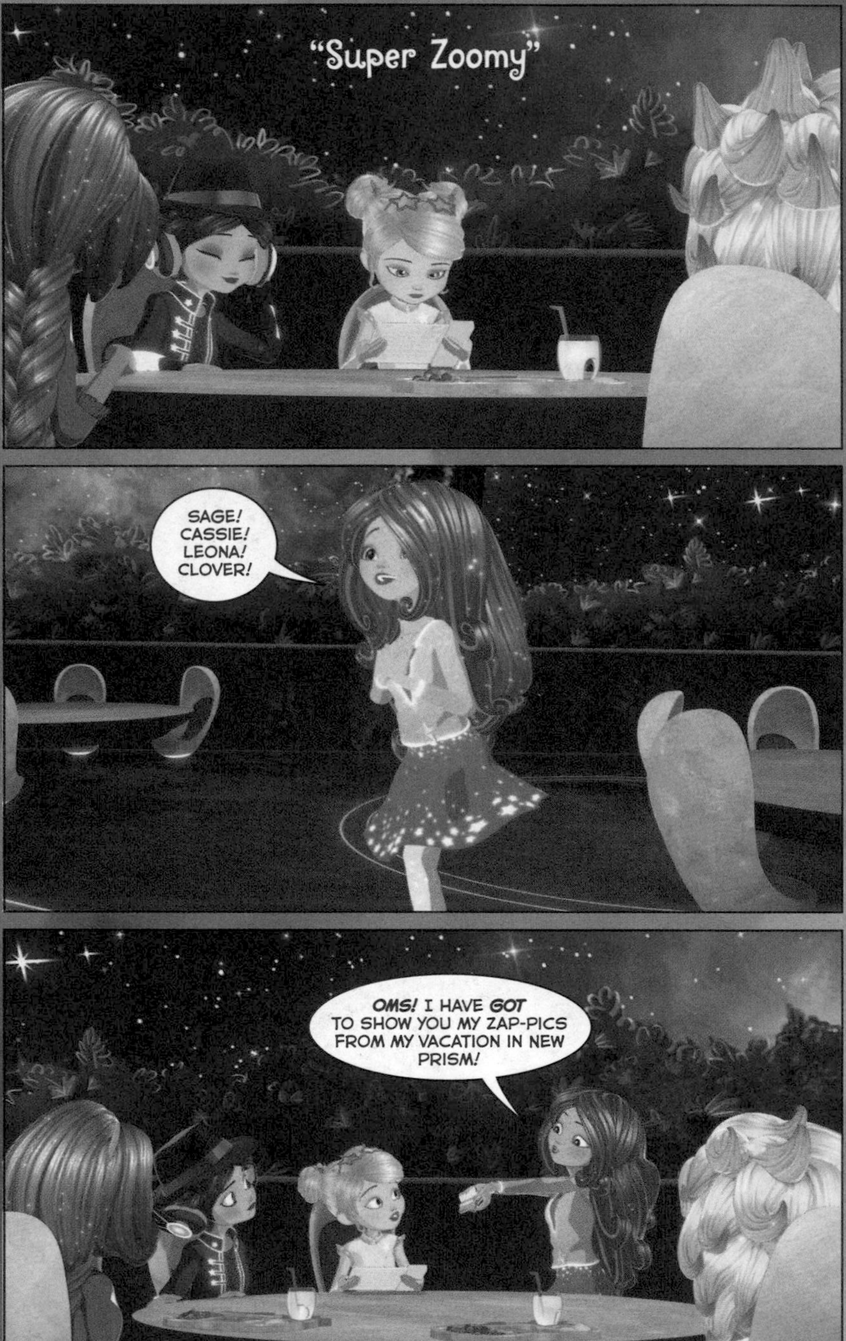
"Super Zoomy"
SAGE! CASSIE! LEONA! CLOVER!
OMS! I HAVE GOT TO SHOW YOU MY ZAP-PICS FROM MY VACATION IN NEW PRISM!

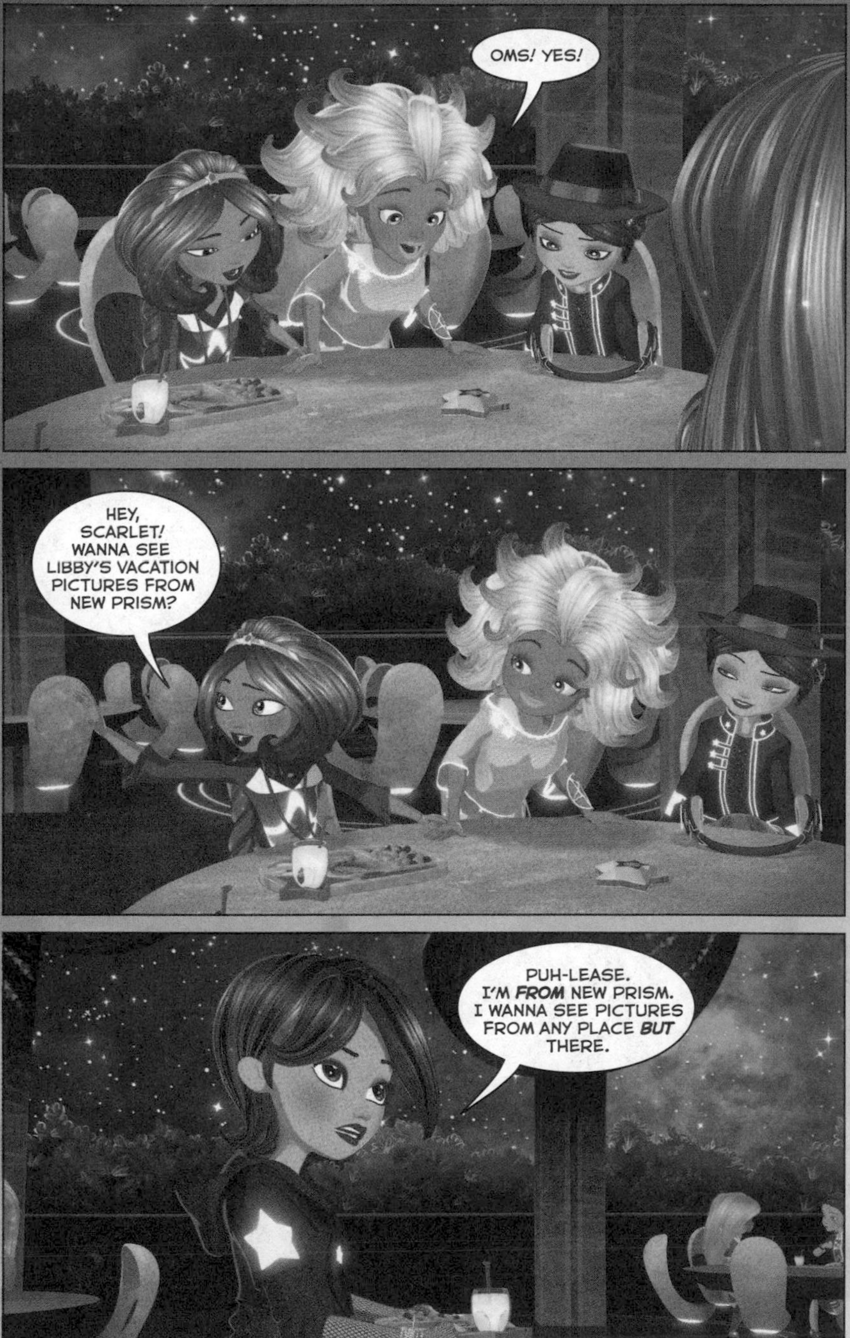
OMS! YES!
HEY, SCARLET! WANNA SEE LIBBY'S VACATION PICTURES FROM NEW PRISM?
PUH-LEASE. I'M *FROM* NEW PRISM. I WANNA SEE PICTURES FROM ANY PLACE *BUT* THERE.

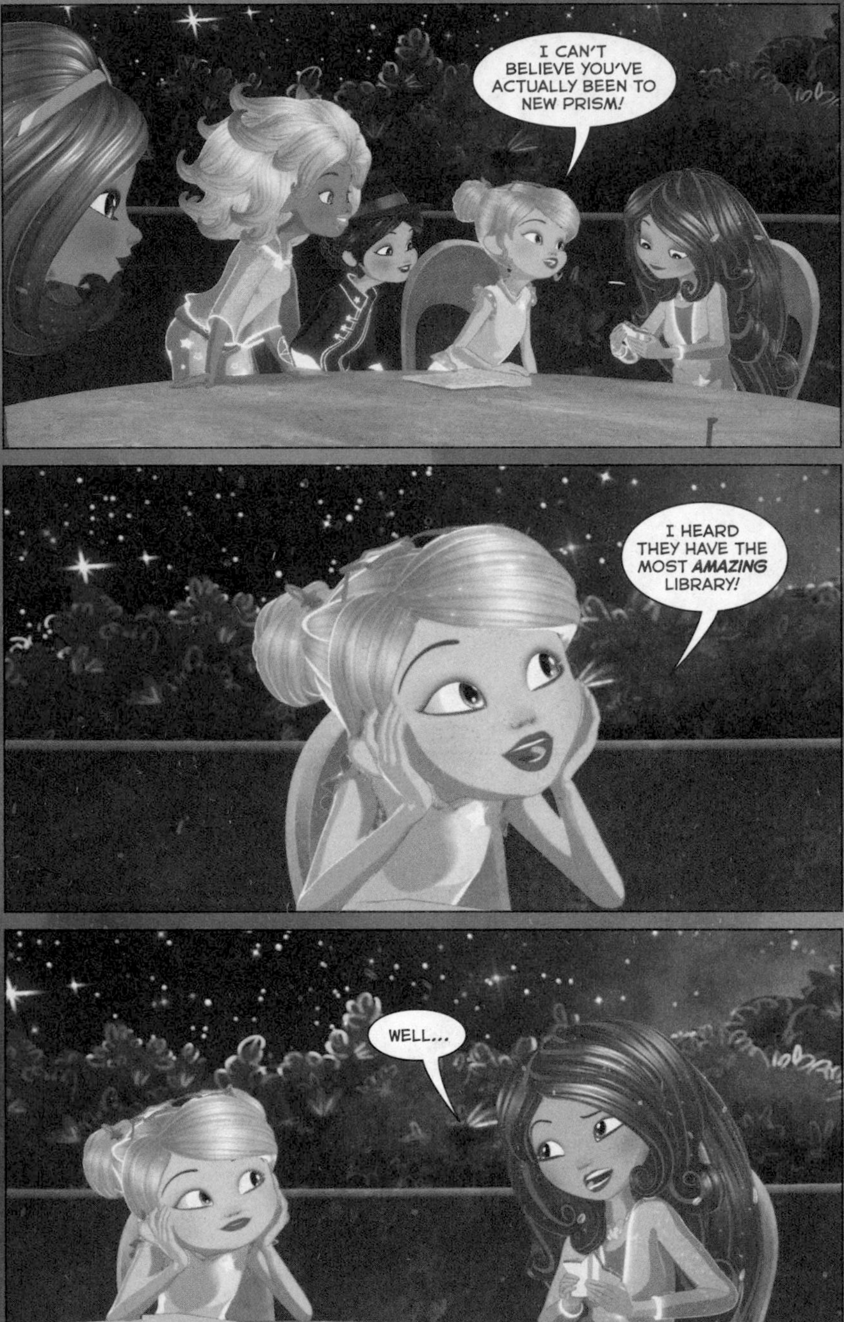
I CAN'T BELIEVE YOU'VE ACTUALLY BEEN TO NEW PRISM!
I HEARD THEY HAVE THE MOST *AMAZING* LIBRARY!
WELL...

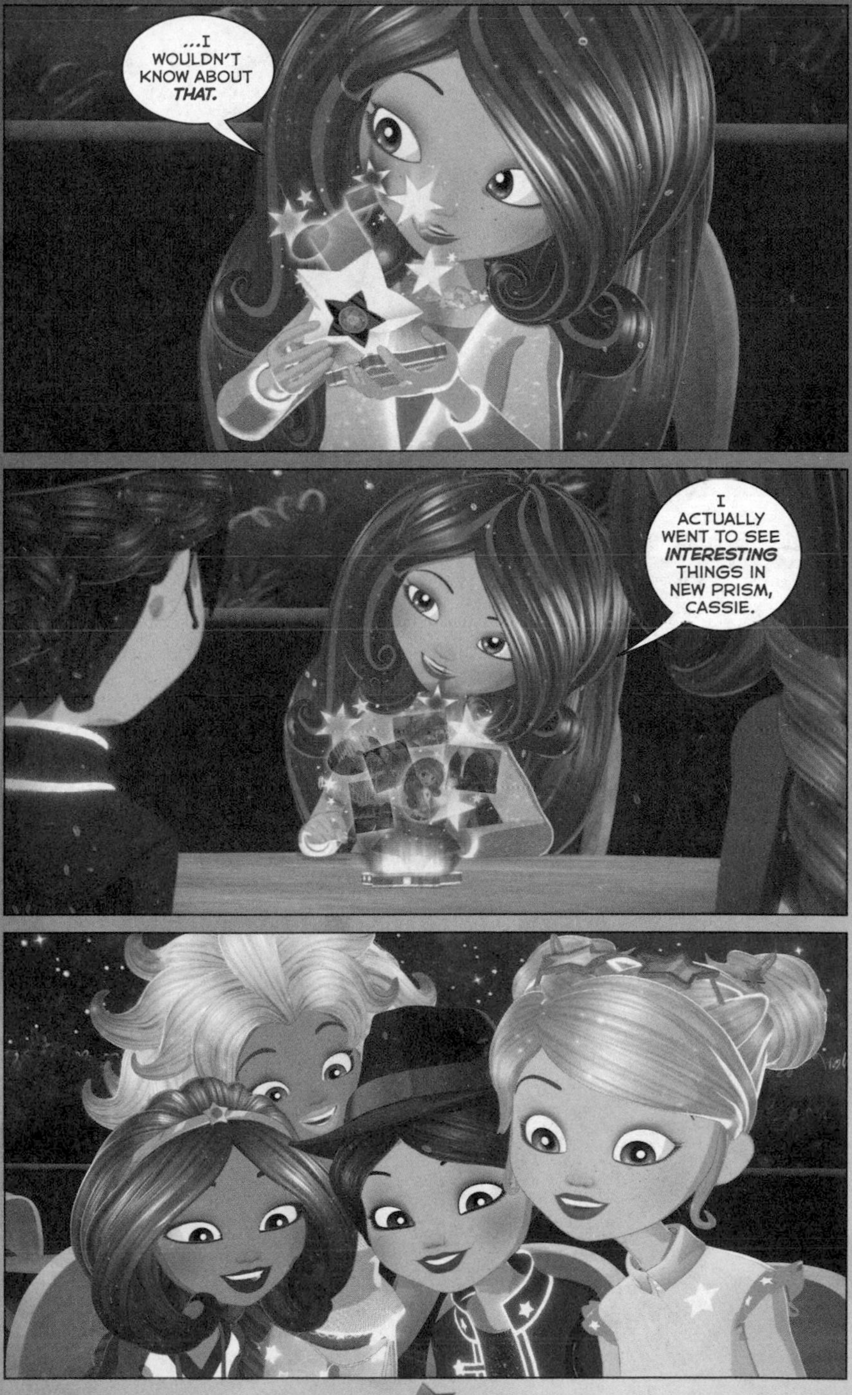
...I WOULDN'T KNOW ABOUT *THAT.*
I ACTUALLY WENT TO SEE *INTERESTING* THINGS IN NEW PRISM, CASSIE.

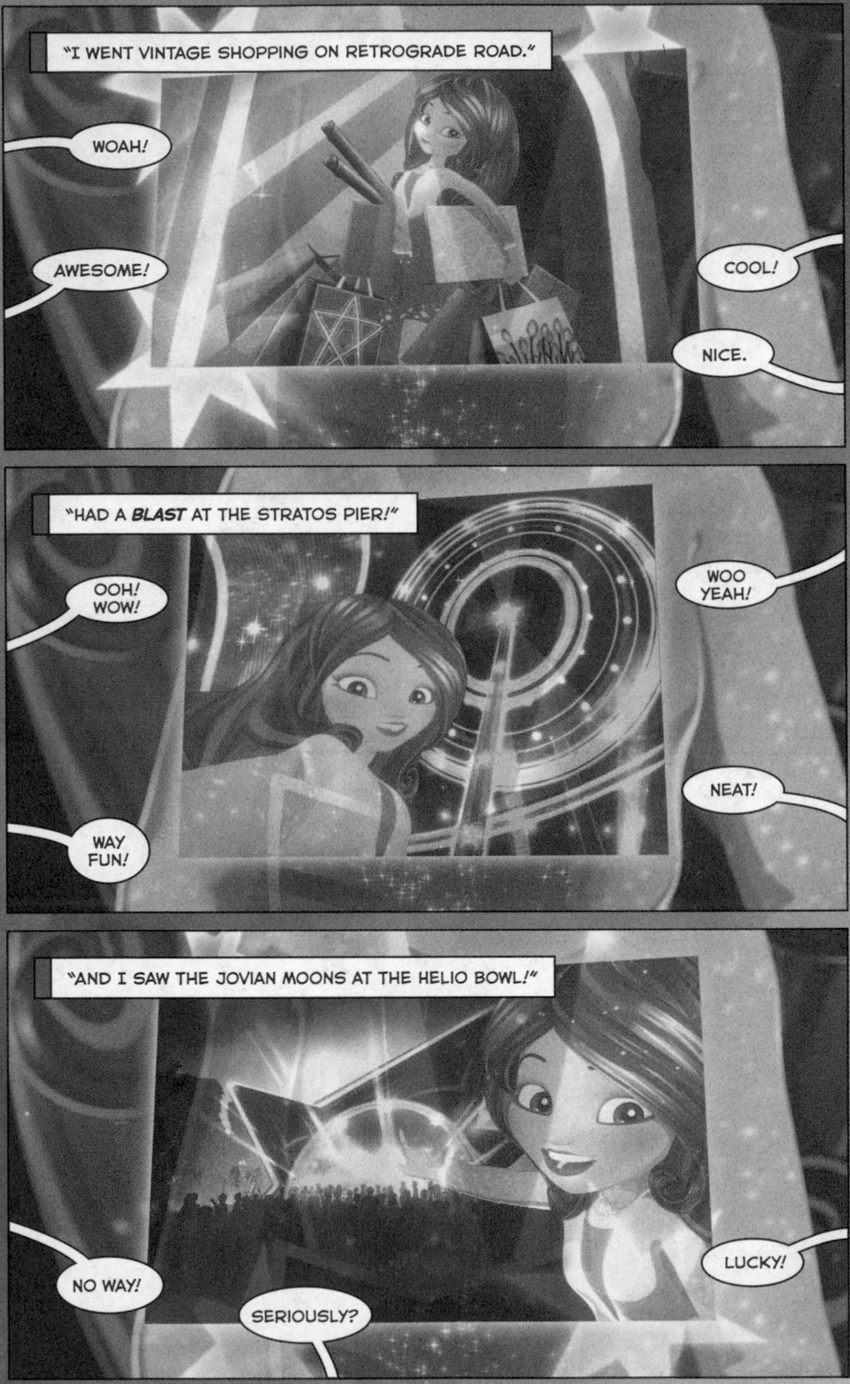
"I WENT VINTAGE SHOPPING ON RETROGRADE ROAD."
WOAH!
AWESOME!
COOL!
NICE.
"HAD A *BLAST* AT THE STRATOS PIER!"
OOH! WOW!
WAY FUN!
WOO YEAH!
NEAT!
"AND I SAW THE JOVIAN MOONS AT THE HELIO BOWL!"
NO WAY!
SERIOUSLY?
LUCKY!

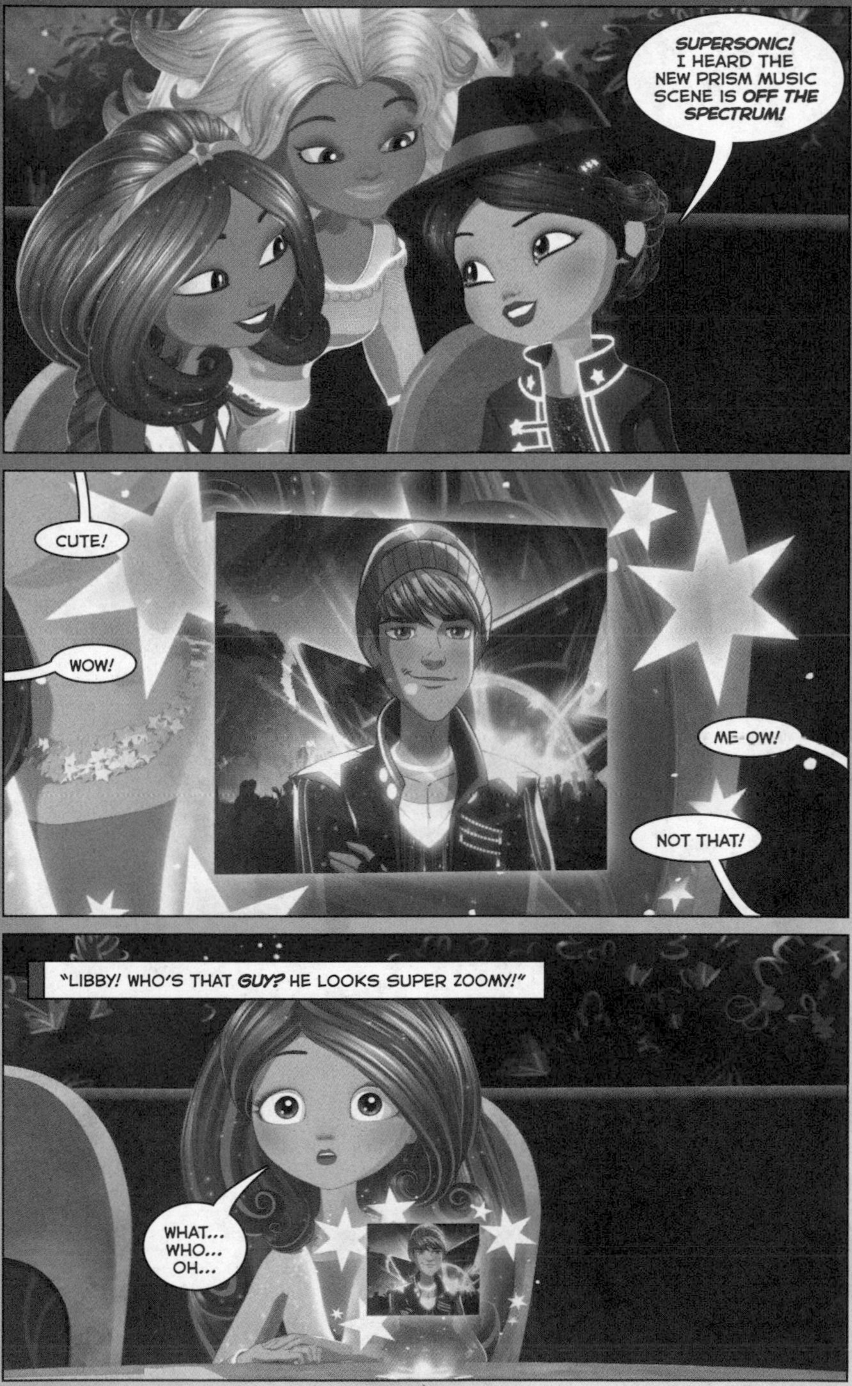
SUPERSONIC! I HEARD THE NEW PRISM MUSIC SCENE IS OFF THE SPECTRUM!
CUTE!
WOW!
ME-OW!
NOT THAT!
"LIBBY! WHO'S THAT GUY? HE LOOKS SUPER ZOOMY!"
WHAT... WHO... OH...

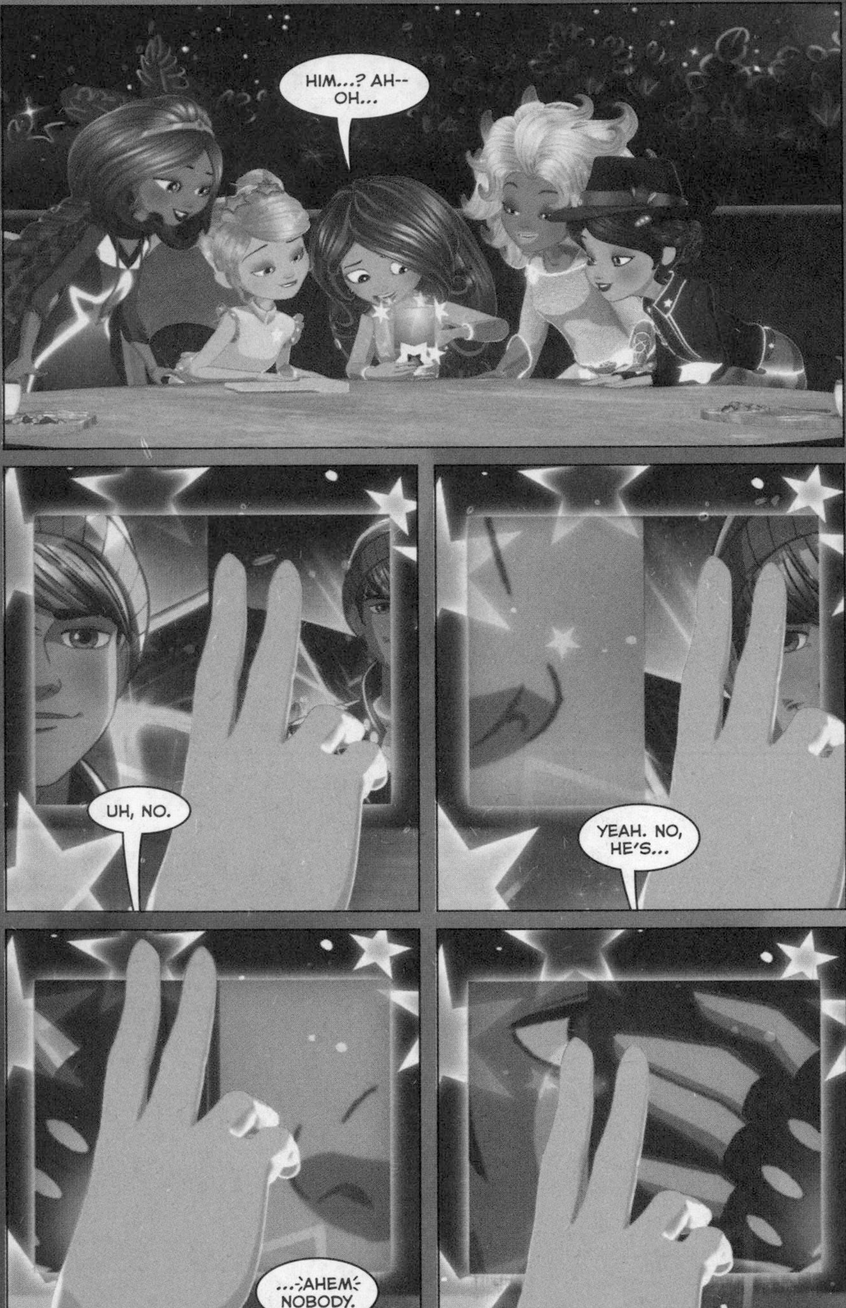
HIM...? AH--
OH...
UH, NO.
YEAH. NO,
HE'S...
...AHEM
NOBODY.

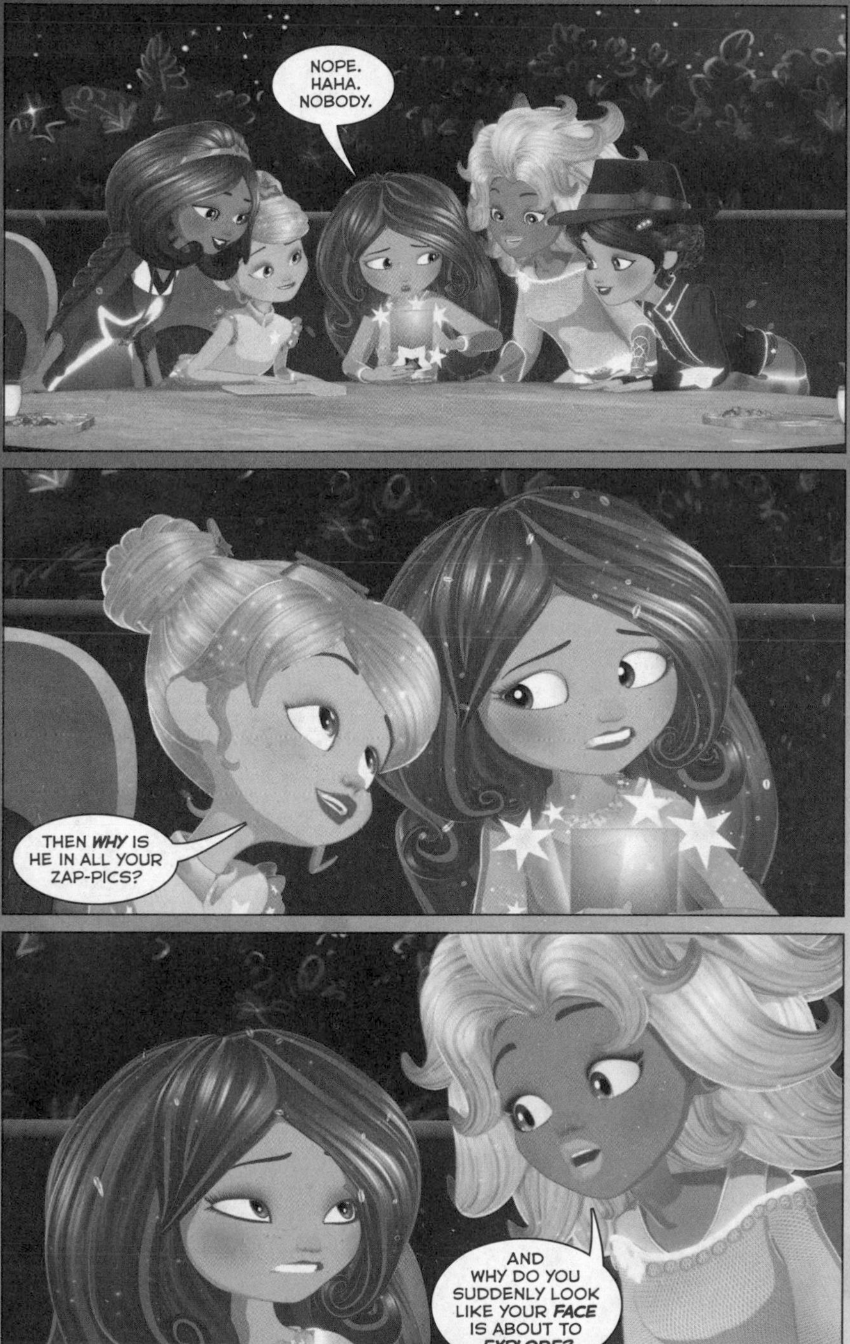
NOPE. HAHA. NOBODY.
THEN *WHY* IS HE IN ALL YOUR ZAP-PICS?
AND WHY DO YOU SUDDENLY LOOK LIKE YOUR *FACE* IS ABOUT TO *EXPLODE?*

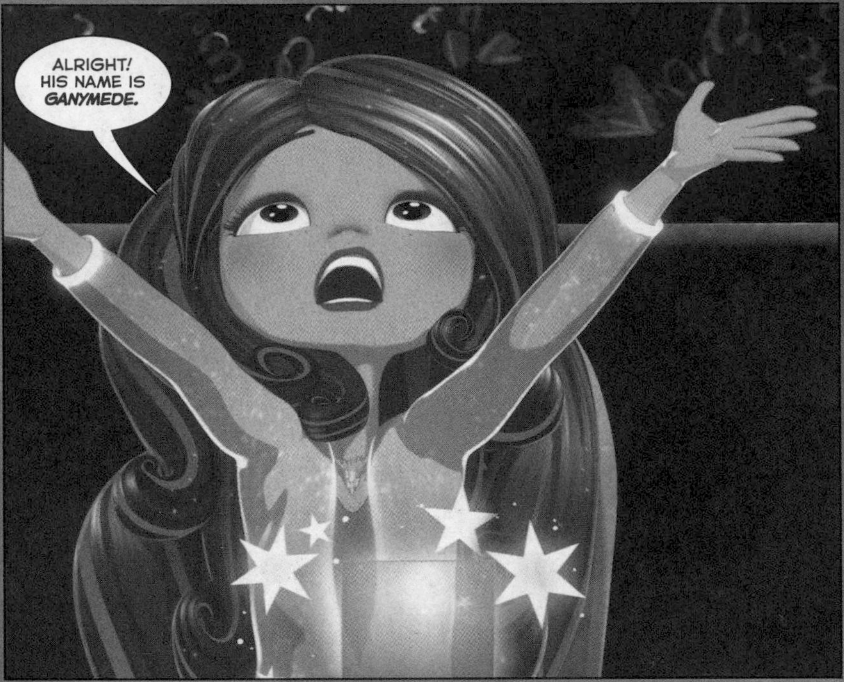
ALRIGHT! HIS NAME IS *GANYMEDE.*

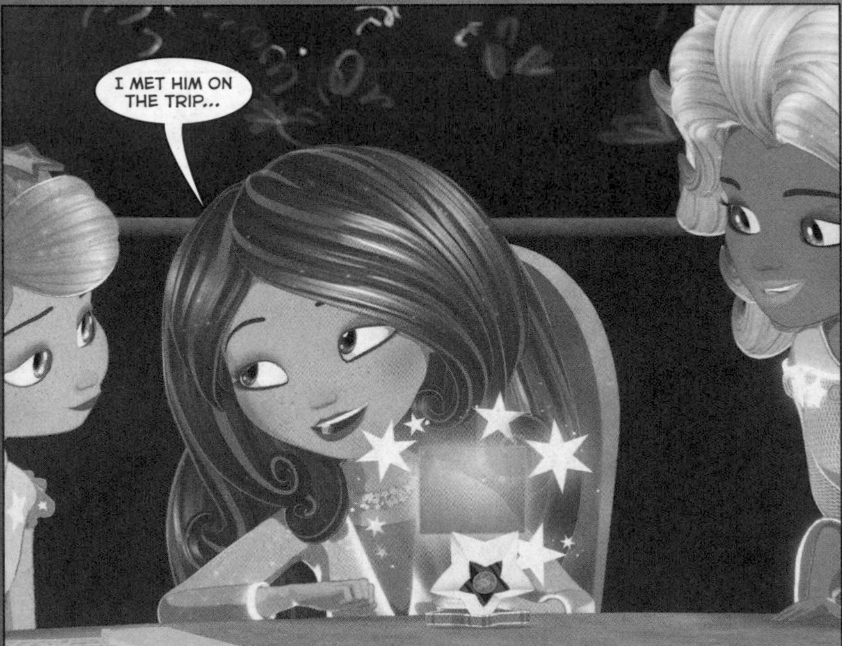
I MET HIM ON THE TRIP...

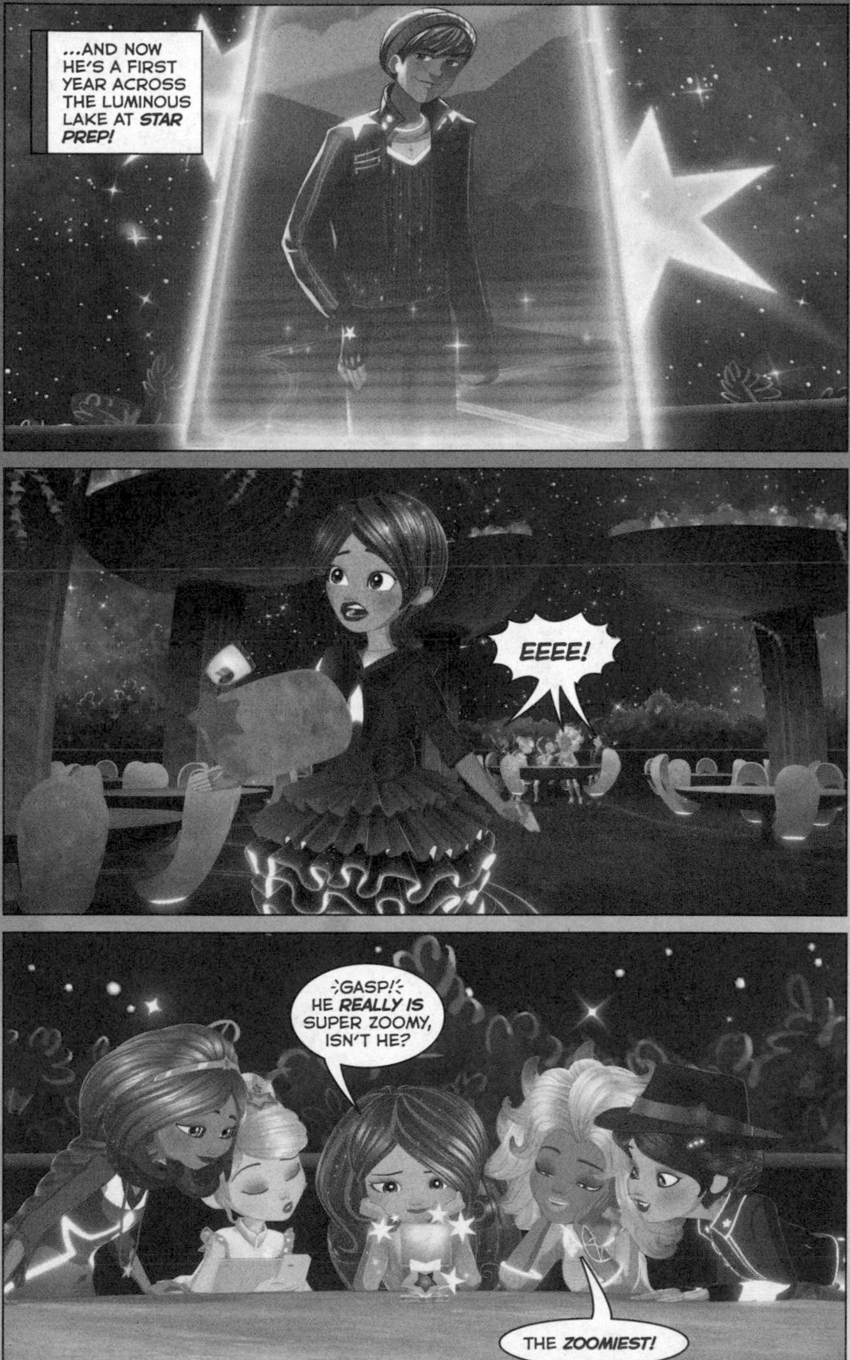
...AND NOW HE'S A FIRST YEAR ACROSS THE LUMINOUS LAKE AT STAR PREP!
EEEE!
GASP! HE REALLY IS SUPER ZOOMY, ISN'T HE?
THE ZOOMIEST!

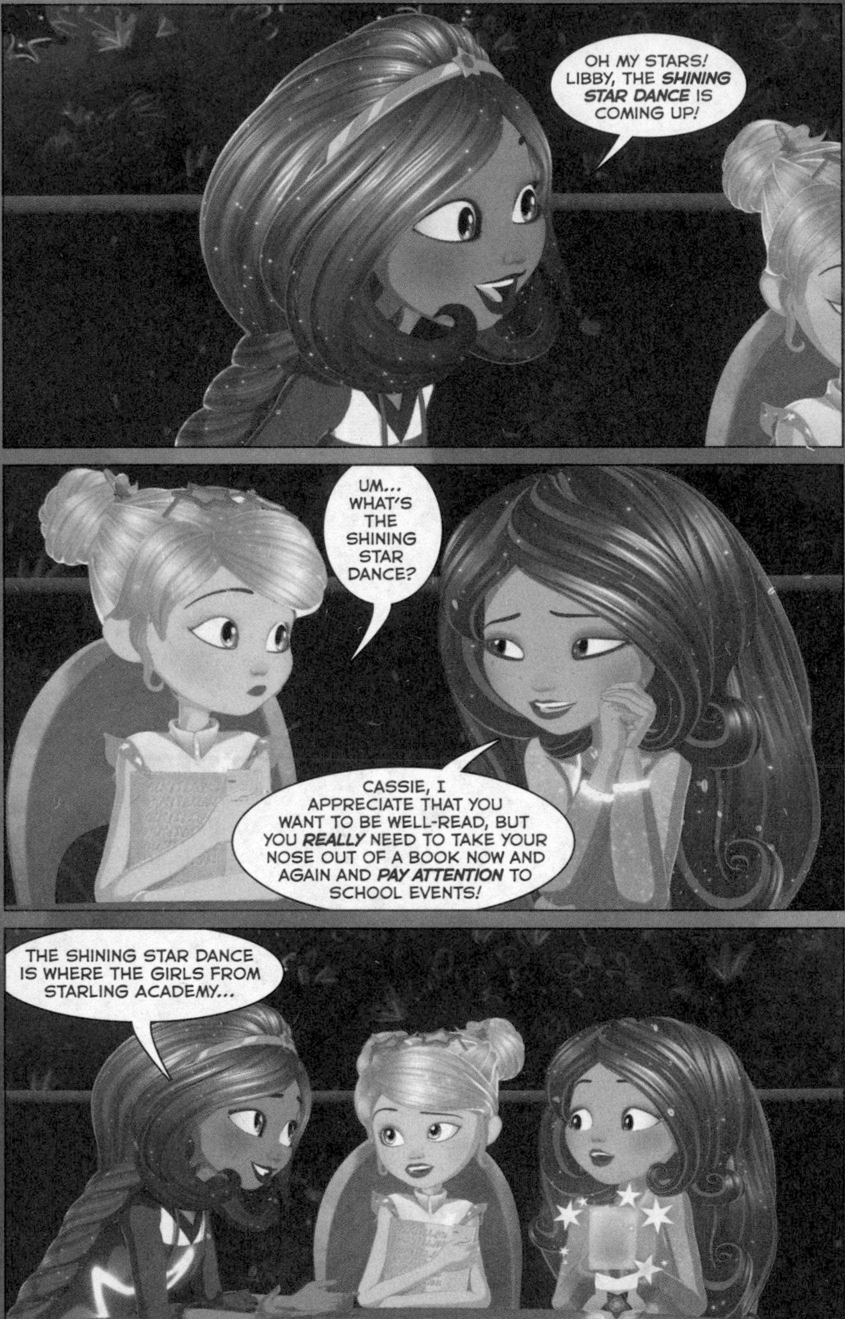
OH MY STARS! LIBBY, THE **SHINING STAR DANCE** IS COMING UP!
UM... WHAT'S THE SHINING STAR DANCE?
CASSIE, I APPRECIATE THAT YOU WANT TO BE WELL-READ, BUT YOU **REALLY** NEED TO TAKE YOUR NOSE OUT OF A BOOK NOW AND AGAIN AND **PAY ATTENTION** TO SCHOOL EVENTS!
THE SHINING STAR DANCE IS WHERE THE GIRLS FROM STARLING ACADEMY...

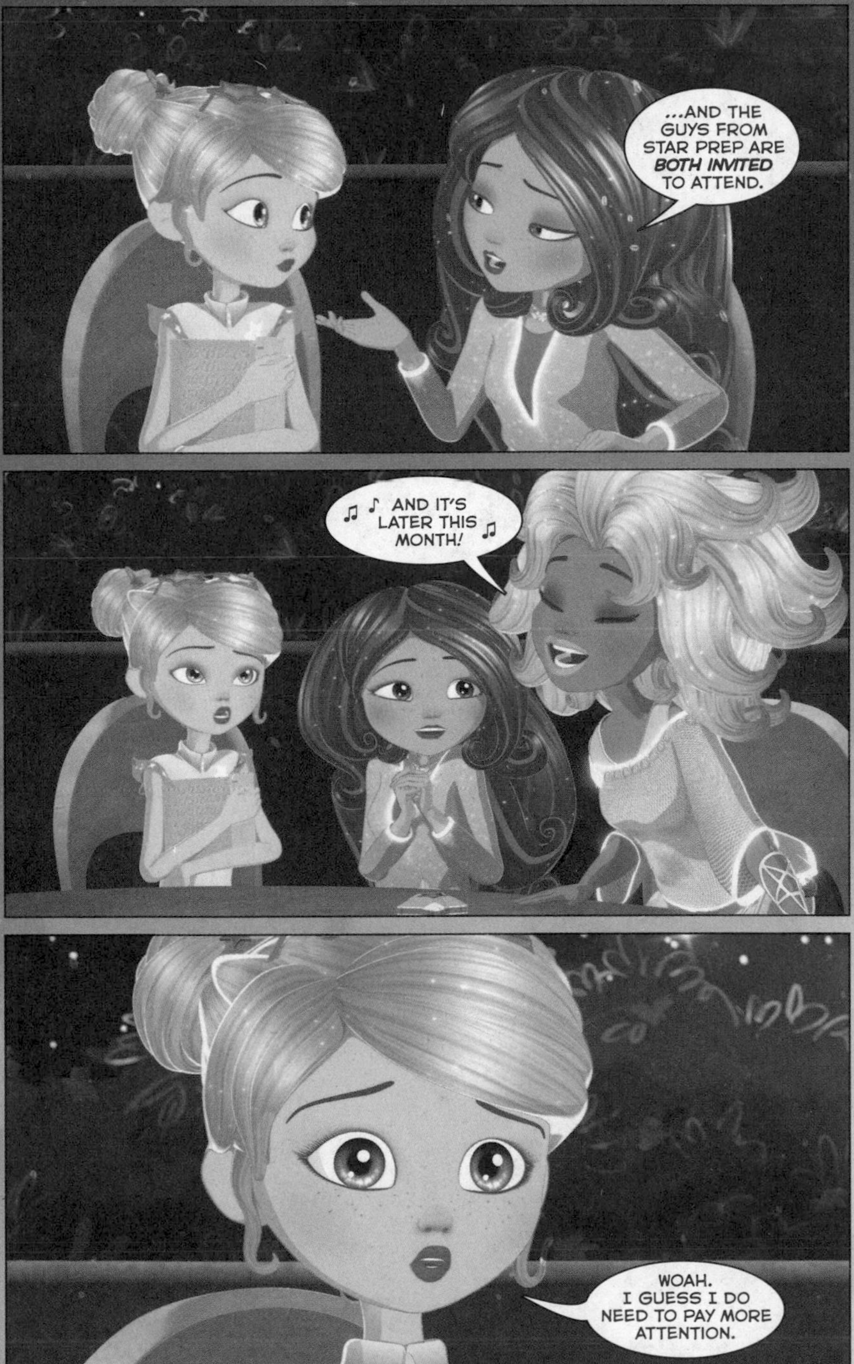
...AND THE GUYS FROM STAR PREP ARE ***BOTH INVITED*** TO ATTEND.
♫ ♪ AND IT'S LATER THIS MONTH! ♫
WOAH. I GUESS I DO NEED TO PAY MORE ATTENTION.

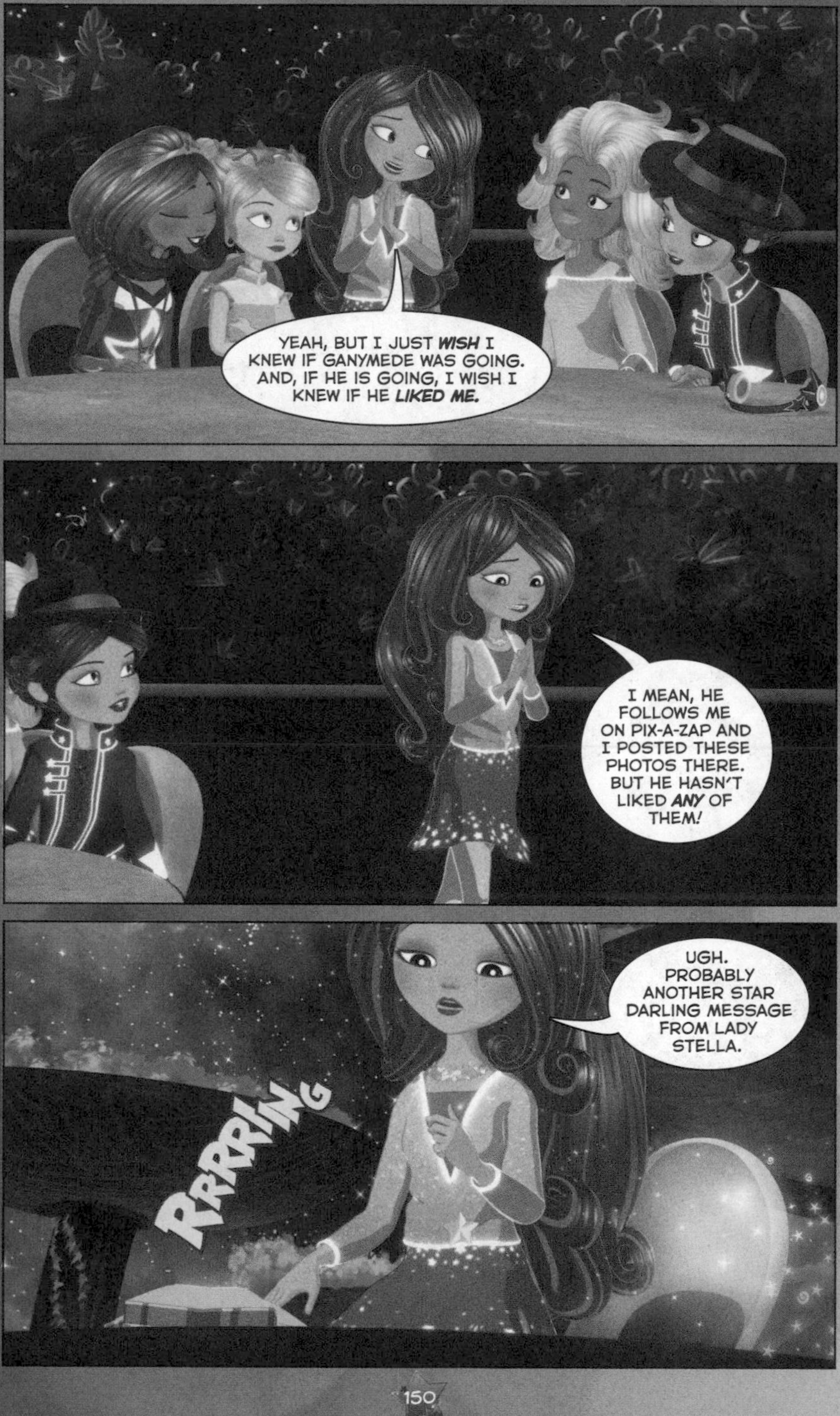
YEAH, BUT I JUST WISH I KNEW IF GANYMEDE WAS GOING. AND, IF HE IS GOING, I WISH I KNEW IF HE LIKED ME.
I MEAN, HE FOLLOWS ME ON PIX-A-ZAP AND I POSTED THESE PHOTOS THERE. BUT HE HASN'T LIKED ANY OF THEM!
UGH. PROBABLY ANOTHER STAR DARLING MESSAGE FROM LADY STELLA.
RRRRING

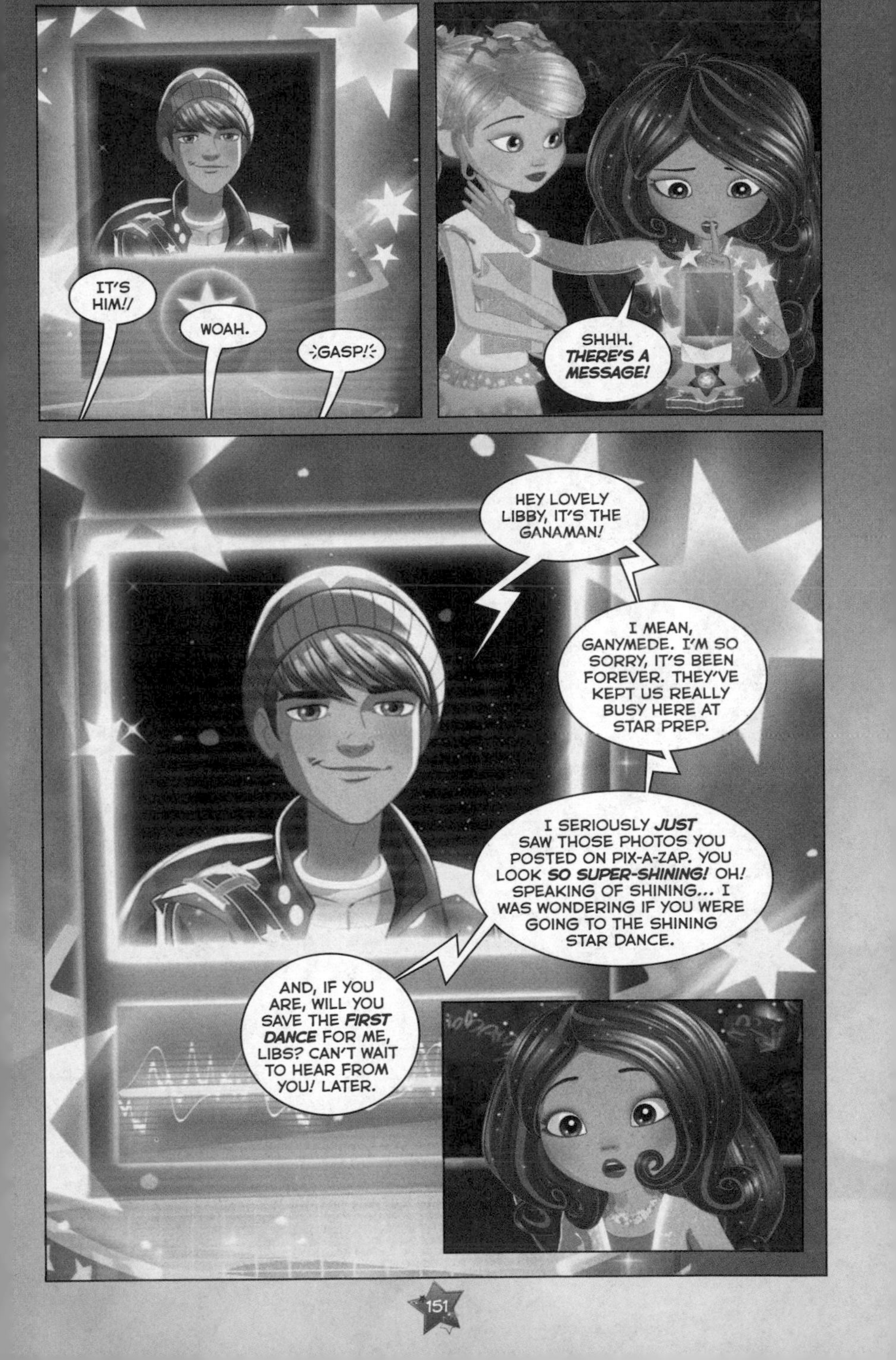
IT'S HIM!!
WOAH.
GASP!
SHHH. THERE'S A MESSAGE!
HEY LOVELY LIBBY, IT'S THE GANAMAN!
I MEAN, GANYMEDE. I'M SO SORRY, IT'S BEEN FOREVER. THEY'VE KEPT US REALLY BUSY HERE AT STAR PREP.
I SERIOUSLY JUST SAW THOSE PHOTOS YOU POSTED ON PIX-A-ZAP. YOU LOOK SO SUPER-SHINING! OH! SPEAKING OF SHINING... I WAS WONDERING IF YOU WERE GOING TO THE SHINING STAR DANCE.
AND, IF YOU ARE, WILL YOU SAVE THE FIRST DANCE FOR ME, LIBS? CAN'T WAIT TO HEAR FROM YOU! LATER.

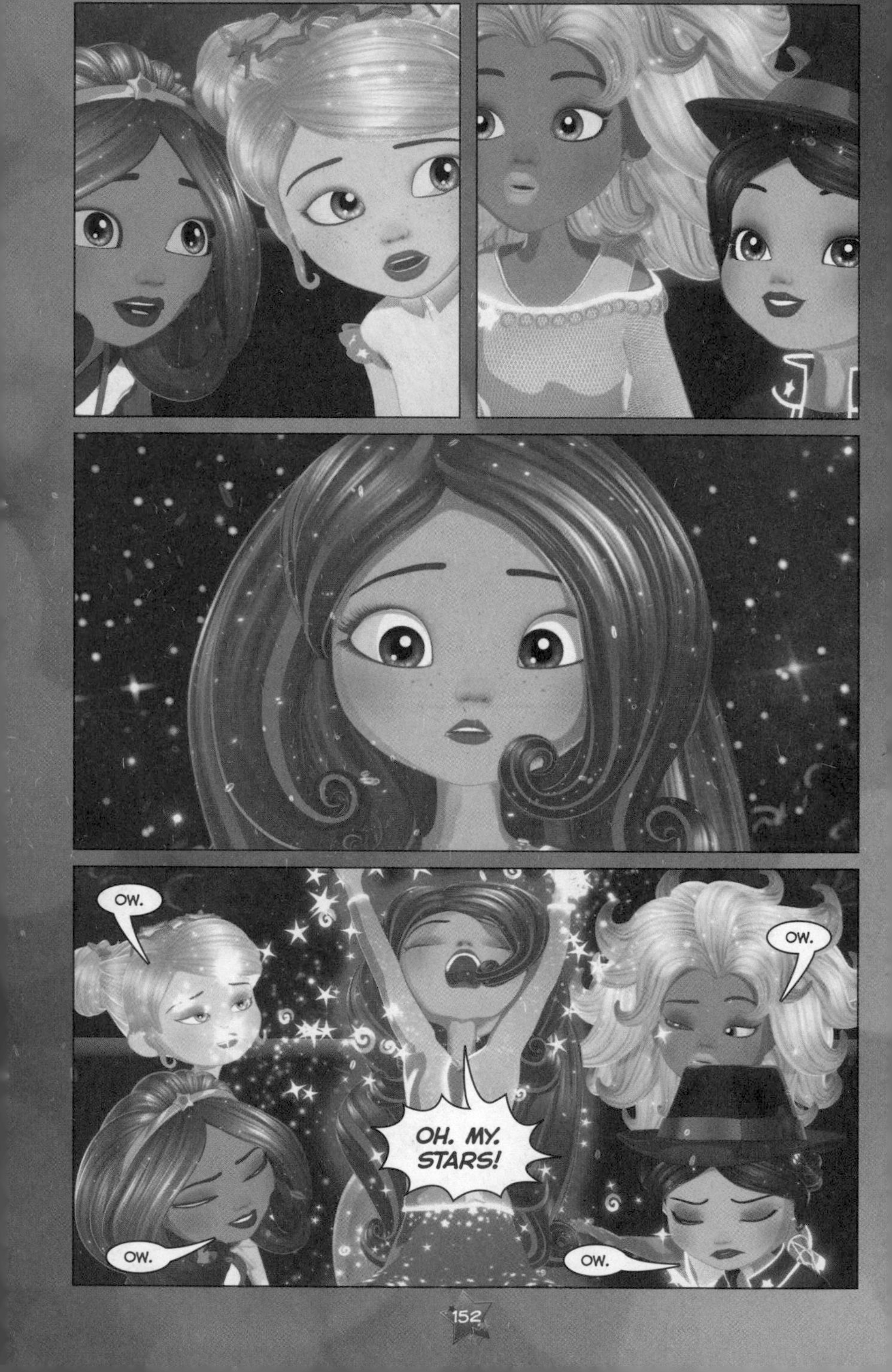
OW.
OW.
OH. MY. STARS!
OW.
OW.

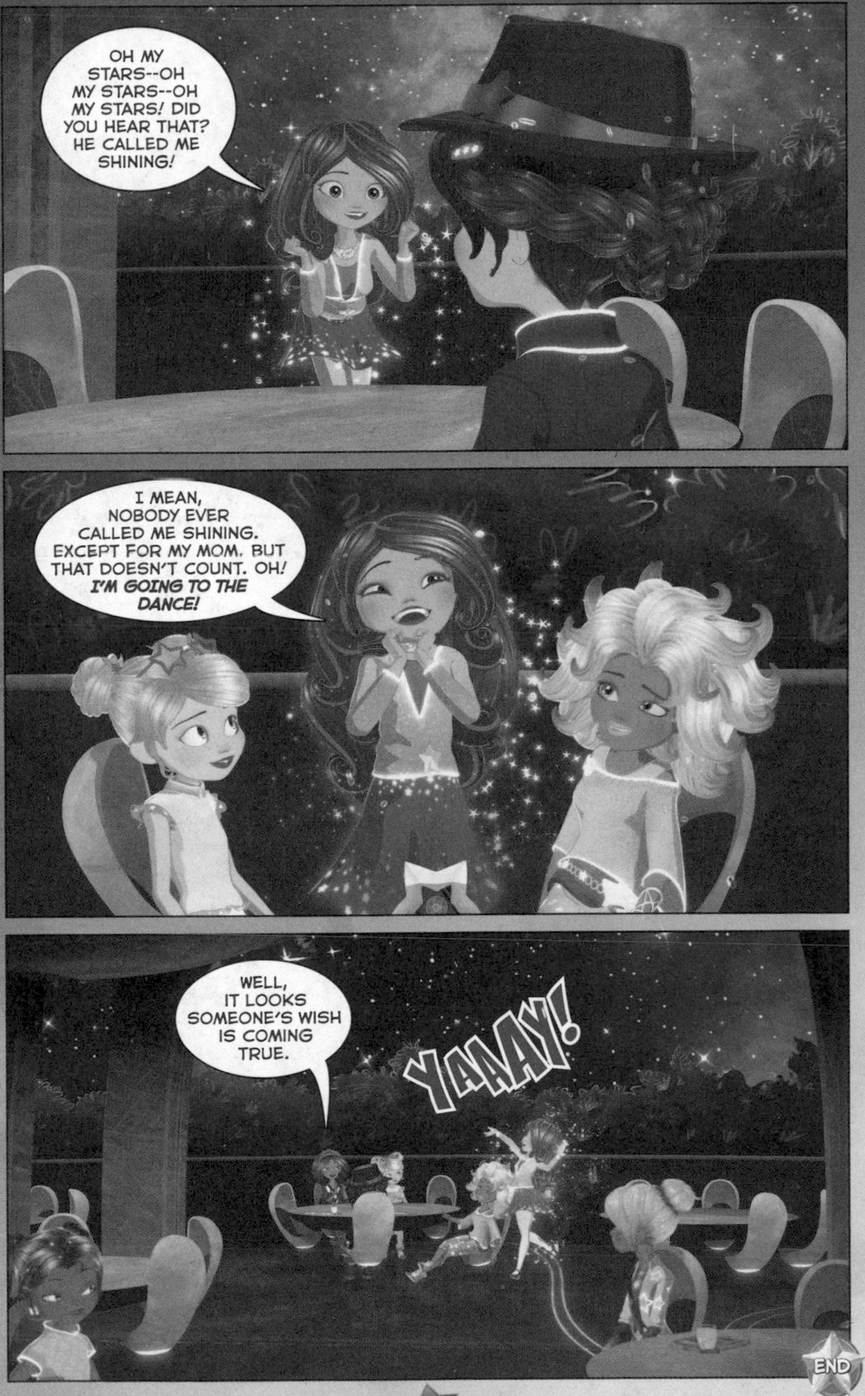
OH MY STARS--OH MY STARS--OH MY STARS! DID YOU HEAR THAT? HE CALLED ME SHINING!
I MEAN, NOBODY EVER CALLED ME SHINING. EXCEPT FOR MY MOM. BUT THAT DOESN'T COUNT. OH! *I'M GOING TO THE DANCE!*
WELL, IT LOOKS SOMEONE'S WISH IS COMING TRUE.
YAAAY!
END

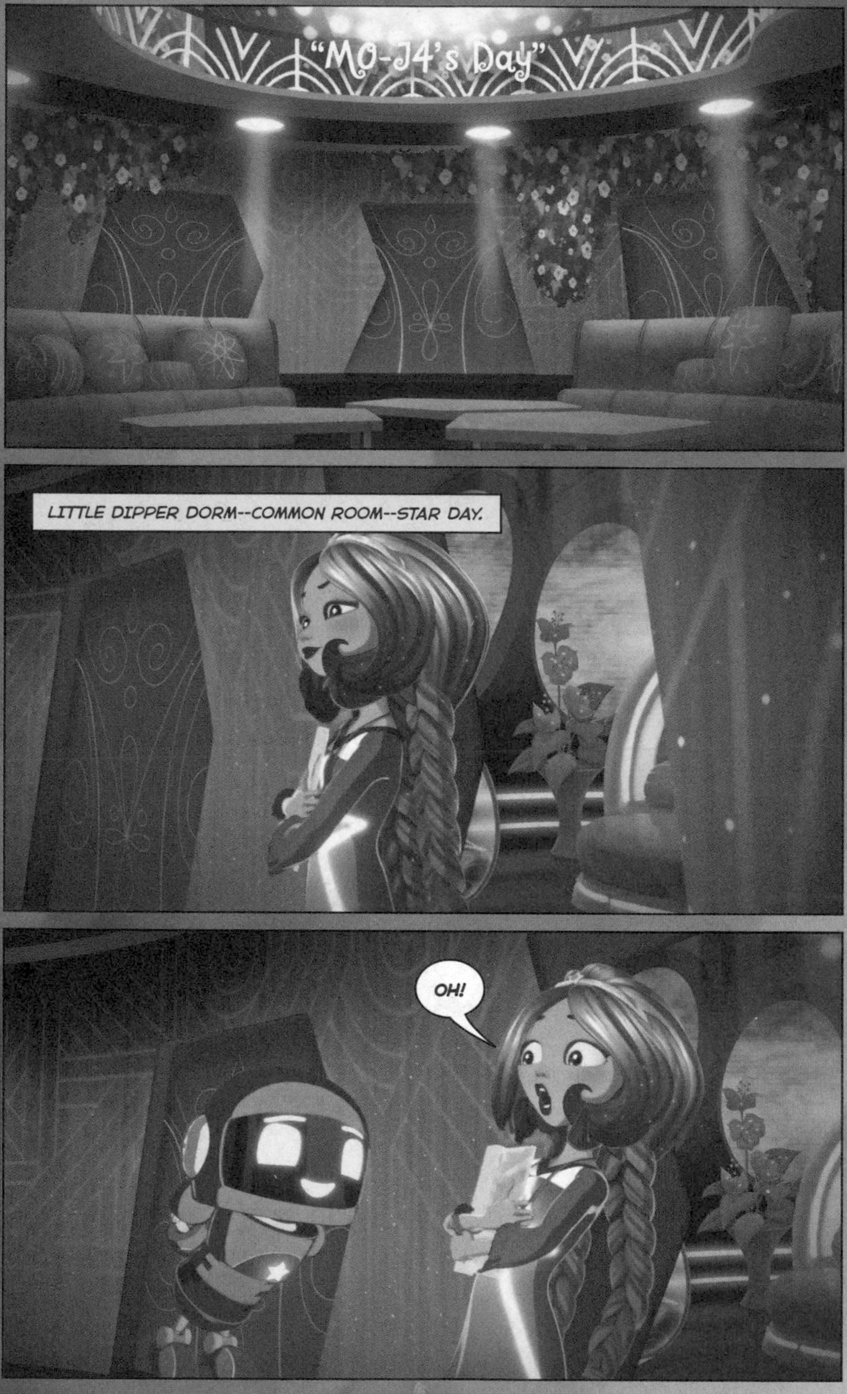
"MO-J4's Day"
LITTLE DIPPER DORM--COMMON ROOM--STAR DAY.
OH!

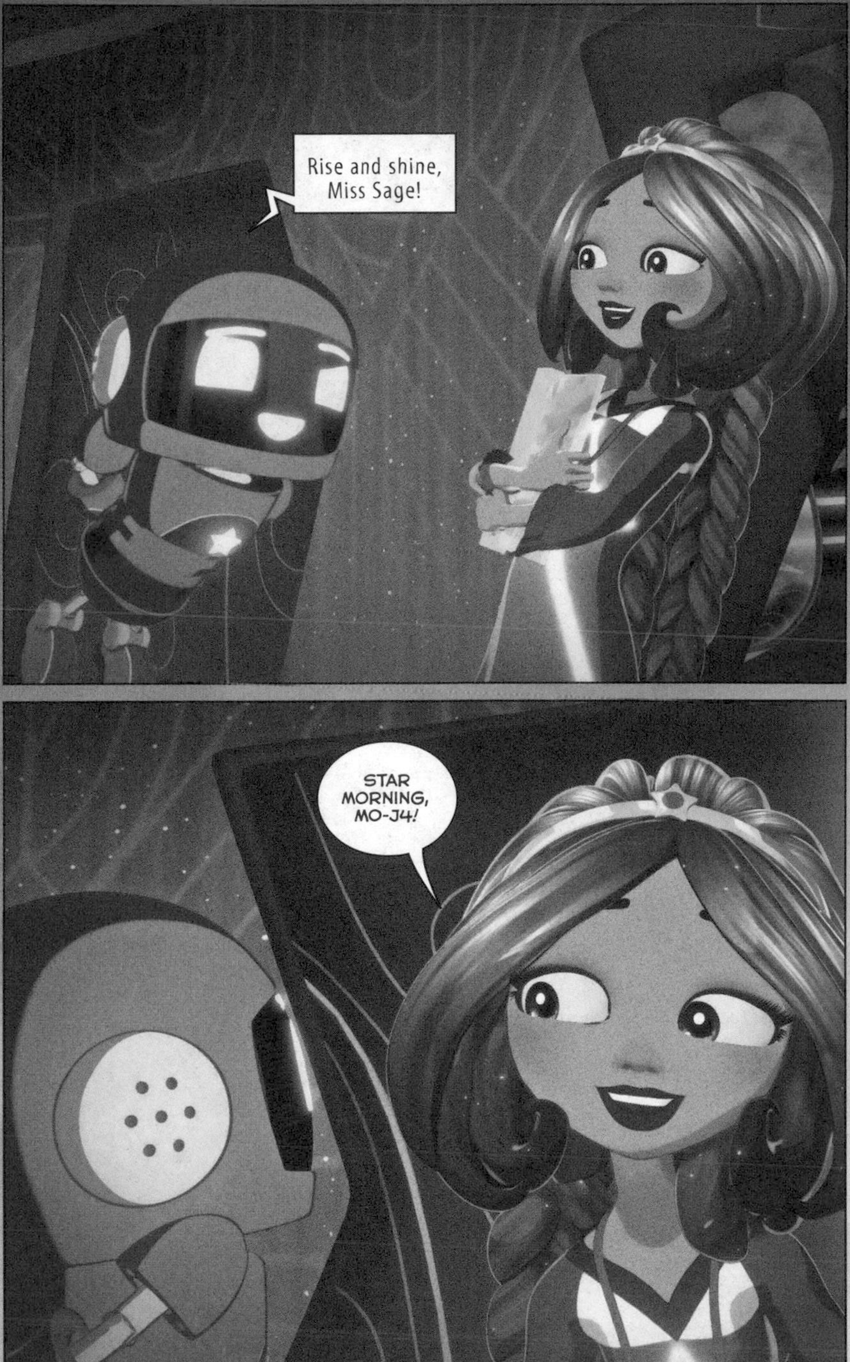
Rise and shine, Miss Sage!
STAR MORNING, MO-J4!

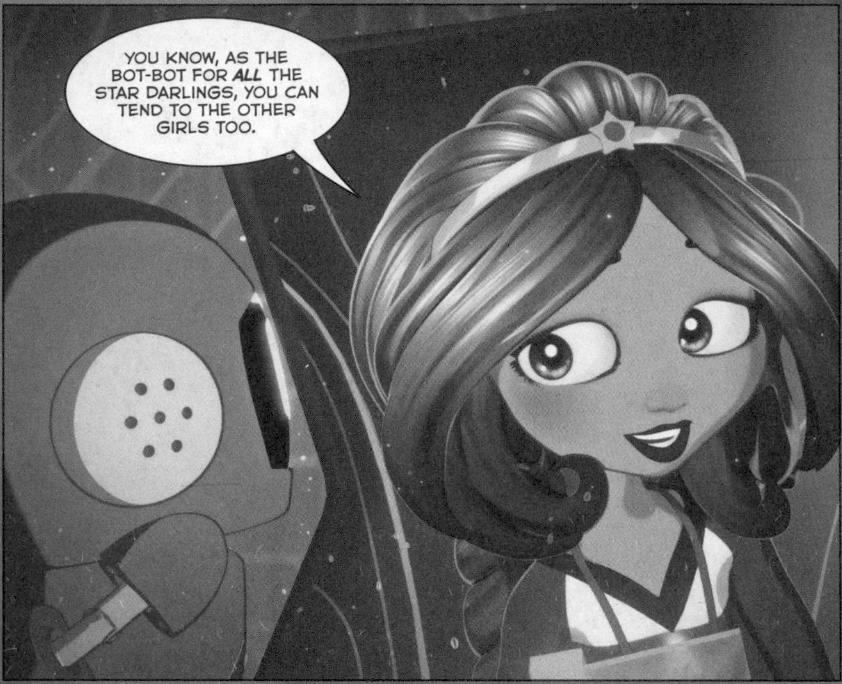
YOU KNOW, AS THE BOT-BOT FOR ALL THE STAR DARLINGS, YOU CAN TEND TO THE OTHER GIRLS TOO.

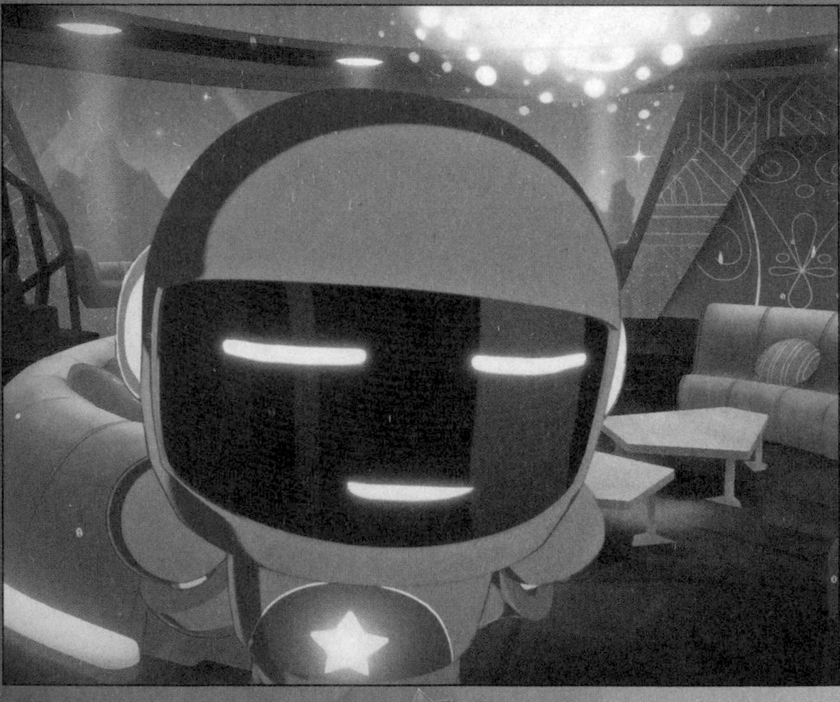

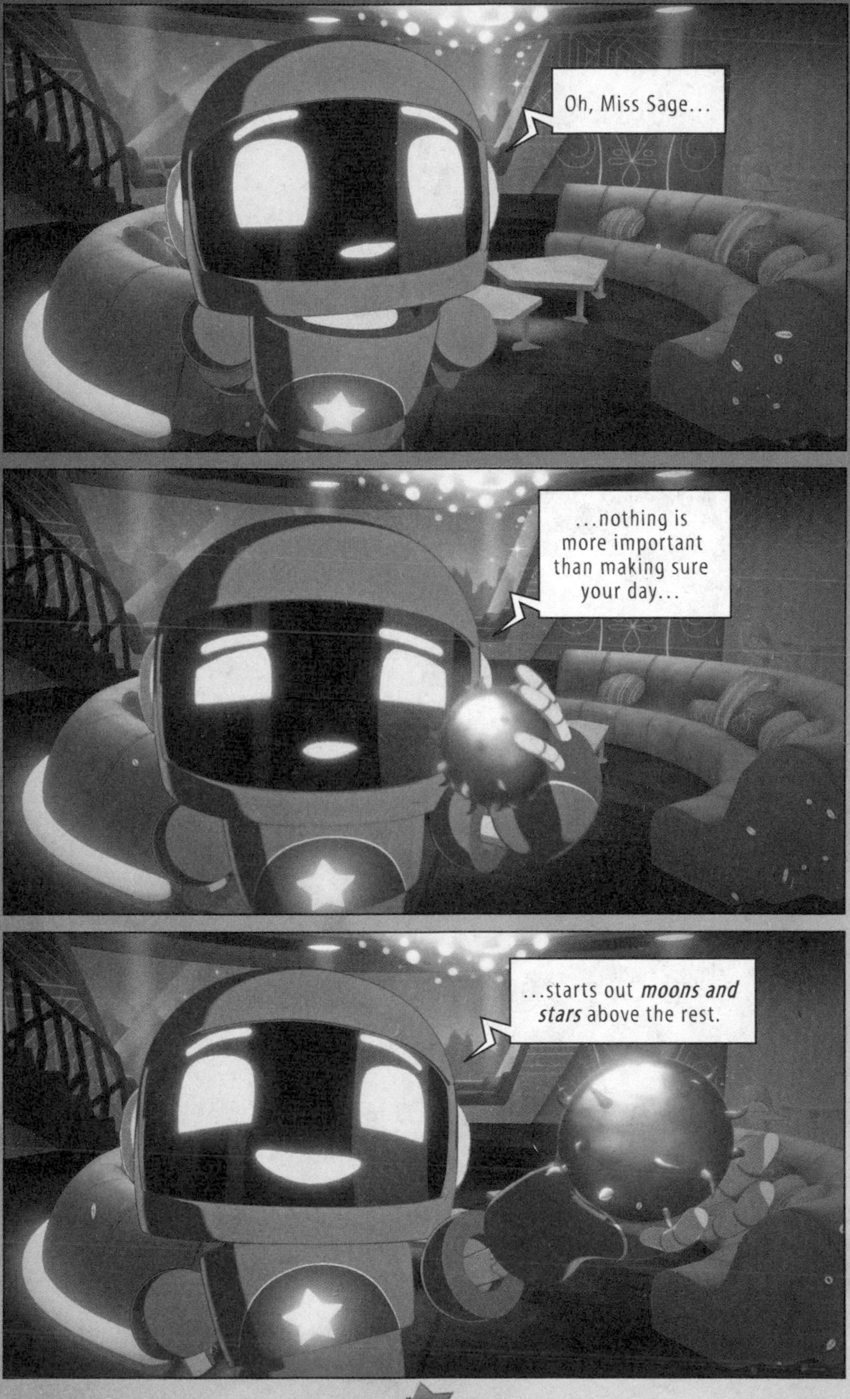
Oh, Miss Sage…
…nothing is more important than making sure your day…
…starts out *moons and stars* above the rest.

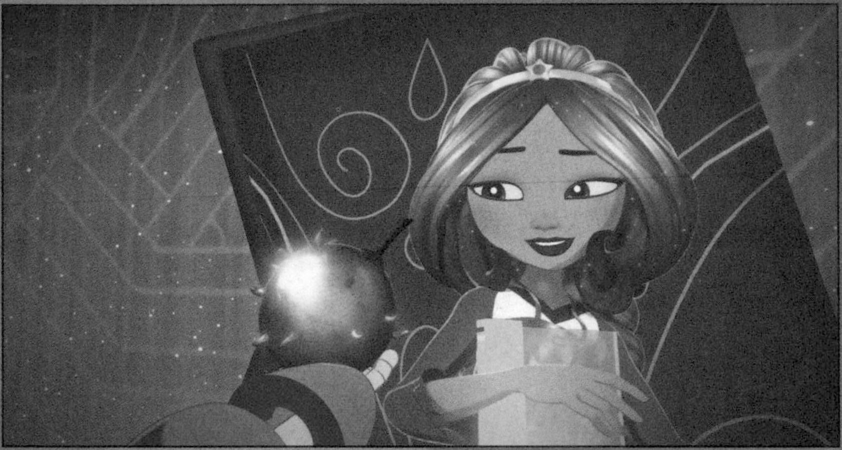

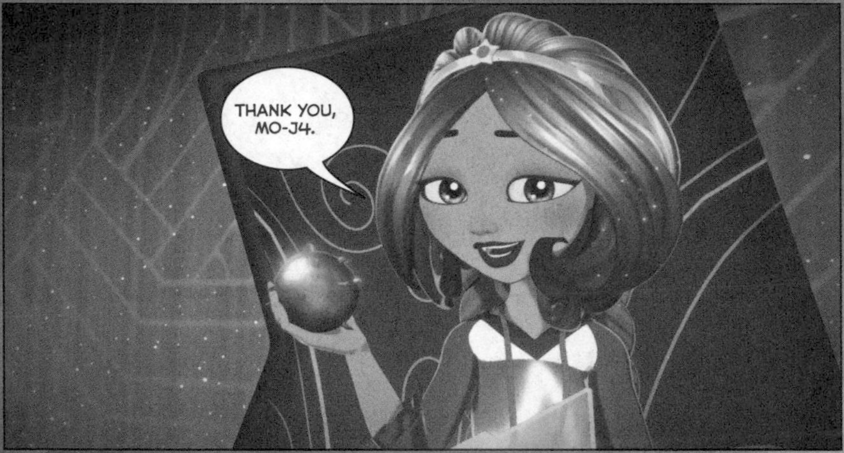
THANK YOU, MO-J4.

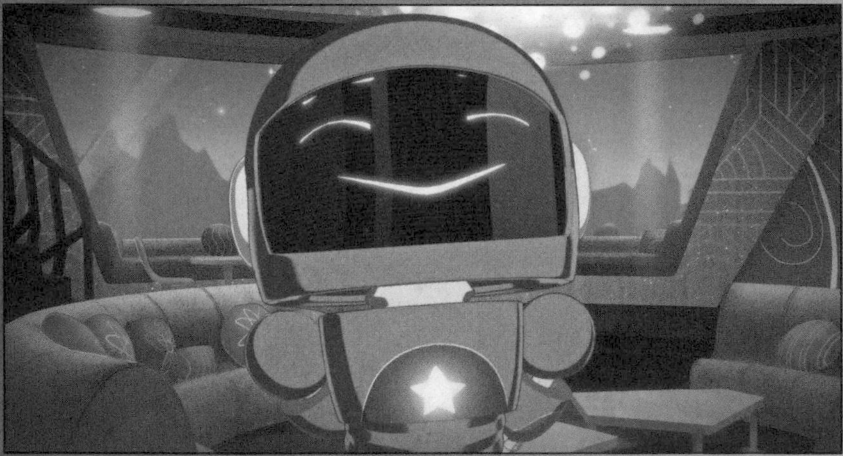

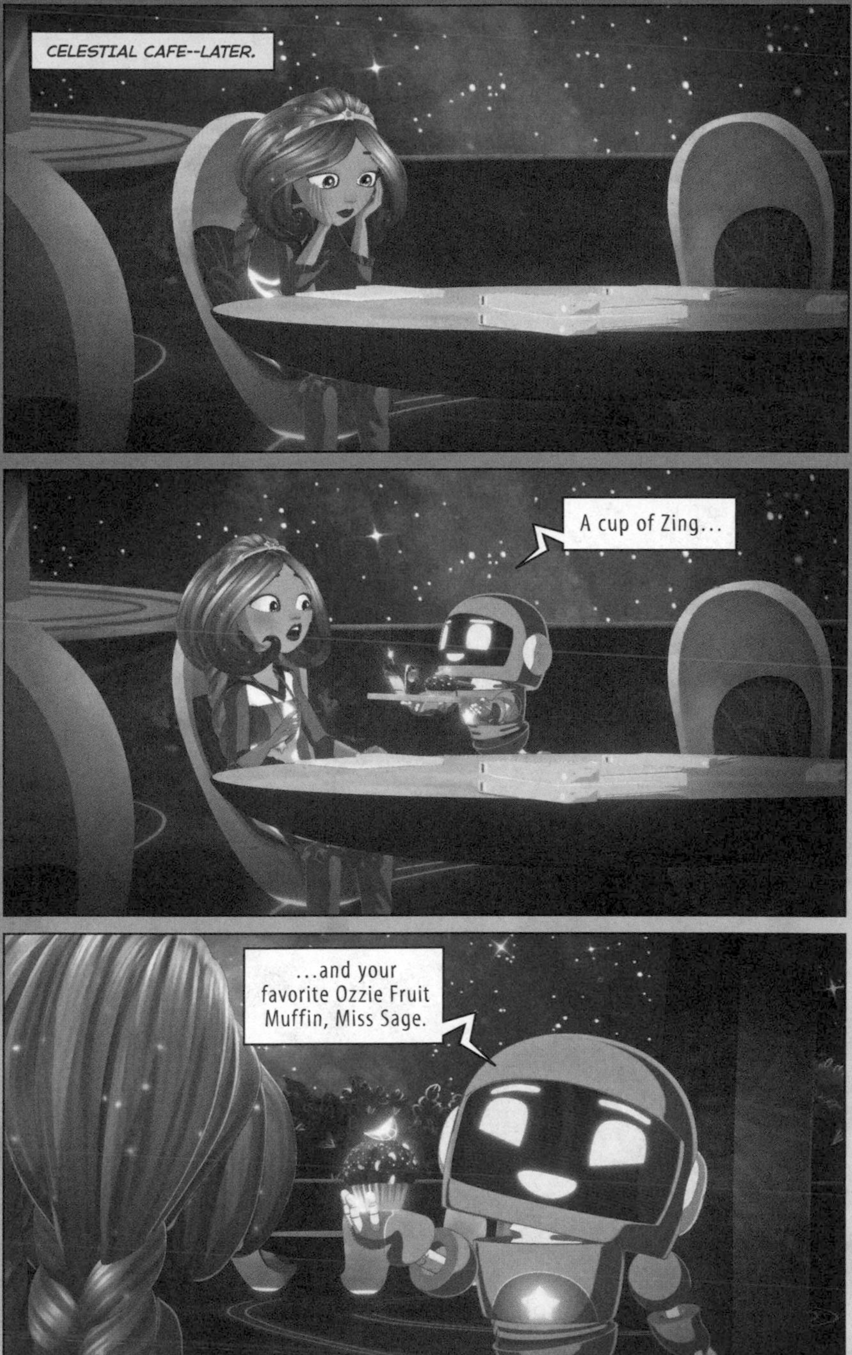
CELESTIAL CAFE--LATER.
A cup of Zing...
...and your favorite Ozzie Fruit Muffin, Miss Sage.

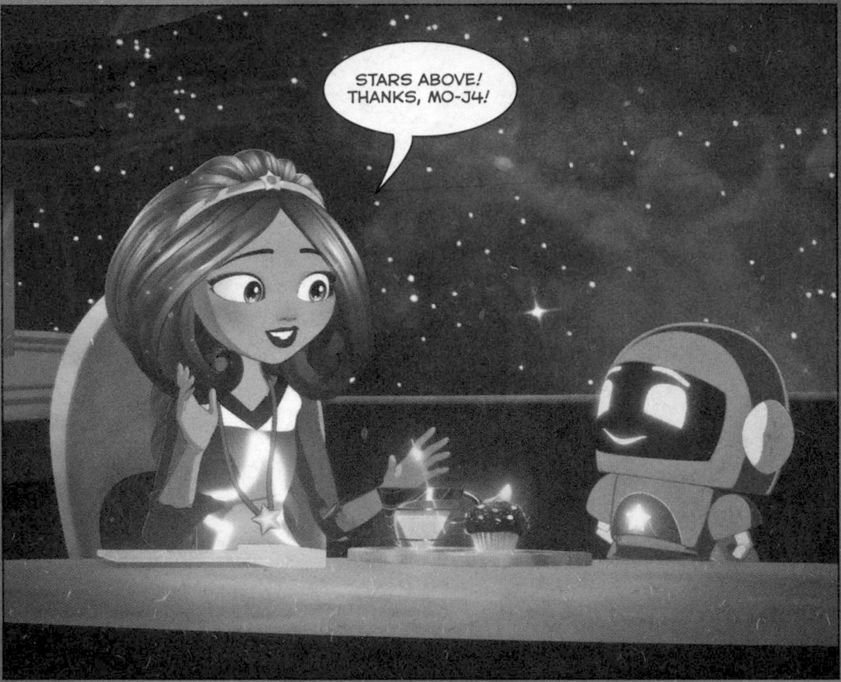
STARS ABOVE! THANKS, MO-J4!

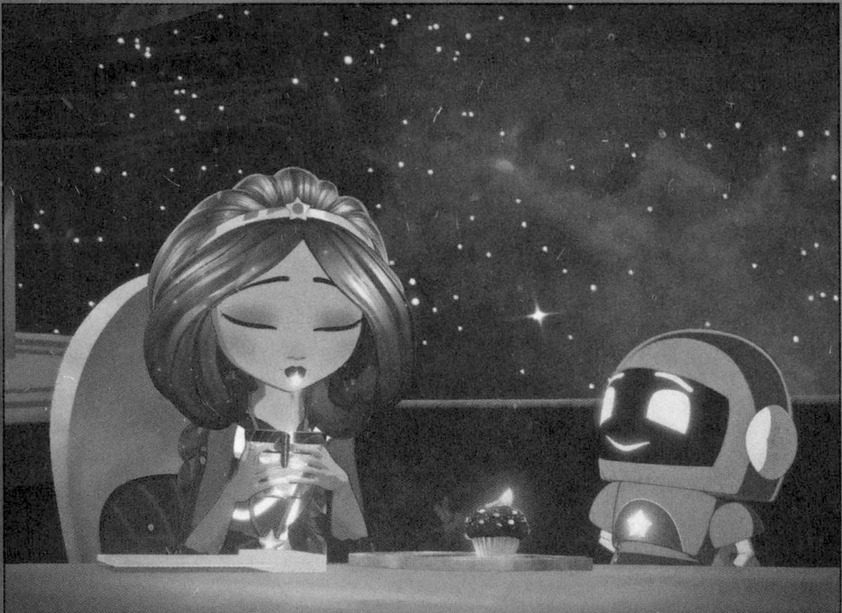

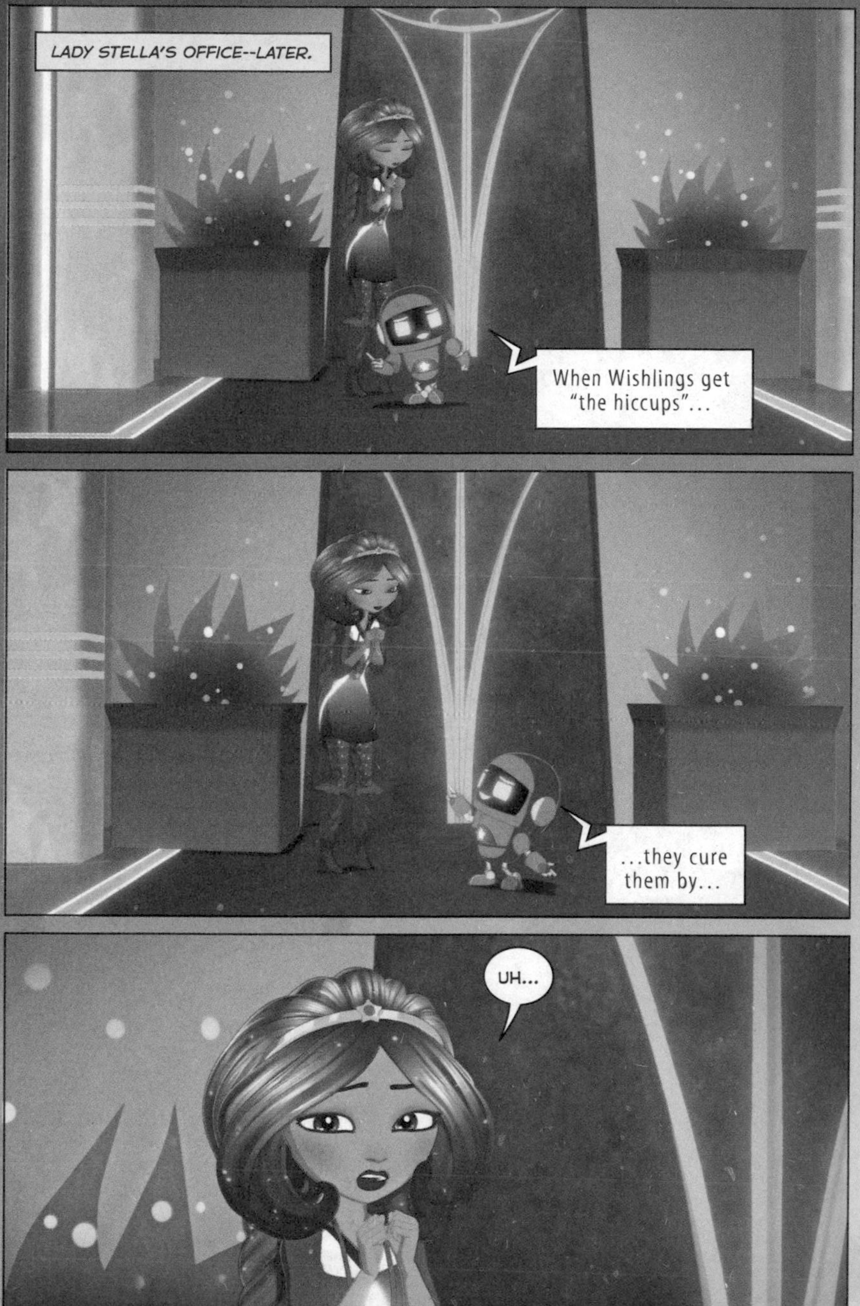
LADY STELLA'S OFFICE--LATER.
When Wishlings get "the hiccups"...
...they cure them by...
UH...

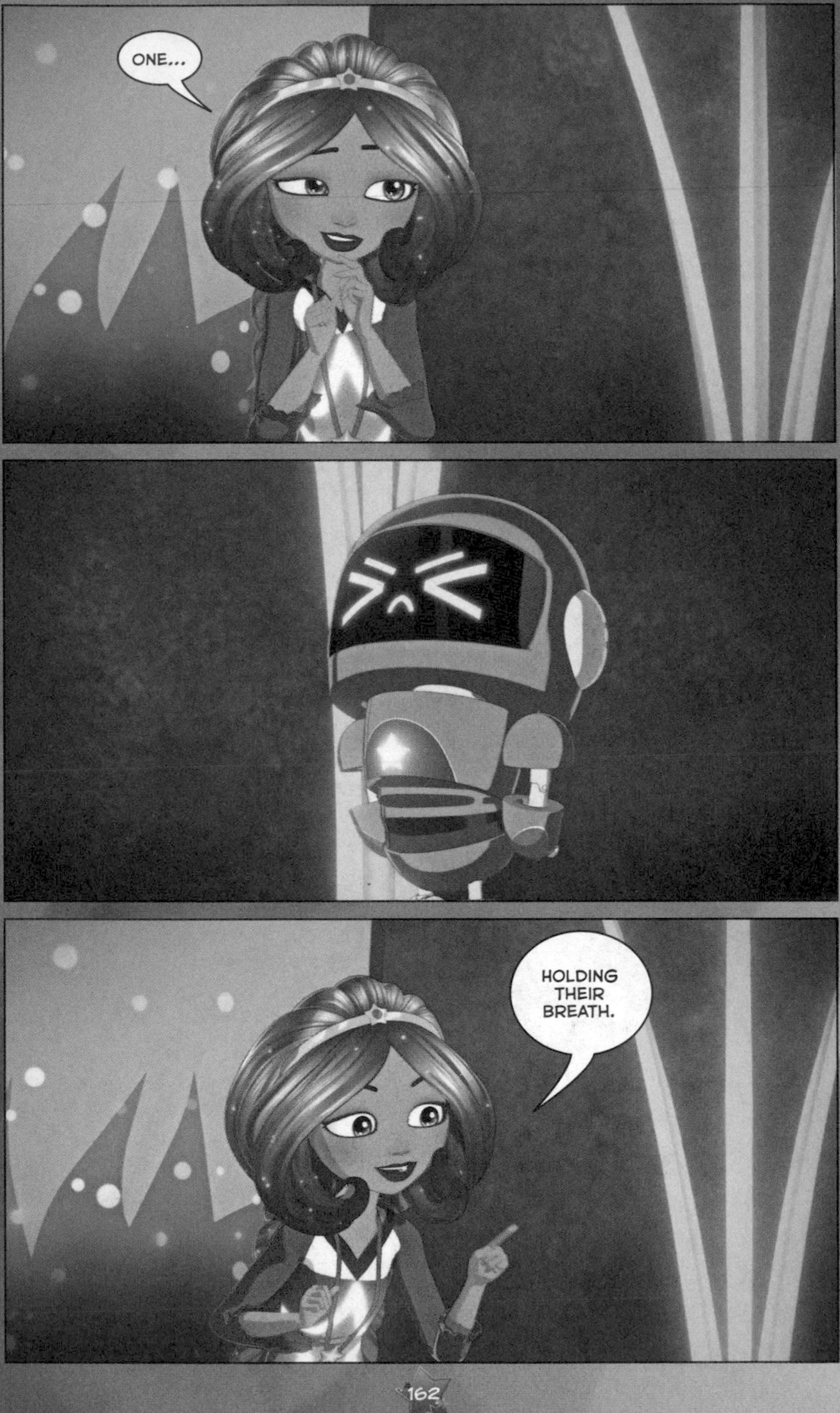
ONE...
HOLDING THEIR BREATH.

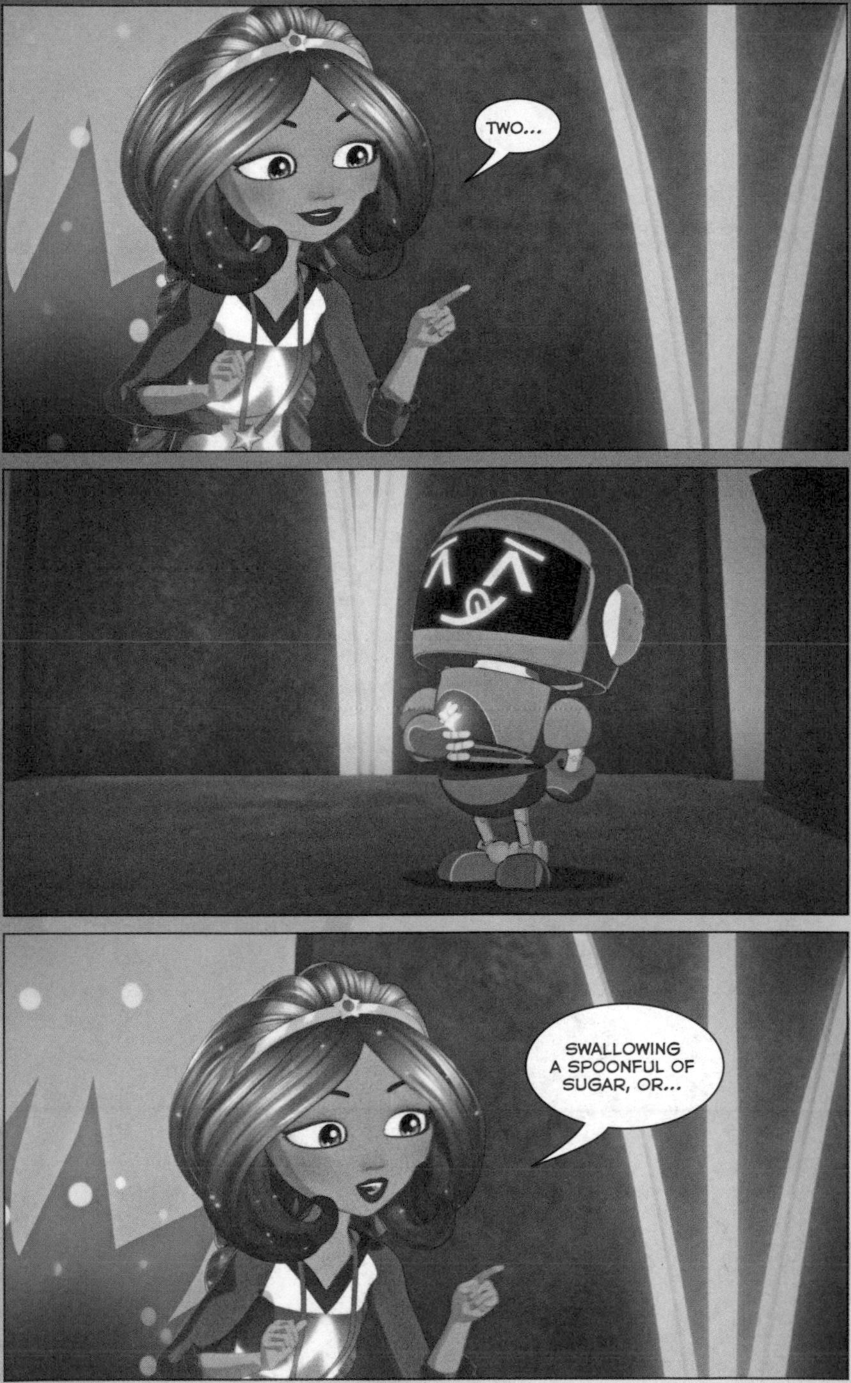
TWO...
SWALLOWING A SPOONFUL OF SUGAR, OR...

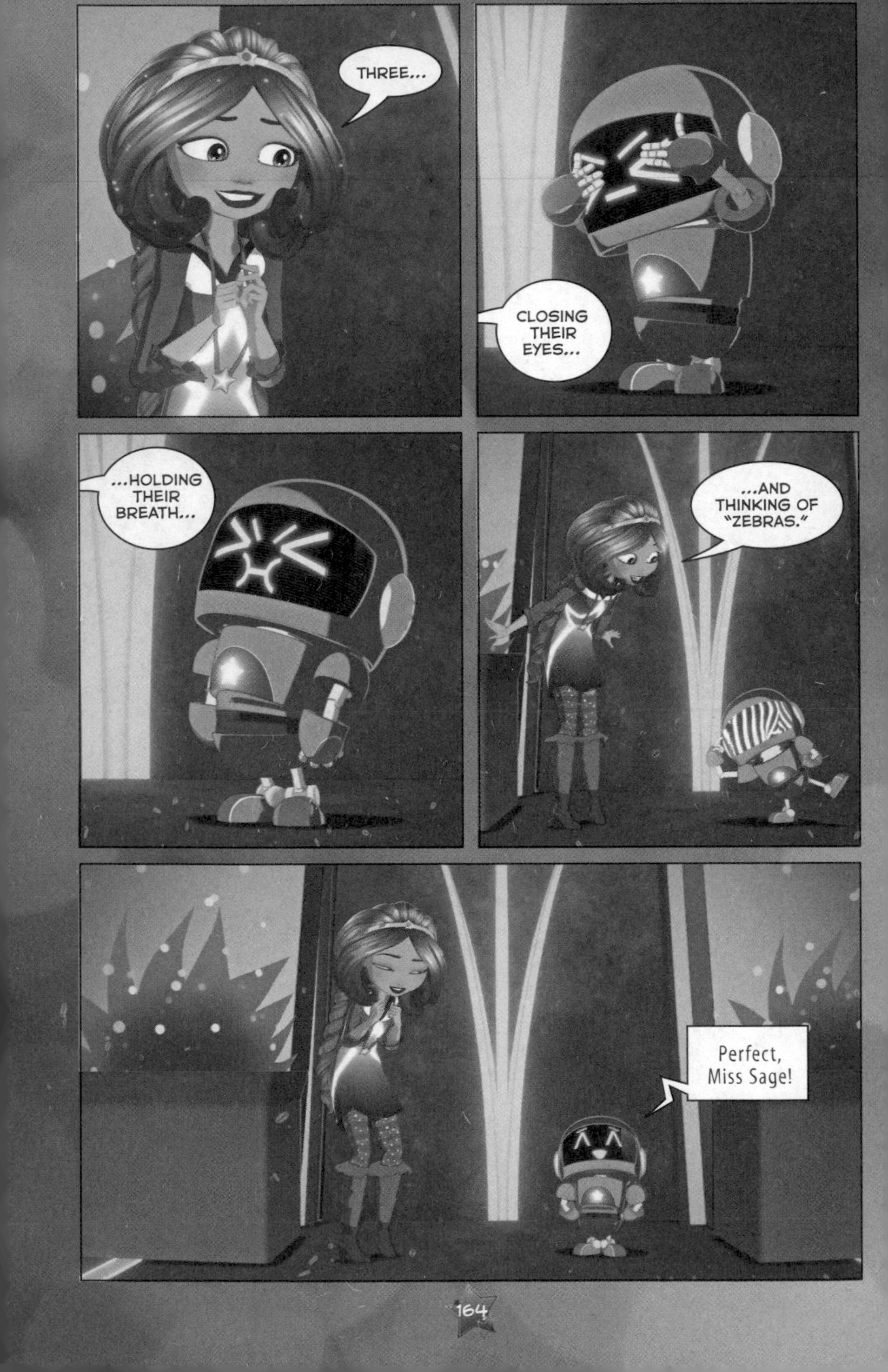
THREE...
CLOSING THEIR EYES...
...HOLDING THEIR BREATH...
...AND THINKING OF "ZEBRAS."
Perfect, Miss Sage!

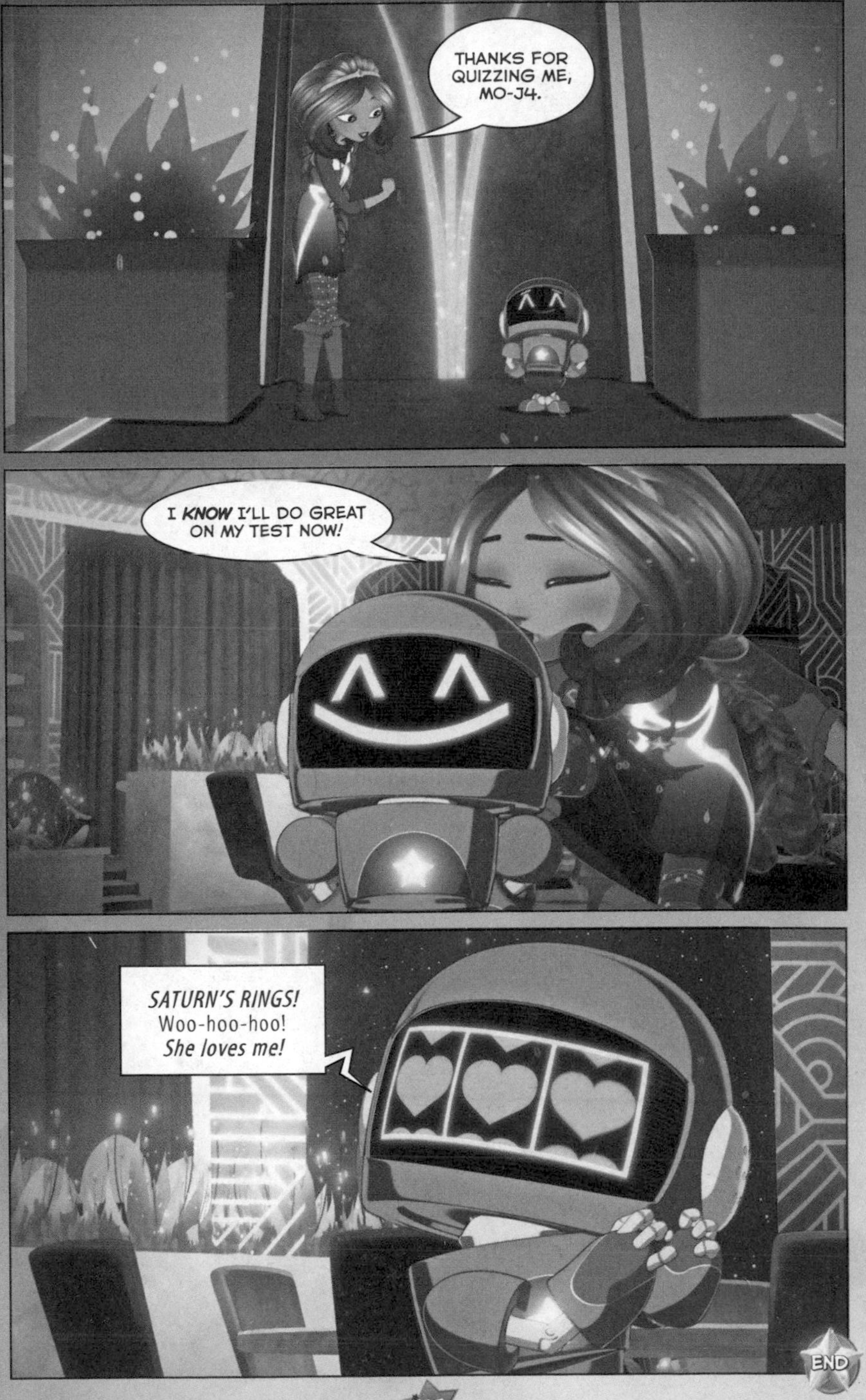
THANKS FOR QUIZZING ME, MO-J4.
I *KNOW* I'LL DO GREAT ON MY TEST NOW!
SATURN'S RINGS! Woo-hoo-hoo! *She loves me!*
END

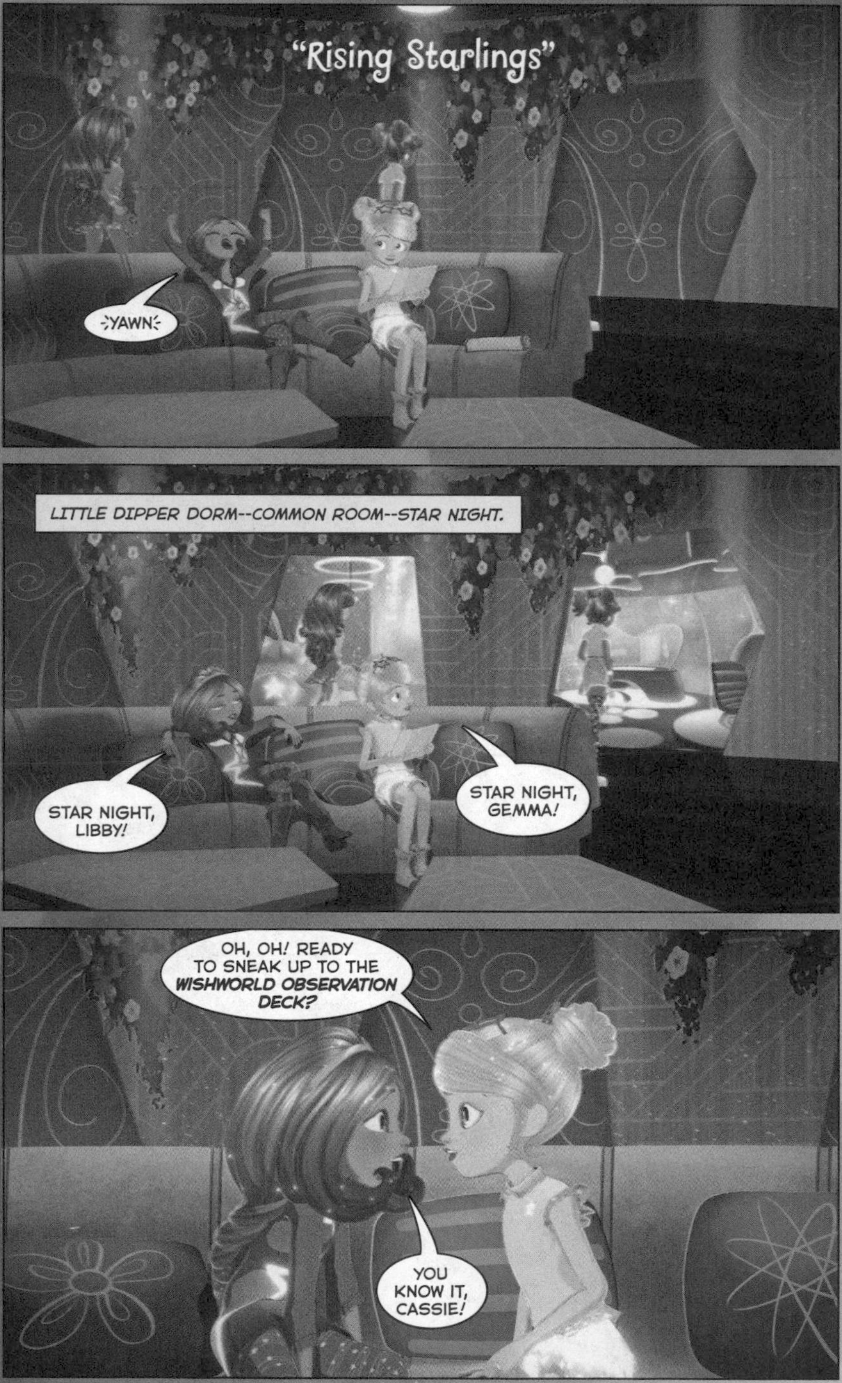
"Rising Starlings"
YAWN
LITTLE DIPPER DORM--COMMON ROOM--STAR NIGHT.
STAR NIGHT, LIBBY!
STAR NIGHT, GEMMA!
OH, OH! READY TO SNEAK UP TO THE WISHWORLD OBSERVATION DECK?
YOU KNOW IT, CASSIE!

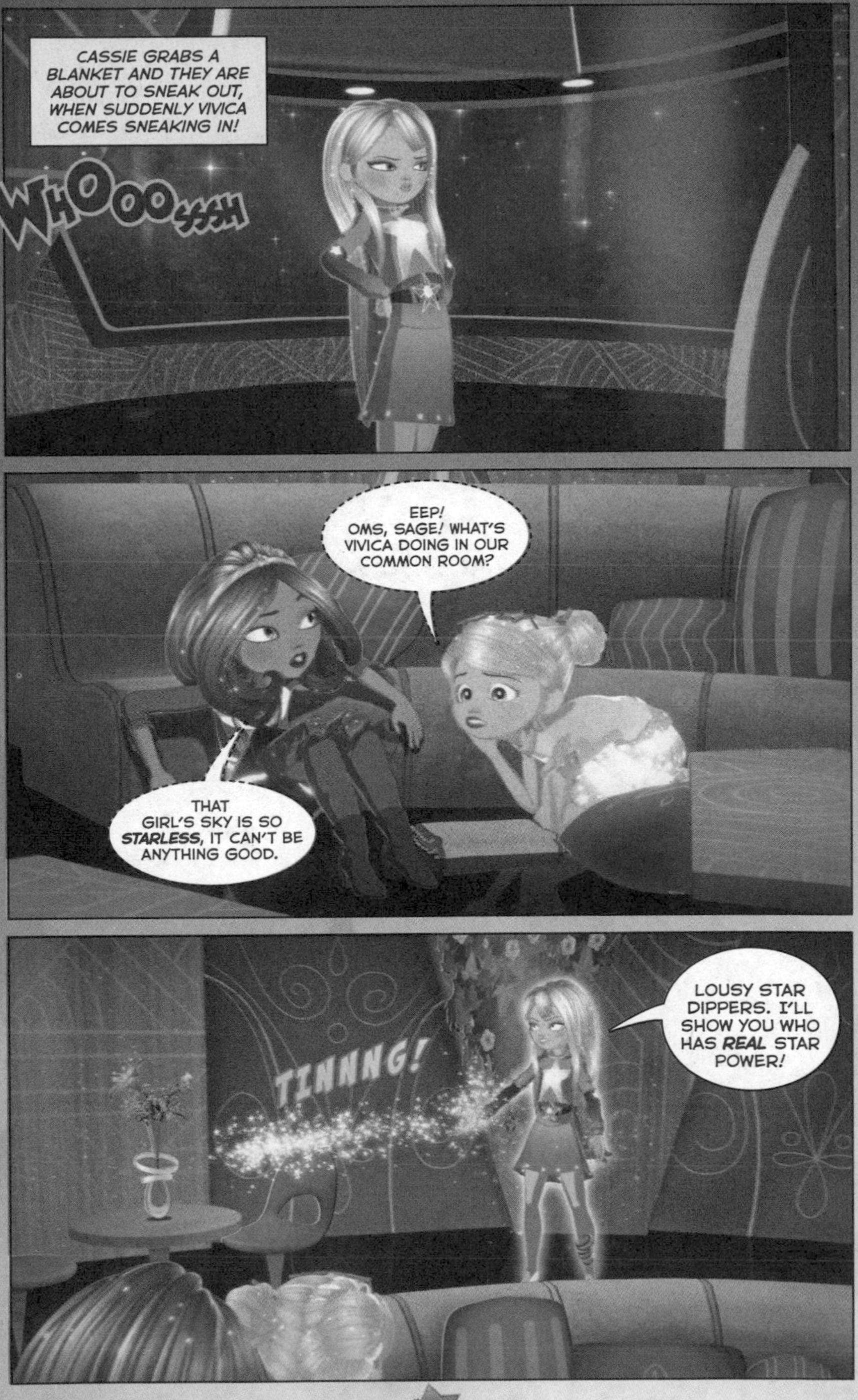
CASSIE GRABS A BLANKET AND THEY ARE ABOUT TO SNEAK OUT, WHEN SUDDENLY VIVICA COMES SNEAKING IN!
WHOOOOSSSH
EEP! OMS, SAGE! WHAT'S VIVICA DOING IN OUR COMMON ROOM?
THAT GIRL'S SKY IS SO STARLESS, IT CAN'T BE ANYTHING GOOD.
TINNNG!
LOUSY STAR DIPPERS. I'LL SHOW YOU WHO HAS REAL STAR POWER!

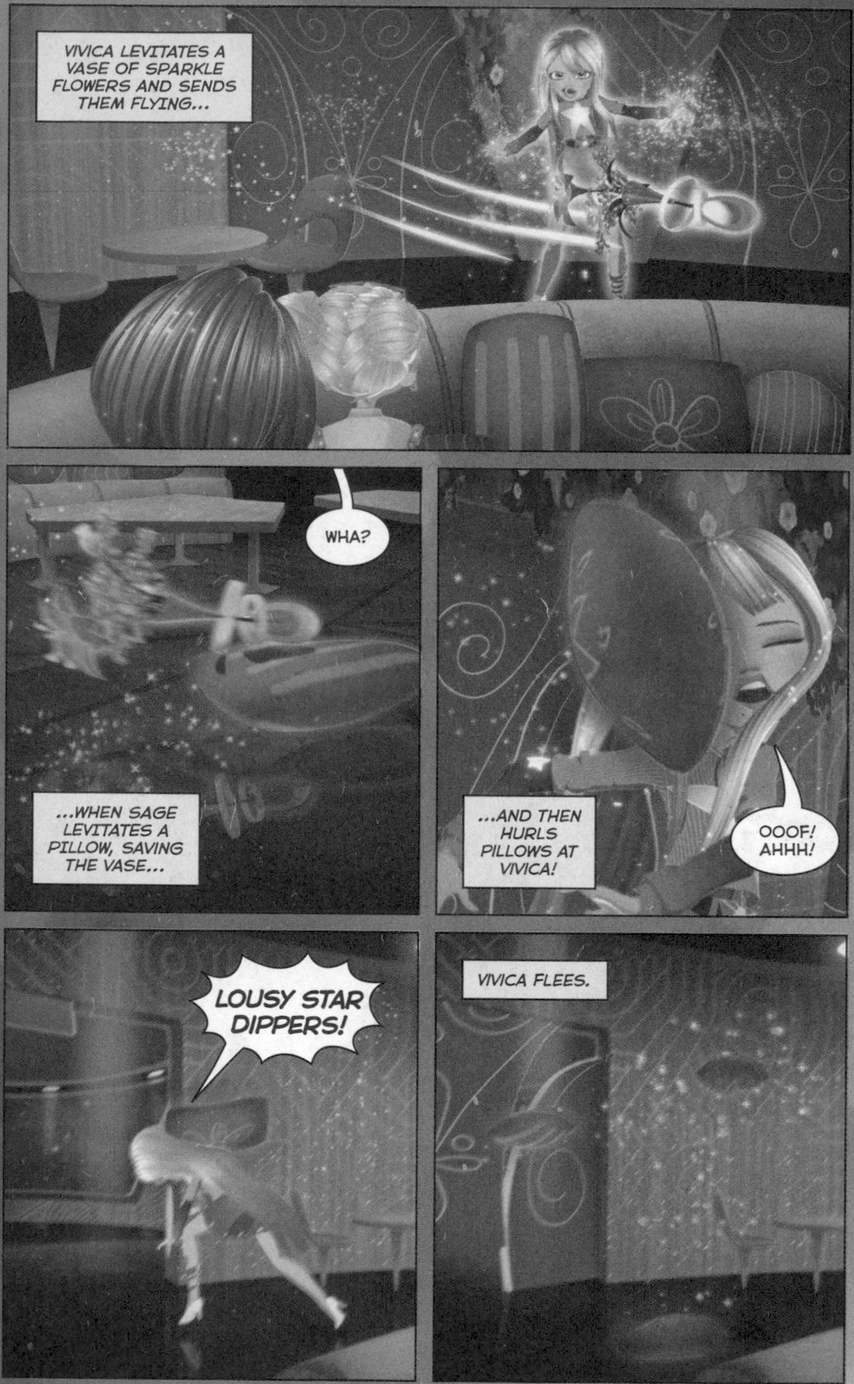
VIVICA LEVITATES A VASE OF SPARKLE FLOWERS AND SENDS THEM FLYING...
WHA?
...WHEN SAGE LEVITATES A PILLOW, SAVING THE VASE...
...AND THEN HURLS PILLOWS AT VIVICA!
OOOF! AHHH!
LOUSY STAR DIPPERS!
VIVICA FLEES.

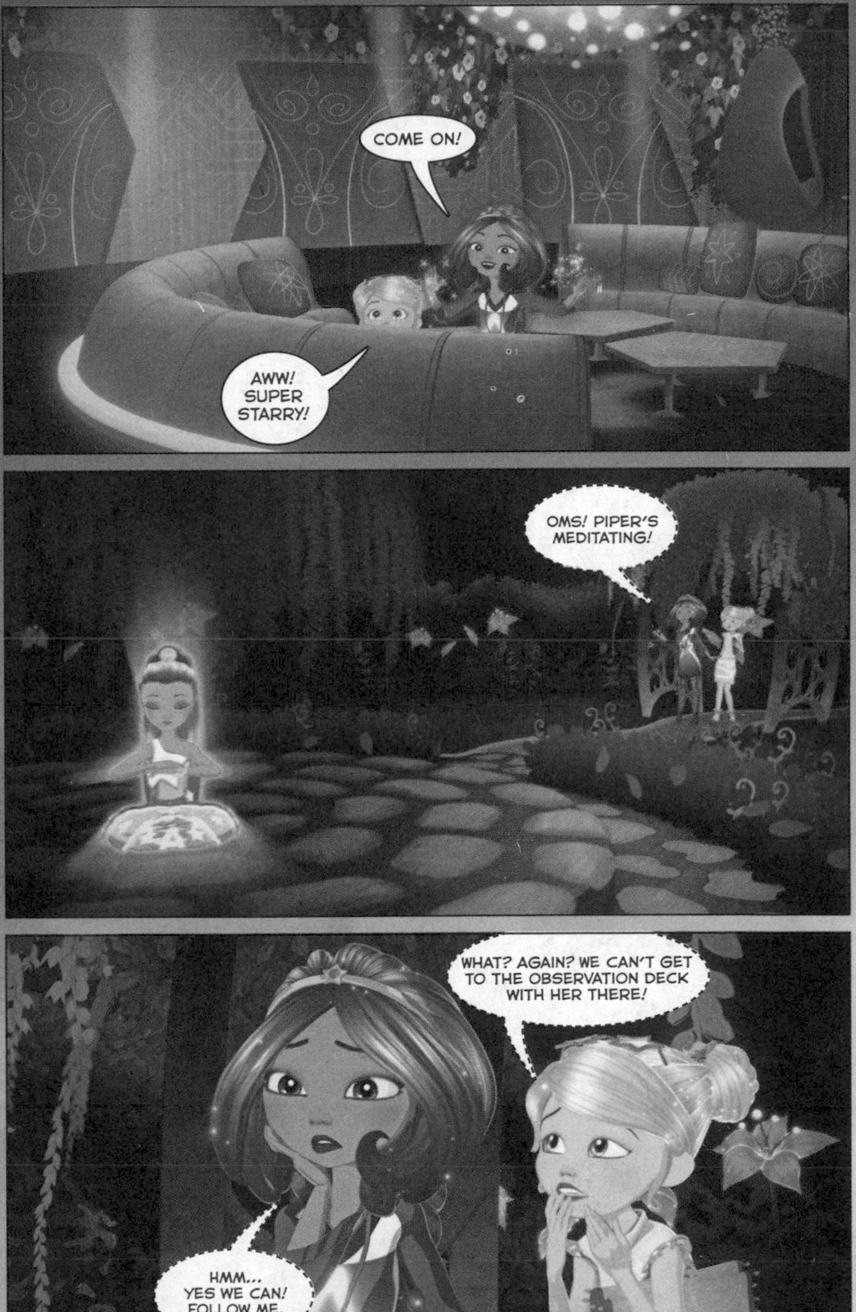
COME ON!
AWW! SUPER STARRY!
OMS! PIPER'S MEDITATING!
WHAT? AGAIN? WE CAN'T GET TO THE OBSERVATION DECK WITH HER THERE!
HMM... YES WE CAN! FOLLOW ME.

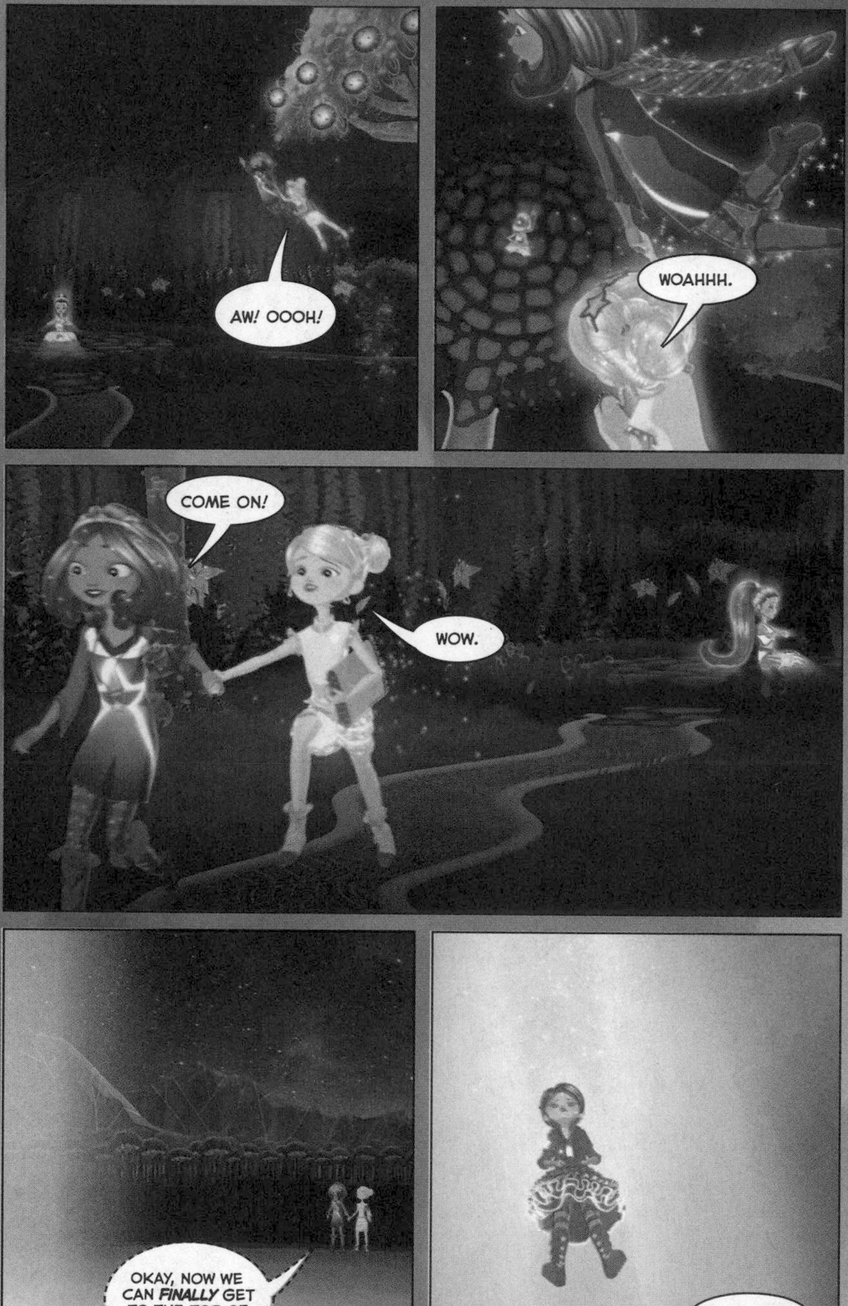
AW! OOOH!
WOAHHH.
COME ON!
WOW.
OKAY, NOW WE CAN *FINALLY* GET TO THE TOP OF THE DECK!
SCARLET?

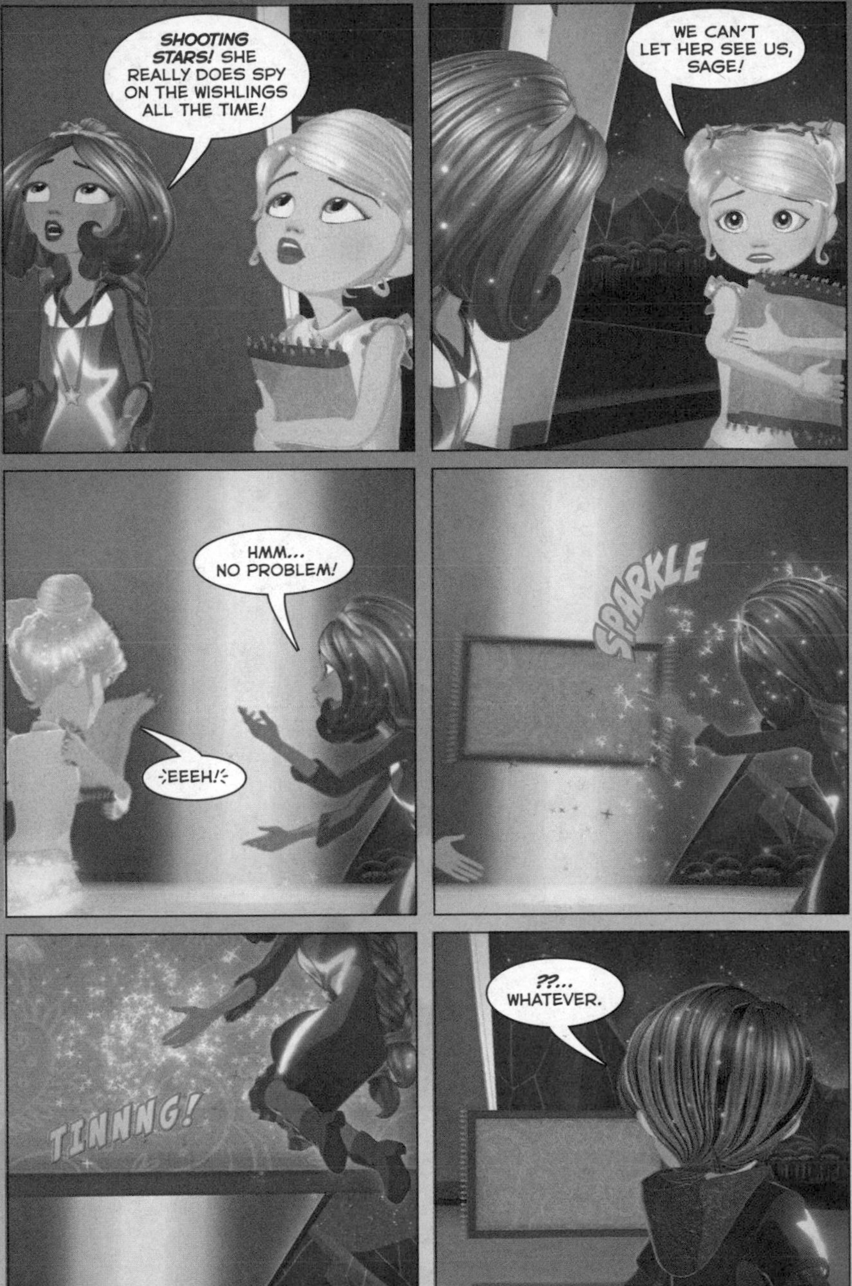
SHOOTING STARS! SHE REALLY DOES SPY ON THE WISHLINGS ALL THE TIME!
WE CAN'T LET HER SEE US, SAGE!
HMM... NO PROBLEM!
EEEH!
SPARKLE
TINNNG!
??... WHATEVER.

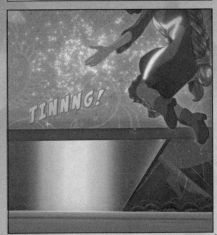

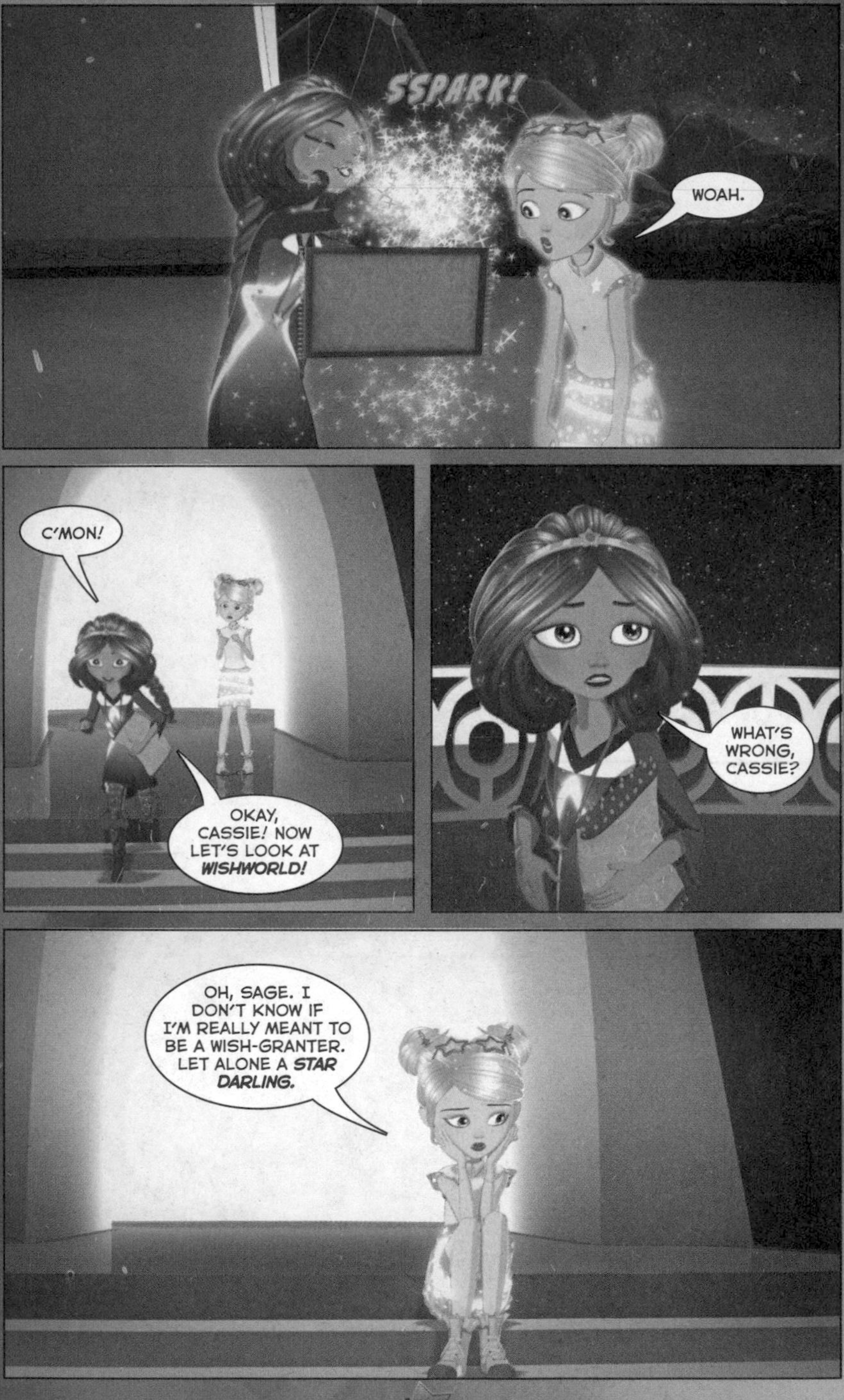
SSPARK!
WOAH.
C'MON!
OKAY, CASSIE! NOW LET'S LOOK AT WISHWORLD!
WHAT'S WRONG, CASSIE?
OH, SAGE. I DON'T KNOW IF I'M REALLY MEANT TO BE A WISH-GRANTER. LET ALONE A STAR DARLING.

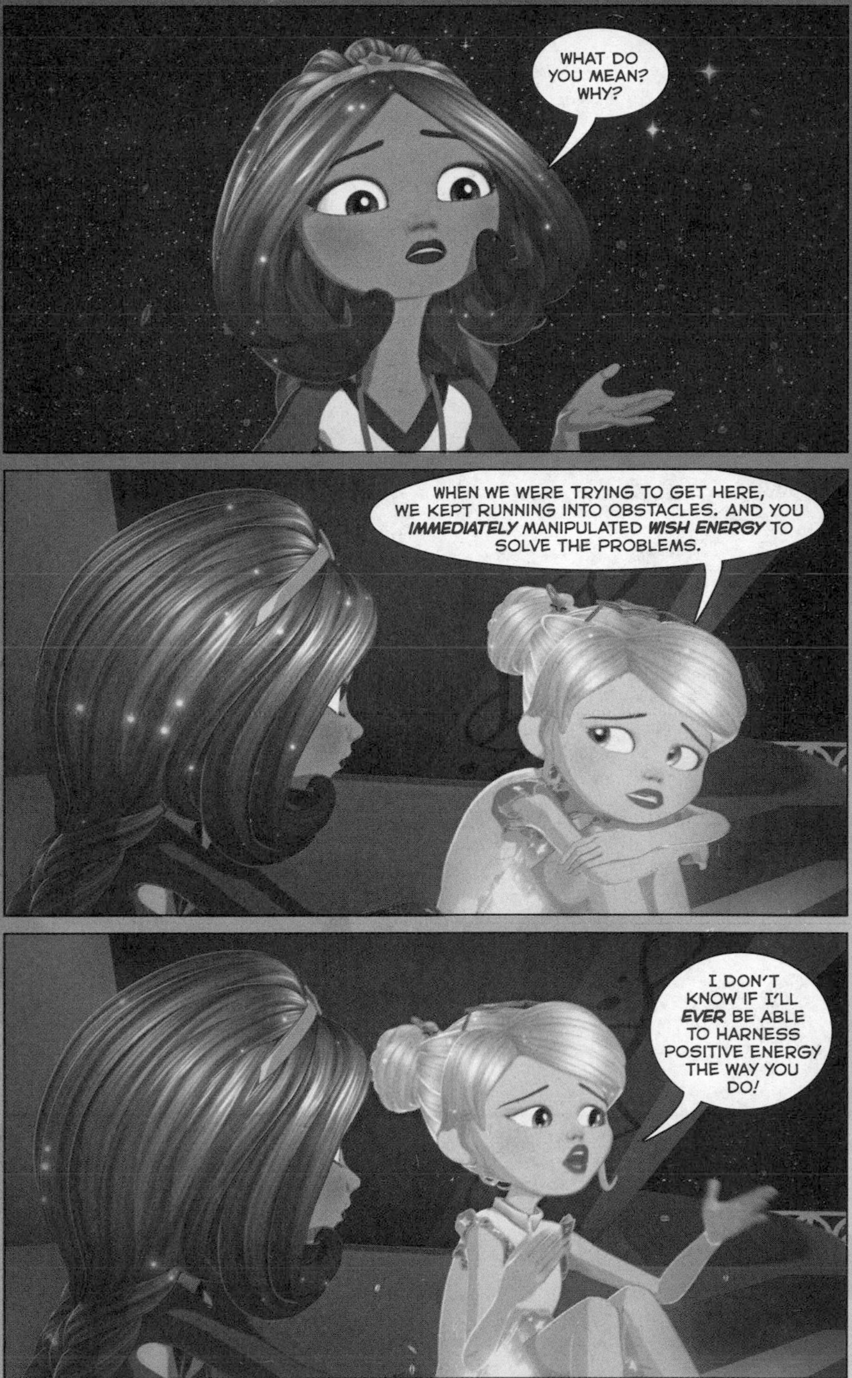
WHAT DO YOU MEAN? WHY?
WHEN WE WERE TRYING TO GET HERE, WE KEPT RUNNING INTO OBSTACLES. AND YOU ***IMMEDIATELY*** MANIPULATED ***WISH ENERGY*** TO SOLVE THE PROBLEMS.
I DON'T KNOW IF I'LL ***EVER*** BE ABLE TO HARNESS POSITIVE ENERGY THE WAY YOU DO!

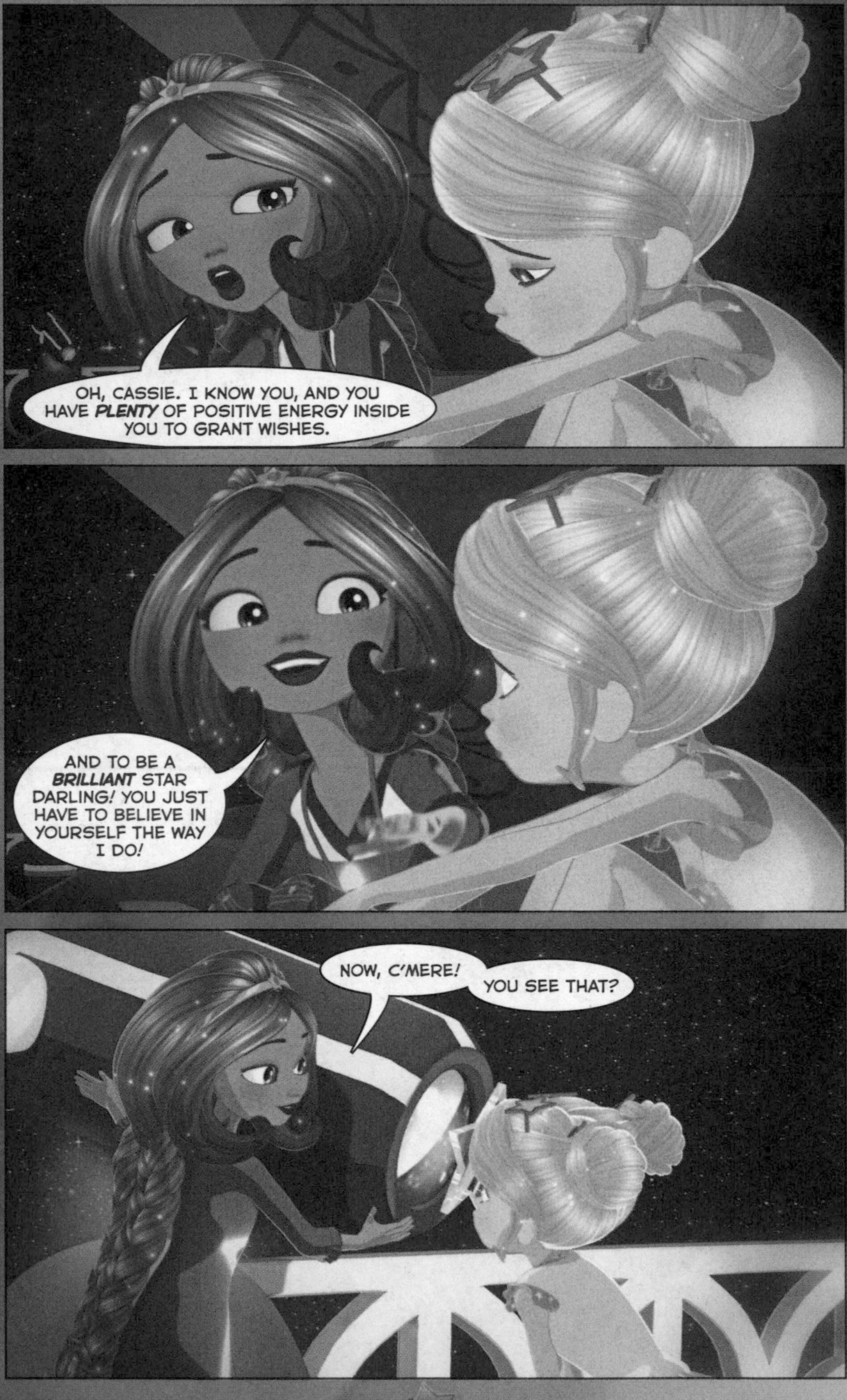
OH, CASSIE. I KNOW YOU, AND YOU HAVE *PLENTY* OF POSITIVE ENERGY INSIDE YOU TO GRANT WISHES.
AND TO BE A *BRILLIANT* STAR DARLING! YOU JUST HAVE TO BELIEVE IN YOURSELF THE WAY I DO!
NOW, C'MERE!
YOU SEE THAT?

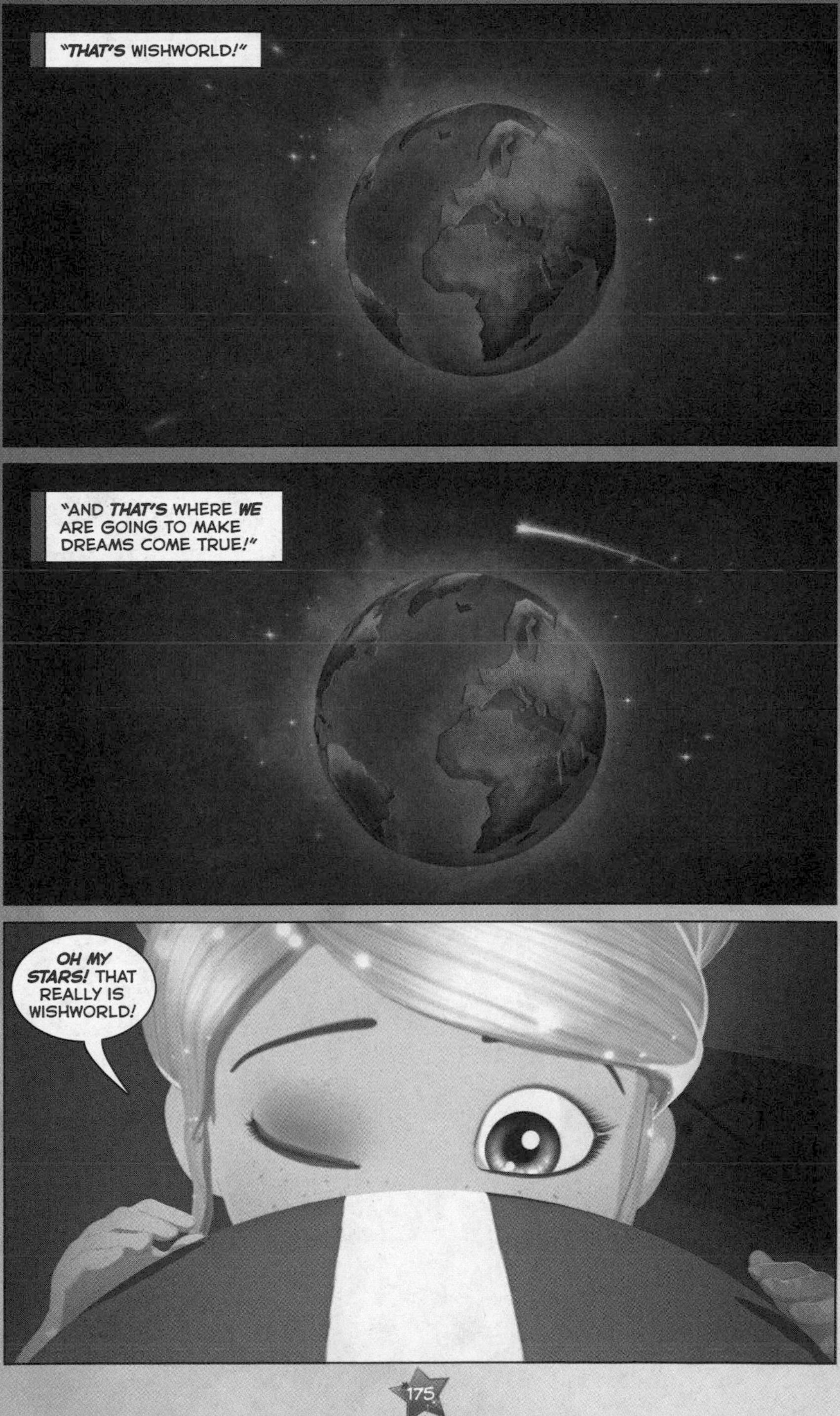
"THAT'S WISHWORLD!"
"AND THAT'S WHERE WE ARE GOING TO MAKE DREAMS COME TRUE!"
OH MY STARS! THAT REALLY IS WISHWORLD!

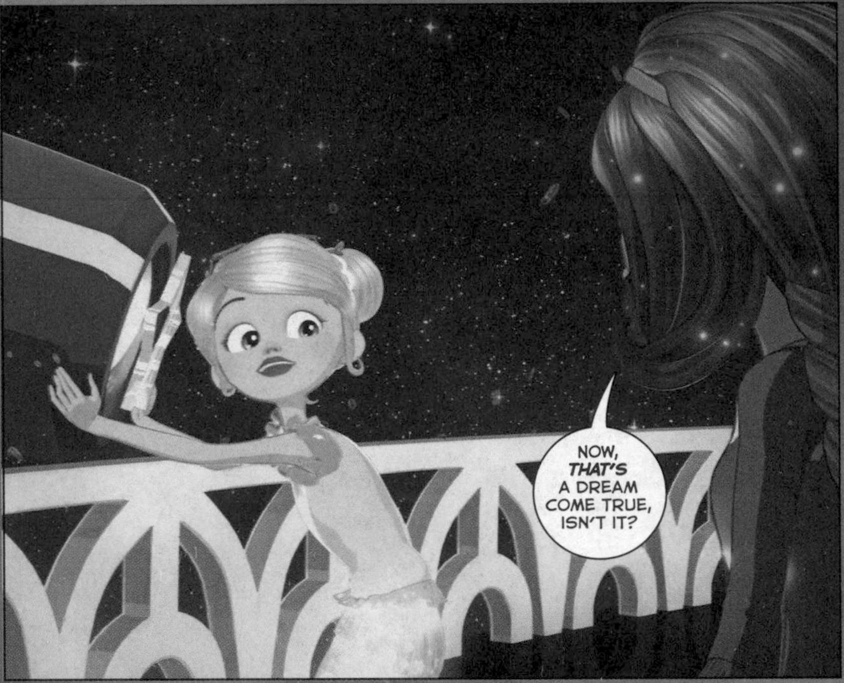
NOW, *THAT'S* A DREAM COME TRUE, ISN'T IT?

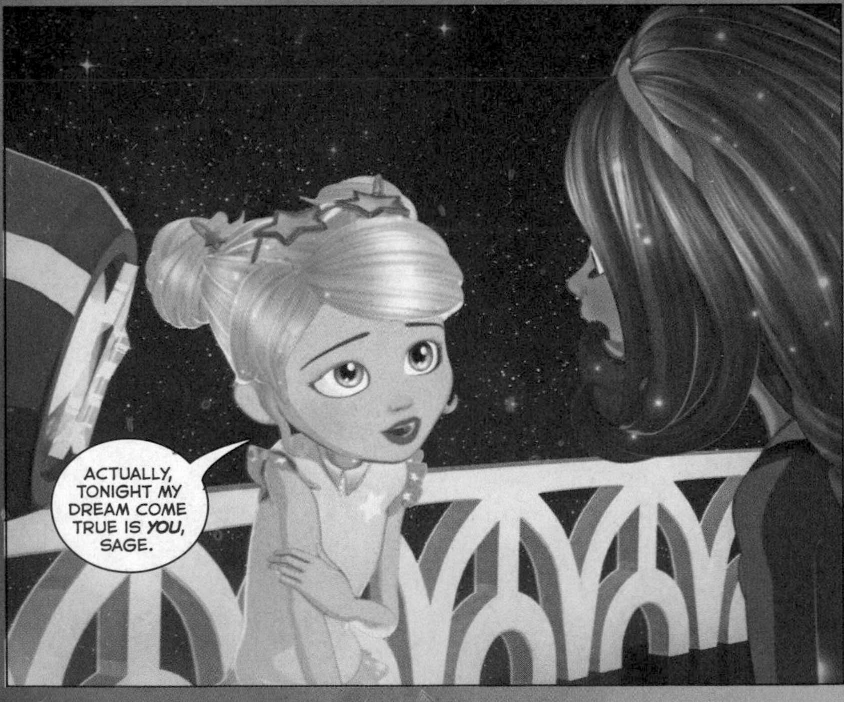
ACTUALLY, TONIGHT MY DREAM COME TRUE IS *YOU*, SAGE.

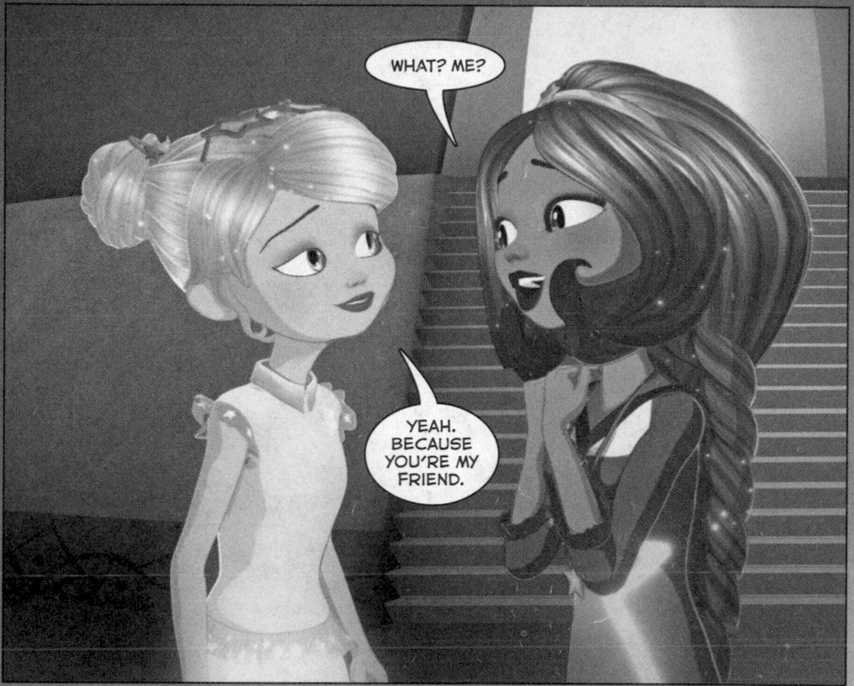
WHAT? ME?
YEAH. BECAUSE YOU'RE MY FRIEND.

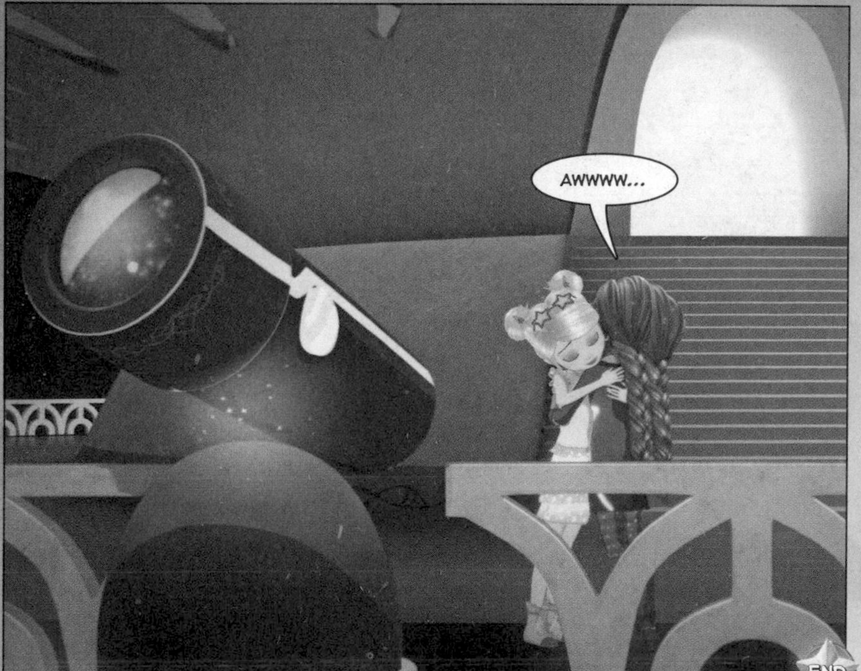
AWWWW...
END

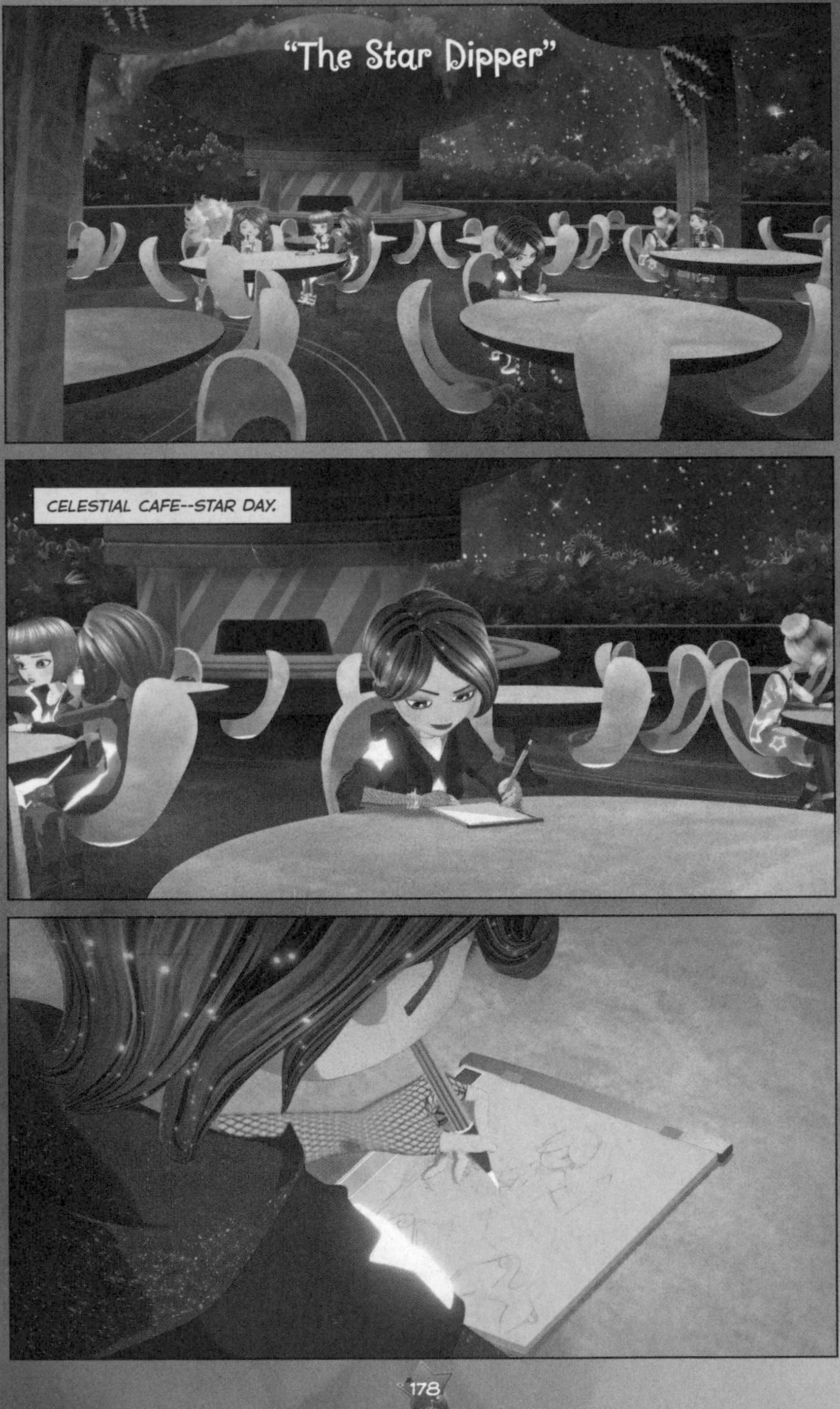
"The Star Dipper"
CELESTIAL CAFE--STAR DAY.

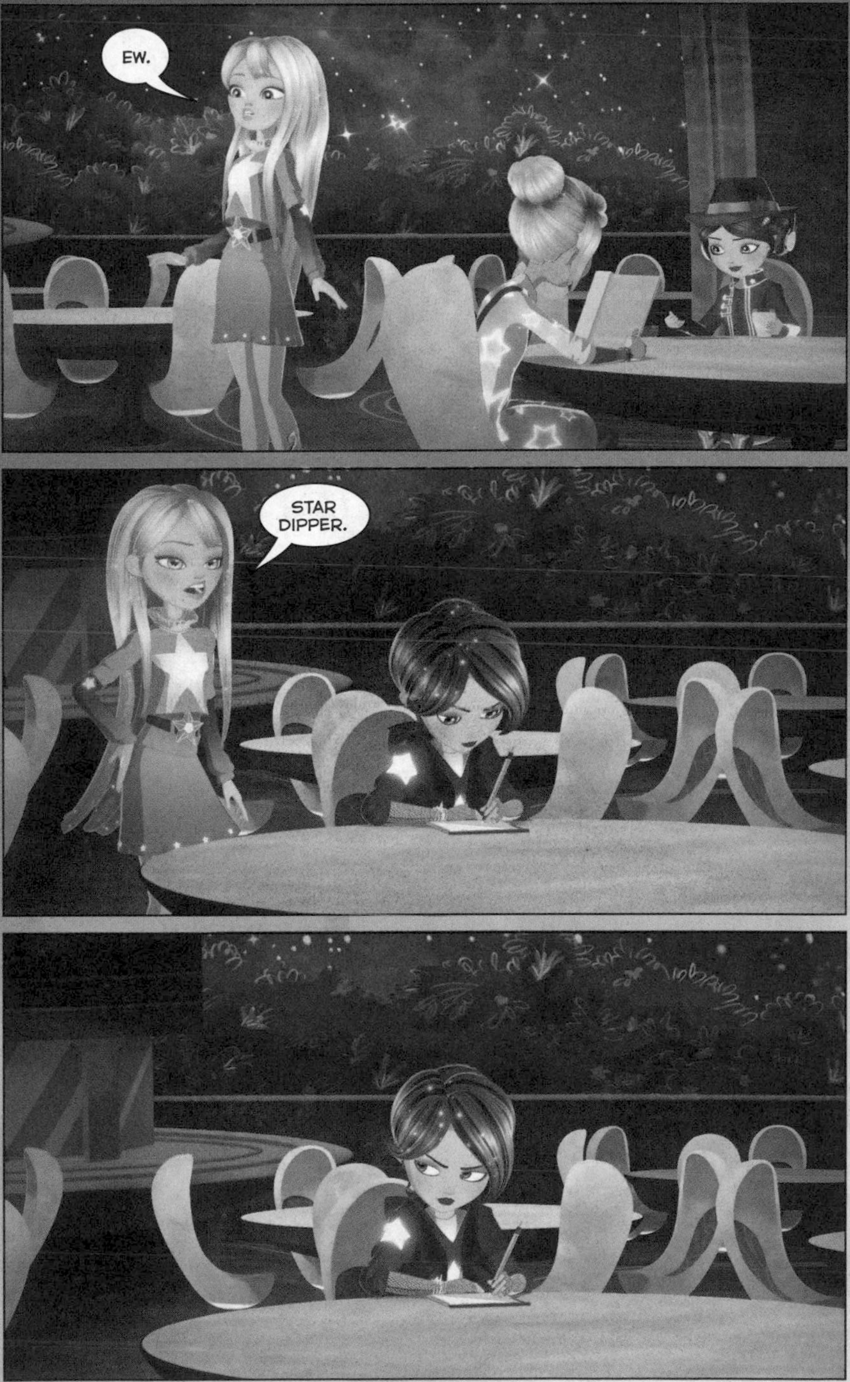
EW.
STAR DIPPER.

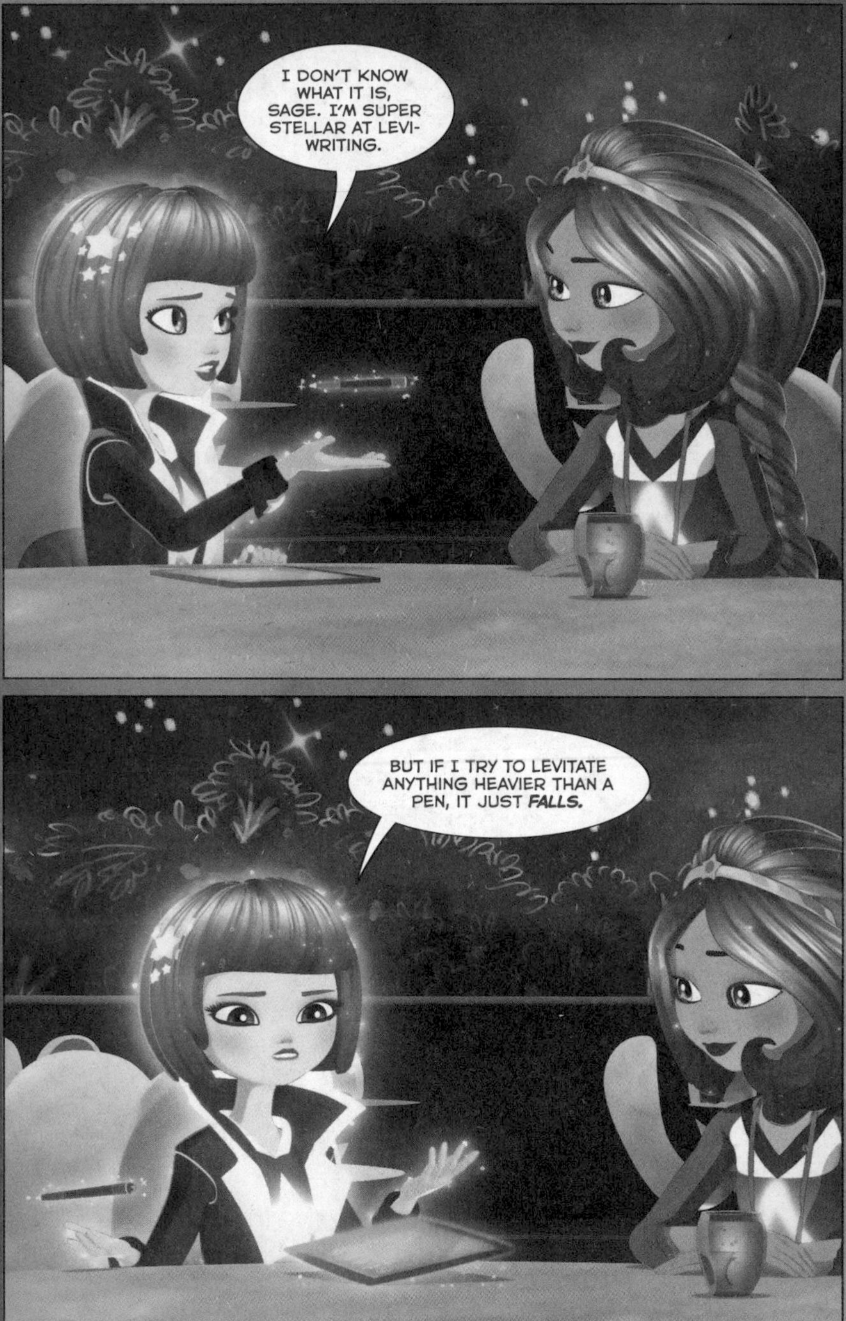
I DON'T KNOW WHAT IT IS, SAGE. I'M SUPER STELLAR AT LEVI-WRITING.
BUT IF I TRY TO LEVITATE ANYTHING HEAVIER THAN A PEN, IT JUST *FALLS.*

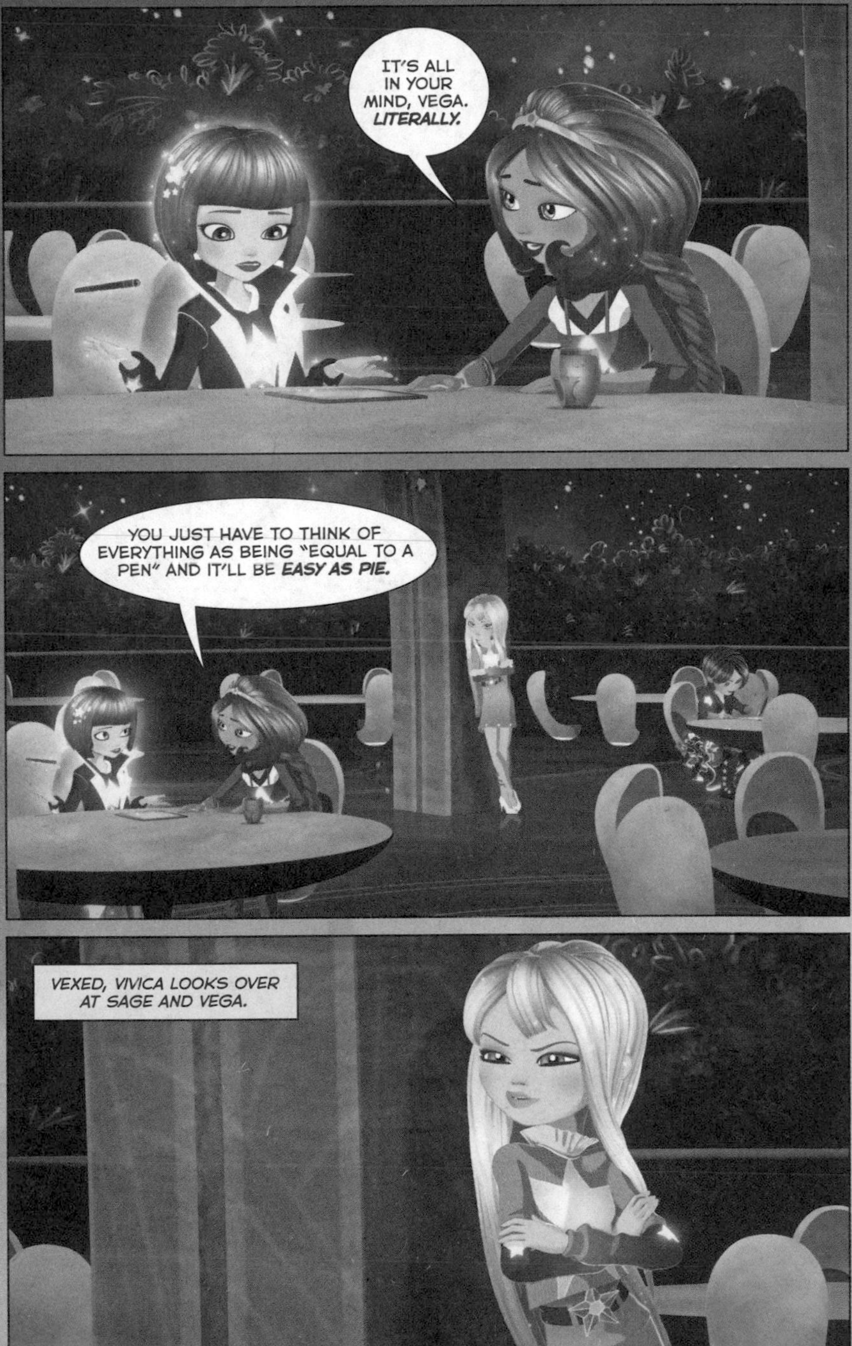
IT'S ALL IN YOUR MIND, VEGA. ***LITERALLY.***
YOU JUST HAVE TO THINK OF EVERYTHING AS BEING "EQUAL TO A PEN" AND IT'LL BE ***EASY AS PIE.***
VEXED, VIVICA LOOKS OVER AT SAGE AND VEGA.

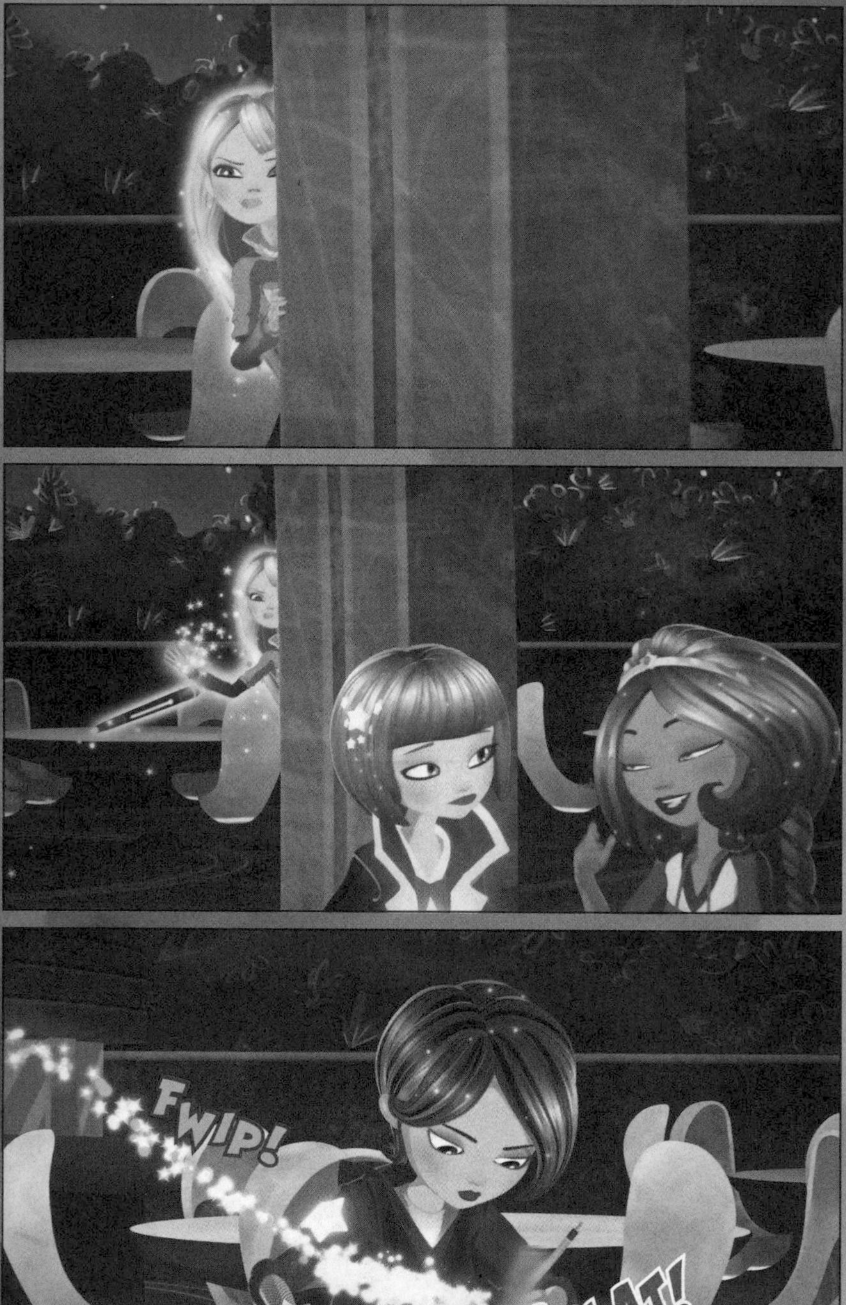
FWIP!
SPLAT!

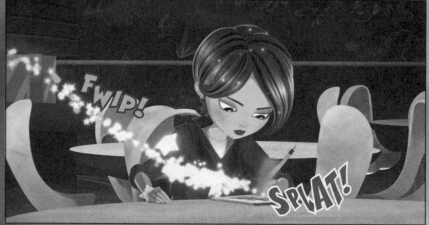

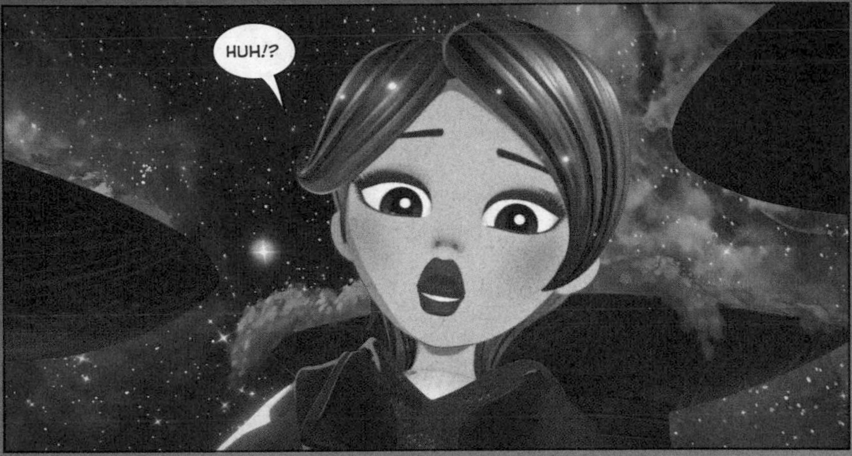
HUH!?

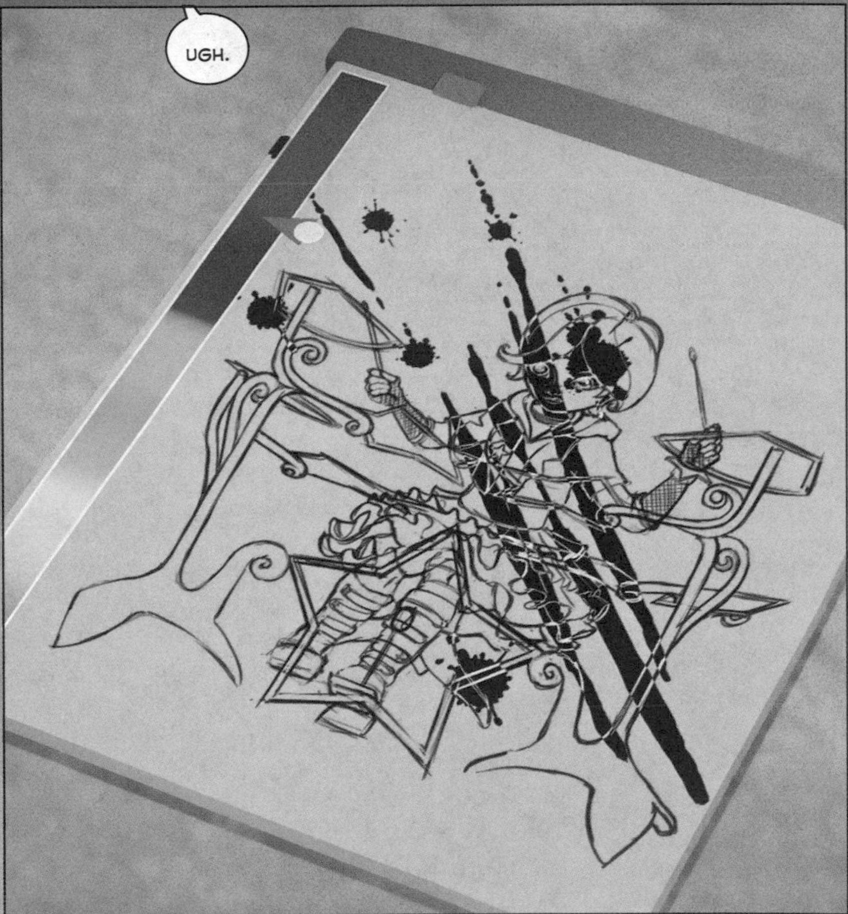
UGH.

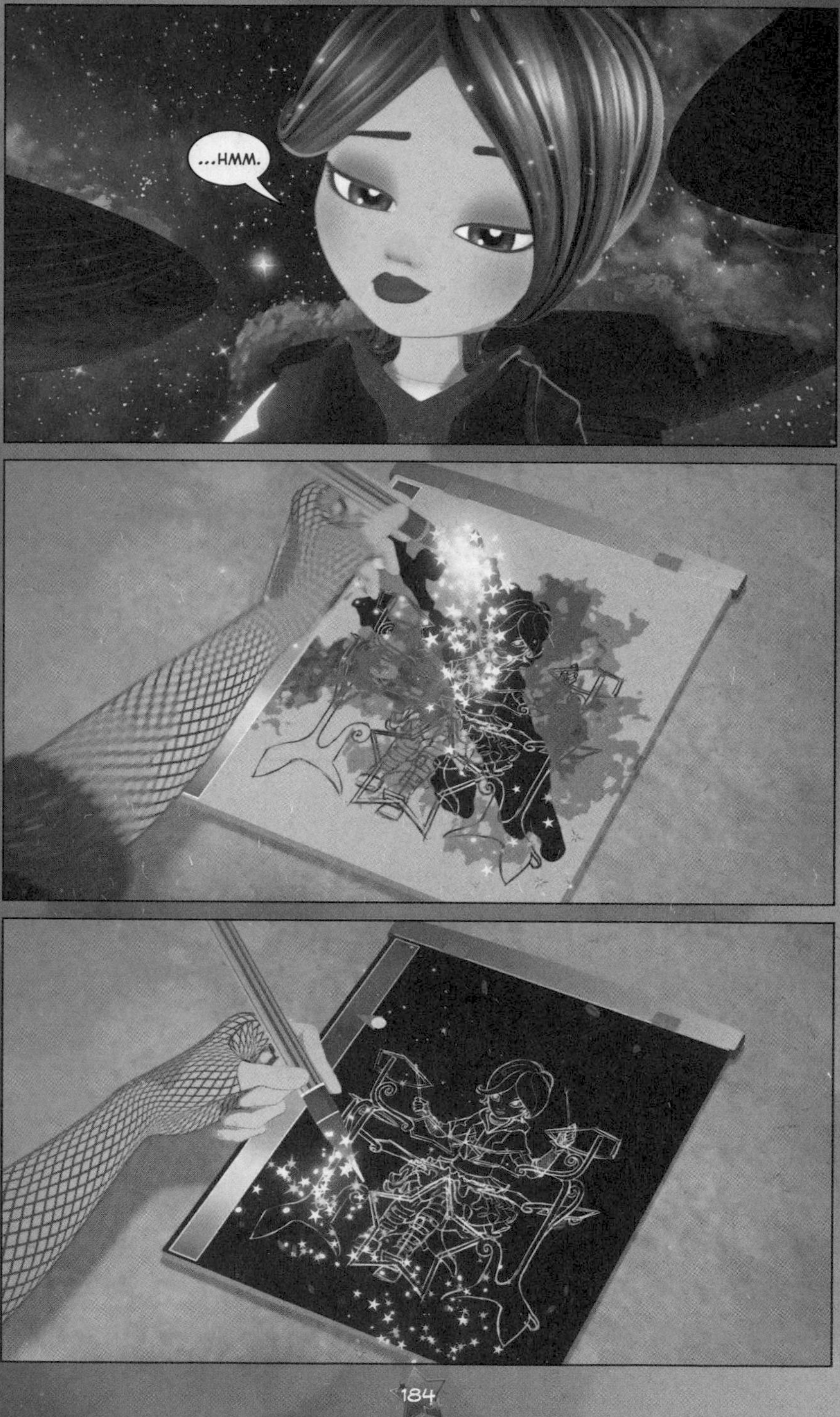
...HMM.

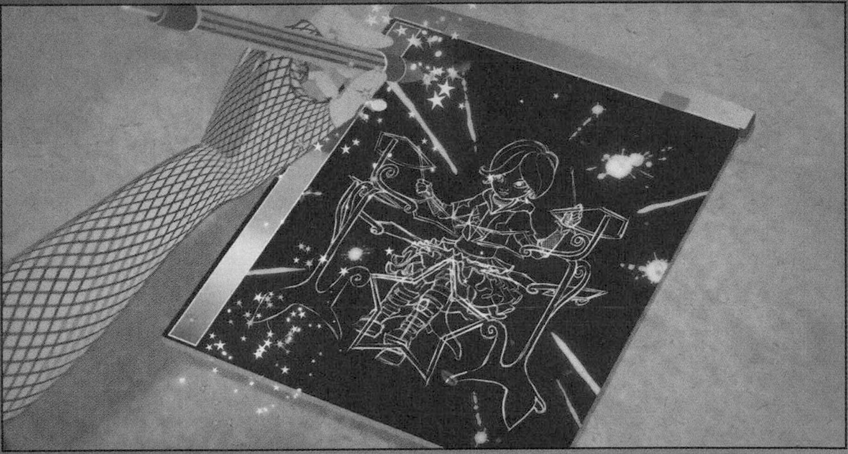

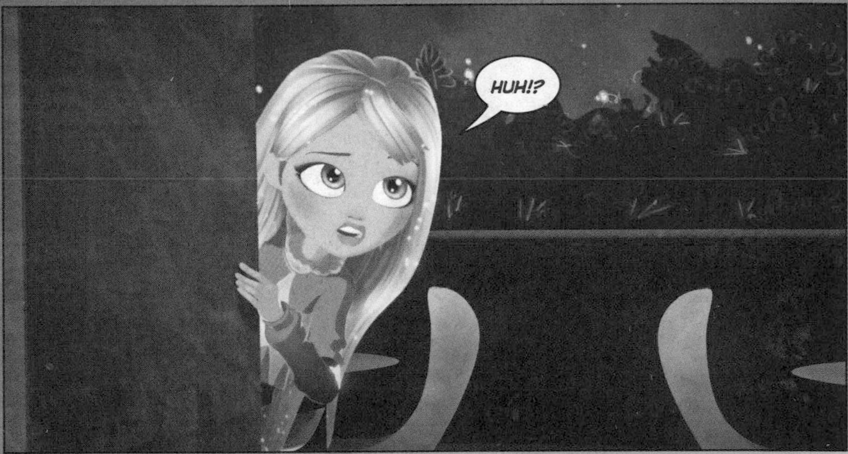
HUH!?

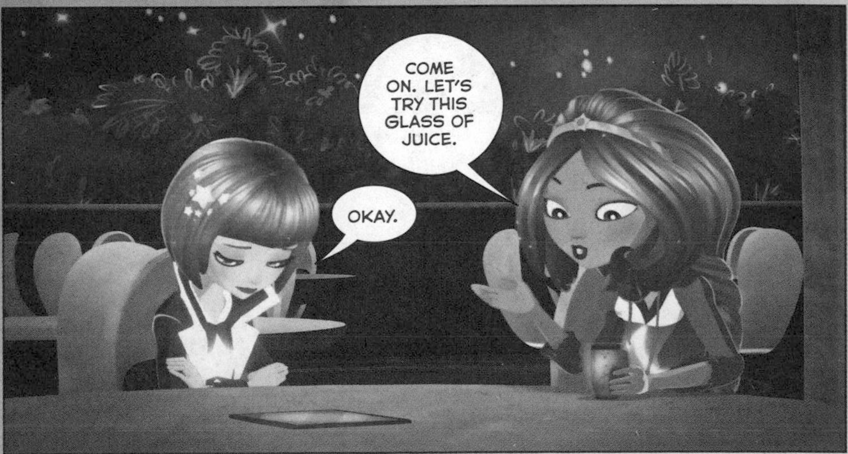
COME ON. LET'S TRY THIS GLASS OF JUICE.
OKAY.

AY.

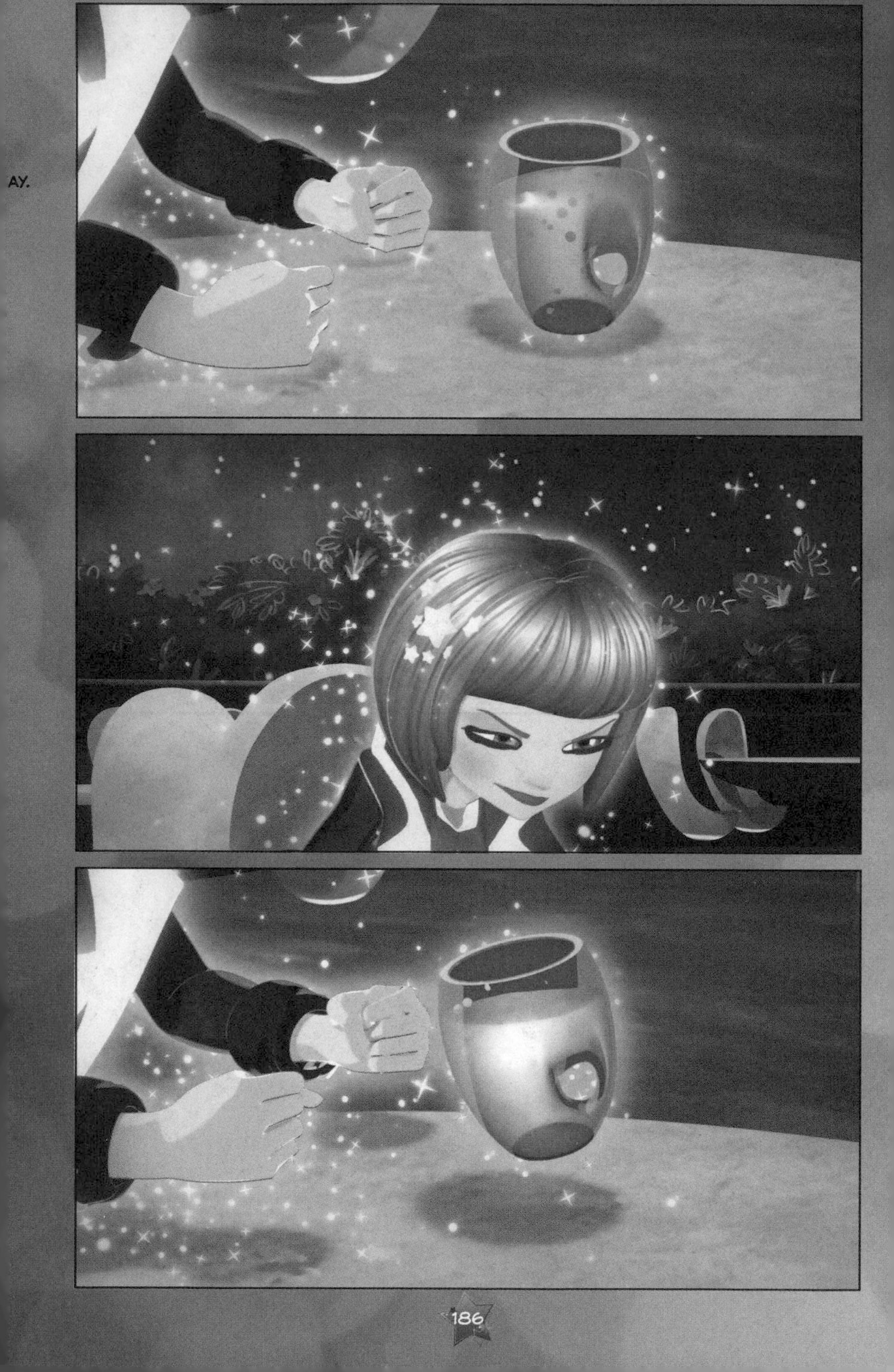

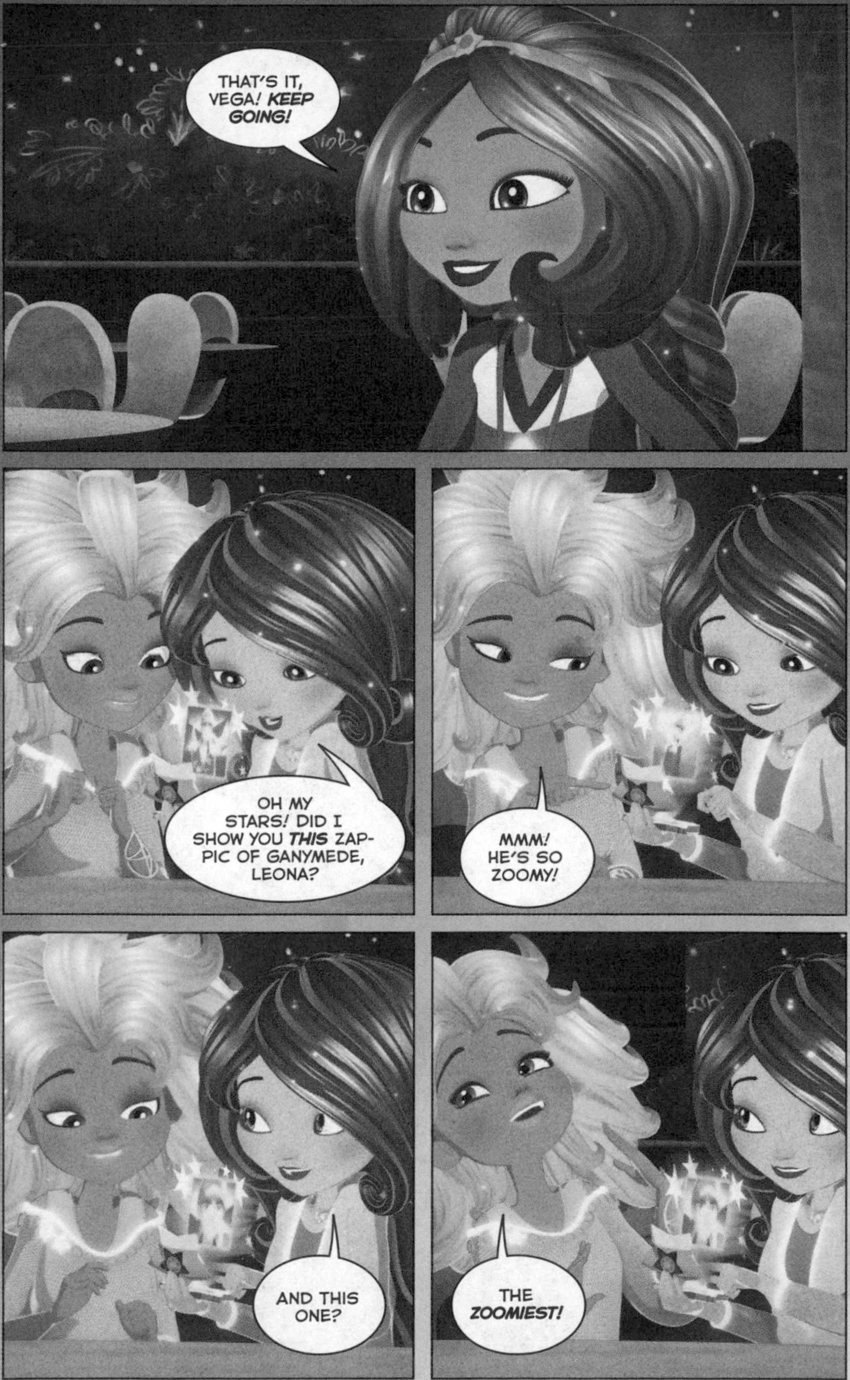
THAT'S IT, VEGA! KEEP GOING!
OH MY STARS! DID I SHOW YOU THIS ZAP-PIC OF GANYMEDE, LEONA?
MMM! HE'S SO ZOOMY!
AND THIS ONE?
THE ZOOMIEST!

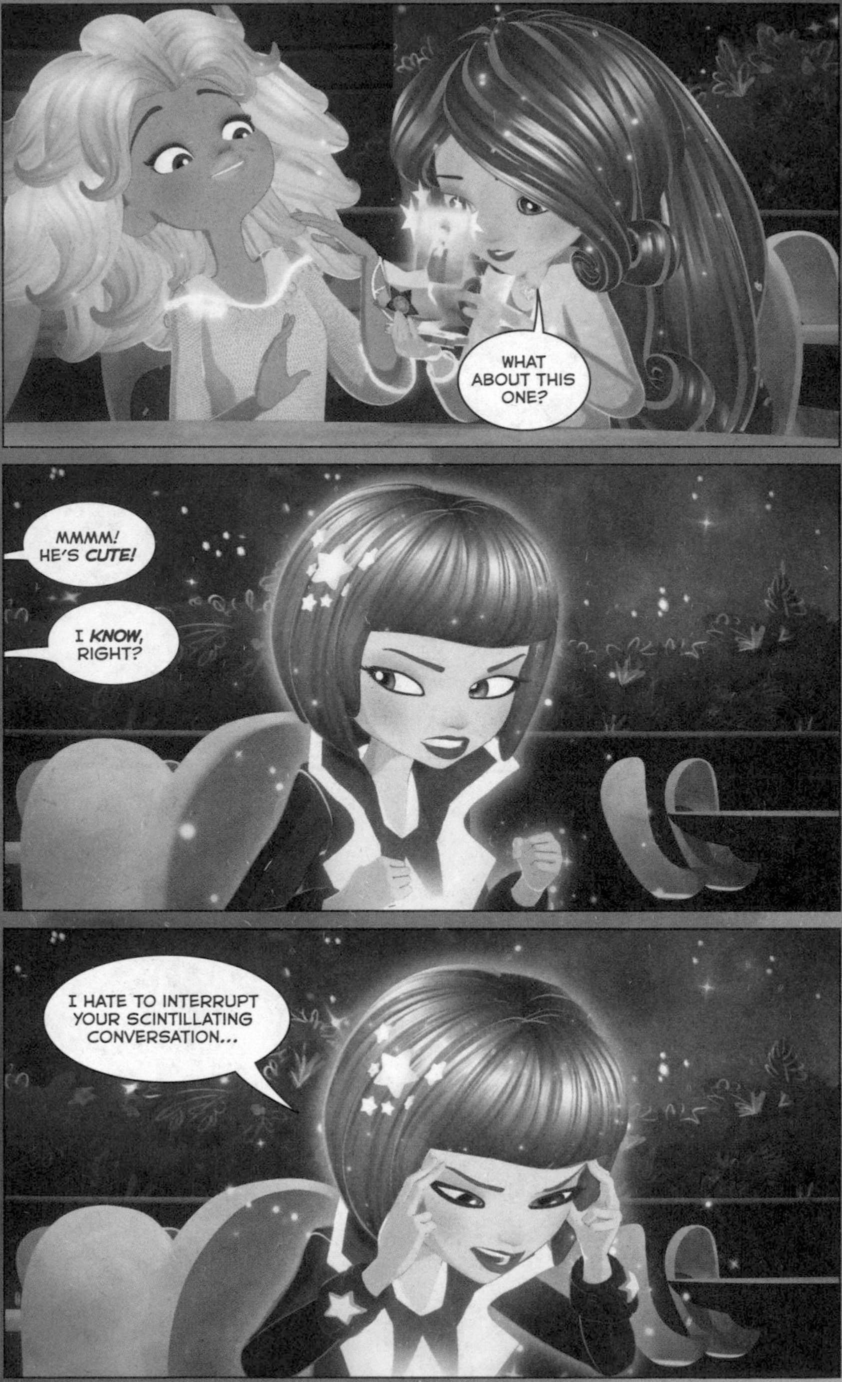
WHAT ABOUT THIS ONE?
MMMM! HE'S *CUTE!*
I *KNOW,* RIGHT?
I HATE TO INTERRUPT YOUR SCINTILLATING CONVERSATION...

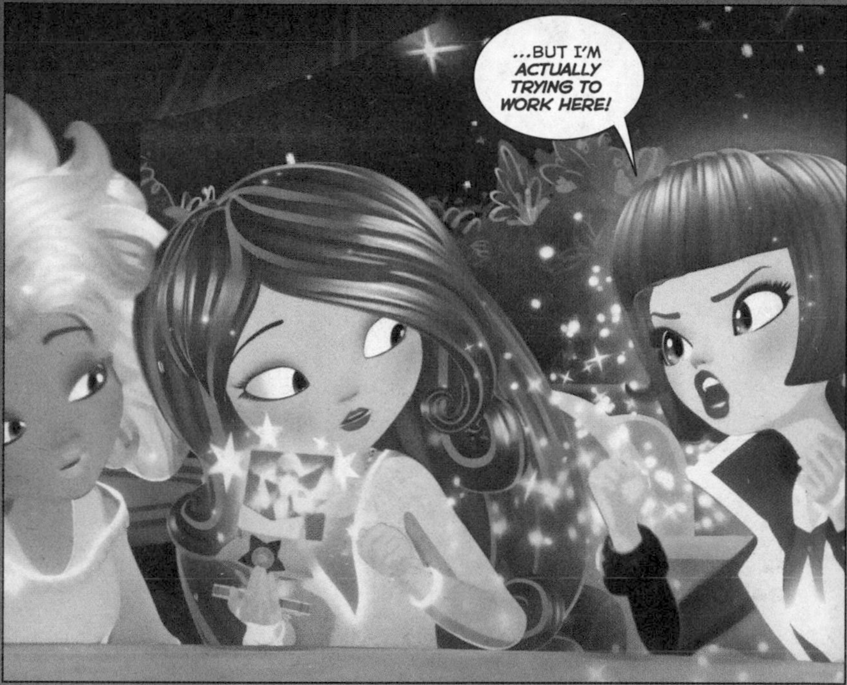
...BUT I'M ACTUALLY TRYING TO WORK HERE!

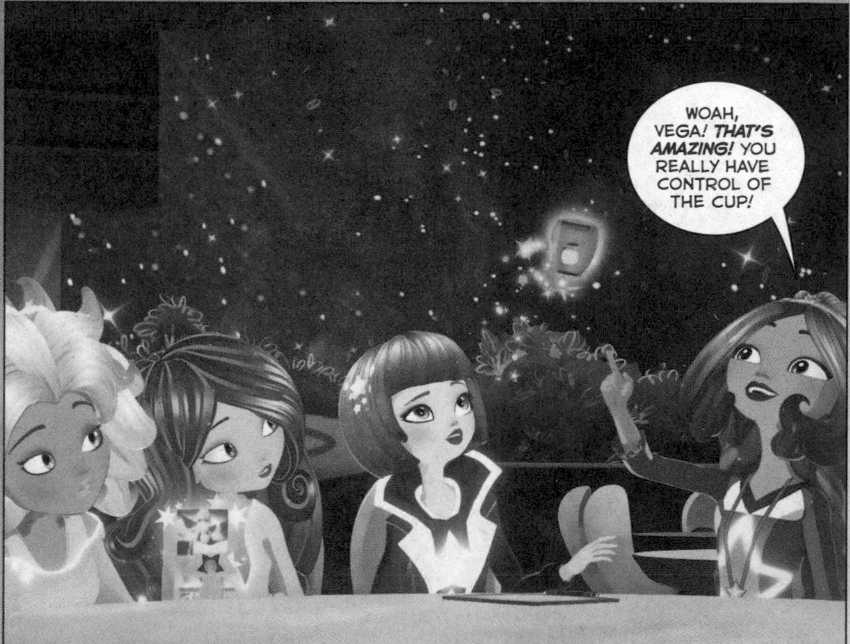
WOAH, VEGA! THAT'S AMAZING! YOU REALLY HAVE CONTROL OF THE CUP!

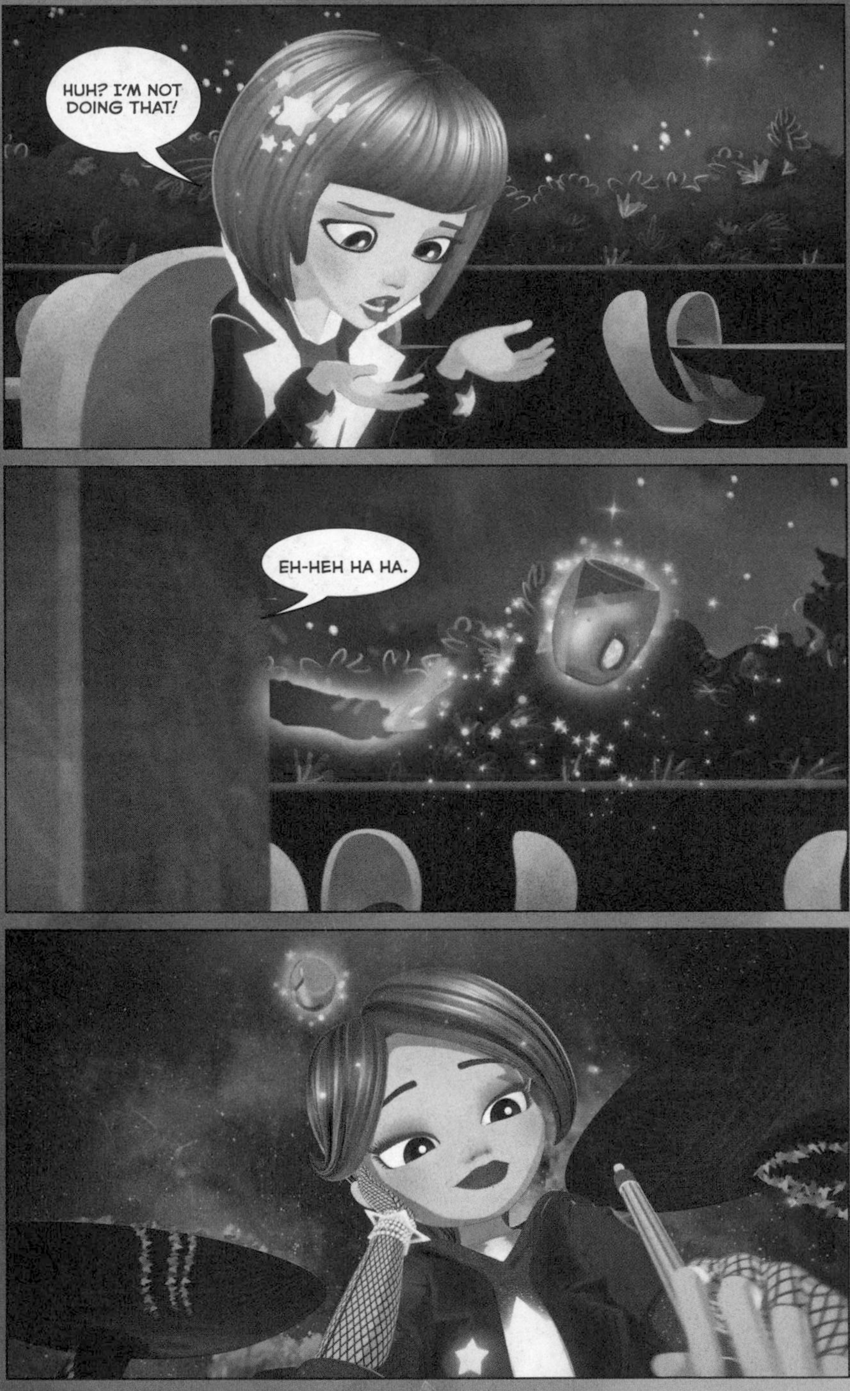
HUH? I'M NOT DOING THAT!
EH-HEH HA HA.

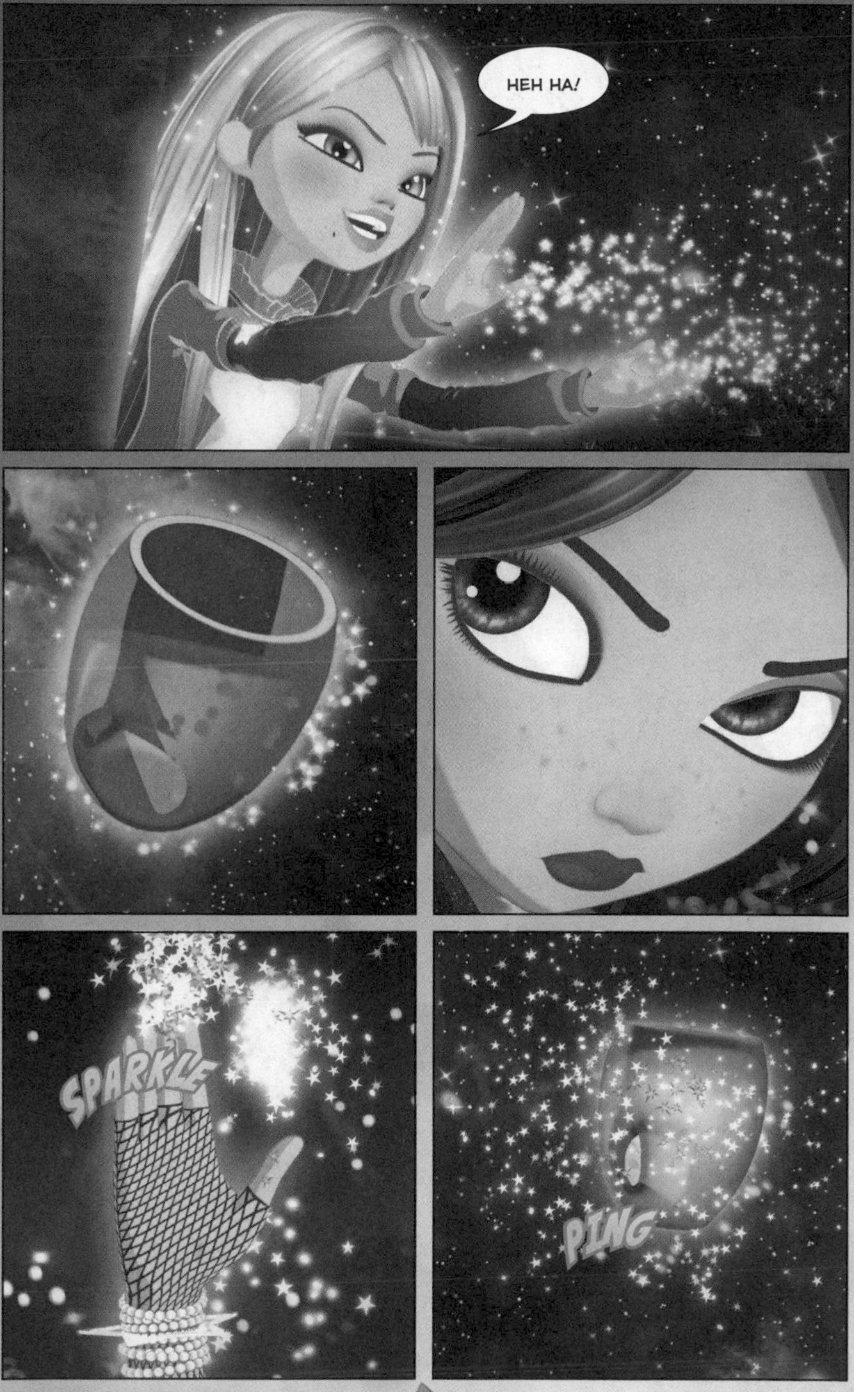
HEH HA!
SPARKLE
PING

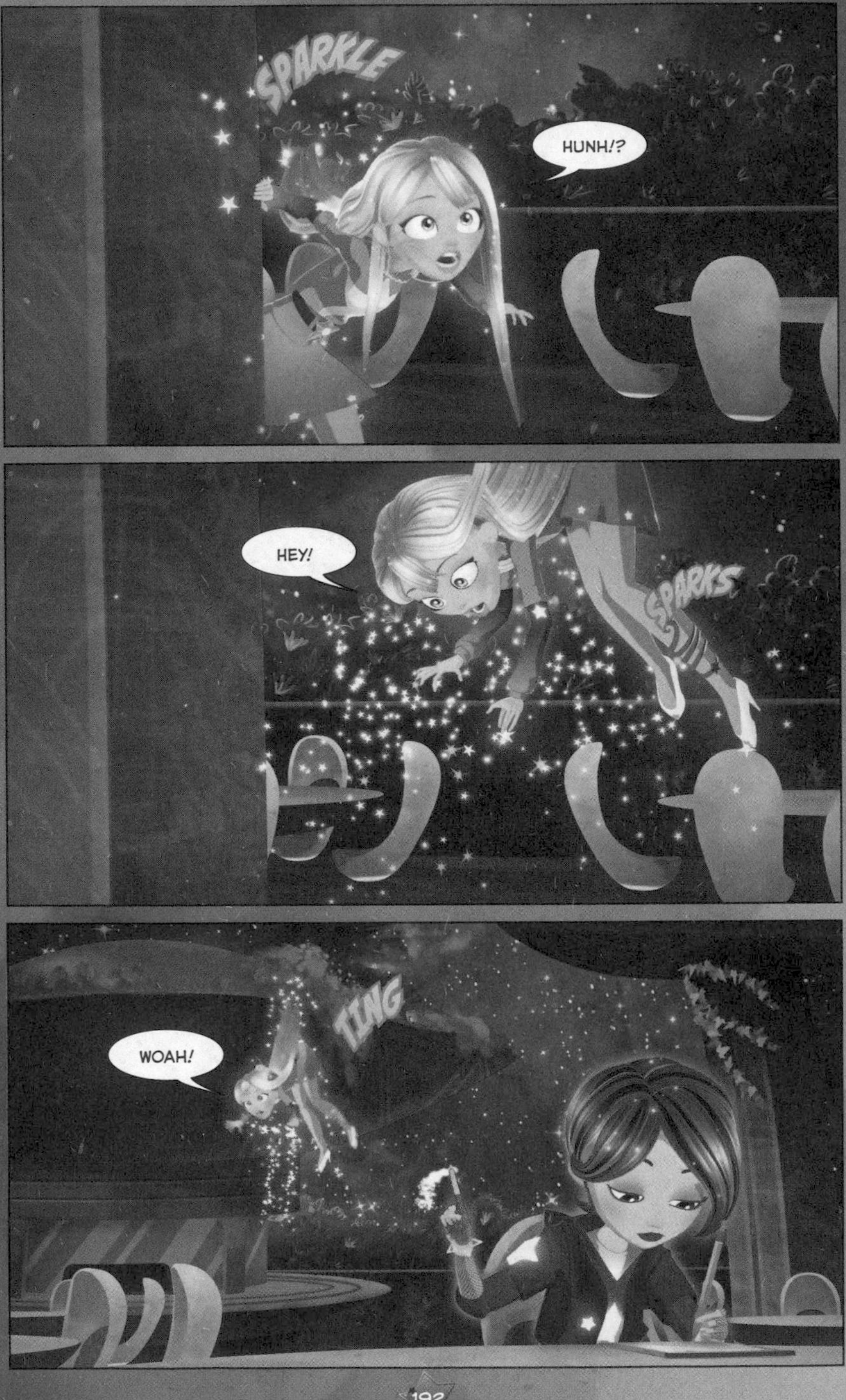
SPARKLE
HUNH!?
HEY!
SPARKS
TING
WOAH!

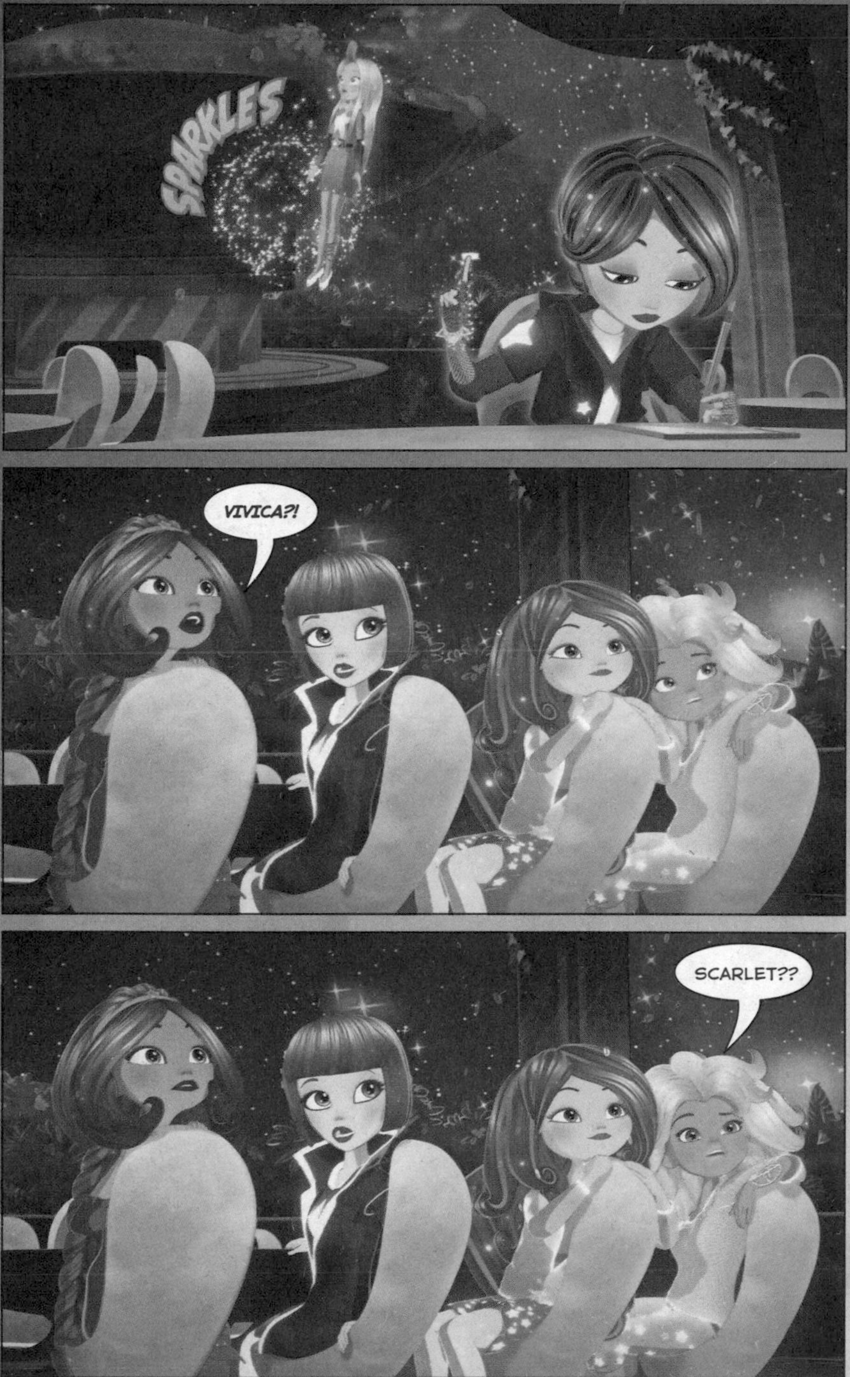
SPARKLES
VIVICA?!
SCARLET??

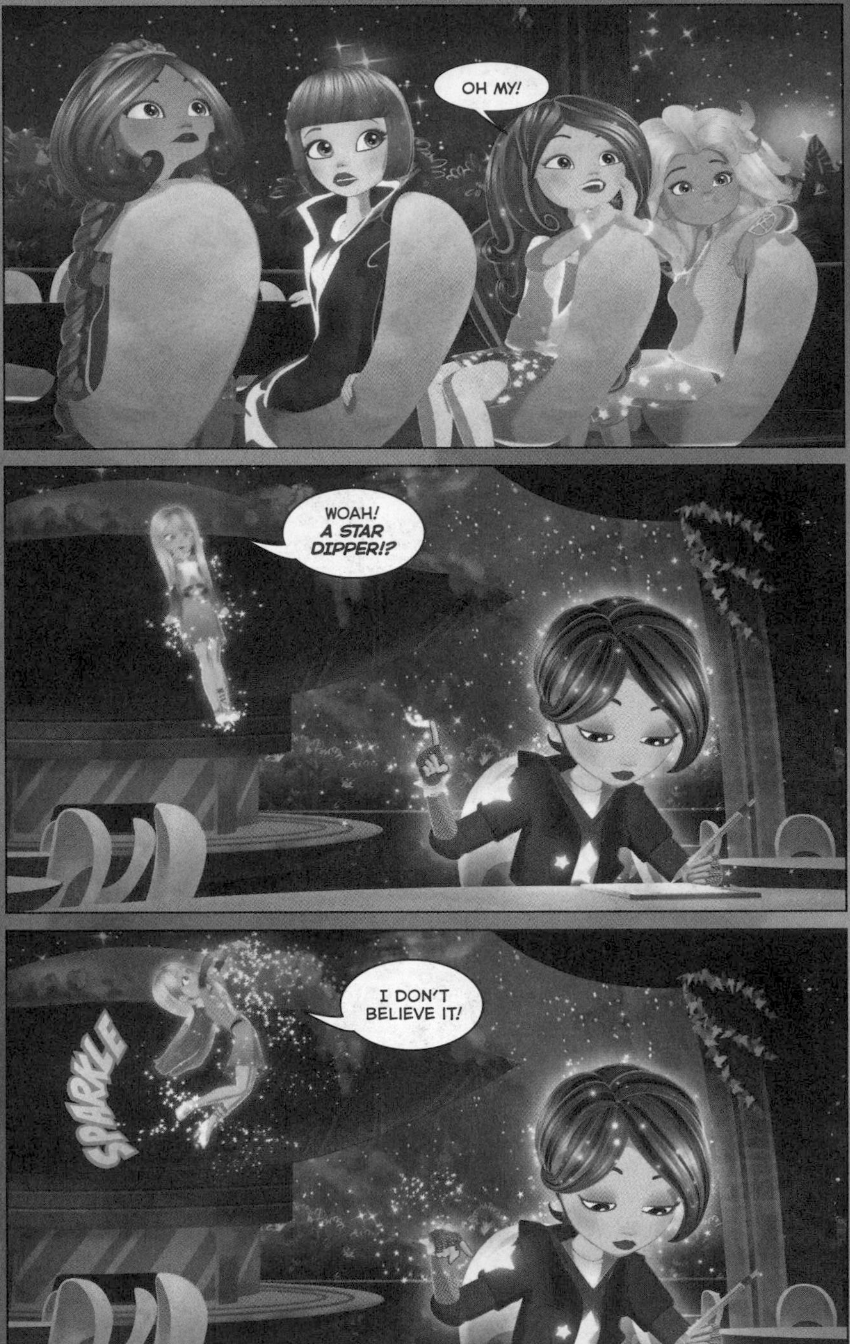
OH MY!
WOAH! A STAR DIPPER!?
SPARKLE
I DON'T BELIEVE IT!

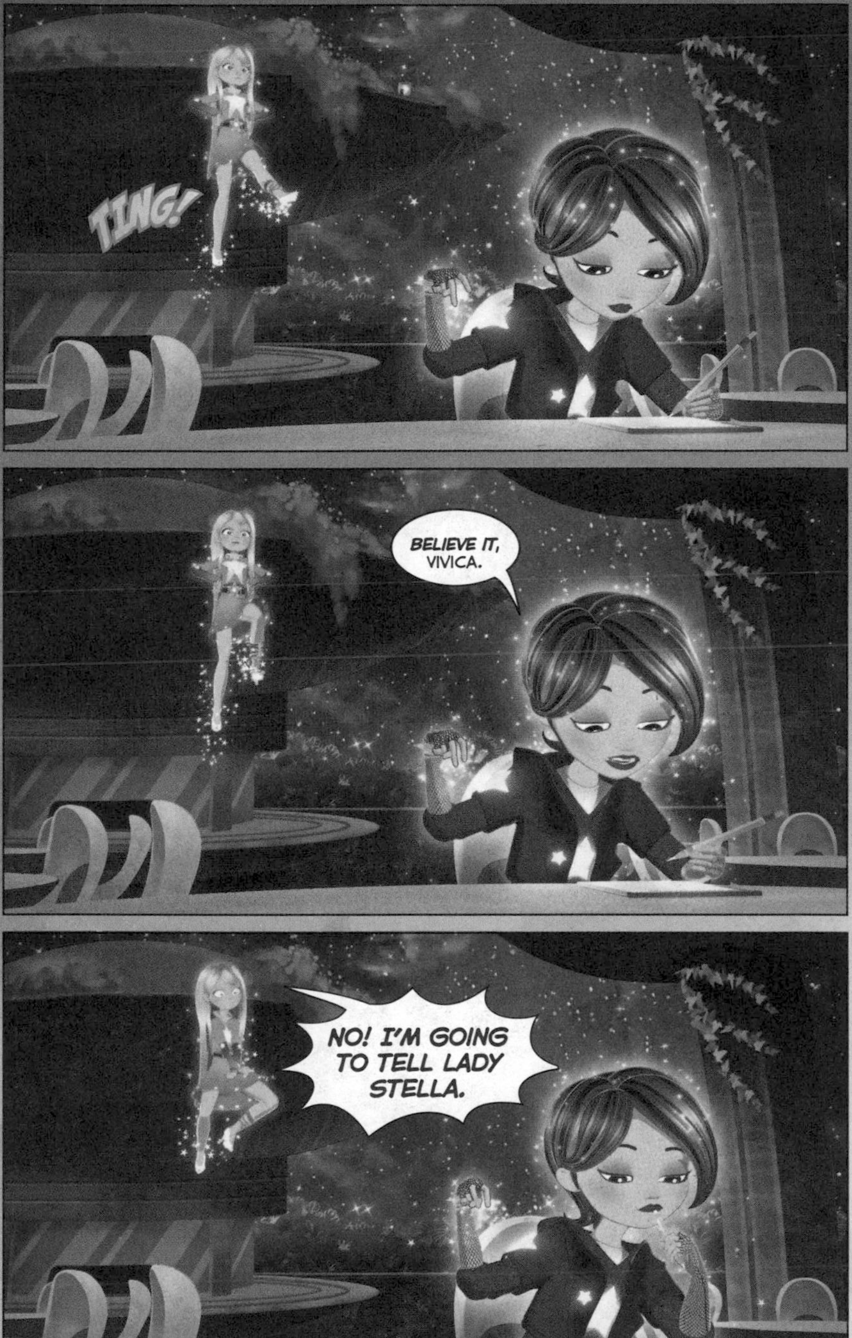
TING!
BELIEVE IT, VIVICA.
NO! I'M GOING TO TELL LADY STELLA.

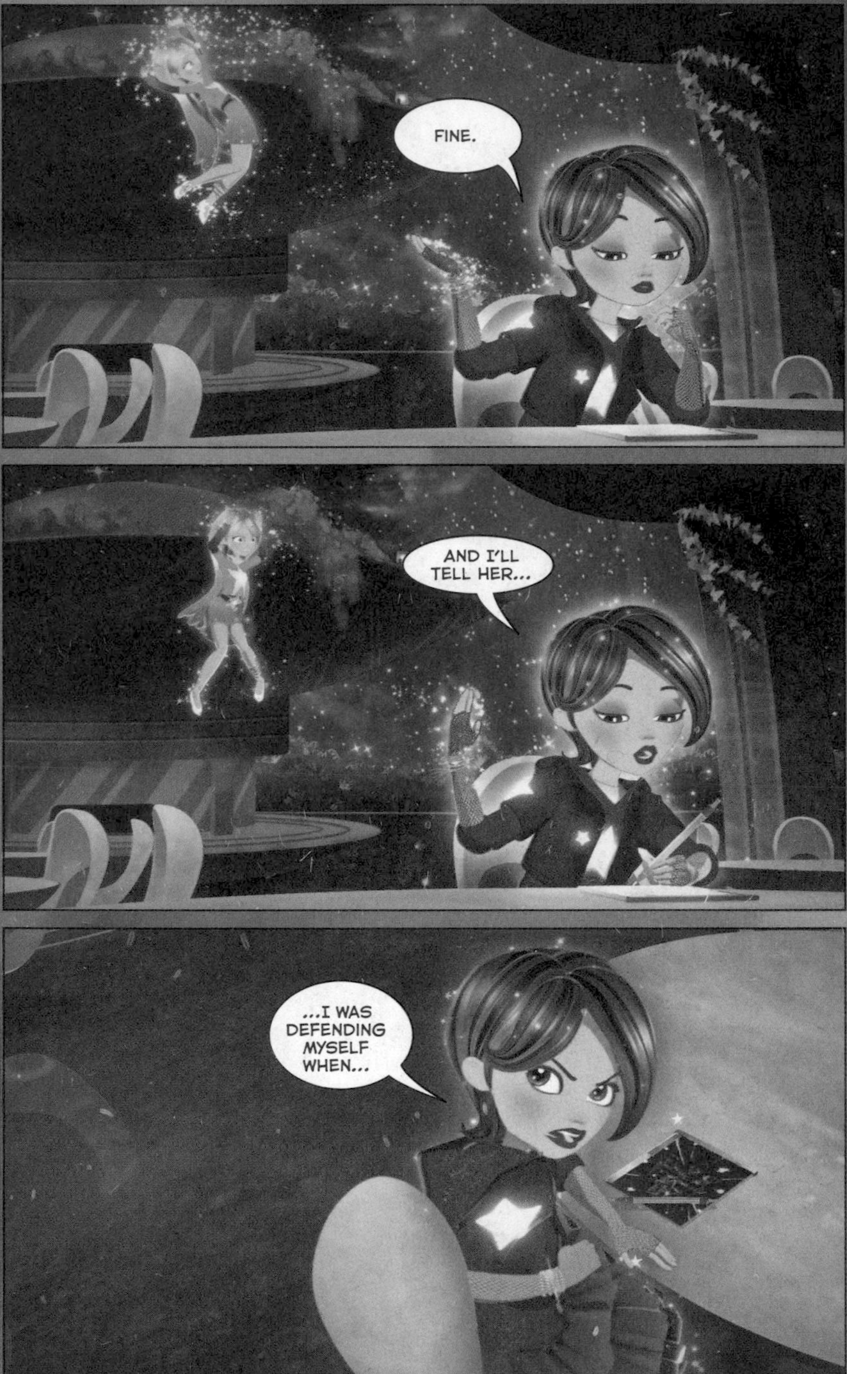
FINE.
AND I'LL TELL HER...
...I WAS DEFENDING MYSELF WHEN...

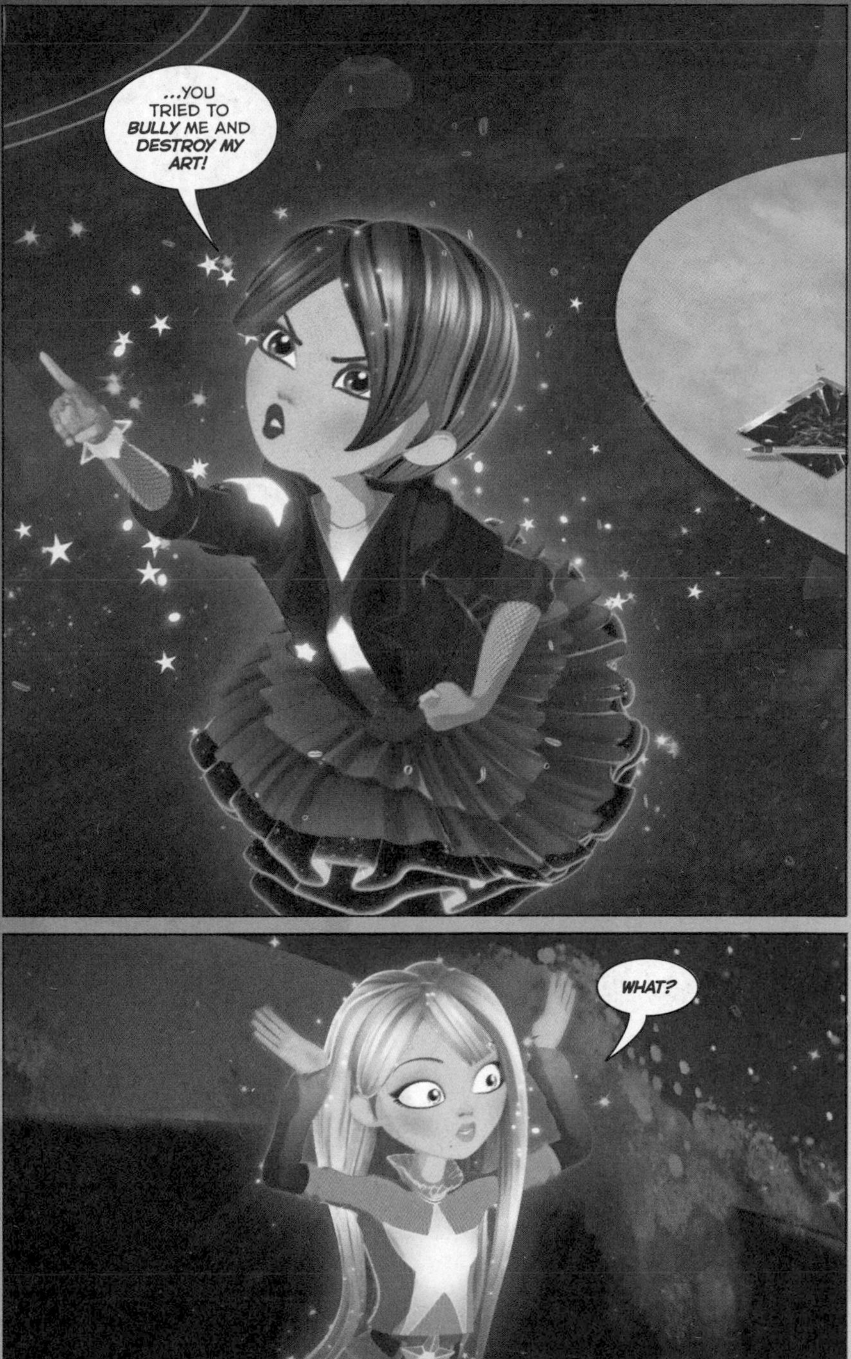
...YOU TRIED TO BULLY ME AND DESTROY MY ART!
WHAT?

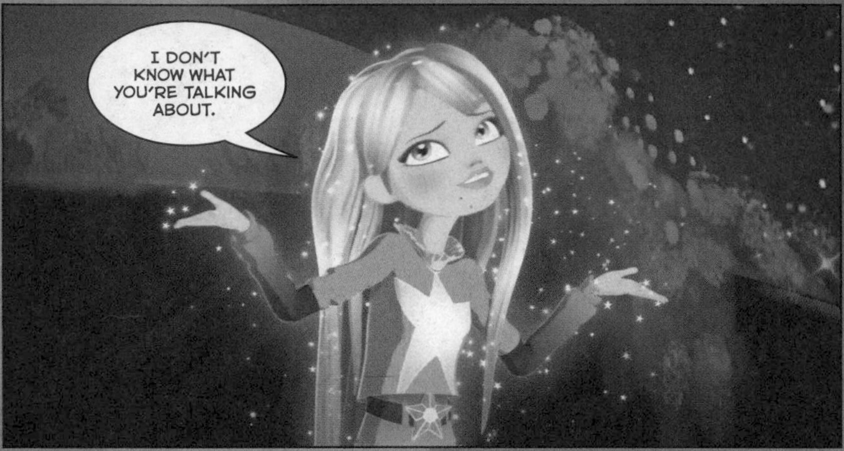
I DON'T KNOW WHAT YOU'RE TALKING ABOUT.

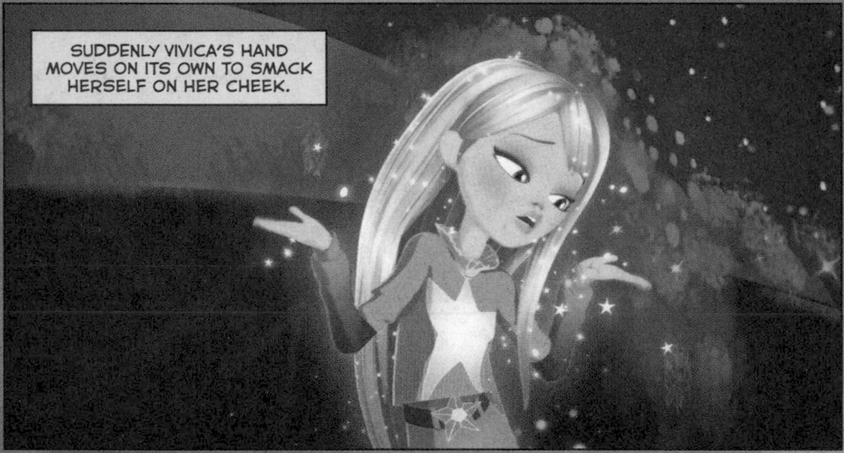
SUDDENLY VIVICA'S HAND MOVES ON ITS OWN TO SMACK HERSELF ON HER CHEEK.

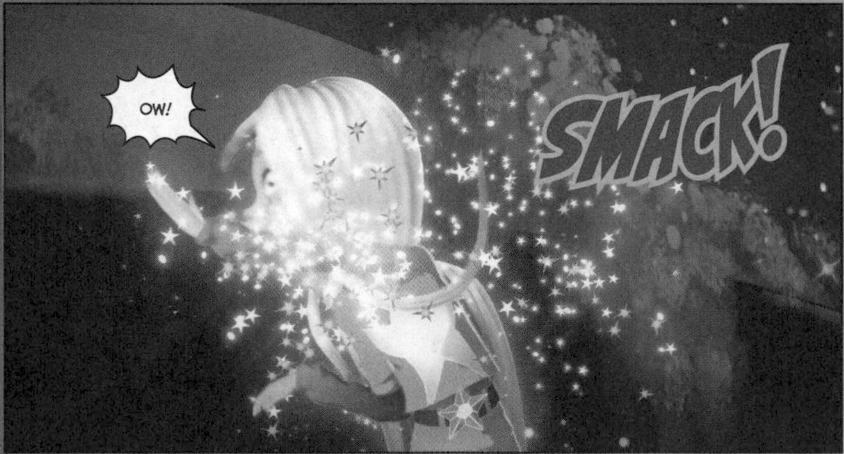
OW!
SMACK!

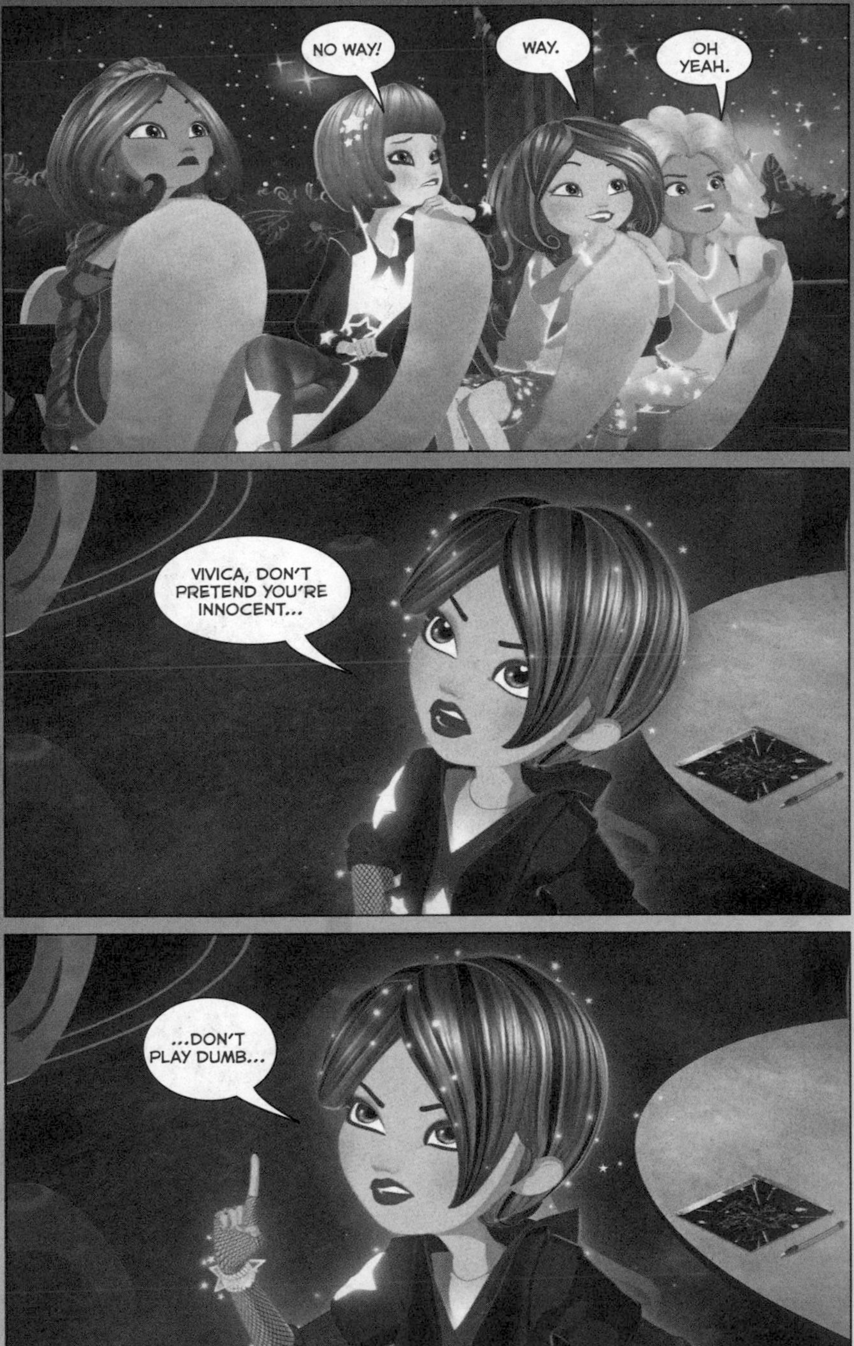
NO WAY!
WAY.
OH YEAH.
VIVICA, DON'T PRETEND YOU'RE INNOCENT...
...DON'T PLAY DUMB...

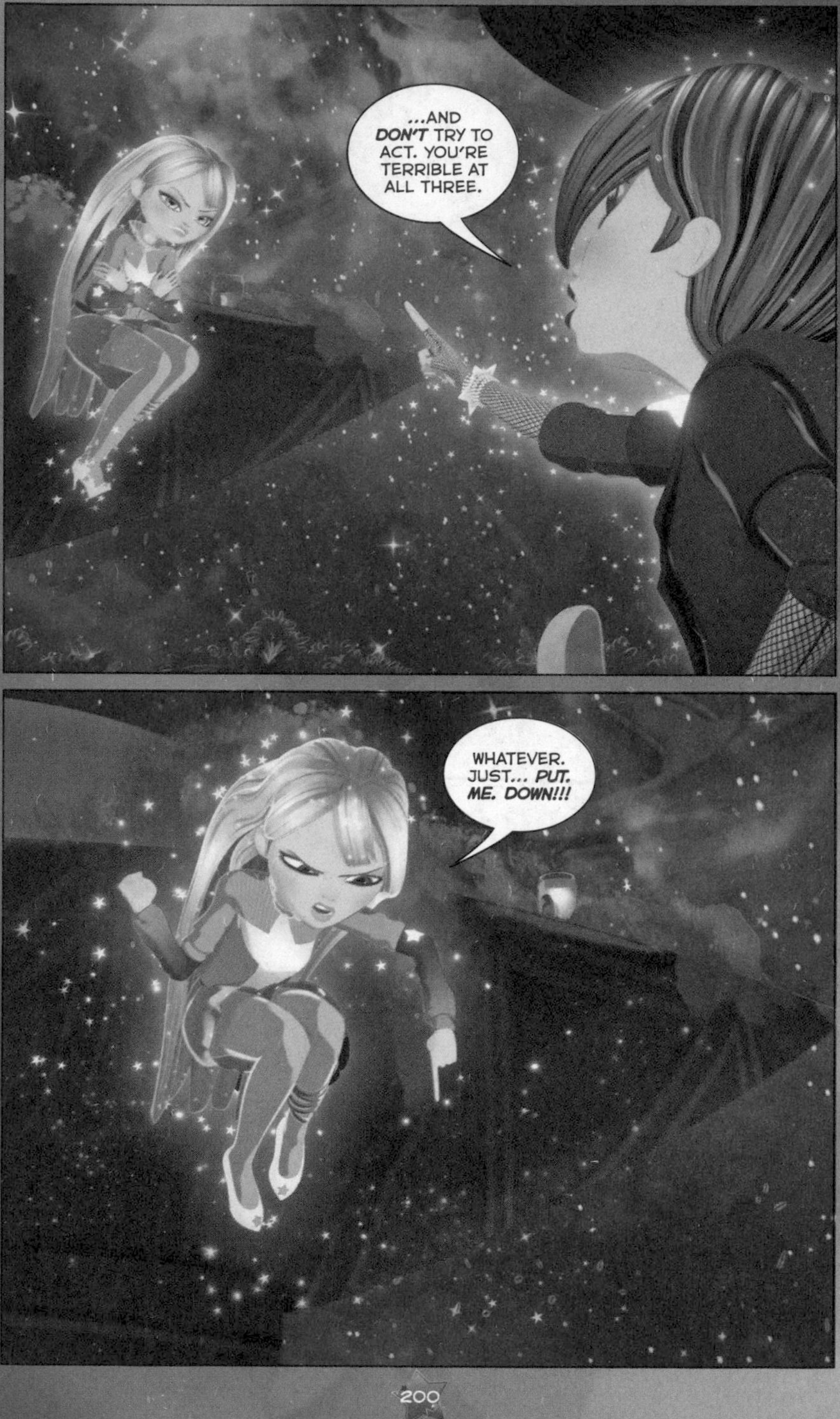
...AND DON'T TRY TO ACT. YOU'RE TERRIBLE AT ALL THREE.
WHATEVER. JUST... PUT. ME. DOWN!!!

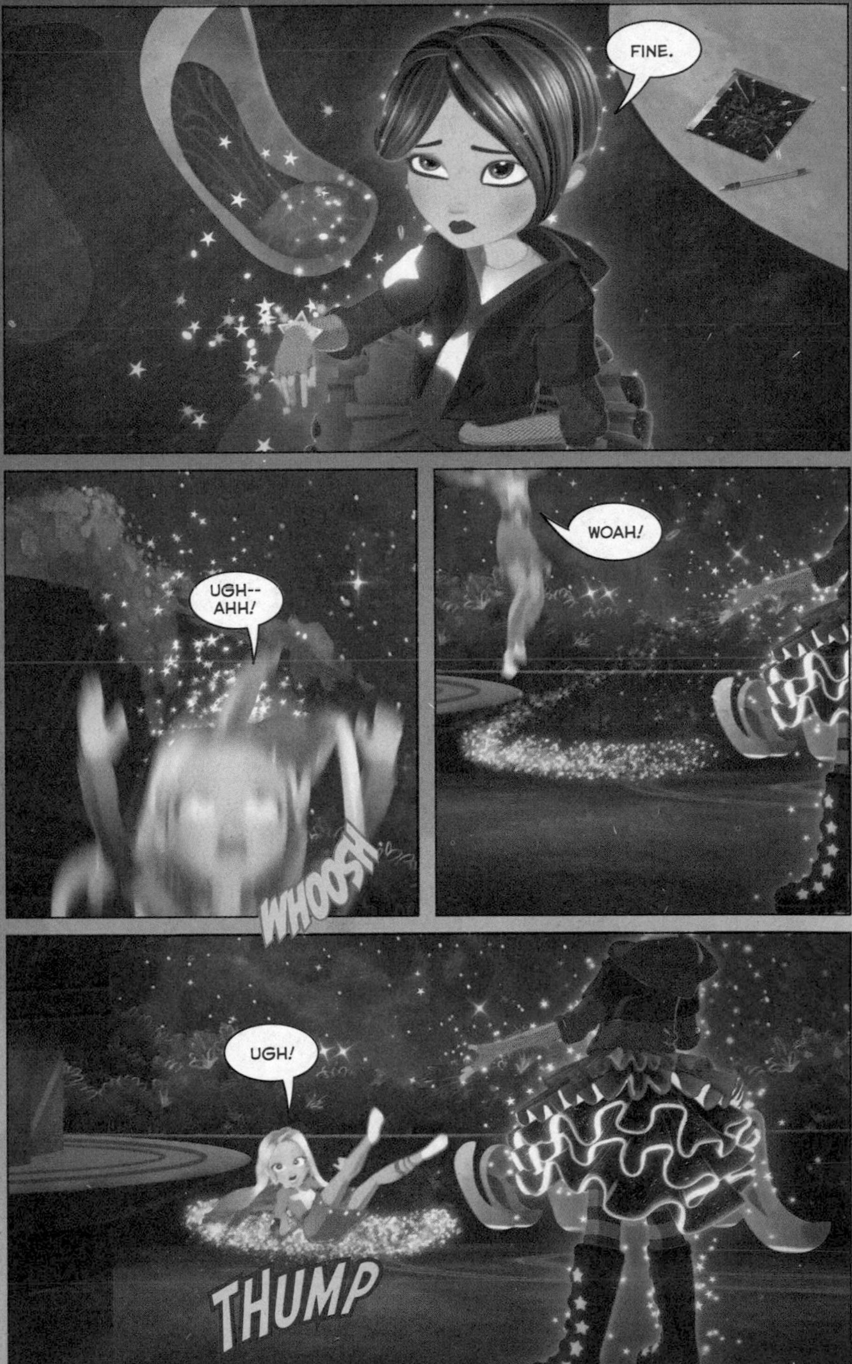
FINE.
UGH--
AHH!
WHOOSH
WOAH!
UGH!
THUMP

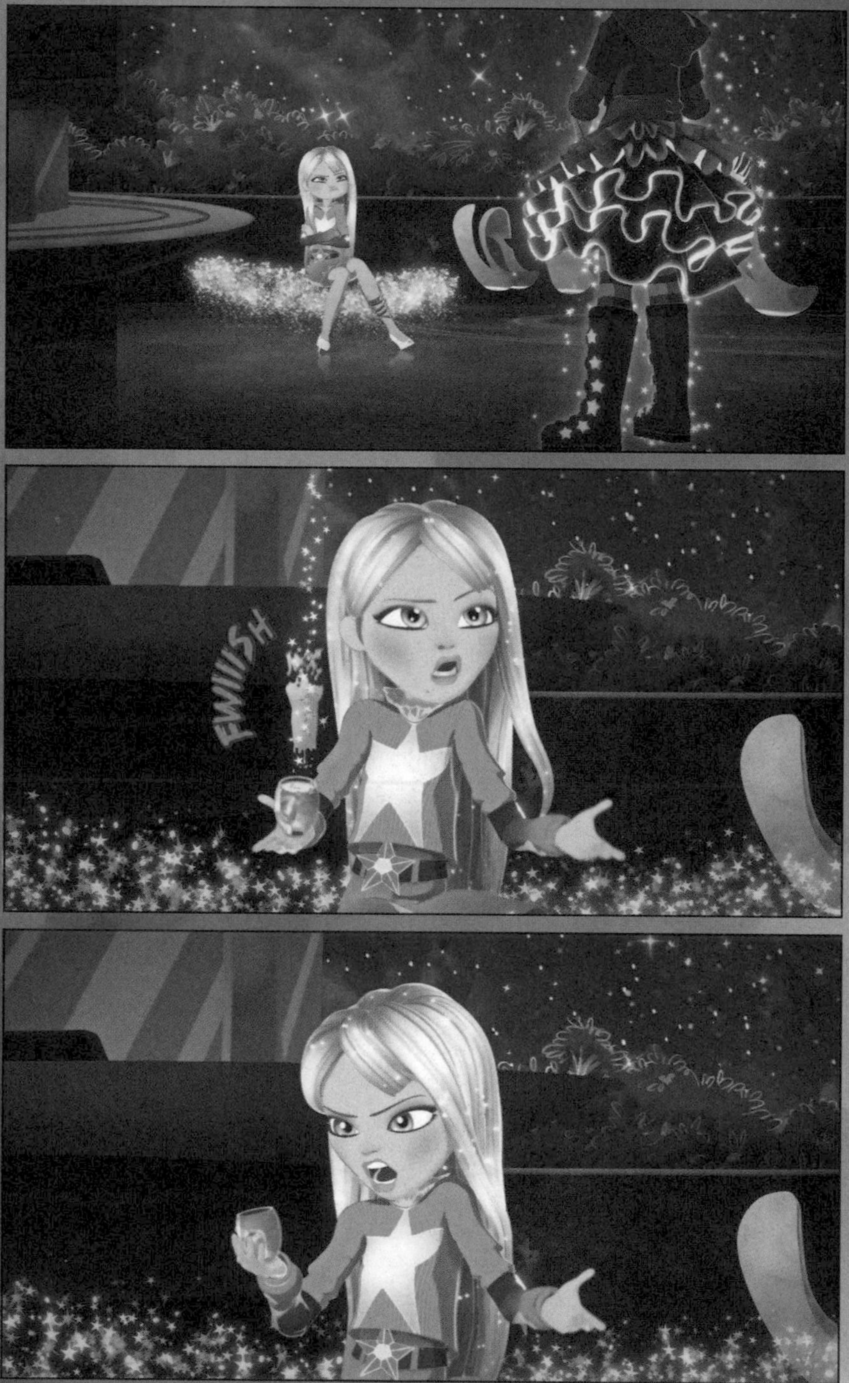
FWIIISH

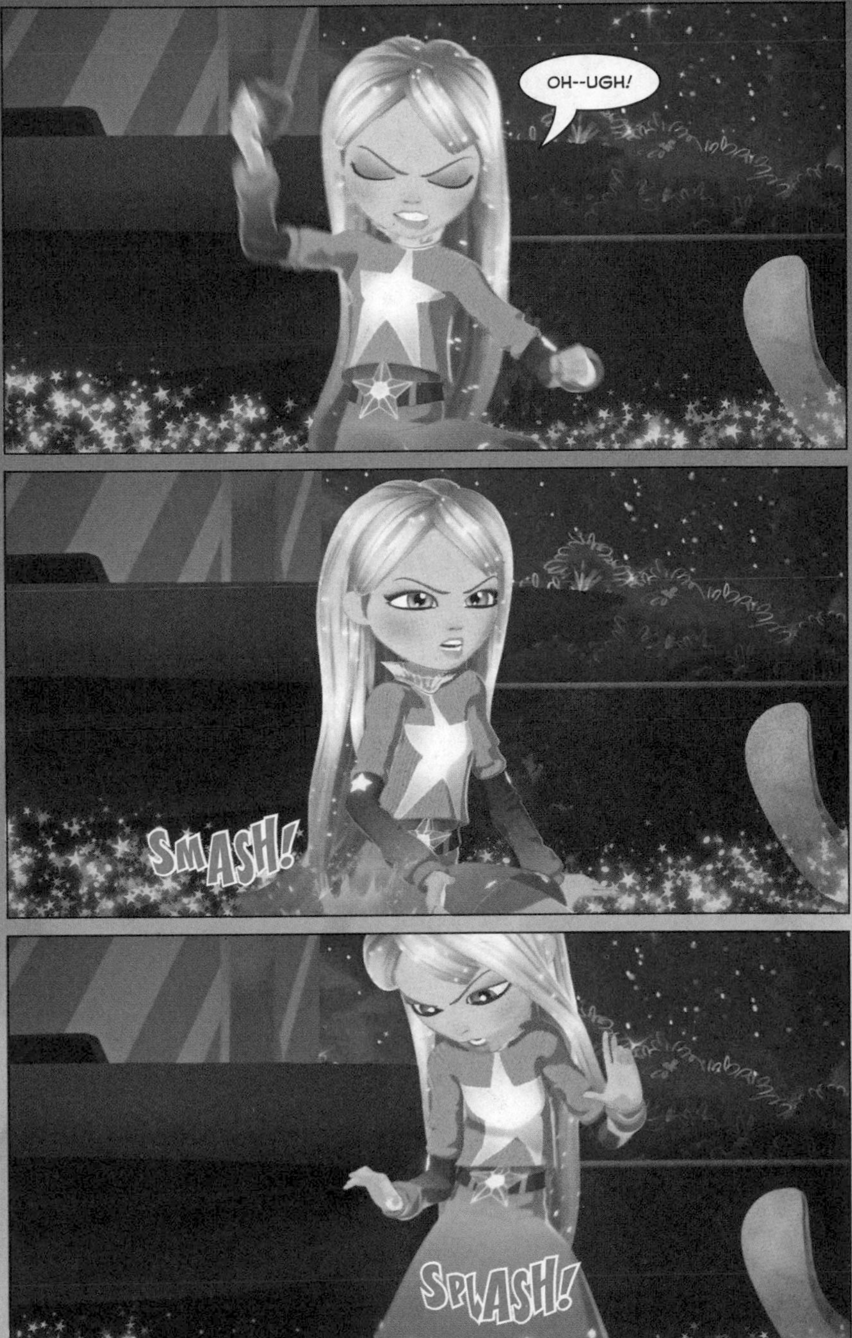
OH--UGH!
SMASH!
SPLASH!

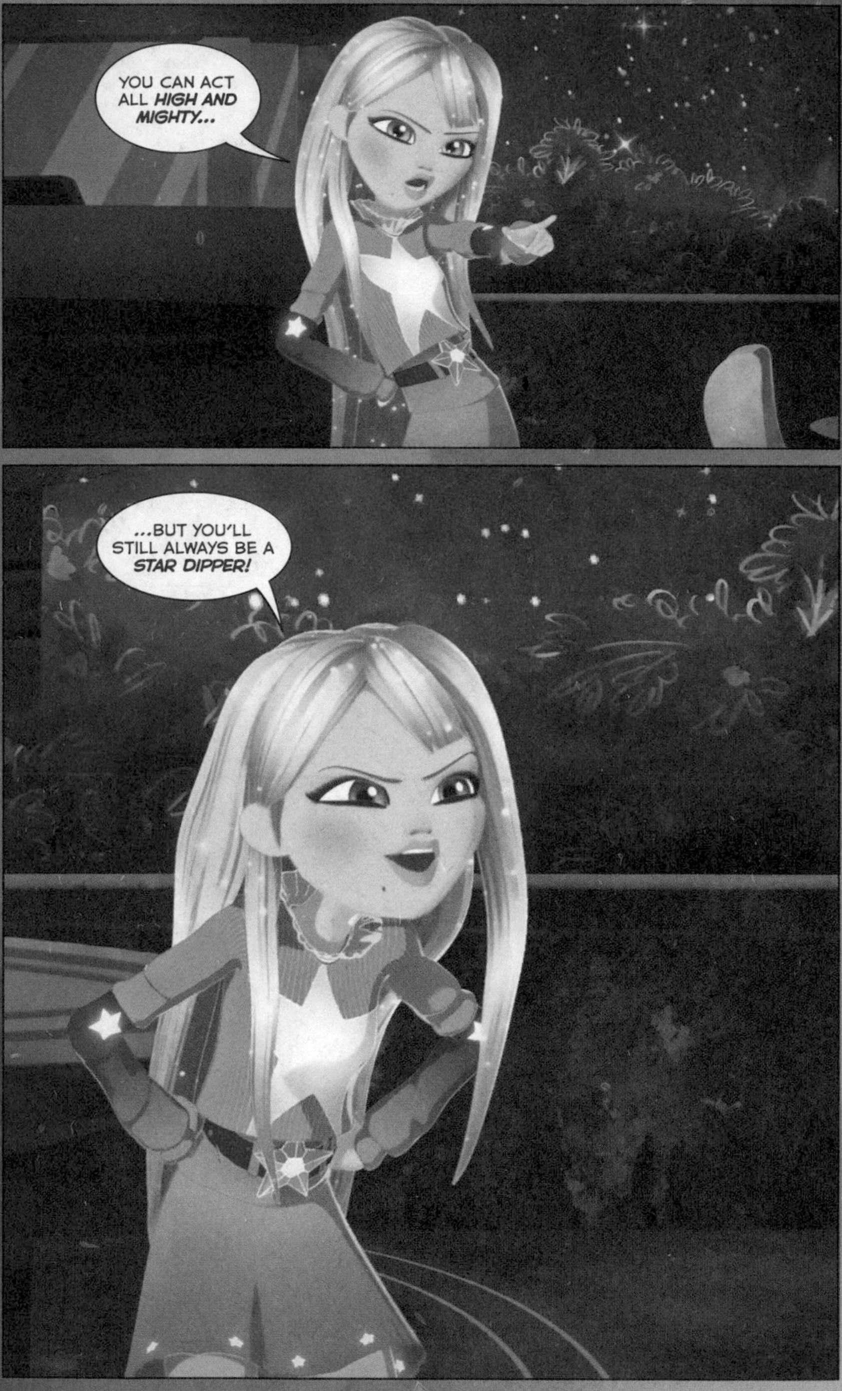
YOU CAN ACT ALL HIGH AND MIGHTY...
...BUT YOU'LL STILL ALWAYS BE A STAR DIPPER!

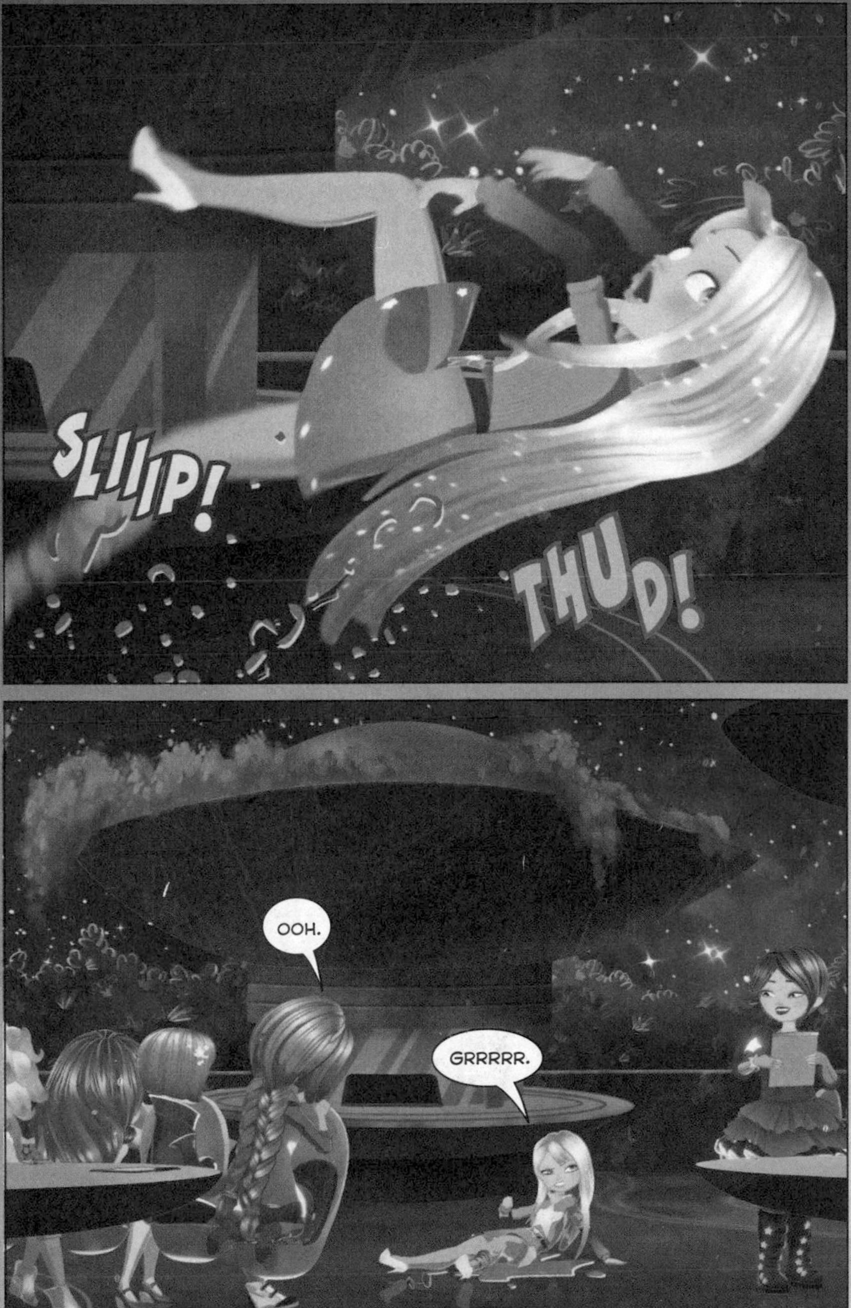
SLIIIP!
THUD!
OOH.
GRRRRR.

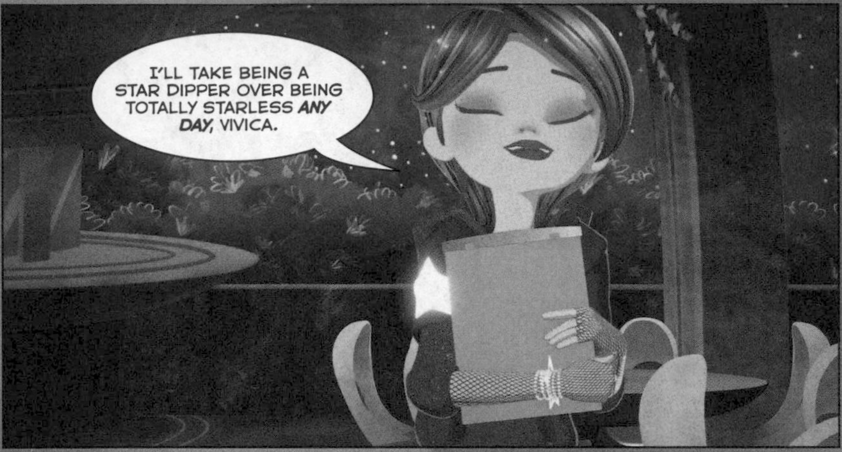
I'LL TAKE BEING A STAR DIPPER OVER BEING TOTALLY STARLESS ANY DAY, VIVICA.

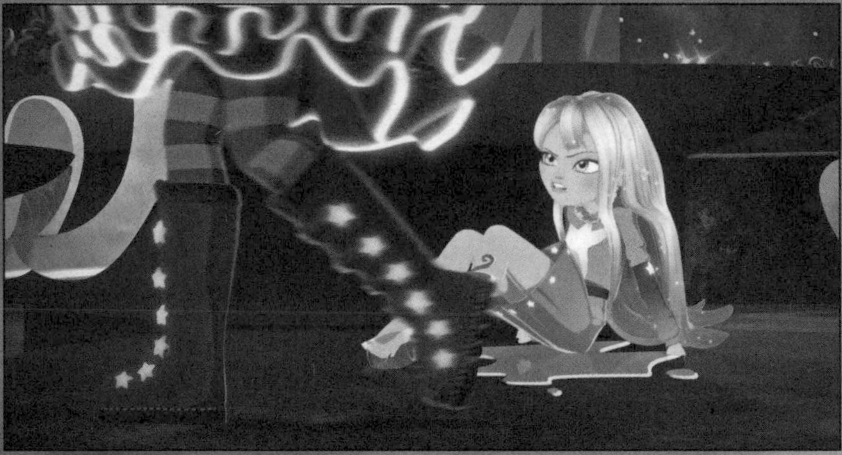

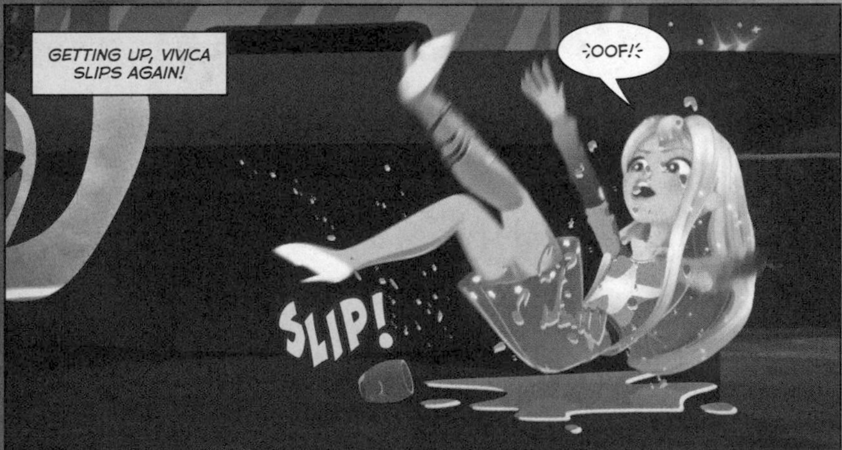
GETTING UP, VIVICA SLIPS AGAIN!
OOF!
SLIP!

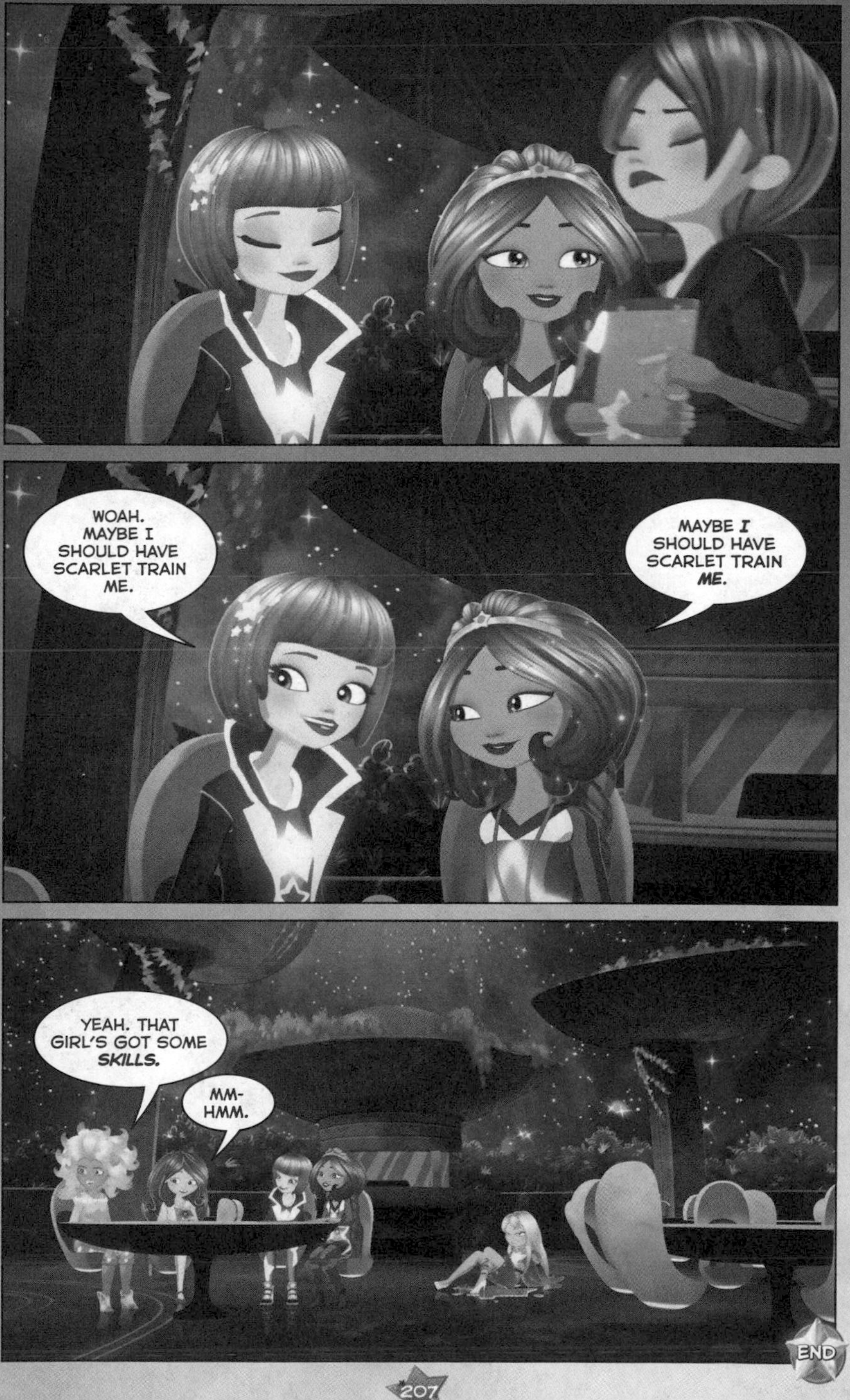
WOAH. MAYBE I SHOULD HAVE SCARLET TRAIN ME.
MAYBE *I* SHOULD HAVE SCARLET TRAIN ***ME.***
YEAH. THAT GIRL'S GOT SOME ***SKILLS.***
MM-HMM.
END

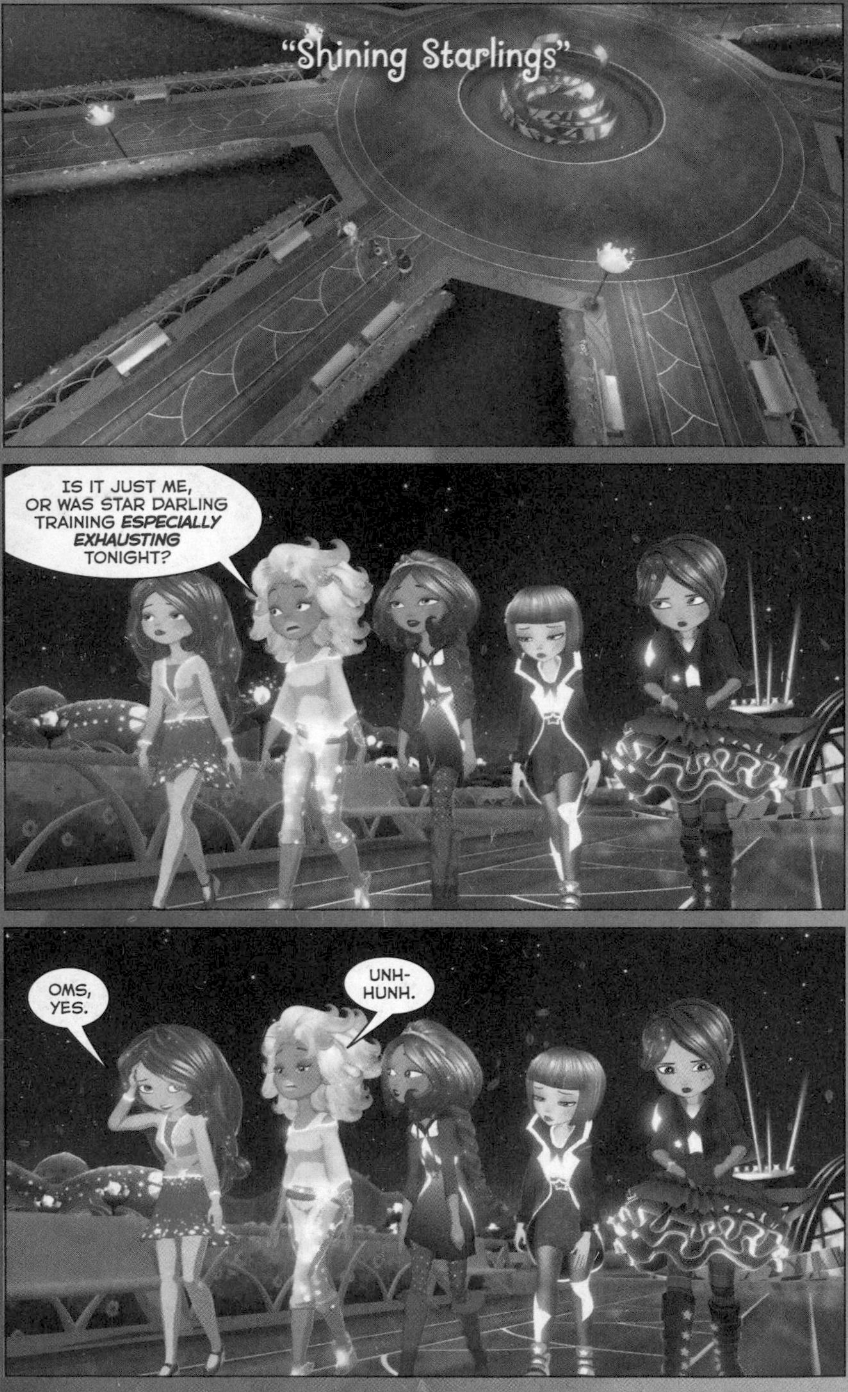
"Shining Starlings"
IS IT JUST ME, OR WAS STAR DARLING TRAINING *ESPECIALLY EXHAUSTING* TONIGHT?
OMS, YES.
UNH-HUNH.

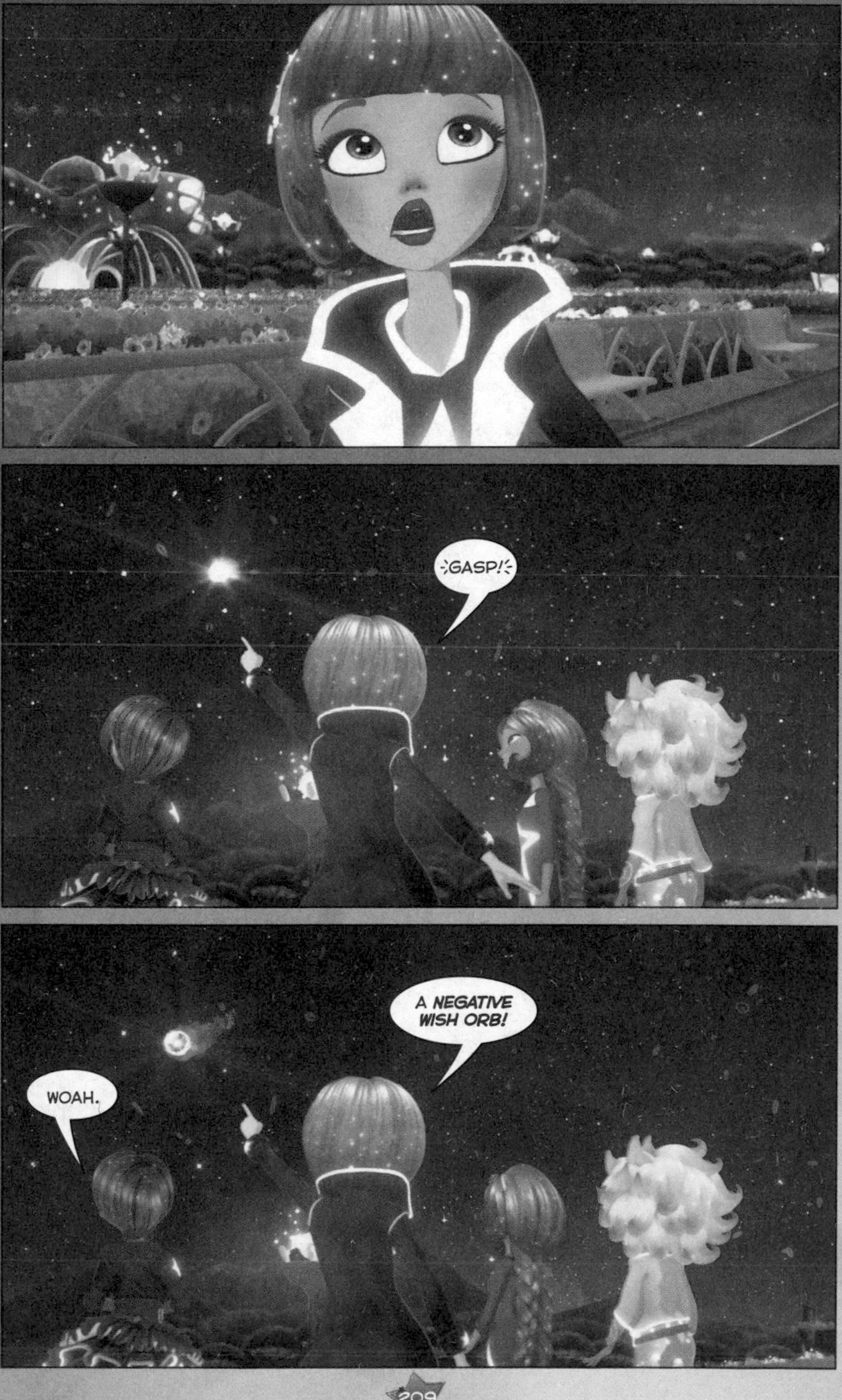
GASP!
A NEGATIVE WISH ORB!
WOAH.

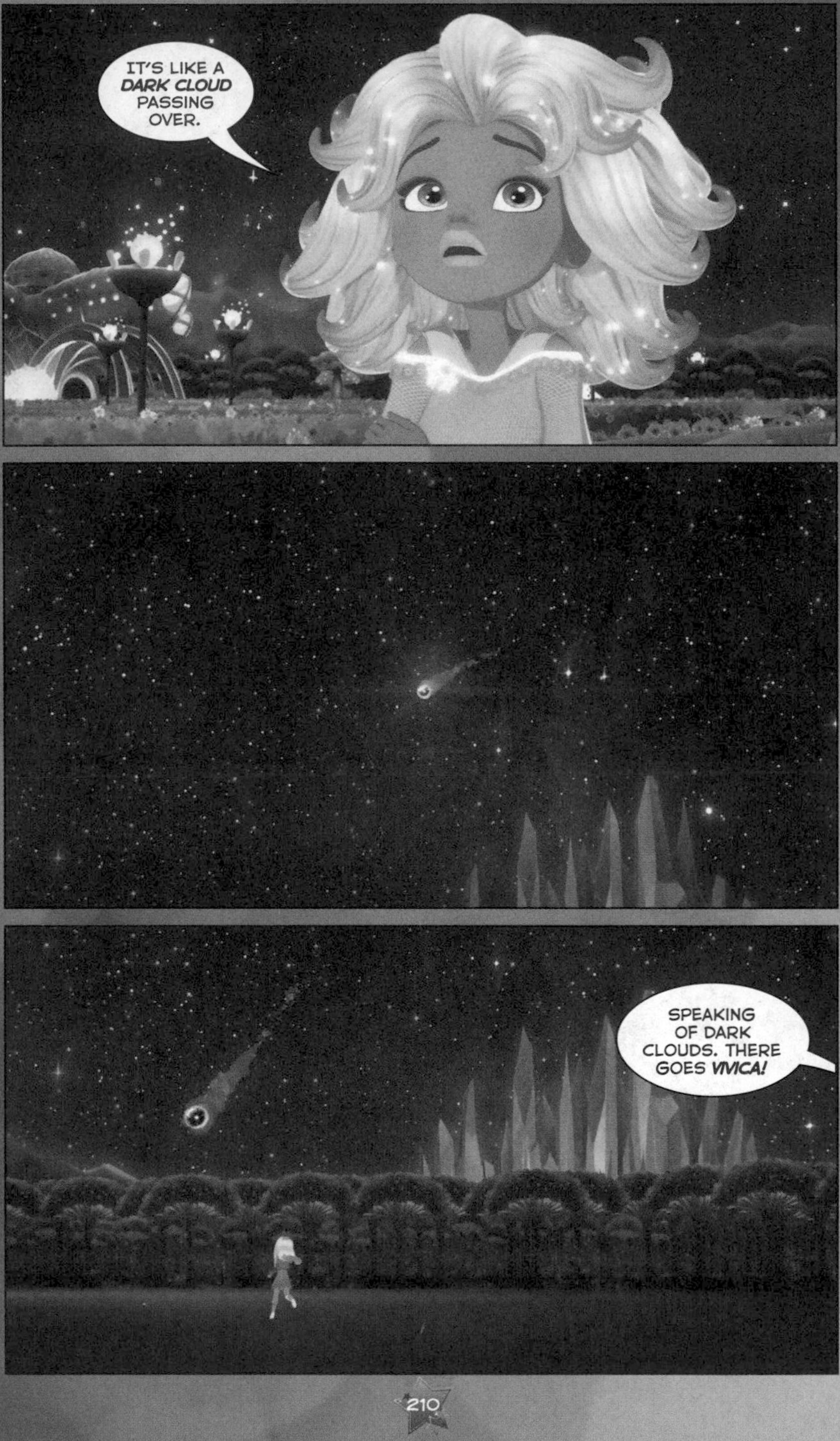
IT'S LIKE A *DARK CLOUD* PASSING OVER.
SPEAKING OF DARK CLOUDS. THERE GOES *VIVICA!*

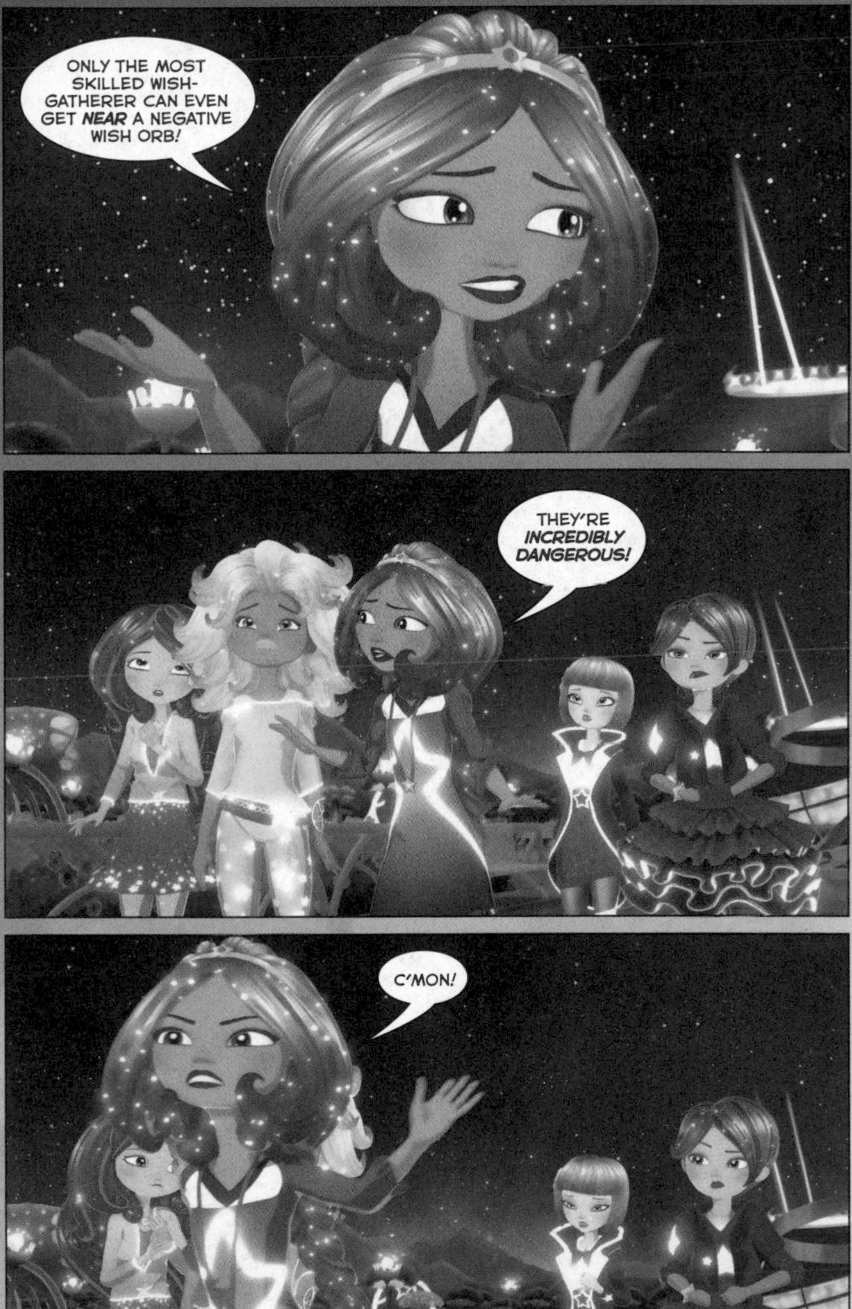
ONLY THE MOST SKILLED WISH-GATHERER CAN EVEN GET *NEAR* A NEGATIVE WISH ORB!
THEY'RE *INCREDIBLY DANGEROUS!*
C'MON!

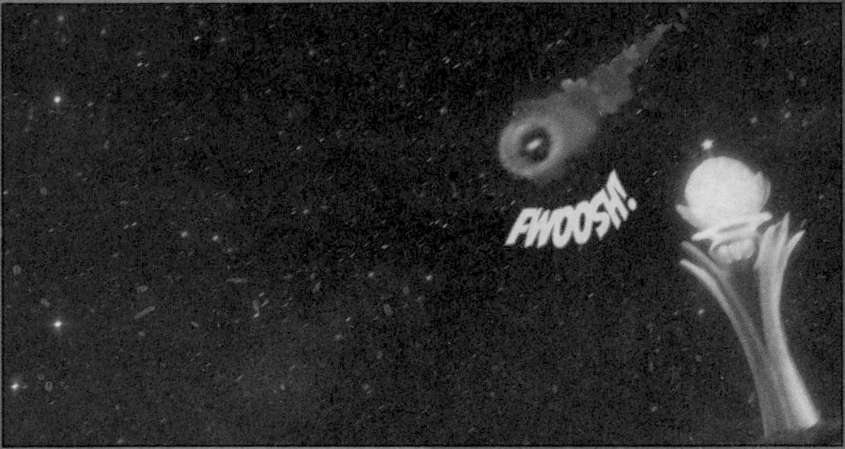
FWOOSH!

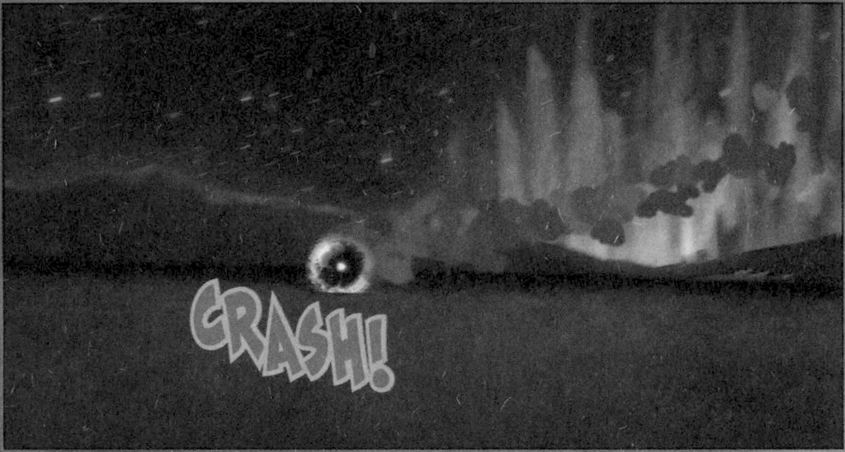
CRASH!

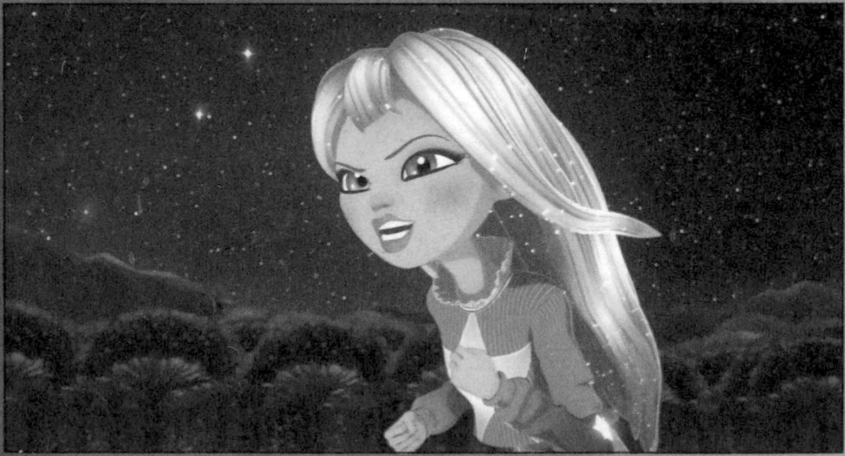

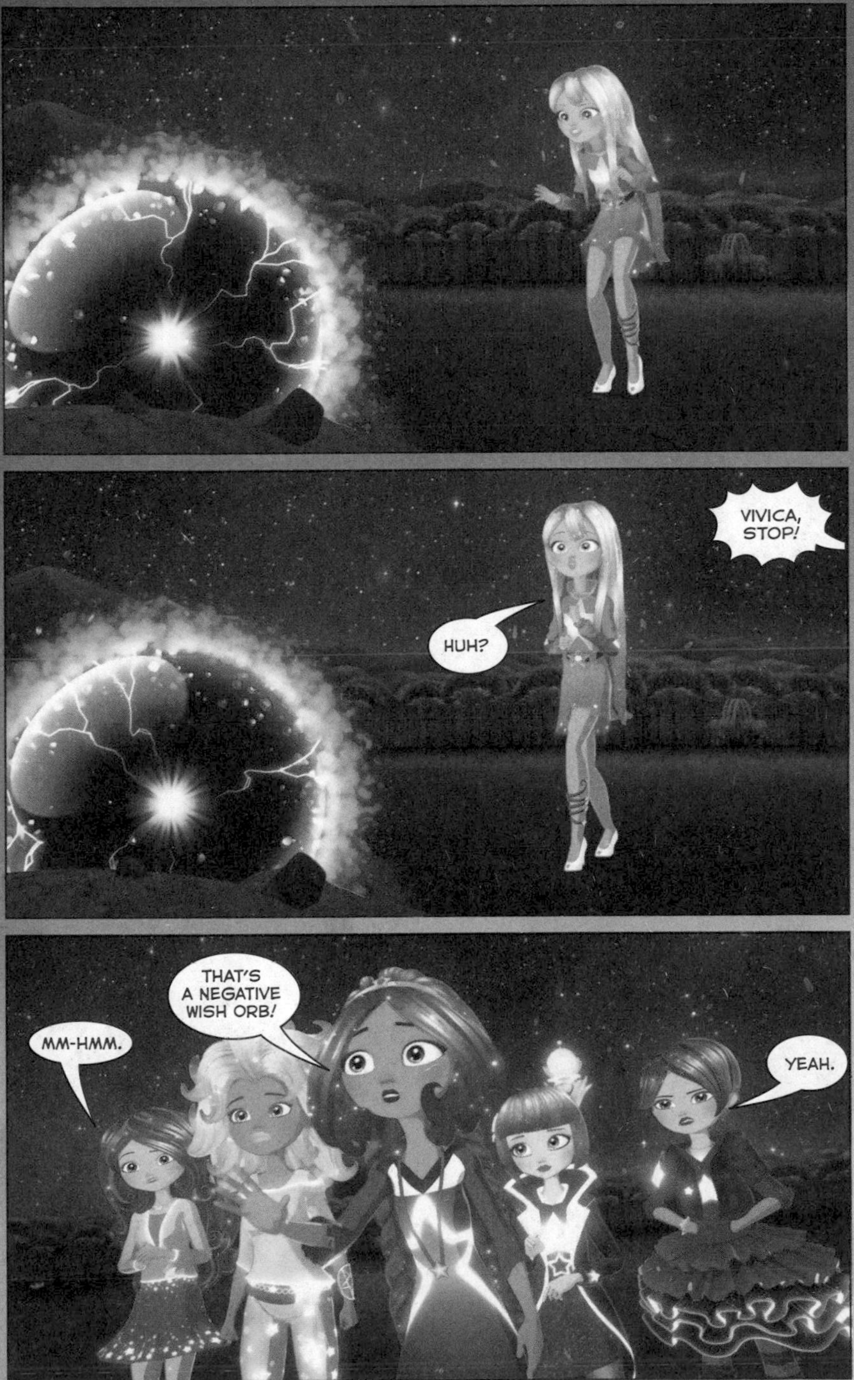
VIVICA, STOP!
HUH?
MM-HMM.
THAT'S A NEGATIVE WISH ORB!
YEAH.

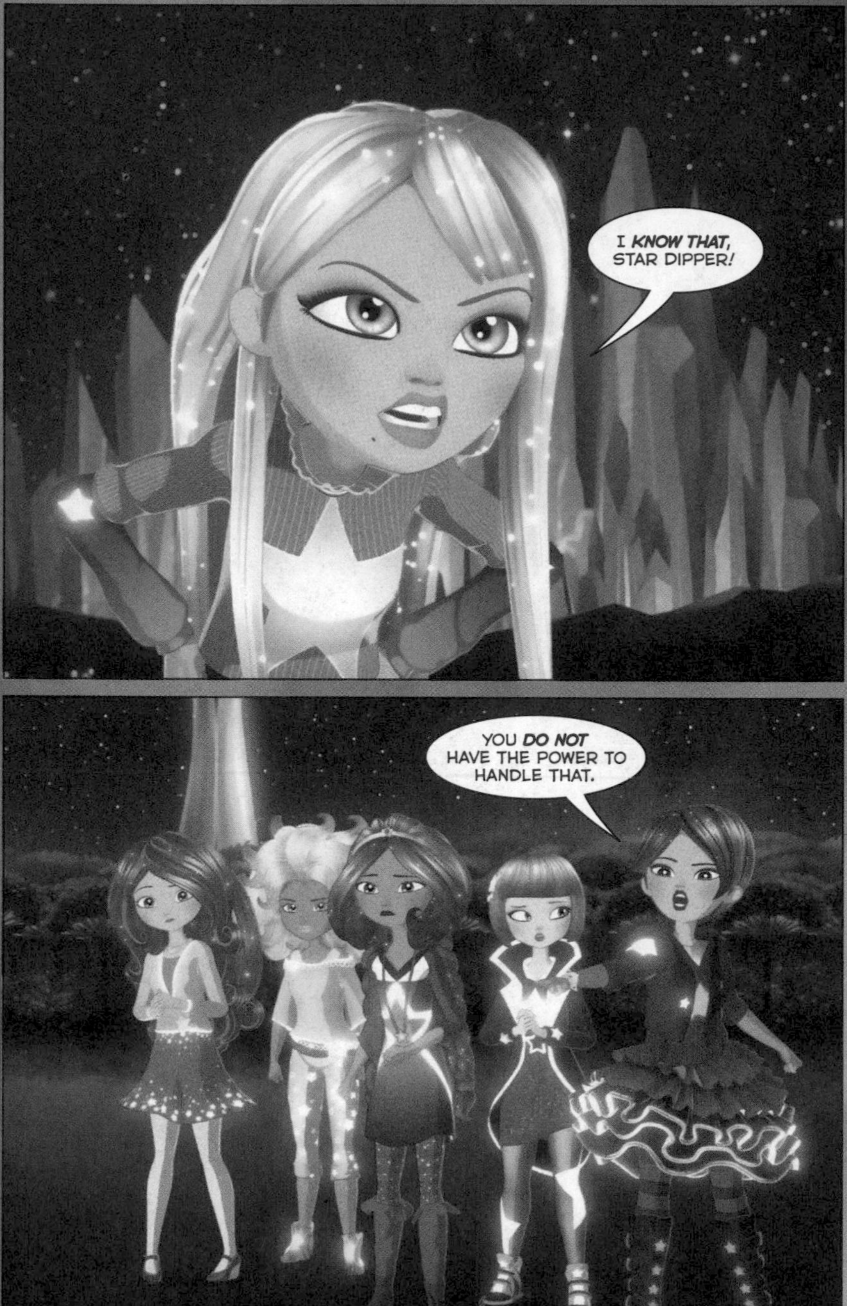
I KNOW THAT, STAR DIPPER!
YOU DO NOT HAVE THE POWER TO HANDLE THAT.

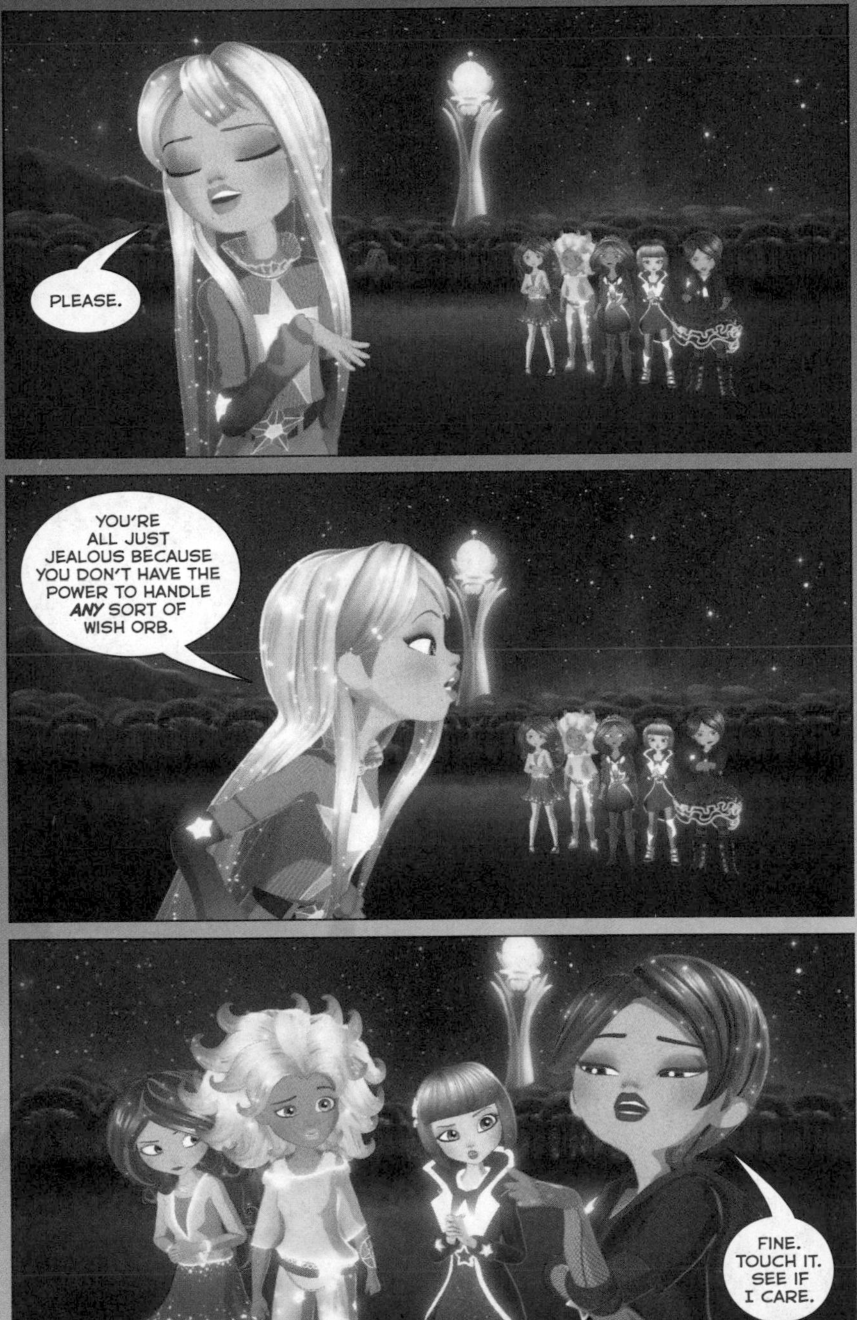
PLEASE.
YOU'RE ALL JUST JEALOUS BECAUSE YOU DON'T HAVE THE POWER TO HANDLE *ANY* SORT OF WISH ORB.
FINE. TOUCH IT. SEE IF I CARE.

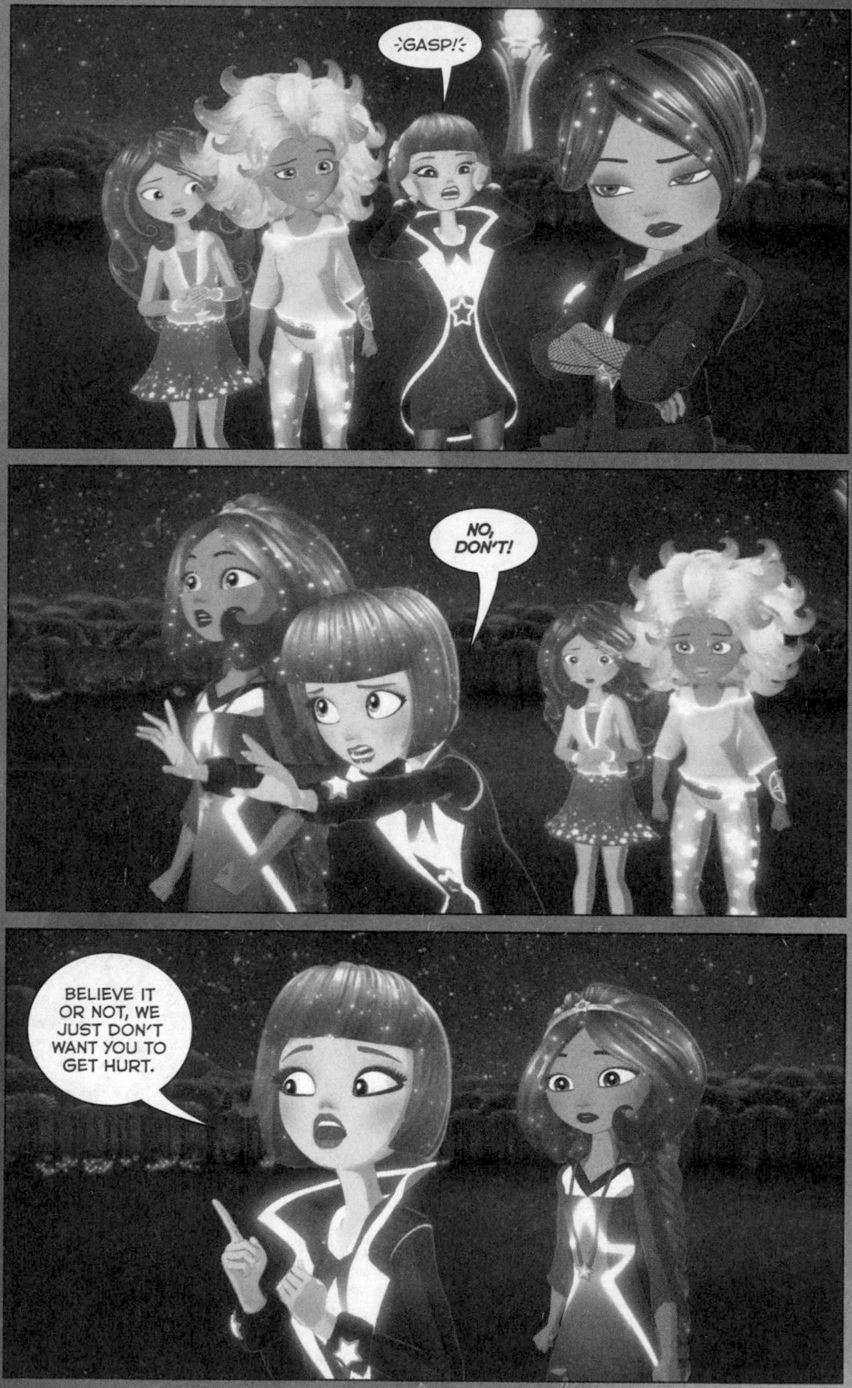
GASP!
NO, DON'T!
BELIEVE IT OR NOT, WE JUST DON'T WANT YOU TO GET HURT.

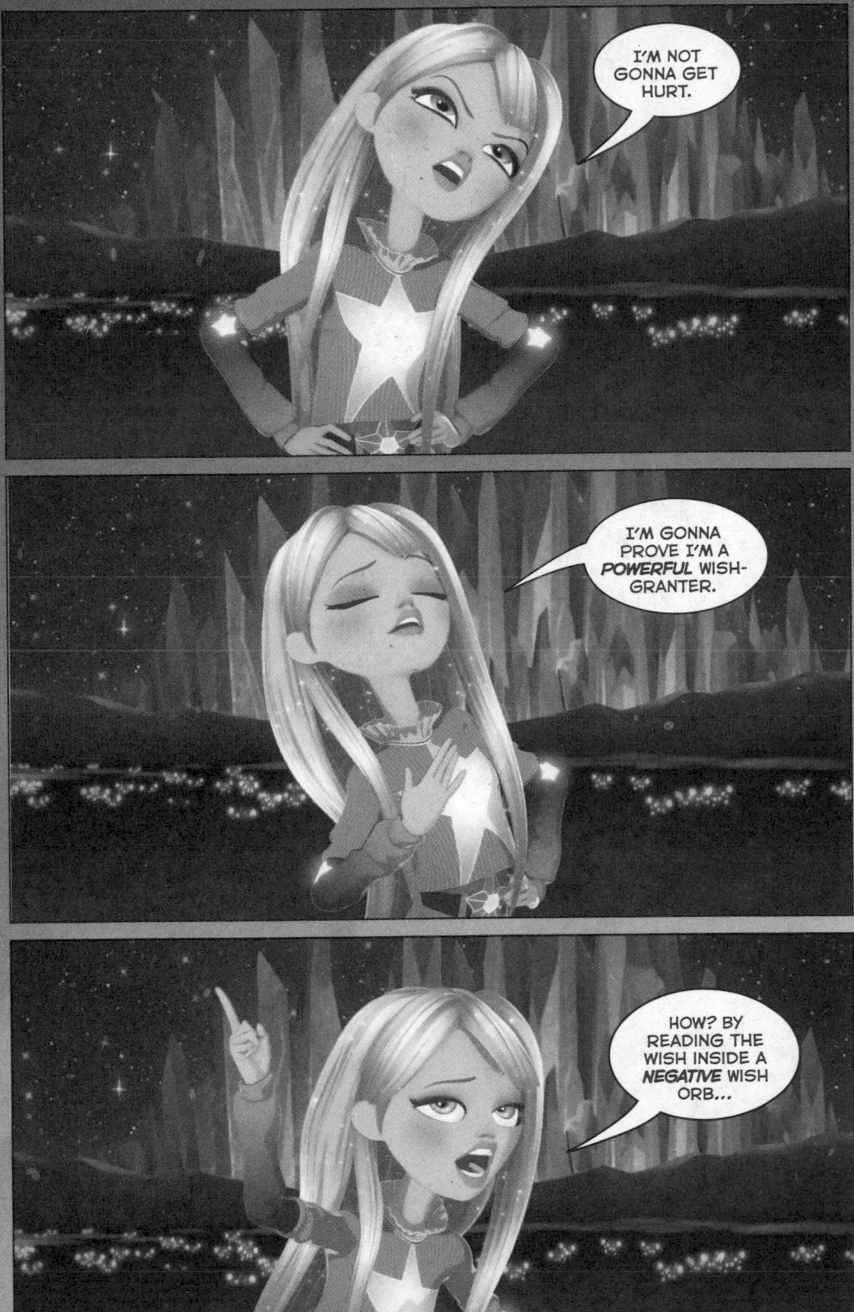
I'M NOT GONNA GET HURT.
I'M GONNA PROVE I'M A **POWERFUL** WISH-GRANTER.
HOW? BY READING THE WISH INSIDE A **NEGATIVE** WISH ORB...

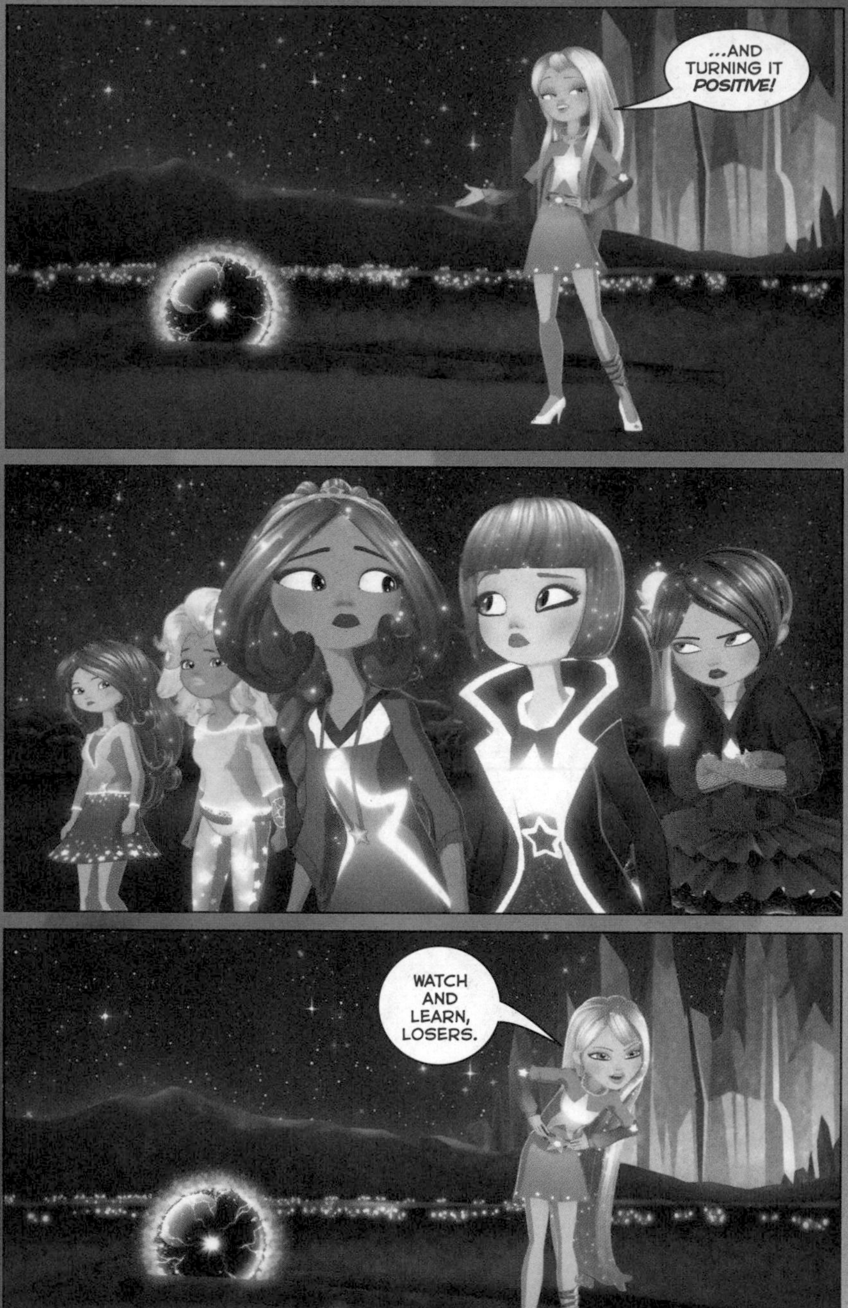
...AND TURNING IT *POSITIVE!*
WATCH AND LEARN, LOSERS.

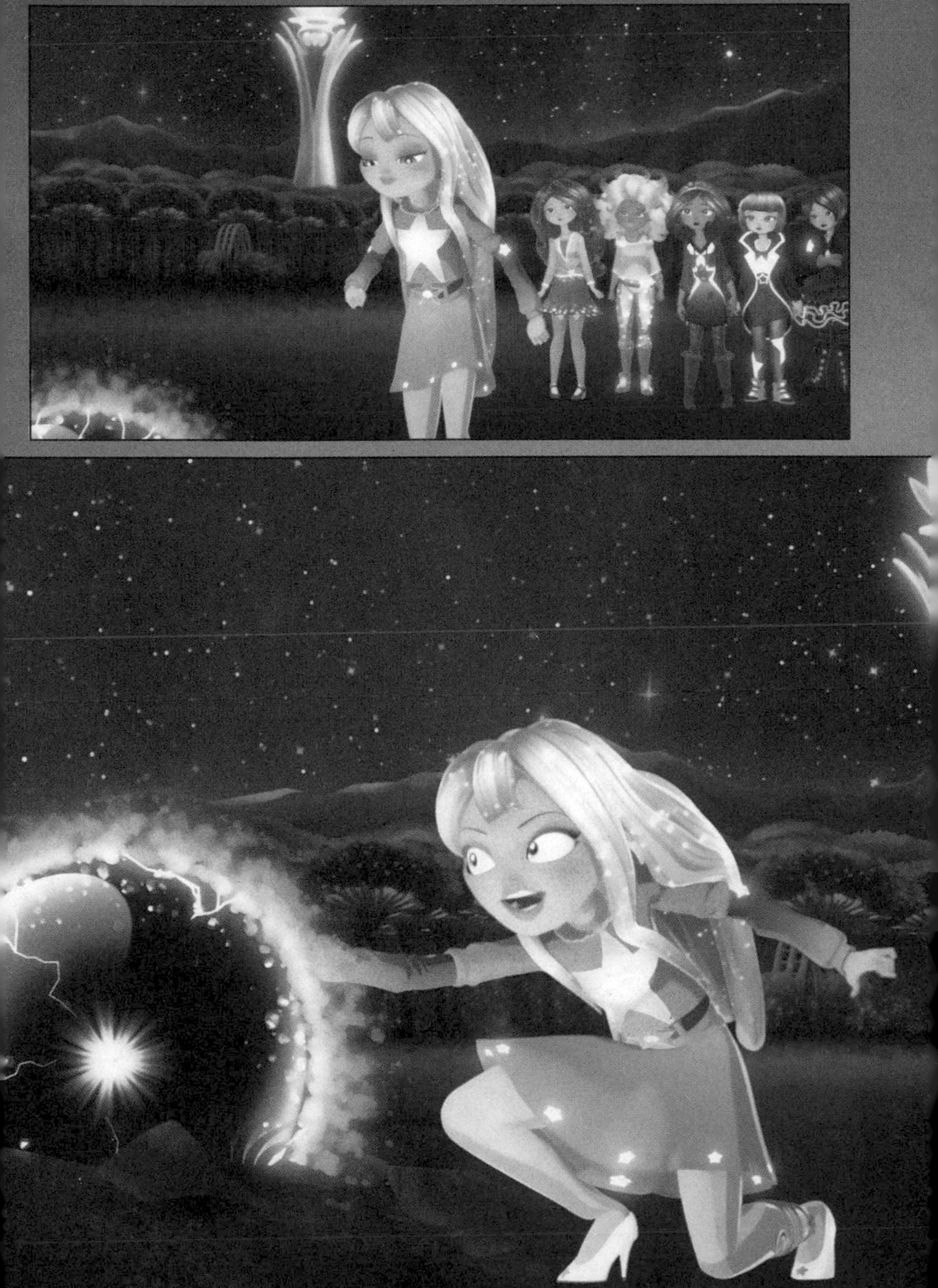

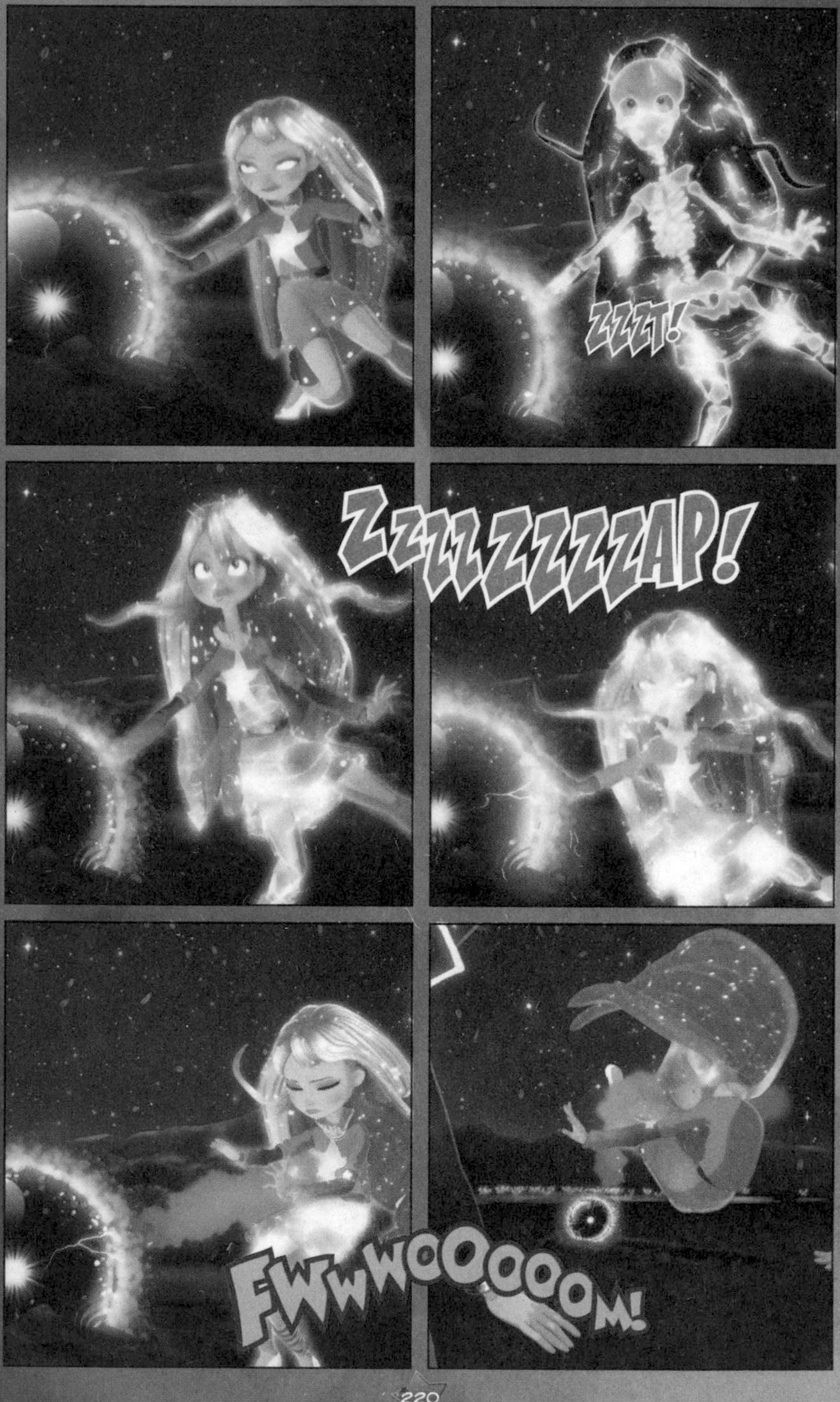
ZZZT!
ZZZZZZZZZAP!
FWWWOOOOOOM!

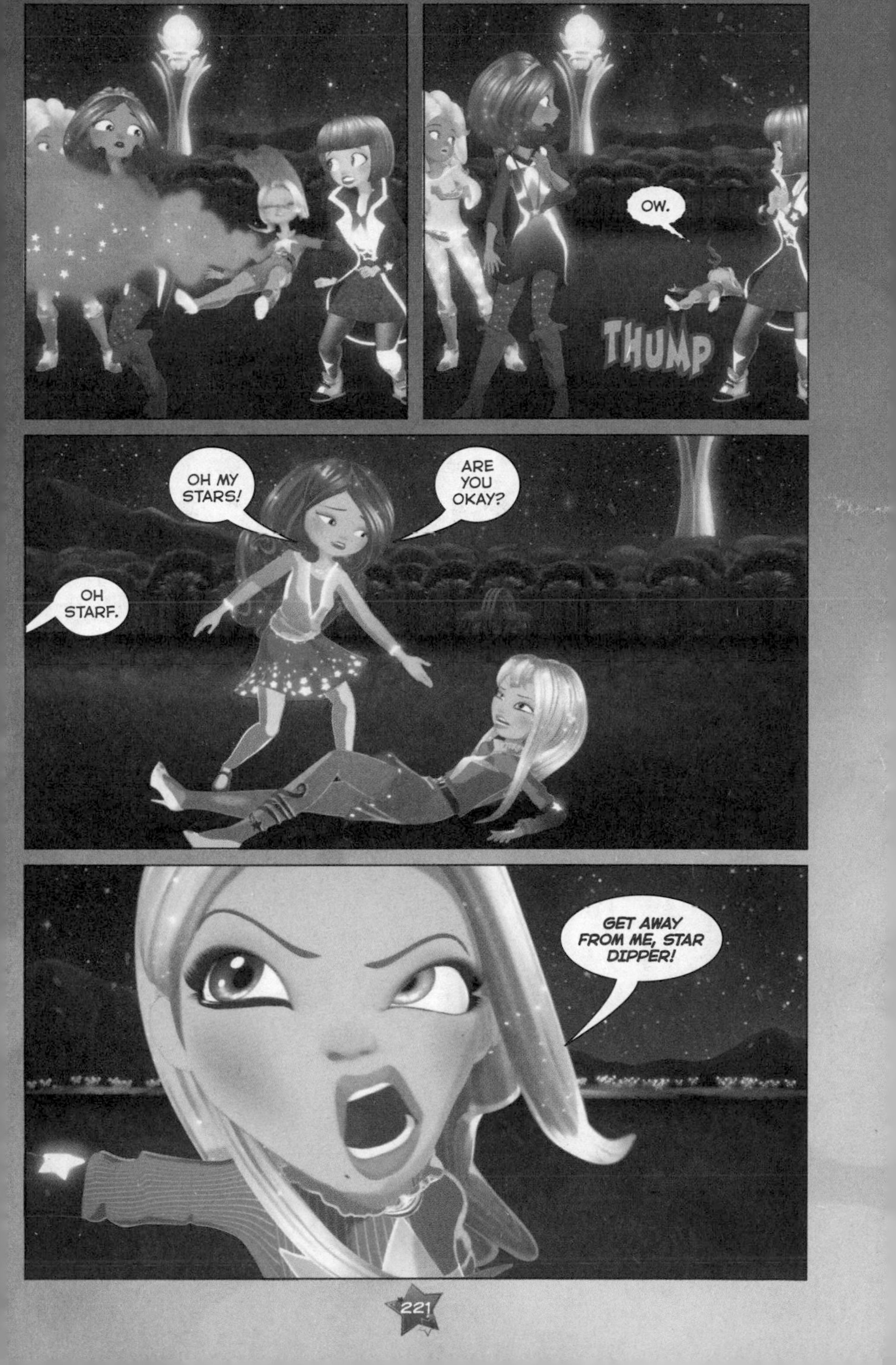
OW.
THUMP
OH MY STARS!
ARE YOU OKAY?
OH STARF.
GET AWAY FROM ME, STAR DIPPER!

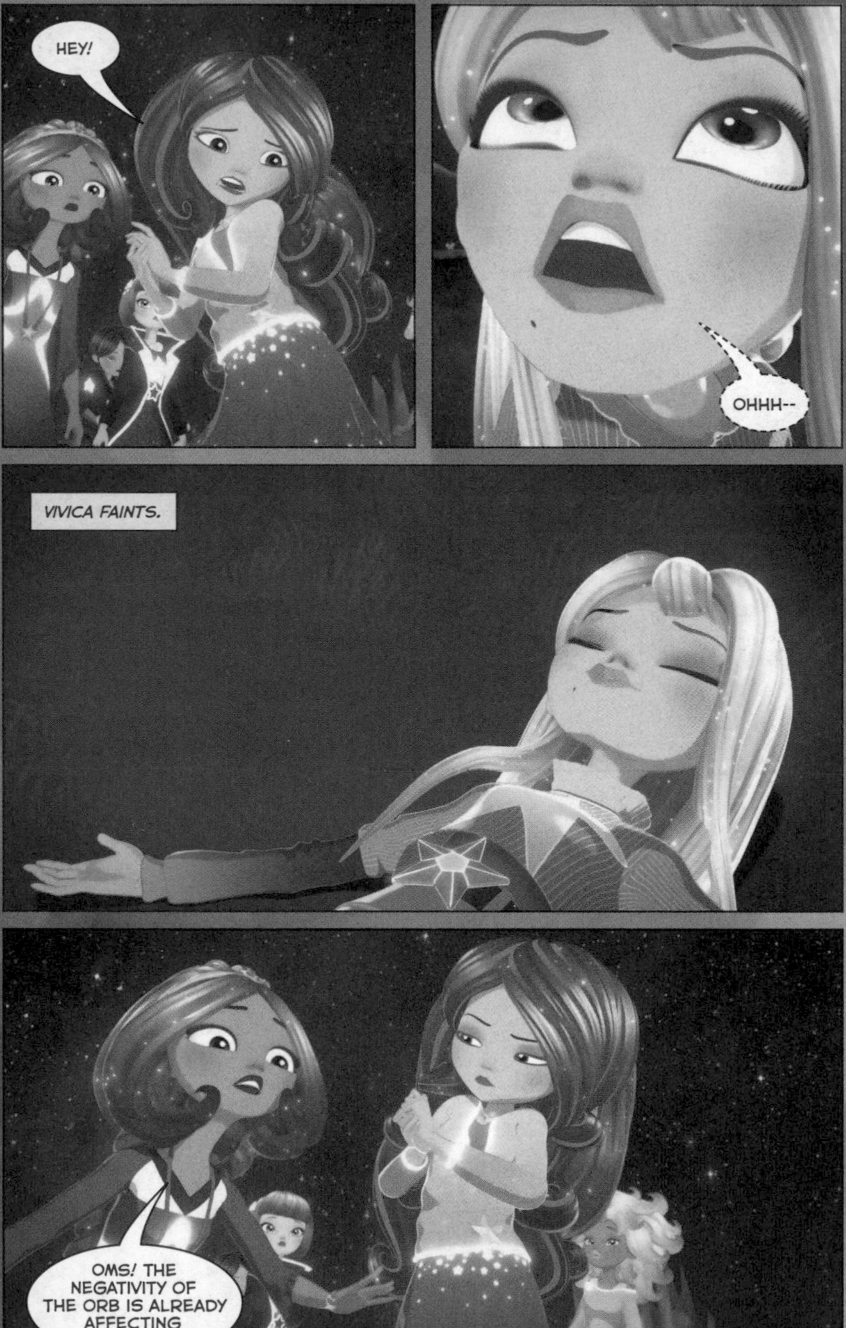
HEY!
OHHH--
VIVICA FAINTS.
OMS! THE NEGATIVITY OF THE ORB IS ALREADY AFFECTING HER.

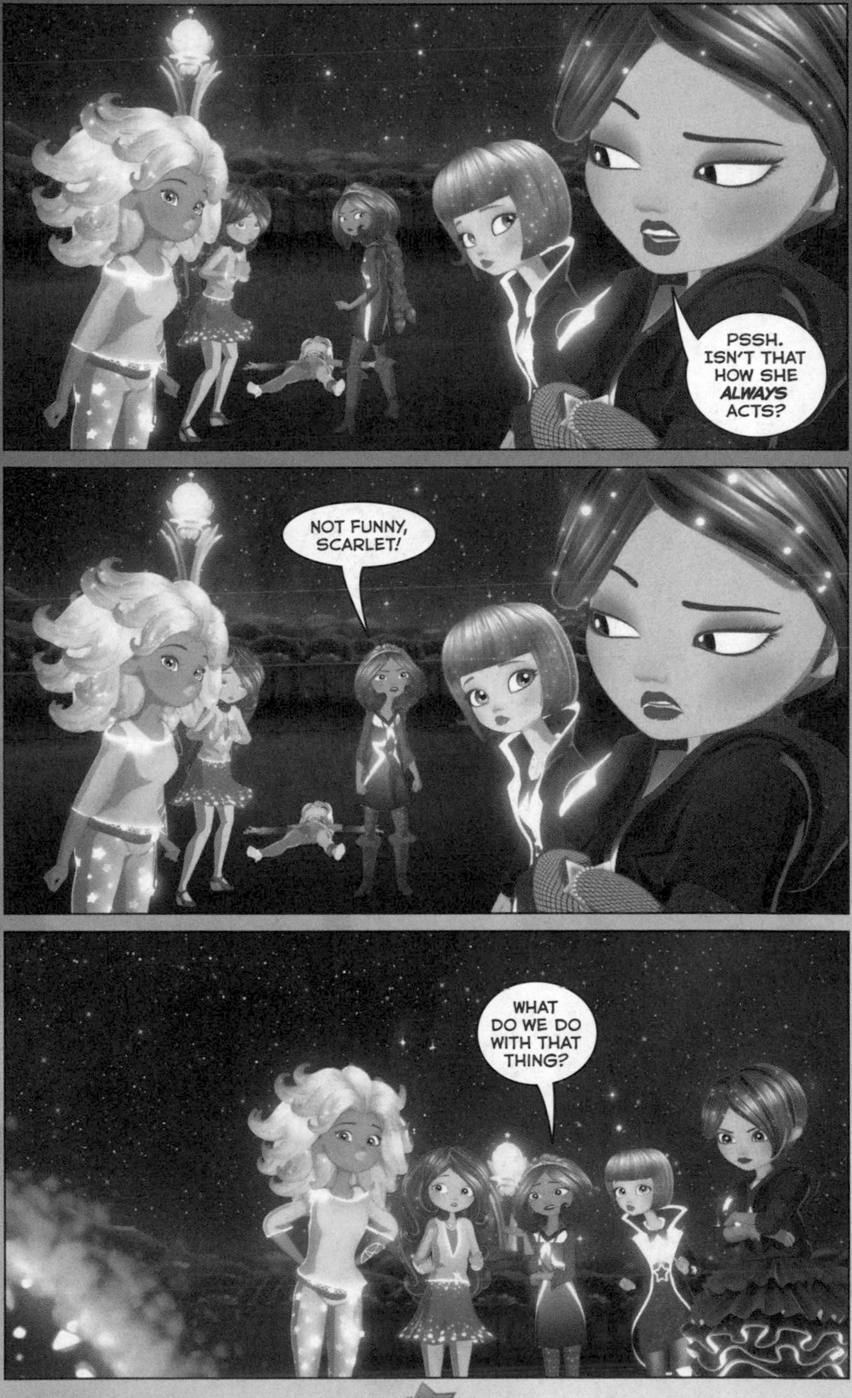
PSSH. ISN'T THAT HOW SHE *ALWAYS* ACTS?
NOT FUNNY, SCARLET!
WHAT DO WE DO WITH THAT THING?

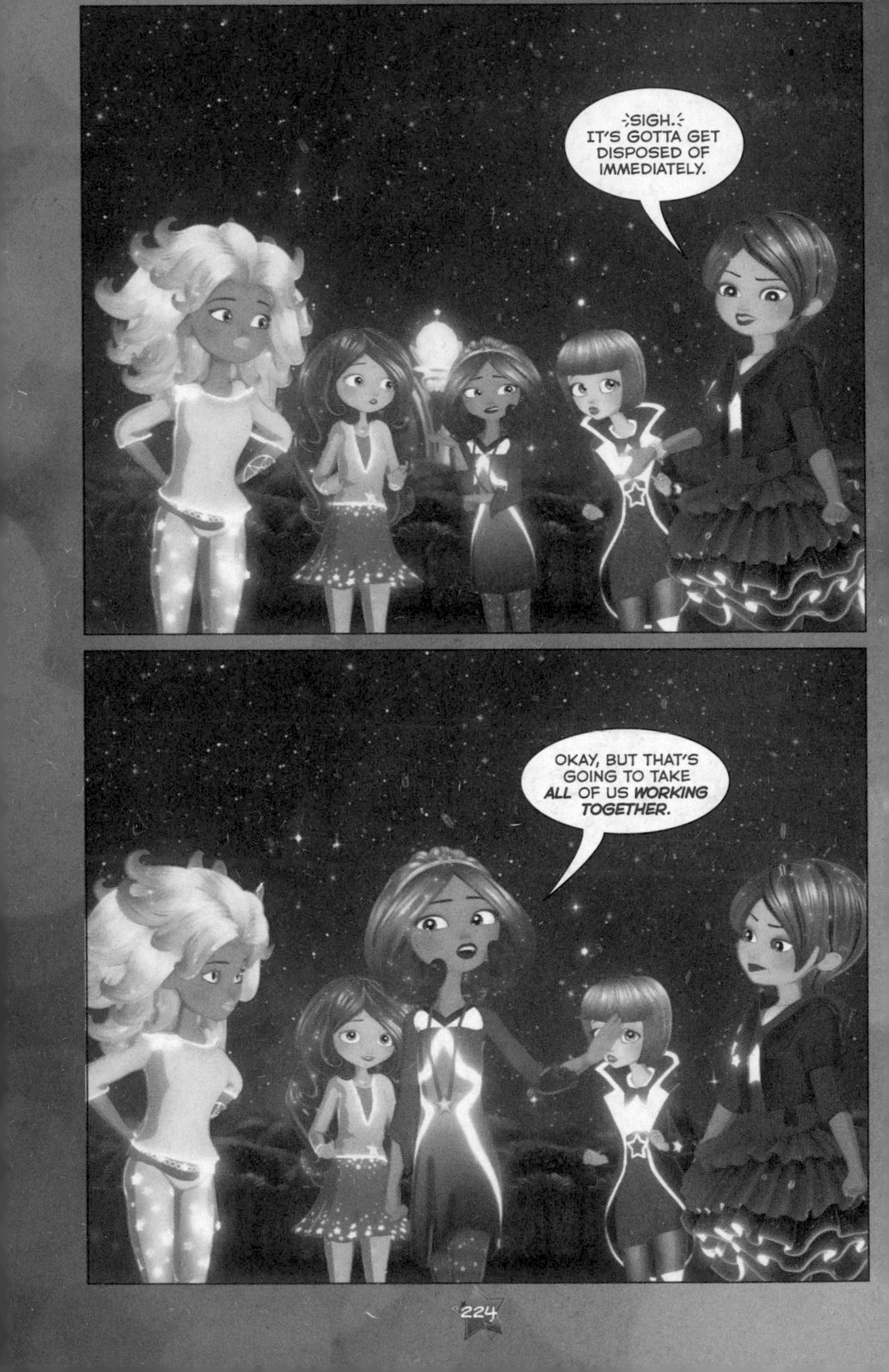
SIGH. IT'S GOTTA GET DISPOSED OF IMMEDIATELY.
OKAY, BUT THAT'S GOING TO TAKE ***ALL*** OF US ***WORKING TOGETHER.***

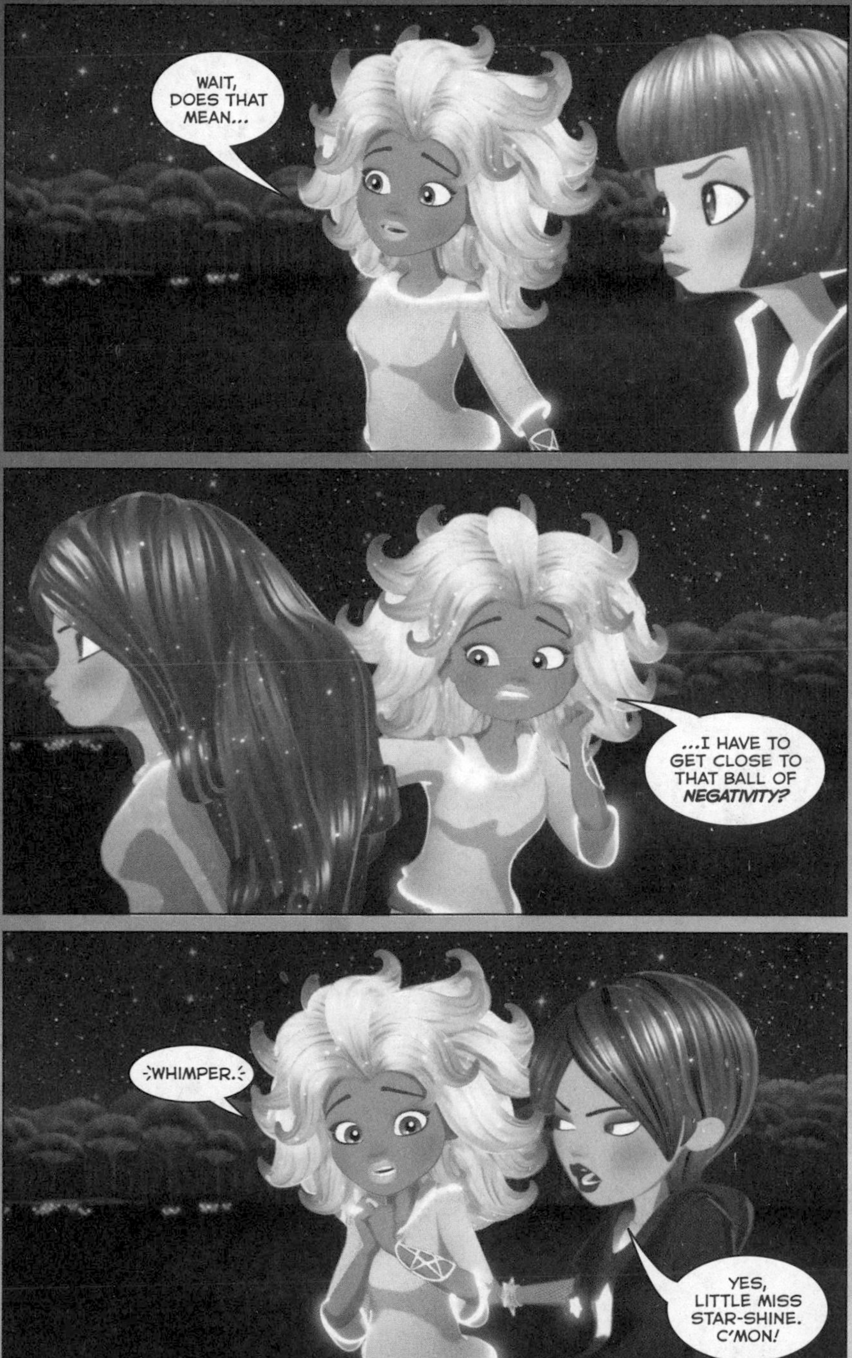
WAIT, DOES THAT MEAN...
...I HAVE TO GET CLOSE TO THAT BALL OF *NEGATIVITY?*
WHIMPER.
YES, LITTLE MISS STAR-SHINE. C'MON!

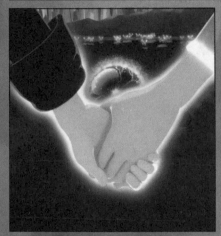

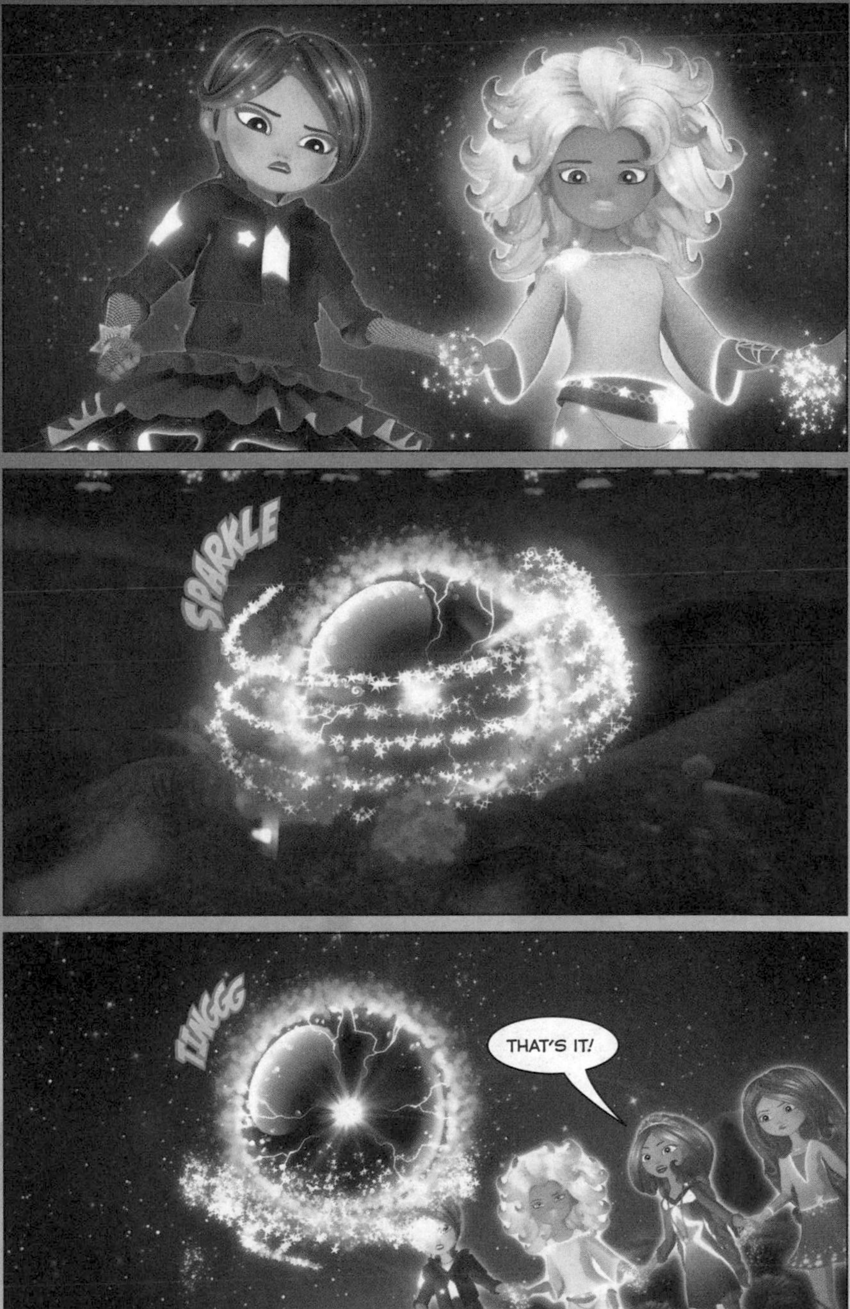
SPARKLE
TINGGG
THAT'S IT!

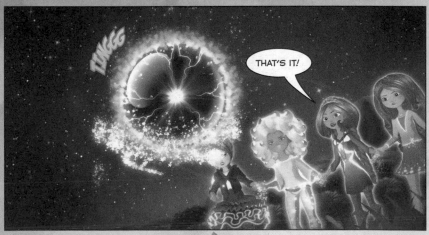

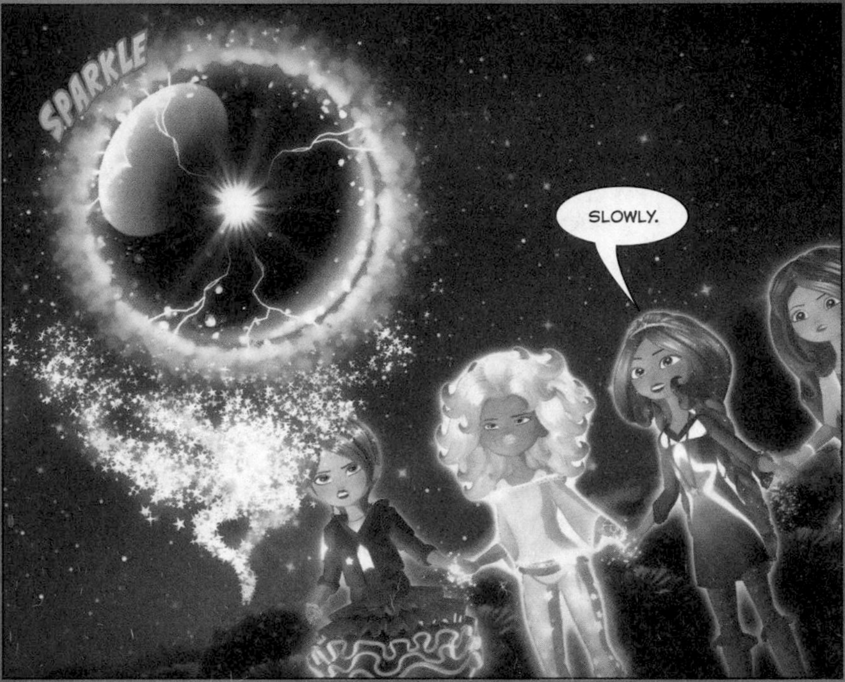
SPARKLE
SLOWLY.

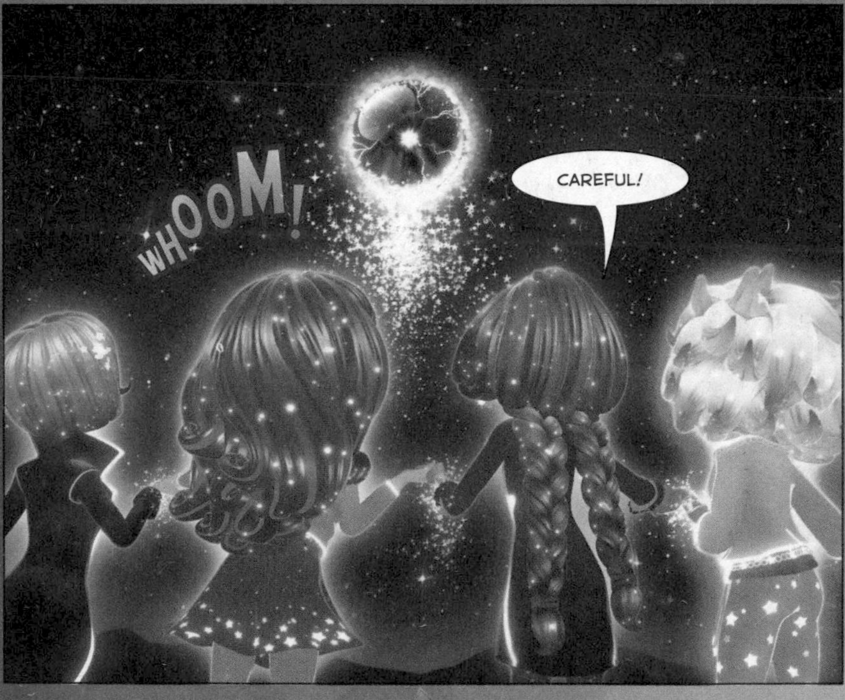
WHOOM!
CAREFUL!

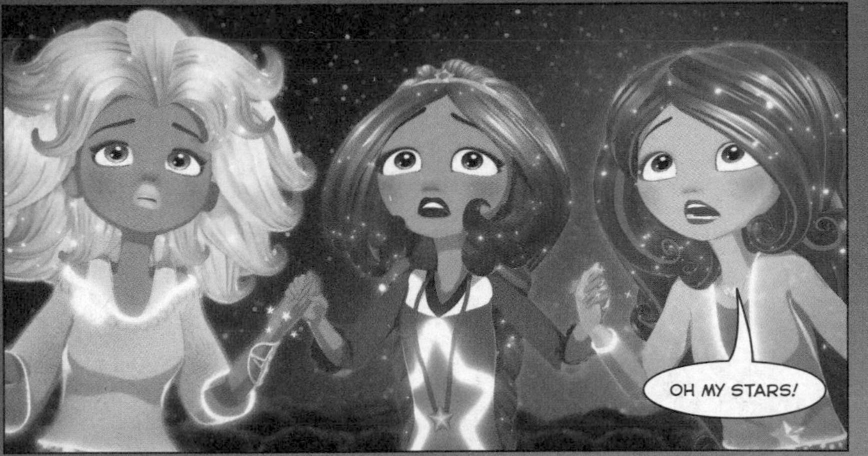
OH MY STARS!

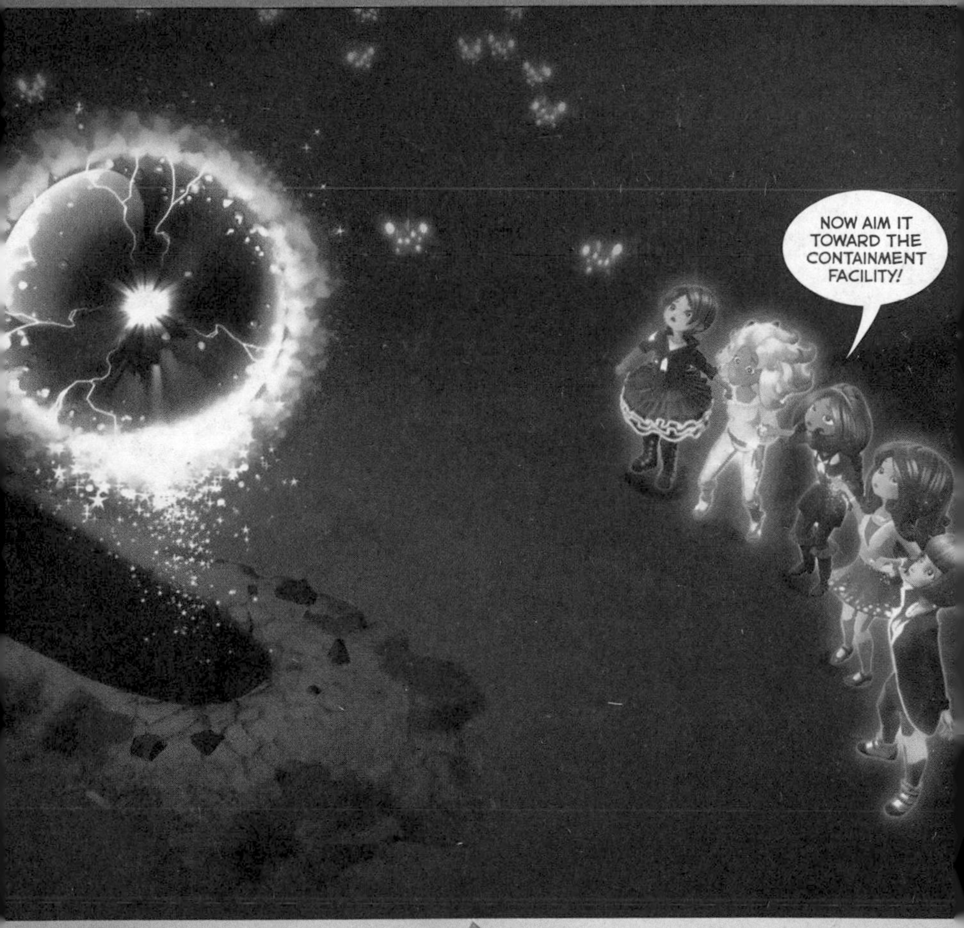
NOW AIM IT TOWARD THE CONTAINMENT FACILITY!

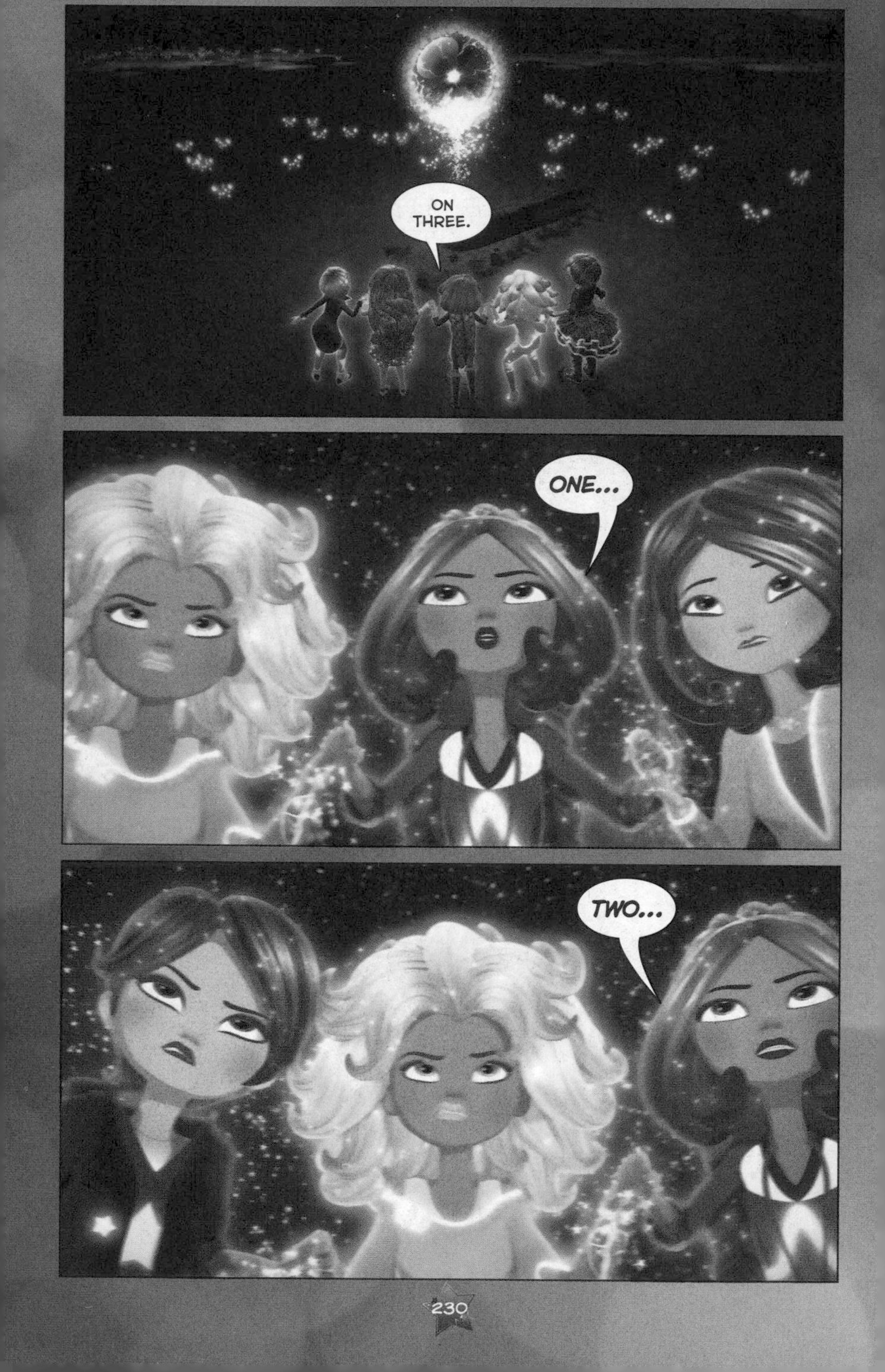
ON THREE.
ONE...
TWO...

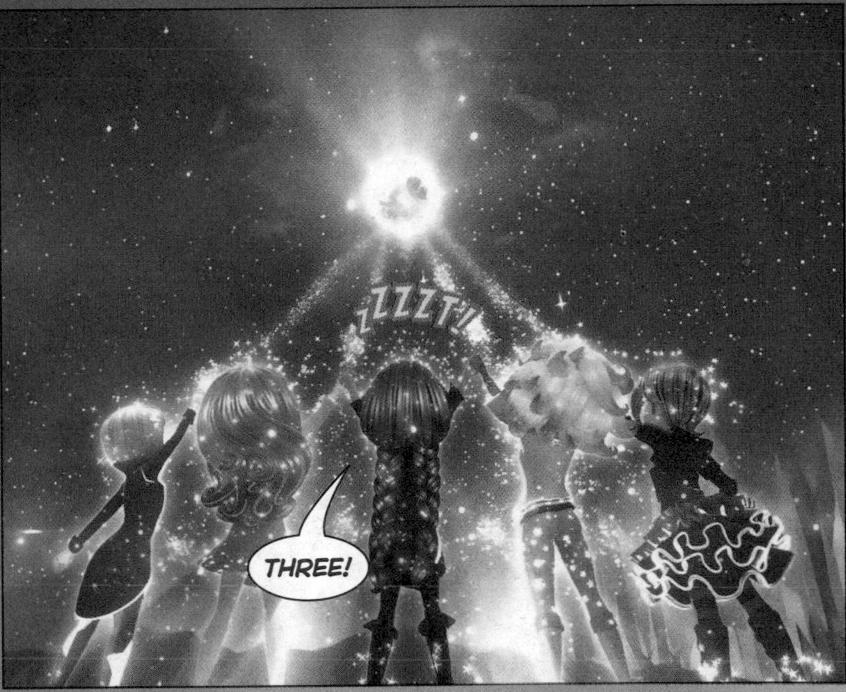
ZZZZT!!
THREE!

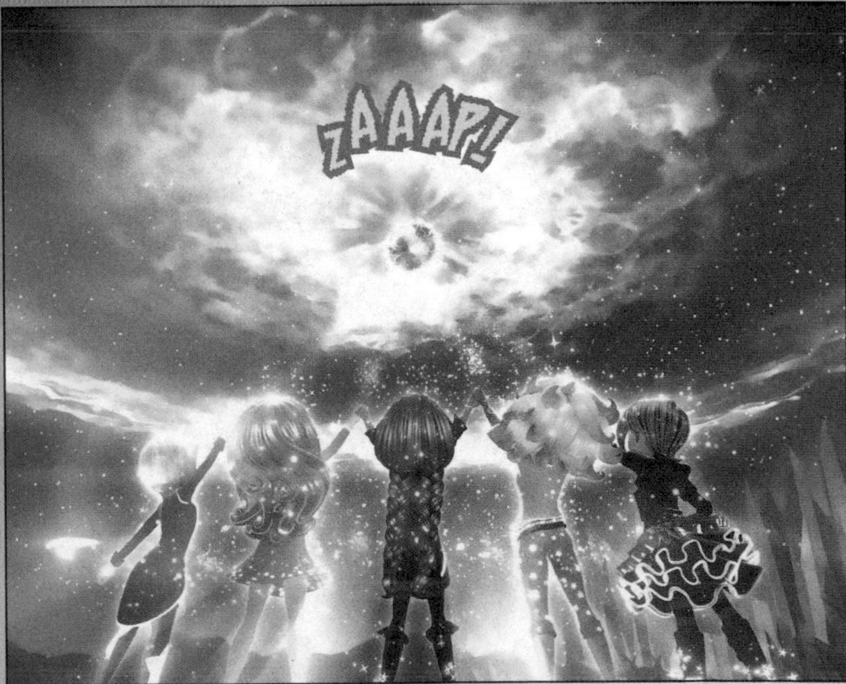
ZAAAP!

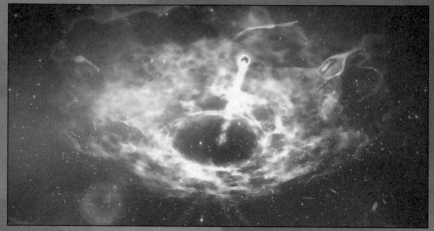

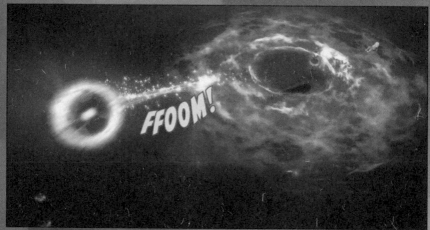

FFOOM!

FWOOSH!

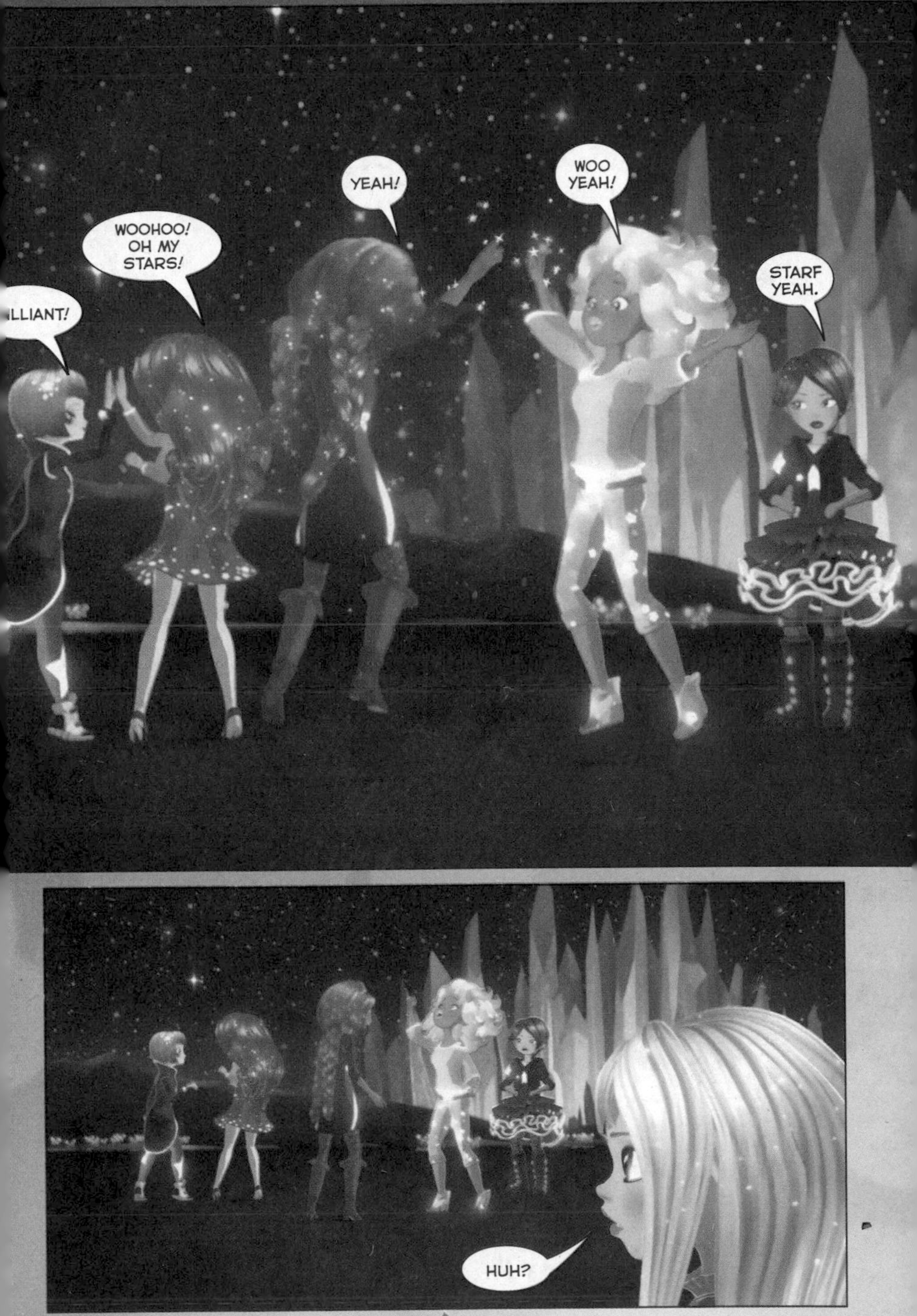
LLIANT!
WOOHOO! OH MY STARS!
YEAH!
WOO YEAH!
STARF YEAH.
HUH?

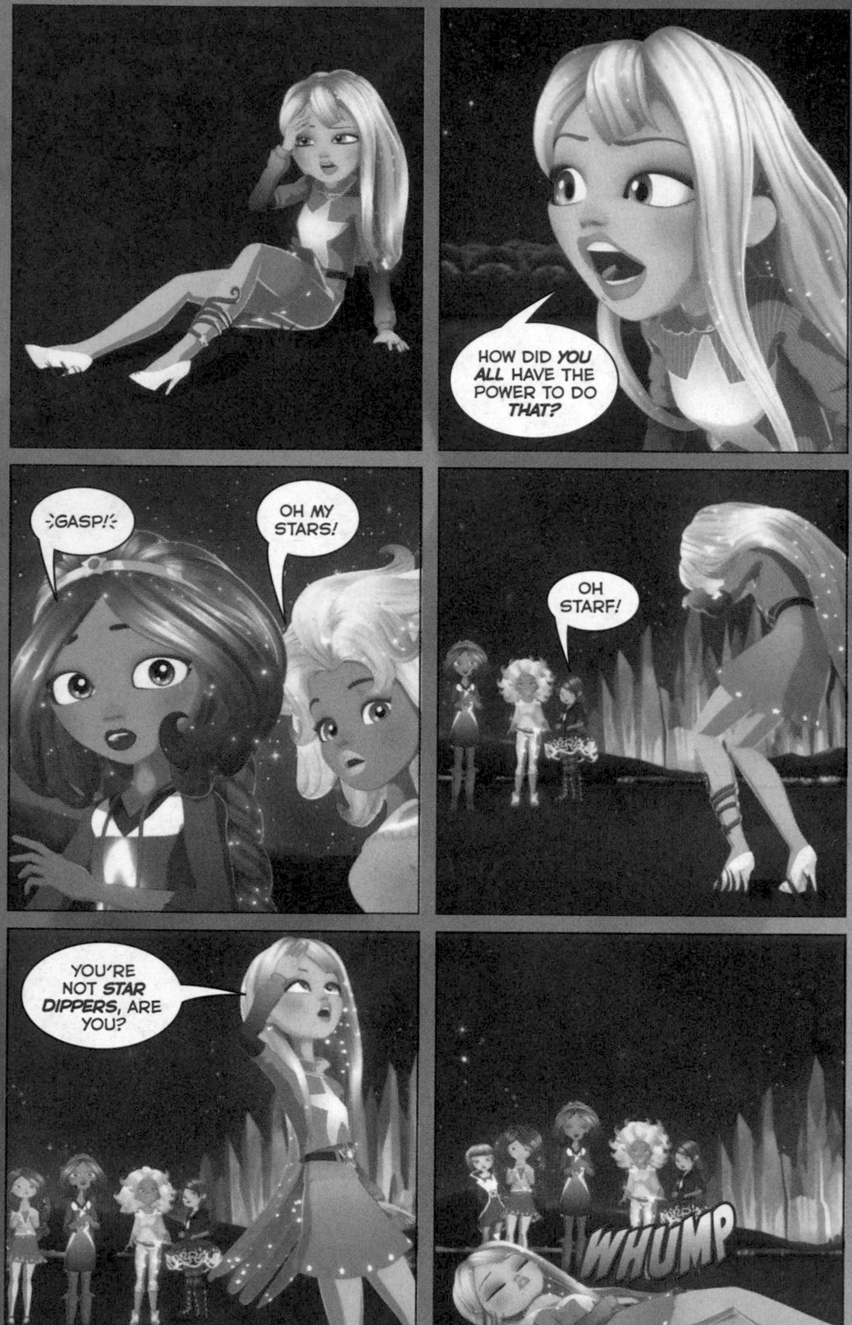
HOW DID YOU ALL HAVE THE POWER TO DO THAT?
-GASP!-
OH MY STARS!
OH STARF!
YOU'RE NOT STAR DIPPERS, ARE YOU?
WHUMP

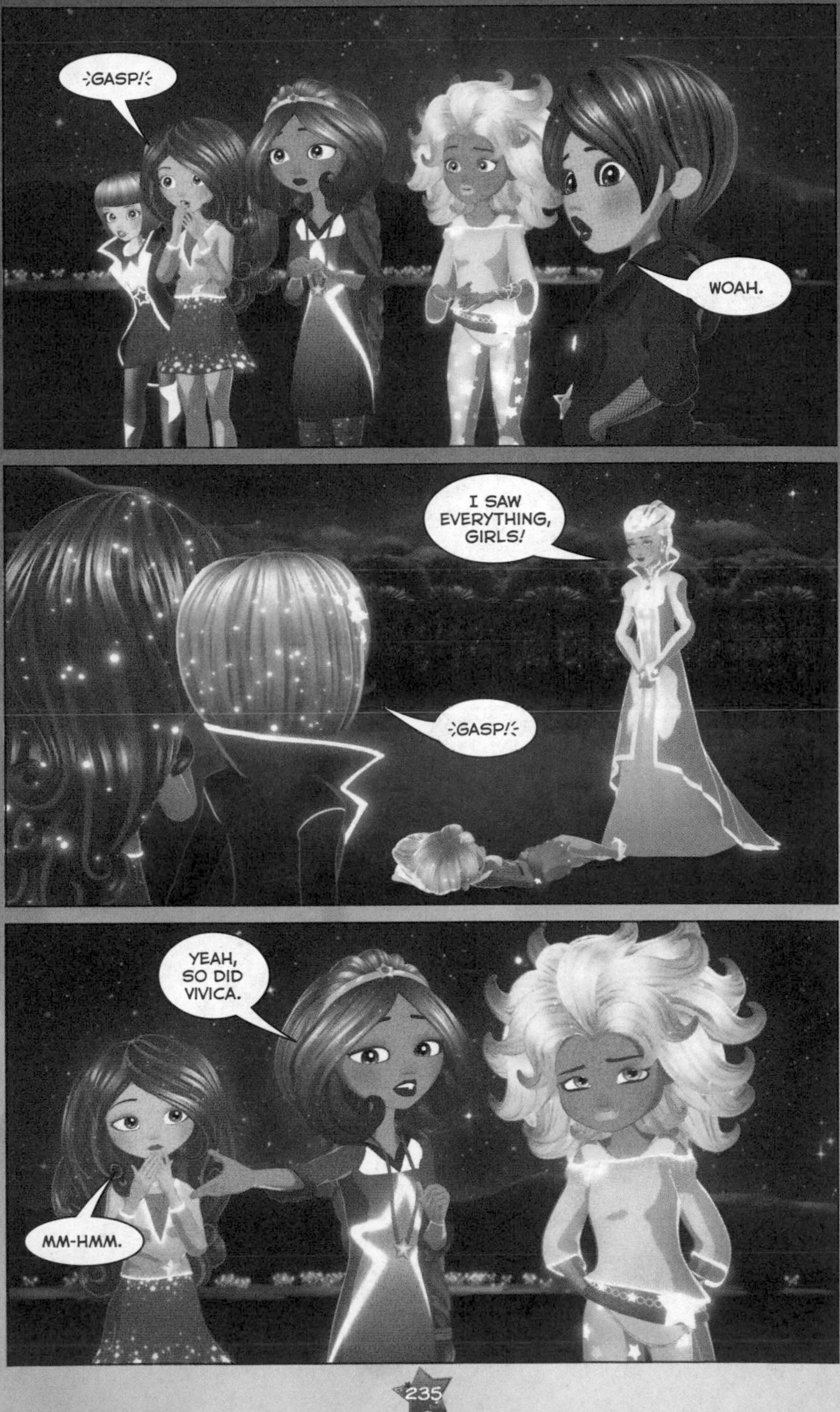

-GASP!-
WOAH.
I SAW EVERYTHING, GIRLS!
-GASP!-
YEAH, SO DID VIVICA.
MM-HMM.

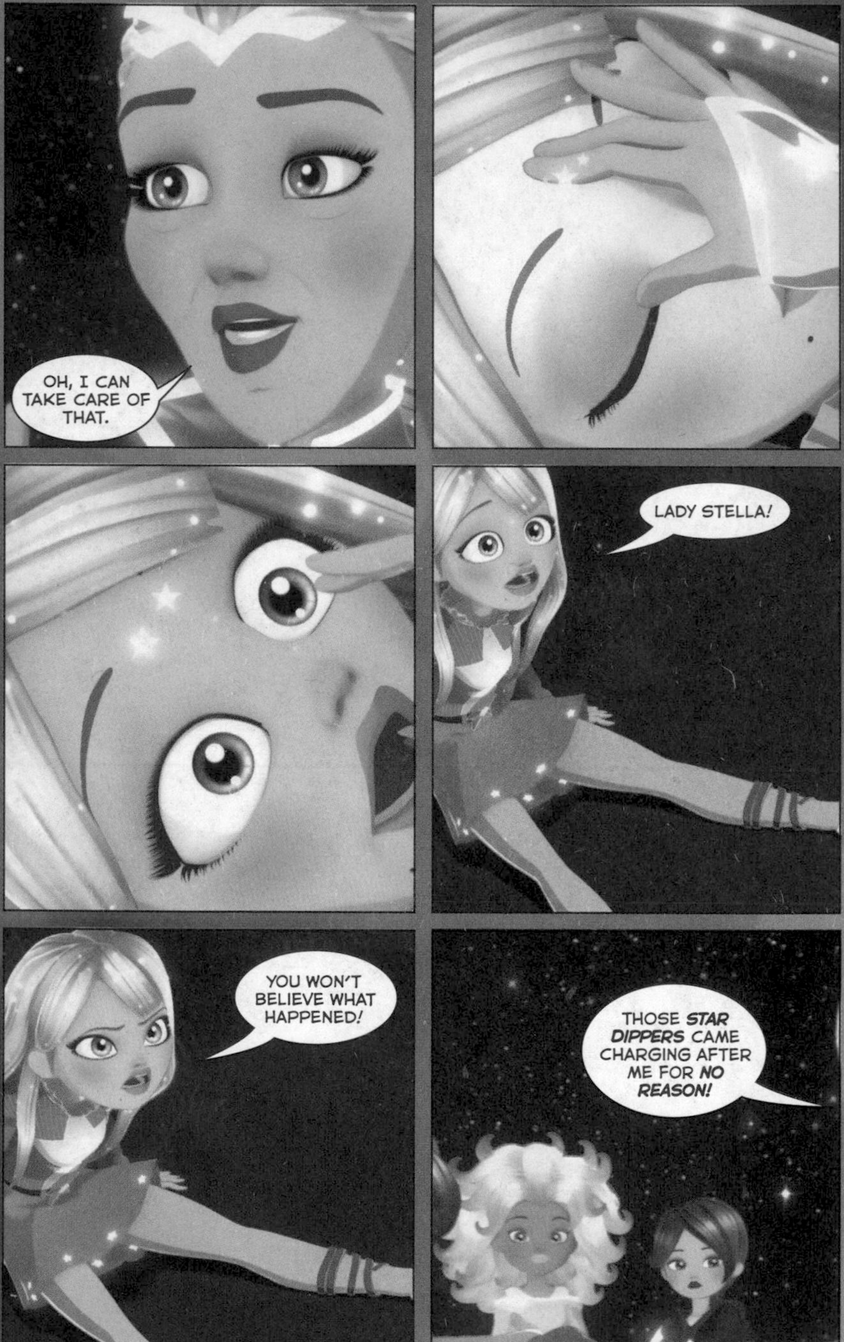
OH, I CAN TAKE CARE OF THAT.
LADY STELLA!
YOU WON'T BELIEVE WHAT HAPPENED!
THOSE STAR DIPPERS CAME CHARGING AFTER ME FOR NO REASON!

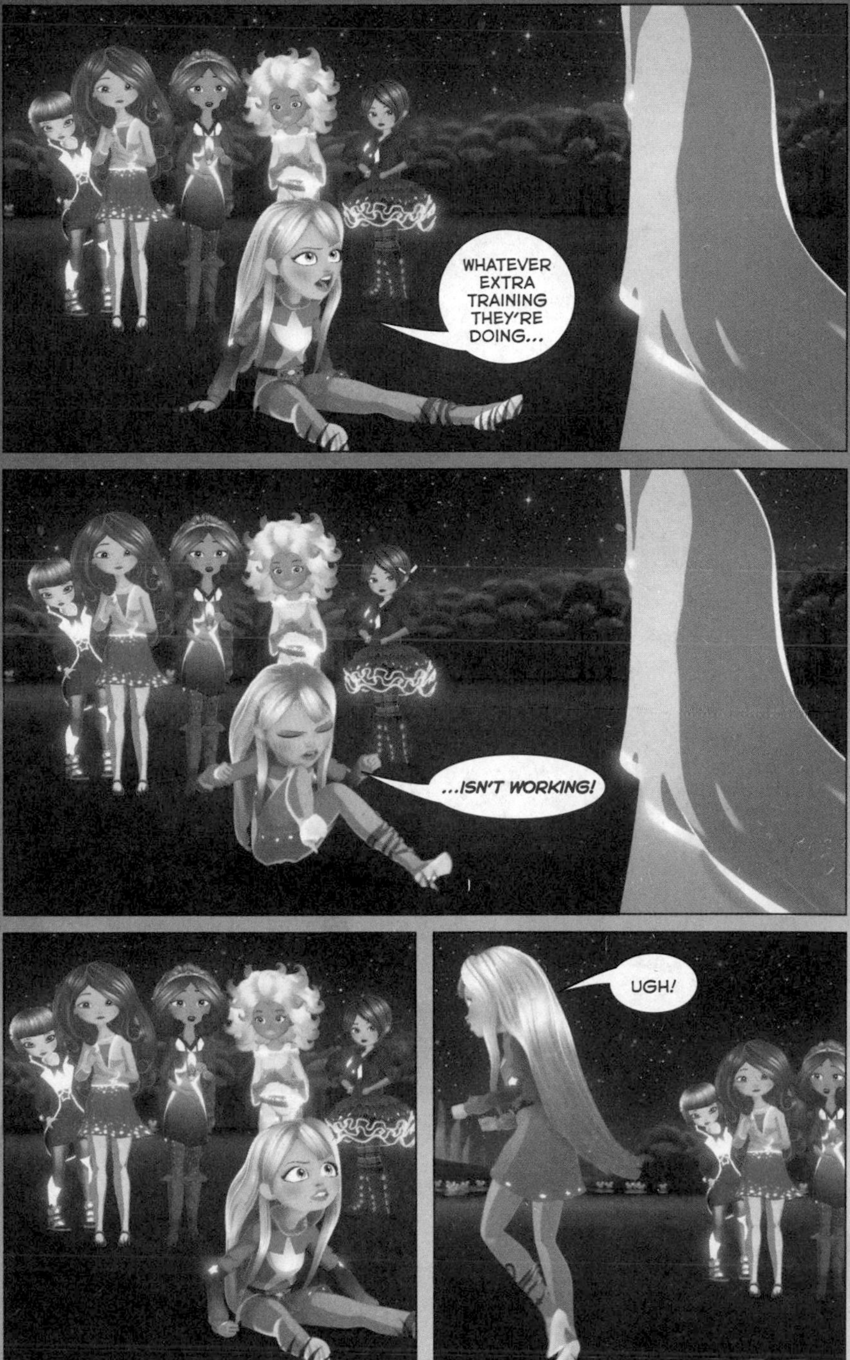
WHATEVER EXTRA TRAINING THEY'RE DOING...
...ISN'T WORKING!
UGH!

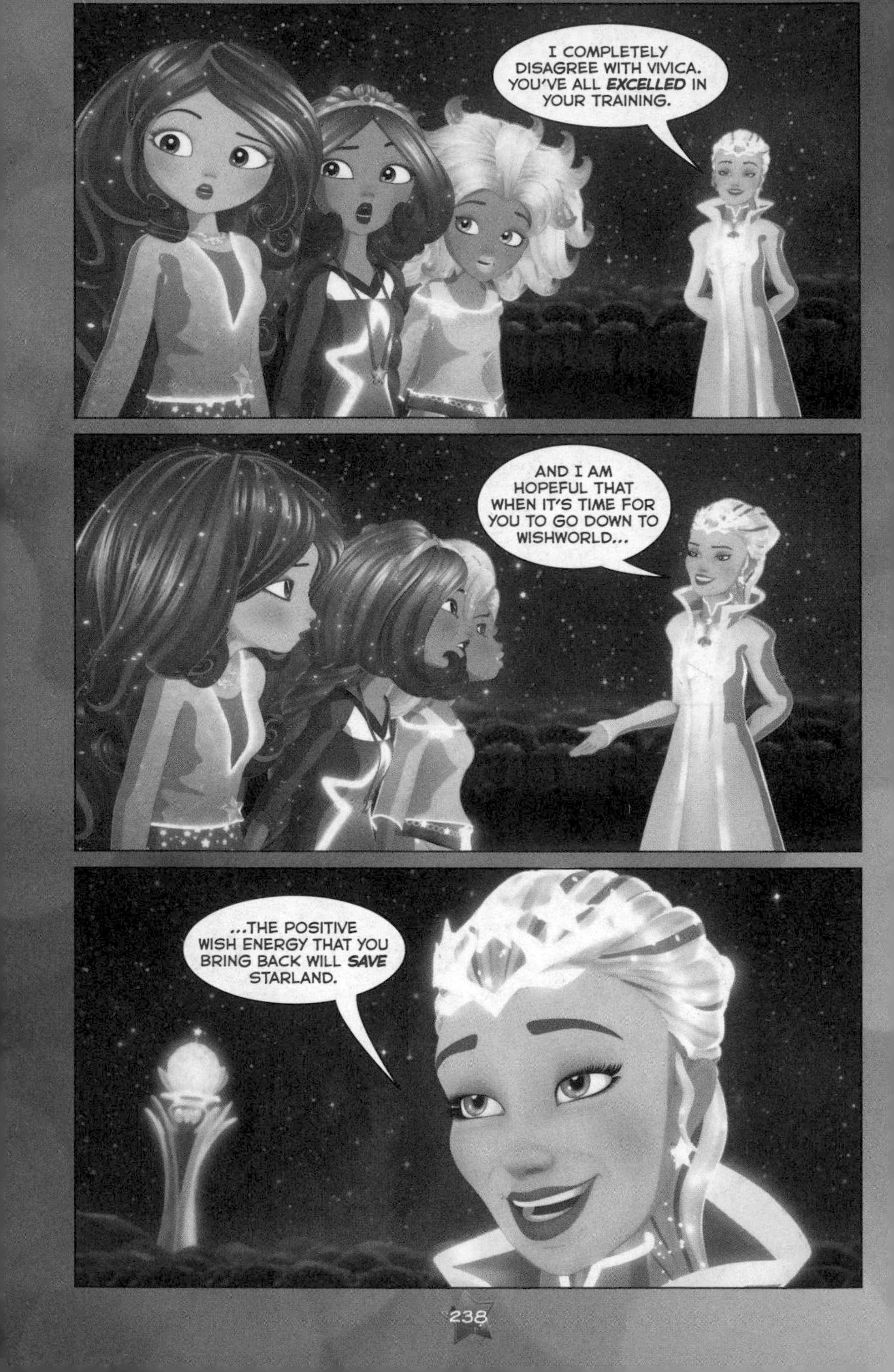
I COMPLETELY DISAGREE WITH VIVICA. YOU'VE ALL *EXCELLED* IN YOUR TRAINING.
AND I AM HOPEFUL THAT WHEN IT'S TIME FOR YOU TO GO DOWN TO WISHWORLD...
...THE POSITIVE WISH ENERGY THAT YOU BRING BACK WILL *SAVE* STARLAND.

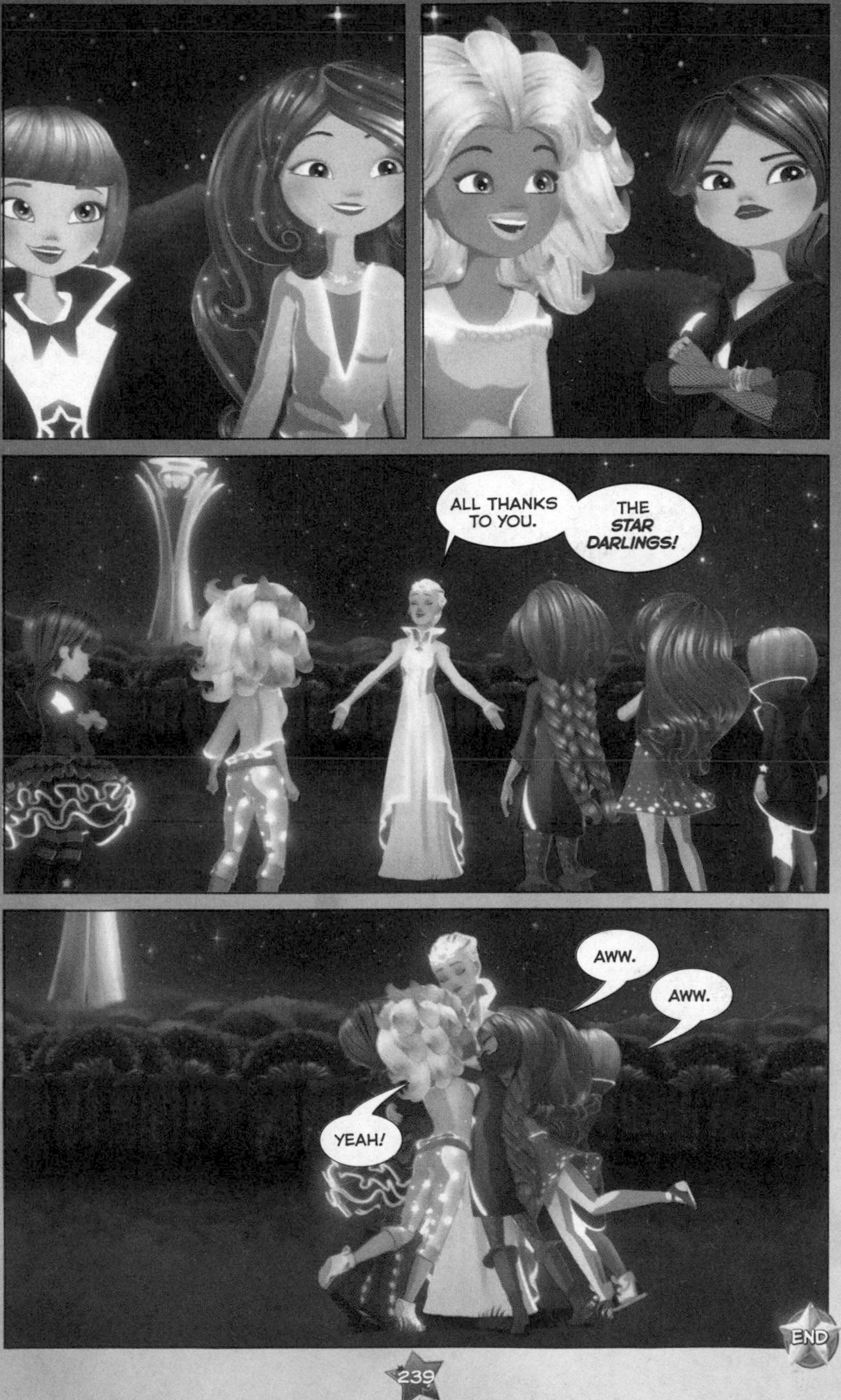
ALL THANKS TO YOU.
THE *STAR DARLINGS!*
AWW.
AWW.
YEAH!
END

CREDITS

Based on Characters Created By
SHANA MULDOON ZAPPA, AHMET ZAPPA

Written By
AMY KEATING ROGERS

Executive Producer
KAREN CHAU

Supervising Producer
TIM YOON

Project Associate
KOHEI OBARA

Special Thanks
ANDREW SUGERMAN, JEANNE MOSURE, GIANFRANCO CORDARA

Art Director
JEAN-PAUL ORPINAS

Artists
CAROLINE EGAN, SOPHIA LIN, JEFFREY THOMAS

With the Voice Talents of
(In Order of Appearance)
PARVESH CHEENA, LIBE BARER, STEPHANIE SHEH,
SARAH NICOLE ROBLES, CORBIN REID, ALISHA
WAINWRIGHT, JENNIFER HALE, ROMI DAMES,
MARIEVE HERINGTON, APRIL STEWART, KATE
MICUCCI, JULIE NATHANSON, CHRIS HAMILTON

Dialogue Director
LISA SCHAFFER

Casting By
AARON DROWN, BRIAN MATHIAS

ODDBOT, INC.

Directed By
YVETTE KAPLAN

Storyboards By
COLE HARRINGTON, ERIN HUMISTON, GLORIA
JENKINS, STEPHEN SAWRAN, CAITLIN ELISE WILLIS

Producer
CHRIS HAMILTON

Co-Producer
FRED SCHAEFER

Line Producer
GREG CHALEKIAN

Animation Art Director
CHRIS HAMILTON

Animation Background
ERIC GONZALEZ, ANNETTE HUCKELL, JOEY
MASON, COLLEEN POLICE

Animation Character Design
MEGAN PHONESAVANH, KENNY THOMPKINS

Effects Design
MEGAN PHONESAVANH

Prop Design
MEGAN PHONESAVANH, COLLEEN POLICE

Background Paint
ALEX FALLAS
ERIC GONZALEZ
COLLEEN POLICE

Storyboard Revisions
DASHAWN MAHONE

Production Manager
TIMOTHY PATTERSON

Production Associate
SEAN JACKSON

Music By
GABRIEL HAYS

Main Title Theme:
Wish Now
Performed by Star Darlings
Written by Andy Dodd, Melissa Peirce,
Ahmet Zappa, and Shana Muldoon Zappa

Animation Production By
SNOWBALL STUDIOS

Editor
ZACH AUFDEMBERG

Animatic Editors
ZACH AUFDEMBERG
MILES COPELAND IV
CARLOS MENDEZ

Sound Effects and Dialogue Editor
BARRY LAWSON

Dialogue Recording Studio
OUTLOUD AUDIO

Post Production Supervisor
KURT WELDON

Post Services By
WESTWIND MEDIA, INC.
PRODUCT FACTORY, LLC